George MacDonald (10 December 1824 – 18 September 1905) was a Scottish author, poet and Christian minister. He was a pioneering figure in the field of fantasy literature and the mentor of fellow writer Lewis Carroll. In addition to his fairy tales, MacDonald wrote several works on Christian apologetics. His writings have been cited as a major literary influence by many notable authors including W. H. Auden, J. M. Barrie, Lord Dunsany, Hope Mirrlees, Robert E. Howard, L. Frank Baum, T.H. White, Lloyd Alexander, C. S. Lewis, J. R. R. Tolkien, Walter de la Mare, E. Nesbit, Peter S. Beagle, Neil Gaiman and Madeleine L'Engle. C. S. Lewis wrote that he regarded MacDonald as his "master": "Picking up a copy of Phantastes one day at a train-station bookstall, I began to read. A few hours later", said Lewis, "I knew that I had crossed a great frontier." G. K. Chesterton cited The Princess and the Goblin as a book that had "made a difference to my whole existence". (Source: Wikipedia)

Literary works:
Phantastes: A Fairie Romance for
Men and Women (1858)
"Cross Purposes" (1862)
"The Second Sight" (1864)
Dealings with the Fairies (1867)
At the Back of the North Wind (1871)
Works of Fancy and Imagination (1871)
The Princess and the Goblin (1872)
The Wise Woman: A Parable (1875)
The Gifts of the Child Christ and Other Tales
The Day Boy and the Night Girl (1882)
The Princess and Curdie (1883)

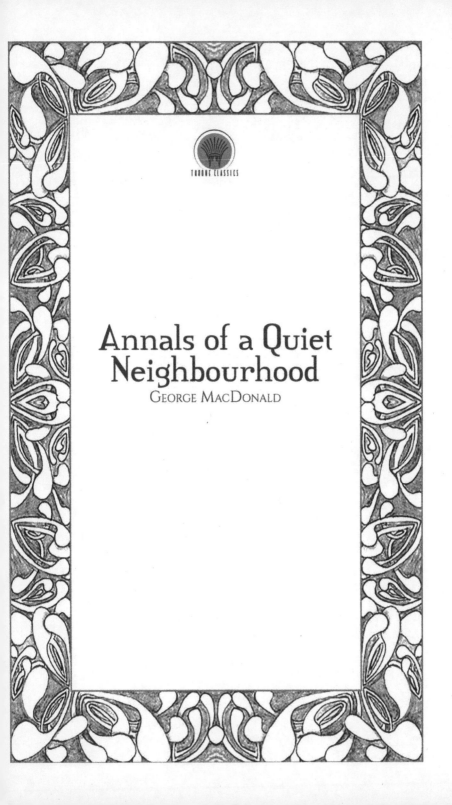

THRONE CLASSICS

Annals of a Quiet Neighbourhood

GEORGE MACDONALD

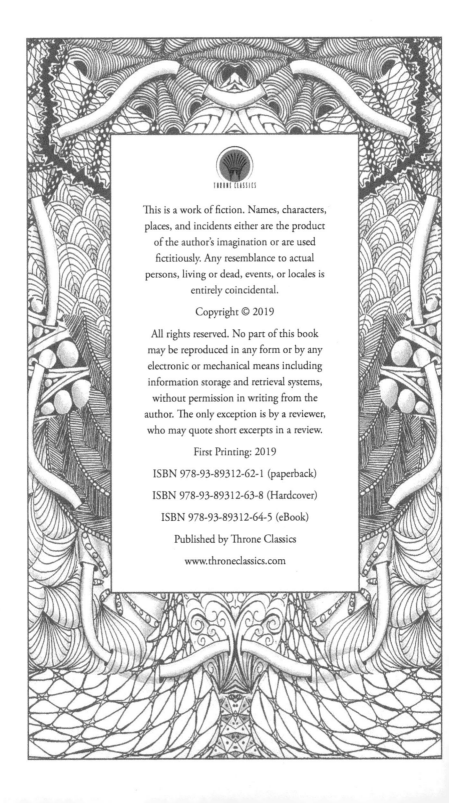

First Printing: 2019

ISBN 978-93-89312-62-1 (paperback)

ISBN 978-93-89312-63-8 (Hardcover)

ISBN 978-93-89312-64-5 (eBook)

Published by Throne Classics

www.throneclassics.com

Contents

Annals of a Quiet Neighbourhood

CHAPTER I. DESPONDENCY AND CONSOLATION.

Before I begin to tell you some of the things I have seen and heard, in both of which I have had to take a share, now from the compulsion of my office, now from the leading of my own heart, and now from that destiny which, including both, so often throws the man who supposed himself a mere on-looker, into the very vortex of events—that destiny which took form to the old pagans as a gray mist high beyond the heads of their gods, but to us is known as an infinite love, revealed in the mystery of man—I say before I begin, it is fitting that, in the absence of a common friend to do that office for me, I should introduce myself to your acquaintance, and I hope coming friendship. Nor can there be any impropriety in my telling you about myself, seeing I remain concealed behind my own words. You can never look me in the eyes, though you may look me in the soul. You may find me out, find my faults, my vanities, my sins, but you will not SEE me, at least in this world. To you I am but a voice of revealing, not a form of vision; therefore I am bold behind the mask, to speak to you heart to heart; bold, I say, just so much the more that I do not speak to you face to face. And when we meet in heaven— well, there I know there is no hiding; there, there is no reason for hiding anything; there, the whole desire will be alternate revelation and vision.

I am now getting old—faster and faster. I cannot help my gray hairs, nor the wrinkles that gather so slowly yet ruthlessly; no, nor the quaver that will come in my voice, not the sense of being feeble in the knees, even when I walk only across the floor of my study. But I have not got used to age yet. I do not FEEL one atom older than I did at three-and-twenty. Nay, to tell all the truth, I feel a good deal younger.—For then I only felt that a man had to take up his cross; whereas now I feel that a man has to follow Him; and that makes an unspeakable difference.—When my voice quavers, I feel that it is mine and not mine; that it just belongs to me like my watch, which does not go well-now, though it went well thirty years ago—not more than a minute out in a month. And when I feel my knees shake, I think of them with a kind of pity, as I used to think of an old mare of my father's of which

I was very fond when I was a lad, and which bore me across many a field and over many a fence, but which at last came to have the same weakness in her knees that I have in mine; and she knew it too, and took care of them, and so of herself, in a wise equine fashion. These things are not me—or I, if the grammarians like it better, (I always feel a strife between doing as the scholar does and doing as other people do;) they are not me, I say; I HAVE them— and, please God, shall soon have better. For it is not a pleasant thing for a young man, or a young woman either, I venture to say, to have an old voice, and a wrinkled face, and weak knees, and gray hair, or no hair at all. And if any moral Philistine, as our queer German brothers over the Northern fish- pond would call him, say that this is all rubbish, for that we ARE old, I would answer: "Of all children how can the children of God be old?"

So little do I give in to calling this outside of me, ME, that I should not mind presenting a minute description of my own person such as would at once clear me from any suspicion of vanity in so introducing myself. Not that my honesty would result in the least from indifference to the external—but from comparative indifference to the transitional; not to the transitional in itself, which is of eternal significance and result, but to the particular form of imperfection which it may have reached at any individual moment of its infinite progression towards the complete. For no sooner have I spoken the word NOW, than that NOW is dead and another is dying; nay, in such a regard, there is no NOW—only a past of which we know a little, and a future of which we know far less and far more. But I will not speak at all of this body of my earthly tabernacle, for it is on the whole more pleasant to forget all about it. And besides, I do not want to set any of my readers to whom I would have the pleasure of speaking far more openly and cordially than if they were seated on the other side of my writing-table—I do not want to set them wondering whether the vicar be this vicar or that vicar; or indeed to run the risk of giving the offence I might give, if I were anything else than "a wandering voice."

I did not feel as I feel now when first I came to this parish. For, as I have said, I am now getting old very fast. True, I was thirty when I was made a vicar, an age at which a man might be expected to be beginning to grow wise;

but even then I had much yet to learn.

I well remember the first evening on which I wandered out from the vicarage to take a look about me—to find out, in short, where I was, and what aspect the sky and earth here presented. Strangely enough, I had never been here before; for the presentation had been made me while I was abroad.—I was depressed. It was depressing weather. Grave doubts as to whether I was in my place in the church, would keep rising and floating about, like rain-clouds within me. Not that I doubted about the church; I only doubted about myself. "Were my motives pure?" "What were my motives?" And, to tell the truth, I did not know what my motives were, and therefore I could not answer about the purity of them. Perhaps seeing we are in this world in order to become pure, it would be expecting too much of any young man that he should be absolutely certain that he was pure in anything. But the question followed very naturally: "Had I then any right to be in the Church—to be eating her bread and drinking her wine without knowing whether I was fit to do her work?" To which the only answer I could find was, "The Church is part of God's world. He makes men to work; and work of some sort must be done by every honest man. Somehow or other, I hardly know how, I find myself in the Church. I do not know that I am fitter for any other work. I see no other work to do. There is work here which I can do after some fashion. With God's help I will try to do it well."

This resolution brought me some relief, but still I was depressed. It was depressing weather.—I may as well say that I was not married then, and that I firmly believed I never should be married—not from any ambition taking the form of self-denial; nor yet from any notion that God takes pleasure in being a hard master; but there was a lady—Well, I WILL be honest, as I would be.—I had been refused a few months before, which I think was the best thing ever happened to me except one. That one, of course, was when I was accepted. But this is not much to the purpose now. Only it was depressing weather.

For is it not depressing when the rain is falling, and the steam of it is rising? when the river is crawling along muddily, and the horses stand stock-still in the meadows with their spines in a straight line from the ears to where

11

they fail utterly in the tails? I should only put on goloshes now, and think of the days when I despised damp. Ah! it was mental waterproof that I needed then; for let me despise damp as much as I would, I could neither keep it out of my mind, nor help suffering the spiritual rheumatism which it occasioned. Now, the damp never gets farther than my goloshes and my Macintosh. And for that worst kind of rheumatism—I never feel it now.

But I had begun to tell you about that first evening.—I had arrived at the vicarage the night before, and it had rained all day, and was still raining, though not so much. I took my umbrella and went out.

For as I wanted to do my work well (everything taking far more the shape of work to me, then, and duty, than it does now—though, even now, I must confess things have occasionally to be done by the clergyman because there is no one else to do them, and hardly from other motive than a sense of duty,—a man not being able to shirk work because it may happen to be dirty)—I say, as I wanted to do my work well, or rather, perhaps, because I dreaded drudgery as much as any poor fellow who comes to the treadmill in consequence—I wanted to interest myself in it; and therefore I would go and fall in love, first of all, if I could, with the country round about. And my first step beyond my own gate was up to the ankles, in mud.

Therewith, curiously enough, arose the distracting thought how I could possibly preach TWO good sermons a Sunday to the same people, when one of the sermons was in the afternoon instead of the evening, to which latter I had been accustomed in the large town in which I had formerly officiated as curate in a proprietary chapel. I, who had declaimed indignantly against excitement from without, who had been inclined to exalt the intellect at the expense even of the heart, began to fear that there must be something in the darkness, and the gas-lights, and the crowd of faces, to account for a man's being able to preach a better sermon, and for servant girls preferring to go out in the evening. Alas! I had now to preach, as I might judge with all probability beforehand, to a company of rustics, of thought yet slower than of speech, unaccustomed in fact to THINK at all, and that in the sleepiest, deadest part of the day, when I could hardly think myself, and when, if the weather should be at all warm, I could not expect many of them to be awake. And what good might I look for as the result of my labour? How could I hope in these men and women to kindle that fire which, in the old days of the outpouring of the Spirit, made men live with the sense of the kingdom of heaven about them, and the expectation of something glorious at hand just outside that invisible door which lay between the worlds?

I have learned since, that perhaps I overrated the spirituality of those times, and underrated, not being myself spiritual enough to see all about me, the spirituality of these times. I think I have learned since, that the parson of a parish must be content to keep the upper windows of his mind open to the holy winds and the pure lights of heaven; and the side windows of tone, of speech, of behaviour open to the earth, to let forth upon his fellow-men the tenderness and truth which those upper influences bring forth in any region exposed to their operation. Believing in his Master, such a servant shall not make haste; shall feel no feverous desire to behold the work of his hands; shall be content to be as his Master, who waiteth long for the fruits of His earth.

But surely I am getting older than I thought; for I keep wandering away from my subject, which is this, my first walk in my new cure. My excuse is, that I want my reader to understand something of the state of my mind, and the depression under which I was labouring. He will perceive that I desired to do some work worth calling by the name of work, and that I did not see how to get hold of a beginning.

I had not gone far from my own gate before the rain ceased, though it was still gloomy enough for any amount to follow. I drew down my umbrella, and began to look about me. The stream on my left was so swollen that I could see its brown in patches through the green of the meadows along its banks. A little in front of me, the road, rising quickly, took a sharp turn to pass along an old stone bridge that spanned the water with a single fine arch, somewhat pointed; and through the arch I could see the river stretching away up through the meadows, its banks bordered with pollards. Now, pollards always made me miserable. In the first place, they look ill-used; in the next place, they look tame; in the third place, they look very ugly. I had not learned then to honour them on the ground that they yield not a jot to the adversity of their circumstances; that, if they must be pollards, they still will be trees;

and what they may not do with grace, they will yet do with bounty; that, in short, their life bursts forth, despite of all that is done to repress and destroy their individuality. When you have once learned to honour anything, love is not very far off; at least that has always been my experience. But, as I have said, I had not yet learned to honour pollards, and therefore they made me more miserable than I was already.

When, having followed the road, I stood at last on the bridge, and, looking up and down the river through the misty air, saw two long rows of these pollards diminishing till they vanished in both directions, the sight of them took from me all power of enjoying the water beneath me, the green fields around me, or even the old-world beauty of the little bridge upon which I stood, although all sorts of bridges have been from very infancy a delight to me. For I am one of those who never get rid of their infantile predilections, and to have once enjoyed making a mud bridge, was to enjoy all bridges for ever.

I saw a man in a white smock-frock coming along the road beyond, but I turned my back to the road, leaned my arms on the parapet of the bridge, and stood gazing where I saw no visions, namely, at those very poplars. I heard the man's footsteps coming up the crown of the arch, but I would not turn to greet him. I was in a selfish humour if ever I was; for surely if ever one man ought to greet another, it was upon such a comfortless afternoon. The footsteps stopped behind me, and I heard a voice:—

"I beg yer pardon, sir; but be you the new vicar?"

I turned instantly and answered, "I am. Do you want me?"

"I wanted to see yer face, sir, that was all, if ye'll not take it amiss."

Before me stood a tall old man with his hat in his hand, clothed as I have said, in a white smock-frock. He smoothed his short gray hair with his curved palm down over his forehead as he stood. His face was of a red brown, from much exposure to the weather. There was a certain look of roughness, without hardness, in it, which spoke of endurance rather than resistance, although he could evidently set his face as a flint. His features were large and a little coarse, but the smile that parted his lips when he spoke, shone in his gray eyes as well, and lighted up a countenance in which a man might trust.

"I wanted to see yer face, sir, if you'll not take it amiss."

"Certainly not," I answered, pleased with the man's address, as he stood square before me, looking as modest as fearless. "The sight of a man's face is what everybody has a right to; but, for all that, I should like to know why you want to see my face."

"Why, sir, you be the new vicar. You kindly told me so when I axed you."

"Well, then, you'll see my face on Sunday in church—that is, if you happen to be there."

For, although some might think it the more dignified way, I could not take it as a matter of course that he would be at church. A man might have better reasons for staying away from church than I had for going, even though I was the parson, and it was my business. Some clergymen separate between themselves and their office to a degree which I cannot understand. To assert the dignities of my office seems to me very like exalting myself; and when I have had a twinge of conscience about it, as has happened more than once, I have then found comfort in these two texts: "The Son of man came not to be ministered unto but to minister;" and "It is enough that the servant should be as his master." Neither have I ever been able to see the very great difference between right and wrong in a clergyman, and right and wrong in another man. All that I can pretend to have yet discovered comes to this: that what is right in another man is right in a clergyman; and what is wrong in another man is much worse in a clergyman. Here, however, is one more proof of approaching age. I do not mean the opinion, but the digression.

"Well, then," I said, "you'll see my face in church on Sunday, if you happen to be there."

"Yes, sir; but you see, sir, on the bridge here, the parson is the parson like, and I'm Old Rogers; and I looks in his face, and he looks in mine, and I says to myself, 'This is my parson.' But o' Sundays he's nobody's parson; he's got his work to do, and it mun be done, and there's an end on't."

15

That there was a real idea in the old man's mind was considerably clearer than the logic by which he tried to bring it out.

"Did you know parson that's gone, sir?" he went on.

"No," I answered.

"Oh, sir! he wur a good parson. Many's the time he come and sit at my son's bedside—him that's dead and gone, sir—for a long hour, on a Saturday night, too. And then when I see him up in the desk the next mornin', I'd say to myself, 'Old Rogers, that's the same man as sat by your son's bedside last night. Think o' that, Old Rogers!' But, somehow, I never did feel right sure o' that same. He didn't seem to have the same cut, somehow; and he didn't talk a bit the same. And when he spoke to me after sermon, in the church-yard, I was always of a mind to go into the church again and look up to the pulpit to see if he war really out ov it; for this warn't the same man, you see. But you'll know all about it better than I can tell you, sir. Only I always liked parson better out o' the pulpit, and that's how I come to want to make you look at me, sir, instead o' the water down there, afore I see you in the church to-morrow mornin'."

The old man laughed a kindly laugh; but he had set me thinking, and I did not know what to say to him all at once. So after a short pause, he resumed—

"You'll be thinking me a queer kind of a man, sir, to speak to my betters before my betters speaks to me. But mayhap you don't know what a parson is to us poor folk that has ne'er a friend more larned than theirselves but the parson. And besides, sir, I'm an old salt,—an old man-o'-war's man,—and I've been all round the world, sir; and I ha' been in all sorts o' company, pirates and all, sir; and I aint a bit frightened of a parson. No; I love a parson, sir. And I'll tell you for why, sir. He's got a good telescope, and he gits to the masthead, and he looks out. And he sings out, 'Land ahead!' or 'Breakers ahead!' and gives directions accordin'. Only I can't always make out what he says. But when he shuts up his spyglass, and comes down the riggin', and talks to us like one man to another, then I don't know what I should do without the parson. Good evenin' to you, sir, and welcome to Marshmallows."

16

The pollards did not look half so dreary. The river began to glimmer a little; and the old bridge had become an interesting old bridge. The country altogether was rather nice than otherwise. I had found a friend already!—that is, a man to whom I might possibly be of some use; and that was the most precious friend I could think of in my present situation and mood. I had learned something from him too; and I resolved to try all I could to be the same man in the pulpit that I was out of it. Some may be inclined to say that I had better have formed the resolution to be the same man out of the pulpit that I was in it. But the one will go quite right with the other. Out of the pulpit I would be the same man I was in it—seeing and feeling the realities of the unseen; and in the pulpit I would be the same man I was out of it— taking facts as they are, and dealing with things as they show themselves in the world.

One other occurrence before I went home that evening, and I shall close the chapter. I hope I shall not write another so dull as this. I dare not promise, though; for this is a new kind of work to me.

Before I left the bridge,—while, in fact, I was contemplating the pollards with an eye, if not of favour, yet of diminished dismay,—the sun, which, for anything I knew of his whereabouts, either from knowledge of the country, aspect of the evening, or state of my own feelings, might have been down for an hour or two, burst his cloudy bands, and blazed out as if he had just risen from the dead, instead of being just about to sink into the grave. Do not tell me that my figure is untrue, for that the sun never sinks into the grave, else I will retort that it is just as true of the sun as of a man; for that no man sinks into the grave. He only disappears. Life IS a constant sunrise, which death cannot interrupt, any more than the night can swallow up the sun. "God is not the God of the dead, but of the living; for all live unto him."

Well, the sun shone out gloriously. The whole sweep of the gloomy river answered him in gladness; the wet leaves of the pollards quivered and glanced; the meadows offered up their perfect green, fresh and clear out of the trouble of the rain; and away in the distance, upon a rising ground covered with trees, glittered a weathercock. What if I found afterwards that it was only on the roof of a stable? It shone, and that was enough. And when the sun had gone

17

below the horizon, and the fields and the river were dusky once more, there it glittered still over the darkening earth, a symbol of that faith which is "the evidence of things not seen," and it made my heart swell as at a chant from the prophet Isaiah. What matter then whether it hung over a stable-roof or a church-tower?

I stood up and wandered a little farther—off the bridge, and along the road. I had not gone far before I passed a house, out of which came a young woman leading a little boy. They came after me, the boy gazing at the red and gold and green of the sunset sky. As they passed me, the child said—

"Auntie, I think I should like to be a painter."

"Why?" returned his companion.

"Because, then," answered the child, "I could help God to paint the sky."

What his aunt replied I do not know; for they were presently beyond my hearing. But I went on answering him myself all the way home. Did God care to paint the sky of an evening, that a few of His children might see it, and get just a hope, just an aspiration, out of its passing green, and gold, and purple, and red? and should I think my day's labour lost, if it wrought no visible salvation in the earth?

But was the child's aspiration in vain? Could I tell him God did not want his help to paint the sky? True, he could mount no scaffold against the infinite of the glowing west. But might he not with his little palette and brush, when the time came, show his brothers and sisters what he had seen there, and make them see it too? Might he not thus come, after long trying, to help God to paint this glory of vapour and light inside the minds of His children? Ah! if any man's work is not WITH God, its results shall be burned, ruthlessly burned, because poor and bad.

"So, for my part," I said to myself, as I walked home, "if I can put one touch of a rosy sunset into the life of any man or woman of my cure, I shall feel that I have worked with God. He is in no haste; and if I do what I may in earnest, I need not mourn if I work no great work on the earth. Let God make His sunsets: I will mottle my little fading cloud. To help the growth

18

of a thought that struggles towards the light; to brush with gentle hand the earth-stain from the white of one snowdrop—such be my ambition! So shall I scale the rocks in front, not leave my name carved upon those behind me."

People talk about special providences. I believe in the providences, but not in the specialty. I do not believe that God lets the thread of my affairs go for six days, and on the seventh evening takes it up for a moment. The so-called special providences are no exception to the rule—they are common to all men at all moments. But it is a fact that God's care is more evident in some instances of it than in others to the dim and often bewildered vision of humanity. Upon such instances men seize and call them providences. It is well that they can; but it would be gloriously better if they could believe that the whole matter is one grand providence.

I was one of such men at the time, and could not fail to see what I called a special providence in this, that on my first attempt to find where I stood in the scheme of Providence, and while I was discouraged with regard to the work before me, I should fall in with these two—an old man whom I could help, and a child who could help me; the one opening an outlet for my labour and my love, and the other reminding me of the highest source of the most humbling comfort,—that in all my work I might be a fellow-worker with God.

CHAPTER II. MY FIRST SUNDAY AT MARSHMALLOWS.

These events fell on the Saturday night. On the Sunday morning, I read prayers and preached. Never before had I enjoyed so much the petitions of the Church, which Hooker calls "the sending of angels upward," or the reading of the lessons, which he calls "the receiving of angels descended from above." And whether from the newness of the parson, or the love of the service, certainly a congregation more intent, or more responsive, a clergyman will hardly find. But, as I had feared, it was different in the afternoon. The people had dined, and the usual somnolence had followed; nor could I find in my heart to blame men and women who worked hard all the week, for being drowsy on the day of rest. So I curtailed my sermon as much as I could, omitting page after page of my manuscript; and when I came to a close, was rewarded by perceiving an agreeable surprise upon many of the faces round me. I resolved that, in the afternoons at least, my sermons should be as short as heart could wish.

But that afternoon there was at least one man of the congregation who was neither drowsy nor inattentive. Repeatedly my eyes left the page off which I was reading and glanced towards him. Not once did I find his eyes turned away from me.

There was a small loft in the west end of the church, in which stood a little organ, whose voice, weakened by years of praising, and possibly of neglect, had yet, among a good many tones that were rough, wooden, and reedy, a few remaining that were as mellow as ever praiseful heart could wish to praise withal. And these came in amongst the rest like trusting thoughts amidst "eating cares;" like the faces of children borne in the arms of a crowd of anxious mothers; like hopes that are young prophecies amidst the downward sweep of events. For, though I do not understand music, I have a keen ear for the perfection of the single tone, or the completeness of the harmony. But of this organ more by and by.

Now this little gallery was something larger than was just necessary for the organ and its ministrants, and a few of the parishioners had chosen to sit in its fore-front. Upon this occasion there was no one there but the man to whom I have referred.

The space below this gallery was not included in the part of the church used for the service. It was claimed by the gardener of the place, that is the sexton, to hold his gardening tools. There were a few ancient carvings in wood lying in it, very brown in the dusky light that came through a small lancet window, opening, not to the outside, but into the tower, itself dusky with an enduring twilight. And there were some broken old headstones, and the kindly spade and pickaxe—but I have really nothing to do with these now, for I am, as it were, in the pulpit, whence one ought to look beyond such things as these.

Rising against the screen which separated this mouldy portion of the church from the rest, stood an old monument of carved wood, once brilliantly painted in the portions that bore the arms of the family over whose vault it

20

stood, but now all bare and worn, itself gently flowing away into the dust it commemorated. It lifted its gablet, carved to look like a canopy, till its apex was on a level with the book-board on the front of the organ-loft; and over— in fact upon this apex appeared the face of the man whom I have mentioned. It was a very remarkable countenance—pale, and very thin, without any hair, except that of thick eyebrows that far over-hung keen, questioning eyes. Short bushy hair, gray, not white, covered a well formed head with a high narrow forehead. As I have said, those keen eyes kept looking at me from under their gray eyebrows all the time of the sermon—intelligently without doubt, but whether sympathetically or otherwise I could not determine. And indeed I hardly know yet. My vestry door opened upon a little group of graves, simple and green, without headstone or slab; poor graves, the memory of whose occupants no one had cared to preserve. Good men must have preceded me here, else the poor would not have lain so near the chancel and the vestry-door. All about and beyond were stones, with here and there a monument; for mine was a large parish, and there were old and rich families in it, more of which buried their dead here than assembled their living. But close by the vestry-door, there was this little billowy lake of grass. And at the end of the narrow path leading from the door, was the churchyard wall, with a few steps on each side of it, that the parson might pass at once from the churchyard into his own shrubbery, here tangled, almost matted, from luxuriance of growth. But I would not creep out the back way from among my people. That way might do very well to come in by; but to go out, I would use the door of the people. So I went along the church, a fine old place, such as I had never hoped to be presented to, and went out by the door in the north side into the middle of the churchyard. The door on the other side was chiefly used by the few gentry of the neighbourhood; and the Lych-gate, with its covered way, (for the main road had once passed on that side,) was shared between the coffins and the carriages, the dead who had no rank but one, that of the dead, and the living who had more money than their neighbours. For, let the old gentry disclaim it as they may, mere wealth, derived from whatever source, will sooner reach their level than poor antiquity, or the rarest refinement of personal worth; although, to be sure, the oldest of them will sooner give to the rich their sons or their daughters to wed, to love if they can, to have children by, than they will yield a jot of their ancestral preeminence, or acknowledge any equality in their sons or daughters-in-law. The carpenter's son is to them an old myth, not an everlasting fact. To Mammon alone will they yield a little of their rank—none of it to Christ. Let me glorify God that Jesus took not on. Him the nature of nobles, but the seed of Adam; for what could I do without my poor brothers and sisters?

I passed along the church to the northern door, and went out. The churchyard lay in bright sunshine. All the rain and gloom were gone. "If one could only bring this glory of sun and grass into one's hope for the future!" thought I; and looking down I saw the little boy who aspired to paint the sky, looking up in my face with mingled confidence and awe.

"Do you trust me, my little man?" thought I. "You shall trust me then. But I won't be a priest to you, I'll be a big brother."

For the priesthood passes away, the brotherhood endures. The priesthood passes away, swallowed up in the brotherhood. It is because men cannot learn simple things, cannot believe in the brotherhood, that they need a priesthood. But as Dr Arnold said of the Sunday, "They DO need it." And I, for one, am sure that the priesthood needs the people much more than the people needs the priesthood.

So I stooped and lifted the child and held him in my arms. And the little fellow looked at me one moment longer, and then put his arms gently round my neck. And so we were friends. When I had set him down, which I did presently, for I shuddered at the idea of the people thinking that I was showing off the CLERGYMAN, I looked at the boy. In his face was great sweetness mingled with great rusticity, and I could not tell whether he was the child of gentlefolk or of peasants. He did not say a word, but walked away to join his aunt, who was waiting for him at the gate of the churchyard. He kept his head turned towards me, however, as he went, so that, not seeing where he was going, he stumbled over the grave of a child, and fell in the hollow on the other side. I ran to pick him up. His aunt reached him at the same moment.

"Oh, thank you, sir!" she said, as I gave him to her, with an earnestness which seemed to me disproportionate to the deed, and carried him away with a deep blush over all her countenance.

At the churchyard-gate, the old man-of-war's man was waiting to have another look at me. His hat was in his hand, and he gave a pull to the short hair over his forehead, as if he would gladly take that off too, to show his respect for the new parson. I held out my hand gratefully. It could not close around the hard, unyielding mass of fingers which met it. He did not know how to shake hands, and left it all to me. But pleasure sparkled in his eyes.

"My old woman would like to shake hands with you, sir," he said.

Beside him stood his old woman, in a portentous bonnet, beneath whose gay yellow ribbons appeared a dusky old face, wrinkled like a ship's timbers, out of which looked a pair of keen black eyes, where the best beauty, that of loving-kindness, had not merely lingered, but triumphed.

"I shall be in to see you soon," I said, as I shook hands with her. "I shall find out where you live."

"Down by the mill," she said; "close by it, sir. There's one bed in our garden that always thrives, in the hottest summer, by the plash from the mill, sir."

"Ask for Old Rogers, sir," said the man. "Everybody knows Old Rogers. But if your reverence minds what my wife says, you won't go wrong. When you find the river, it takes you to the mill; and when you find the mill, you find the wheel; and when you find the wheel, you haven't far to look for the cottage, sir. It's a poor place, but you'll be welcome, sir."

CHAPTER III. MY FIRST MONDAY AT MARSHMALLOWS.

The next day I might expect some visitors. It is a fortunate thing that English society now regards the parson as a gentleman, else he would have little chance of being useful to the UPPER CLASSES. But I wanted to get a good start of them, and see some of my poor before my rich came to see me. So after breakfast, on as lovely a Monday in the beginning of autumn as ever came to comfort a clergyman in the reaction of his efforts to feed his flock on the Sunday, I walked out, and took my way to the village. I strove to dismiss from my mind every feeling of DOING DUTY, of PERFORMING MY

PART, and all that. I had a horror of becoming a moral policeman as much as of "doing church." I would simply enjoy the privilege, more open to me in virtue of my office, of ministering. But as no servant has a right to force his service, so I would be the NEIGHBOUR only, until such time as the opportunity of being the servant should show itself.

The village was as irregular as a village should be, partly consisting of those white houses with intersecting parallelograms of black which still abound in some regions of our island. Just in the centre, however, grouping about an old house of red brick, which had once been a manorial residence, but was now subdivided in all modes that analytic ingenuity could devise, rose a portion of it which, from one point of view, might seem part of an old town. But you had only to pass round any one of three visible corners to see stacks of wheat and a farm-yard; while in another direction the houses went straggling away into a wood that looked very like the beginning of a forest, of which some of the village orchards appeared to form part. From the street the slow-winding, poplar-bordered stream was here and there just visible.

I did not quite like to have it between me and my village. I could not help preferring that homely relation in which the houses are built up like swallow-nests on to the very walls of the cathedrals themselves, to the arrangement here, where the river flowed, with what flow there was in it, between the church and the people.

A little way beyond the farther end of the village appeared an iron gate, of considerable size, dividing a lofty stone wall. And upon the top of that one of the stone pillars supporting the gate which I could see, stood a creature of stone, whether natant, volant, passant, couchant, or rampant, I could not tell, only it looked like something terrible enough for a quite antediluvian heraldry.

As I passed along the street, wondering with myself what relations between me and these houses were hidden in the future, my eye was caught by the window of a little shop, in which strings of beads and elephants of gingerbread formed the chief samples of the goods within. It was a window much broader than it was high, divided into lozenge-shaped panes. Wondering what kind of old woman presided over the treasures in this cave of Aladdin, I thought to make a first of my visits by going in and buying something. But I hesitated, because I could not think of anything I was in want of—at least that the old woman was likely to have. To be sure I wanted a copy of Bengel's "Gnomon;" but she was not likely to have that. I wanted the fourth plate in the third volume of Law's "Behmen;" she was not likely to have that either. I did not care for gingerbread; and I had no little girl to take home beads to.

But why should I not go in without an ostensible errand? For this reason: there are dissenters everywhere, and I could not tell but I might be going into the shop of a dissenter. Now, though, I confess, nothing would have pleased me better than that all the dissenters should return to their old home in the Church, I could not endure the suspicion of laying myself out to entice them back by canvassing or using any personal influence. Whether they returned or not, however, (and I did not expect many would,) I hoped still, some day, to stand towards every one of them in the relation of the parson of the parish, that is, one of whom each might feel certain that he was ready to serve him or her at any hour when he might be wanted to render a service. In the meantime, I could not help hesitating.

I had almost made up my mind to ask if she had a small pocket compass, for I had seen such things in little country shops—I am afraid only in France, though—when the door opened, and out came the little boy whom I had already seen twice, and who was therefore one of my oldest friends in the place. He came across the road to me, took me by the hand, and said—

"Come and see mother."

"Where, my dear?" I asked.

"In the shop there," he answered.

"Is it your mother's shop?"

"Yes."

I said no more, but accompanied him. Of course my expectation of seeing an old woman behind the counter had vanished, but I was not in the least prepared for the kind of woman I did see.

The place was half a shop and half a kitchen. A yard or so of counter stretched inwards from the door, just as a hint to those who might be intrusively inclined. Beyond this, by the chimney-corner, sat the mother, who rose as we entered. She was certainly one—I do not say of the most beautiful, but, until I have time to explain further—of the most remarkable women I had ever seen. Her face was absolutely white—no, pale cream-colour—except her lips and a spot upon each cheek, which glowed with a deep carmine. You would have said she had been painting, and painting very inartistically, so little was the red shaded into the surrounding white. Now this was certainly not beautiful. Indeed, it occasioned a strange feeling, almost of terror, at first, for she reminded one of the spectre woman in the "Rime of the Ancient Mariner." But when I got used to her complexion, I saw that the form of her features was quite beautiful. She might indeed have been LOVELY but for a certain hardness which showed through the beauty. This might have been the result of ill health, ill endured; but I doubted it. For there was a certain modelling of the cheeks and lips which showed that the teeth within were firmly closed; and, taken with the look of the eyes and forehead, seemed the expression of a constant and bitter self-command. But there were indubitable marks of ill health upon her, notwithstanding; for not to mention her complexion, her large dark eye was burning as if the lamp of life had broken and the oil was blazing; and there was a slight expansion of the nostrils, which indicated physical unrest. But her manner was perfectly, almost dreadfully, quiet; her voice soft, low, and chiefly expressive of indifference. She spoke without looking me in the face, but did not seem either shy or ashamed. Her figure was remarkably graceful, though too worn to be beautiful.—Here was a strange parishioner for me!—in a country toy-shop, too!

As soon as the little fellow had brought me in, he shrunk away through a half-open door that revealed a stair behind.

"What can I do for you, sir?" said the mother, coldly, and with a kind of book-propriety of speech, as she stood on the other side of the little counter, prepared to open box or drawer at command.

"To tell the truth, I hardly know," I said. "I am the new vicar; but I do not think that I should have come in to see you just to-day, if it had not been that your little boy there—where is he gone to? He asked me to come in and see his mother."

"He is too ready to make advances to strangers, sir."

She said this in an incisive tone.

"Oh, but," I answered, "I am not a stranger to him. I have met him twice before. He is a little darling. I assure you he has quite gained my heart."

No reply for a moment. Then just "Indeed!" and nothing more.

I could not understand it.

But a jar on a shelf, marked TOBACCO, rescued me from the most pressing portion of the perplexity, namely, what to say next.

"Will you give me a quarter of a pound of tobacco?" I said.

The woman turned, took down the jar, arranged the scales, weighed out the quantity, wrapped it up, took the money,—and all without one other word than, "Thank you, sir;" which was all I could return, with the addition of, "Good morning."

For nothing was left me but to walk away with my parcel in my pocket.

The little boy did not show himself again. I had hoped to find him outside.

Pondering, speculating, I now set out for the mill, which, I had already learned, was on the village side of the river. Coming to a lane leading down to the river, I followed it, and then walked up a path outside the row of pollards, through a lovely meadow, where brown and white cows were eating and shining all over the thick deep grass. Beyond the meadow, a wood on the side of a rising ground went parallel with the river a long way. The river flowed on my right. That is, I knew that it was flowing, but I could not have told how I knew, it was so slow. Still swollen, it was of a clear brown, in which you could see the browner trouts darting to and fro with such a slippery gliding, that the motion seemed the result of will, without any such intermediate and complicate arrangement as brain and nerves and muscles. The water-beetles went spinning about over the surface; and one glorious dragon-fly made a mist about him with his long wings. And over all, the sun hung in the sky, pouring down life; shining on the roots of the willows at the bottom of the stream; lighting up the black head of the water-rat as he hurried across to the opposite bank; glorifying the rich green lake of the grass; and giving to the whole an utterance of love and hope and joy, which was, to him who could read it, a more certain and full revelation of God than any display of power in thunder, in avalanche, in stormy sea. Those with whom the feeling of religion is only occasional, have it most when the awful or grand breaks out of the common; the meek who inherit the earth, find the God of the whole earth more evidently present—I do not say more present, for there is no measuring of His presence—more evidently present in the commonest things. That which is best He gives most plentifully, as is reason with Him. Hence the quiet fulness of ordinary nature; hence the Spirit to them that ask it.

I soon came within sound of the mill; and presently, crossing the stream that flowed back to the river after having done its work on the corn, I came in front of the building, and looked over the half-door into the mill. The floor was clean and dusty. A few full sacks, tied tight at the mouth—they always look to me as if Joseph's silver cup were just inside—stood about. In the farther corner, the flour was trickling down out of two wooden spouts into a wooden receptacle below. The whole place was full of its own faint but pleasant odour. No man was visible. The spouts went on pouring the slow torrent of flour, as if everything could go on with perfect propriety of itself. I could not even see how a man could get at the stones that I heard grinding away above, except he went up the rope that hung from the ceiling. So I walked round the corner of the place, and found myself in the company of the water-wheel, mossy and green with ancient waterdrops, looking so furred and overgrown and lumpy, that one might have thought the wood of it had taken to growing again in its old days, and so the wheel was losing by slow degrees the shape of a wheel, to become some new awful monster of a pollard. As yet, however, it was going round; slowly, indeed, and with the gravity of age, but doing its work, and casting its loose drops in the alms-giving of a gentle rain upon a little plot of Master Rogers's garden, which was therefore full of moisture-loving flowers. This plot was divided from the mill-wheel by a small stream which carried away the surplus water, and was now full and running rapidly.

Beyond the stream, beside the flower bed, stood a dusty young man, talking to a young woman with a rosy face and clear honest eyes. The moment they saw me they parted. The young man came across the stream at a step, and the young woman went up the garden towards the cottage.

"That must be Old Rogers's cottage?" I said to the miller.

"Yes, sir," he answered, looking a little sheepish.

"Was that his daughter—that nice-looking young woman you were talking to?"

"Yes, sir, it was."

And he stole a shy pleased look at me out of the corners of his eyes.

"It's a good thing," I said, "to have an honest experienced old mill like yours, that can manage to go on of itself for a little while now and then."

This gave a great help to his budding confidence. He laughed.

"Well, sir, it's not very often it's left to itself. Jane isn't at her father's above once or twice a week at most."

"She doesn't live with them, then?"

"No, sir. You see they're both hearty, and they ain't over well to do, and Jane lives up at the Hall, sir. She's upper housemaid, and waits on one of the young ladies.—Old Rogers has seen a great deal of the world, sir."

"So I imagine. I am just going to see him. Good morning."

I jumped across the stream, and went up a little gravel-walk, which led me in a few yards to the cottage-door. It was a sweet place to live in, with honeysuckle growing over the house, and the sounds of the softly-labouring mill-wheel ever in its little porch and about its windows.

The door was open, and Dame Rogers came from within to meet me.

She welcomed me, and led the way into her little kitchen. As I entered, Jane went out at the back-door. But it was only to call her father, who presently came in.

"I'm glad to see ye, sir. This pleasure comes of having no work to-day. After harvest there comes slack times for the likes of me. People don't care about a bag of old bones when they can get hold of young men. Well, well, never mind, old woman. The Lord'll take us through somehow. When the wind blows, the ship goes; when the wind drops, the ship stops; but the sea is His all the same, for He made it; and the wind is His all the same too."

He spoke in the most matter-of-fact tone, unaware of anything poetic in what he said. To him it was just common sense, and common sense only.

"I am sorry you are out of work," I said. "But my garden is sadly out of order, and I must have something done to it. You don't dislike gardening, do you?"

"Well, I beant a right good hand at garden-work," answered the old man, with some embarrassment, scratching his gray head with a troubled scratch.

There was more in this than met the ear; but what, I could not conjecture. I would press the point a little. So I took him at his own word.

"I won't ask you to do any of the more ornamental part," I said,—"only plain digging and hoeing."

"I would rather be excused, sir."

"I am afraid I made you think"—

"I thought nothing, sir. I thank you kindly, sir."

"I assure you I want the work done, and I must employ some one else if you don't undertake it."

"Well, sir, my back's bad now—no, sir, I won't tell a story about it. I would just rather not, sir."

"Now," his wife broke in, "now, Old Rogers, why won't 'ee tell the parson the truth, like a man, downright? If ye won't, I'll do it for 'ee. The fact is, sir," she went on, turning to me, with a plate in her hand, which she was wiping, "the fact is, that the old parson's man for that kind o' work was Simmons, t'other end of the village; and my man is so afeard o' hurtin' e'er another, that he'll turn the bread away from his own mouth and let it fall in the dirt."

"Now, now, old 'oman, don't 'ee belie me. I'm not so bad as that. You see, sir, I never was good at knowin' right from wrong like. I never was good, that is, at tellin' exactly what I ought to do. So when anything comes up, I just says to myself, 'Now, Old Rogers, what do you think the Lord would best like you to do?' And as soon as I ax myself that, I know directly what I've got to do; and then my old woman can't turn me no more than a bull. And she don't like my obstinate fits. But, you see, I daren't sir, once I axed myself that."

"Stick to that, Rogers," I said.

"Besides, sir," he went on, "Simmons wants it more than I do. He's got a sick wife; and my old woman, thank God, is hale and hearty. And there is another thing besides, sir: he might take it hard of you, sir, and think it was turning away an old servant like; and then, sir, he wouldn't be ready to hear what you had to tell him, and might, mayhap, lose a deal o' comfort. And that I would take worst of all, sir."

"Well, well, Rogers, Simmons shall have the job."

"Thank ye, sir," said the old man.

His wife, who could not see the thing quite from her husband's point of view, was too honest to say anything; but she was none the less cordial to me. The daughter stood looking from one to the other with attentive face, which took everything, but revealed nothing.

I rose to go. As I reached the door, I remembered the tobacco in my pocket. I had not bought it for myself. I never could smoke. Nor do I conceive that smoking is essential to a clergyman in the country; though I have occasionally envied one of my brethren in London, who will sit down by the fire, and, lighting his pipe, at the same time please his host and subdue the bad smells of the place. And I never could hit his way of talking to his parishioners either. He could put them at their ease in a moment. I think he must have got the trick out of his pipe. But in reality, I seldom think about how I ought to talk to anybody I am with.

That I didn't smoke myself was no reason why I should not help Old Rogers to smoke. So I pulled out the tobacco.

"You smoke, don't you, Rogers?" I said.

"Well, sir, I can't deny it. It's not much I spend on baccay, anyhow. Is it, dame?"

"No, that it bean't," answered his wife.

"You don't think there's any harm in smoking a pipe, sir?"

"Not the least," I answered, with emphasis.

"You see, sir," he went on, not giving me time to prove how far I was from thinking there was any harm in it; "You see, sir, sailors learns many ways they might be better without. I used to take my pan o' grog with the rest of them; but I give that up quite, 'cause as how I don't want it now."

"'Cause as how," interrupted his wife, "you spend the money on tea for me, instead. You wicked old man to tell stories!"

"Well, I takes my share of the tea, old woman, and I'm sure it's a deal better for me. But, to tell the truth, sir, I was a little troubled in my mind about the baccay, not knowing whether I ought to have it or not. For you see, the parson that's gone didn't more than half like it, as I could tell by the turn of his hawse-holes when he came in at the door and me a-smokin'. Not as he said anything; for, ye see, I was an old man, and I daresay that kep him quiet. But I did hear him blow up a young chap i' the village he come upon promiscus with a pipe in his mouth. He did give him a thunderin' broadside, to be sure! So I was in two minds whether I ought to go on with my pipe or not."

"And how did you settle the question, Rogers?"

"Why, I followed my own old chart, sir."

"Quite right. One mustn't mind too much what other people think."

"That's not exactly what I mean, sir."

"What do you mean then? I should like to know."

"Well, sir, I mean that I said to myself, 'Now, Old Rogers, what do you think the Lord would say about this here baccay business?'"

"And what did you think He would say?"

"Why, sir, I thought He would say, 'Old Rogers, have yer baccay; only mind ye don't grumble when you 'aint got none.'"

Something in this—I could not at the time have told what—touched me more than I can express. No doubt it was the simple reality of the relation in which the old man stood to his Father in heaven that made me feel as if the tears would come in spite of me.

"And this is the man," I said to myself, "whom I thought I should be able to teach! Well, the wisest learn most, and I may be useful to him after all."

As I said nothing, the old man resumed—

"For you see, sir, it is not always a body feels he has a right to spend his ha'pence on baccay; and sometimes, too, he 'aint got none to spend."

"In the meantime," I said, "here is some that I bought for you as I came along. I hope you will find it good. I am no judge."

The old sailor's eyes glistened with gratitude. "Well, who'd ha' thought it. You didn't think I was beggin' for it, sir, surely?"

"You see I had it for you in my pocket."

"Well, that IS good o' you, sir!"

"Why, Rogers, that'll last you a month!" exclaimed his wife, looking nearly as pleased as himself.

"Six weeks at least, wife," he answered. "And ye don't smoke yourself, sir, and yet ye bring baccay to me! Well, it's just like yer Master, sir."

I went away, resolved that Old Rogers should have no chance of "grumbling" for want of tobacco, if I could help it.

CHAPTER IV. THE COFFIN.

On the way back, my thoughts were still occupied with the woman I had seen in the little shop. The old man-of-war's man was probably the nobler being of the two; and if I had had to choose between them, I should no doubt have chosen him. But I had not to choose between them; I had only to think about them; and I thought a great deal more about the one I could not understand than the one I could understand. For Old Rogers wanted little help from me; whereas the other was evidently a soul in pain, and therefore belonged to me in peculiar right of my office; while the readiest way in which I could justify to myself the possession of that office was to make it a shepherding of the sheep. So I resolved to find out what I could about her, as one having a right to know, that I might see whether I could not help her. From herself it was evident that her secret, if she had one, was not to be easily gained; but even the common reports of the village would be some enlightenment to the darkness I was in about her.

As I went again through the village, I observed a narrow lane striking off to the left, and resolved to explore in that direction. It led up to one side of the large house of which I have already spoken. As I came near, I smelt what has been to me always a delightful smell—that of fresh deals under the hands of the carpenter. In the scent of those boards of pine is enclosed all the idea the tree could gather of the world of forest where it was reared. It speaks of many wild and bright but chiefly clean and rather cold things. If I were idling, it would draw me to it across many fields.—Turning a corner, I heard the sound of a saw. And this sound drew me yet more. For a carpenter's shop was the delight of my boyhood; and after I began to read the history of our Lord with something of that sense of reality with which we read other histories, and which, I am sorry to think, so much of the well-meant instruction we receive in our youth tends to destroy, my feeling about such a workshop grew stronger and stronger, till at last I never could go near enough to see the shavings lying on the floor of one, without a spiritual sensation such as I have in entering an old church; which sensation, ever since having been admitted on the usual conditions to a Mohammedan mosque, urges me to pull off, not only my hat, but my shoes likewise. And the feeling has grown upon me, till now it seems at times as if the only cure in the world for social pride would be to go for five silent minutes into a carpenter's shop. How one can think of himself as above his neighbours, within sight, sound, or smell of one, I fear I am getting almost unable to imagine, and one ought not to get out of sympathy with the wrong. Only as I am growing old now, it does not matter so much, for I daresay my time will not be very long.

So I drew near to the shop, feeling as if the Lord might be at work there at one of the benches. And when I reached the door, there was my pale-faced hearer of the Sunday afternoon, sawing a board for a coffin-lid.

As my shadow fell across and darkened his work, he lifted his head and saw me.

I could not altogether understand the expression of his countenance as he stood upright from his labour and touched his old hat with rather a proud than a courteous gesture. And I could not believe that he was glad to see me, although he laid down his saw and advanced to the door. It was the gentleman in him, not the man, that sought to make me welcome, hardly caring whether I saw through the ceremony or not. True, there was a smile on his lips, but the smile of a man who cherishes a secret grudge; of one who does not altogether dislike you, but who has a claim upon you—say, for an apology, of which claim he doubts whether you know the existence. So the smile seemed tightened, and stopped just when it got half-way to its width, and was about to become hearty and begin to shine.

"May I come in?" I said.

"Come in, sir," he answered.

"I am glad I have happened to come upon you by accident," I said.

He smiled as if he did not quite believe in the accident, and considered it a part of the play between us that I should pretend it. I hastened to add—

"I was wandering about the place, making some acquaintance with it,

35

and with my friends in it, when I came upon you quite unexpectedly. You know I saw you in church on Sunday afternoon."

"I know you saw me, sir," he answered, with a motion as if to return to his work; "but, to tell the truth, I don't go to church very often."

I did not quite know whether to take this as proceeding from an honest fear of being misunderstood, or from a sense of being in general superior to all that sort of thing. But I felt that it would be of no good to pursue the inquiry directly. I looked therefore for something to say.

"Ah! your work is not always a pleasant one," I said, associating the feelings of which I have already spoken with the facts before me, and looking at the coffin, the lower part of which stood nearly finished upon trestles on the floor.

"Well, there are unpleasant things in all trades," he answered. "But it does not matter," he added, with an increase of bitterness in his smile.

"I didn't mean," I said, "that the work was unpleasant—only sad. It must always be painful to make a coffin."

"A joiner gets used to it, sir, as you do to the funeral service. But, for my part, I don't see why it should be considered so unhappy for a man to be buried. This isn't such a good job, after all, this world, sir, you must allow."

"Neither is that coffin," said I, as if by a sudden inspiration.

The man seemed taken aback, as Old Rogers might have said. He looked at the coffin and then looked at me.

"Well, sir," he said, after a short pause, which no doubt seemed longer both to him and to me than it would have seemed to any third person, "I don't see anything amiss with the coffin. I don't say it'll last till doomsday, as the gravedigger says to Hamlet, because I don't know so much about doomsday as some people pretend to; but you see, sir, it's not finished yet."

"Thank you," I said; "that's just what I meant. You thought I was hasty in my judgment of your coffin; whereas I only said of it knowingly what you said of the world thoughtlessly. How do you know that the world is finished anymore than your coffin? And how dare you then say that it is a bad job?"

The same respectfully scornful smile passed over his face, as much as to say, "Ah! it's your trade to talk that way, so I must not be too hard upon you."

"At any rate, sir," he said, "whoever made it has taken long enough about it, a person would think, to finish anything he ever meant to finish."

"One day is with the Lord as a thousand years, and a thousand years as one day," I said.

"That's supposing," he answered, "that the Lord did make the world. For my part, I am half of a mind that the Lord didn't make it at all."

"I am very glad to hear you say so," I answered.

Hereupon I found that we had changed places a little. He looked up at me. The smile of superiority was no longer there, and a puzzled questioning, which might indicate either "Who would have expected that from you?" or, "What can he mean?" or both at once, had taken its place. I, for my part, knew that on the scale of the man's judgment I had risen nearer to his own level. As he said nothing, however, and I was in danger of being misunderstood, I proceeded at once.

"Of course it seems to me better that you should not believe God had done a thing, than that you should believe He had not done it well!"

"Ah! I see, sir. Then you will allow there is some room for doubting whether He made the world at all?"

"Yes; for I do not think an honest man, as you seem to me to be, would be able to doubt without any room whatever. That would be only for a fool. But it is just possible, as we are not perfectly good ourselves—you'll allow that, won't you?"

"That I will, sir; God knows."

"Well, I say—as we're not quite good ourselves, it's just possible that things may be too good for us to do them the justice of believing in them."

"But there are things, you must allow, so plainly wrong!"

"So much so, both in the world and in myself, that it would be to me torturing despair to believe that God did not make the world; for then, how would it ever be put right? Therefore I prefer the theory that He has not done making it yet."

"But wouldn't you say, sir, that God might have managed it without so many slips in the making as your way would suppose? I should think myself a bad workman if I worked after that fashion."

"I do not believe that there are any slips. You know you are making a coffin; but are you sure you know what God is making of the world?"

"That I can't tell, of course, nor anybody else."

"Then you can't say that what looks like a slip is really a slip, either in the design or in the workmanship. You do not know what end He has in view; and you may find some day that those slips were just the straight road to that very end."

"Ah! maybe. But you can't be sure of it, you see."

"Perhaps not, in the way you mean; but sure enough, for all that, to try it upon life—to order my way by it, and so find that it works well. And I find that it explains everything that comes near it. You know that no engineer would be satisfied with his engine on paper, nor with any proof whatever except seeing how it will go."

He made no reply.

It is a principle of mine never to push anything over the edge. When I am successful, in any argument, my one dread is of humiliating my opponent. Indeed I cannot bear it. It humiliates me. And if you want him to think about anything, you must leave him room, and not give him such associations with the question that the very idea of it will be painful and irritating to him. Let him have a hand in the convincing of himself. I have been surprised sometimes to see my own arguments come up fresh and green, when I thought the fowls of the air had devoured them up. When a man reasons for victory and not for the truth in the other soul, he is sure of just one ally, the same that Faust had in fighting Gretchen's brother—that is, the Devil. But God and good men are against him. So I never follow up a victory of that kind, for, as I said, the defeat of the intellect is not the object in fighting with the sword of the Spirit, but the acceptance of the heart. In this case, therefore, I drew back.

"May I ask for whom you are making that coffin?"

"For a sister of my own, sir."

"I'm sorry to hear that."

"There's no occasion. I can't say I'm sorry, though she was one of the best women I ever knew."

"Why are you not sorry, then? Life's a good thing in the main, you will allow."

"Yes, when it's endurable at all. But to have a brute of a husband coming home at any hour of the night or morning, drunk upon the money she had earned by hard work, was enough to take more of the shine out of things than church-going on Sundays could put in again, regular as she was, poor woman! I'm as glad as her brute of a husband, that she's out of his way at last."

"How do you know he's glad of it?"

"He's been drunk every night since she died."

"Then he's the worse for losing her?"

"He may well be. Crying like a hypocrite, too, over his own work!"

"A fool he must be. A hypocrite, perhaps not. A hypocrite is a terrible name to give. Perhaps her death will do him good."

"He doesn't deserve to be done any good to. I would have made this coffin for him with a world of pleasure."

"I never found that I deserved anything, not even a coffin. The only claim that I could ever lay to anything was that I was very much in want of it."

The old smile returned—as much as to say, "That's your little game in the church." But I resolved to try nothing more with him at present; and indeed was sorry that I had started the new question at all, partly because thus I had again given him occasion to feel that he knew better than I did, which was not good either for him or for me in our relation to each other.

"This has been a fine old room once," I said, looking round the workshop.

"You can see it wasn't a workshop always, sir. Many a grand dinner-party has sat down in this room when it was in its glory. Look at the chimney-piece there."

"I have been looking at it," I said, going nearer.

"It represents the four quarters of the world, you see."

I saw strange figures of men and women, one on a kneeling camel, one on a crawling crocodile, and others differently mounted; with various besides of Nature's bizarre productions creeping and flying in stone-carving over the huge fire-place, in which, in place of a fire, stood several new and therefore brilliantly red cart-wheels. The sun shone through the upper part of a high window, of which many of the panes were broken, right in upon the cart-wheels, which, glowing thus in the chimney under the sombre chimney-piece, added to the grotesque look of the whole assemblage of contrasts. The coffin and the carpenter stood in the twilight occasioned by the sharp division of light made by a lofty wing of the house that rose flanking the other window. The room was still wainscotted in panels, which, I presume, for the sake of the more light required for handicraft, had been washed all over with white. At the level of labour they were broken in many places. Somehow or other, the whole reminded me of Albert Durer's "Melencholia."

Seeing I was interested in looking about his shop, my new friend—for I could not help feeling that we should be friends before all was over, and so began to count him one already—resumed the conversation. He had never taken up the dropped thread of it before.

"Yes, sir," he said; "the owners of the place little thought it would come to this—the deals growing into a coffin there on the spot where the grand dinner was laid for them and their guests! But there is another thing about it that is odder still; my son is the last male"—

Here he stopped suddenly, and his face grew very red. As suddenly he resumed—

"I'm not a gentleman, sir; but I will tell the truth. Curse it!—I beg your pardon, sir,"—and here the old smile—"I don't think I got that from THEIR side of the house.—My son's NOT the last male descendant."

Here followed another pause.

As to the imprecation, I knew better than to take any notice of a mere expression of excitement under a sense of some injury with which I was not yet acquainted. If I could get his feelings right in regard to other and more important things, a reform in that matter would soon follow; whereas to make a mountain of a molehill would be to put that very mountain between him and me. Nor would I ask him any questions, lest I should just happen to ask him the wrong one; for this parishioner of mine evidently wanted careful handling, if I would do him any good. And it will not do any man good to fling even the Bible in his face. Nay, a roll of bank-notes, which would be more evidently a good to most men, would carry insult with it if presented in that manner. You cannot expect people to accept before they have had a chance of seeing what the offered gift really is.

After a pause, therefore, the carpenter had once more to recommence, or let the conversation lie. I stood in a waiting attitude. And while I looked at him, I was reminded of some one else whom I knew—with whom, too, I had pleasant associations—though I could not in the least determine who that one might be.

"It's very foolish of me to talk so to a stranger," he resumed.

"It is very kind and friendly of you," I said, still careful to make no advances. "And you yourself belong to the old family that once lived in this old house?"

"It would be no boast to tell the truth, sir, even if it were a credit to me, which it is not. That family has been nothing but a curse to ours."

41

I noted that he spoke of that family as different from his, and yet implied that he belonged to it. The explanation would come in time. But the man was again silent, planing away at half the lid of his sister's coffin. And I could not help thinking that the closed mouth meant to utter nothing more on this occasion.

"I am sure there must be many a story to tell about this old place, if only there were any one to tell them," I said at last, looking round the room once more.—"I think I see the remains of paintings on the ceiling."

"You are sharp-eyed, sir. My father says they were plain enough in his young days."

"Is your father alive, then?"

"That he is, sir, and hearty too, though he seldom goes out of doors now. Will you go up stairs and see him? He's past ninety, sir. He has plenty of stories to tell about the old place—before it began to fall to pieces like."

"I won't go to-day," I said, partly because I wanted to be at home to receive any one who might call, and partly to secure an excuse for calling again upon the carpenter sooner than I should otherwise have liked to do. "I expect visitors myself, and it is time I were at home. Good morning."

"Good morning, sir."

And away home I went with a new wonder in my brain. The man did not seem unknown to me. I mean, the state of his mind woke no feeling of perplexity in me. I was certain of understanding it thoroughly when I had learned something of his history; for that such a man must have a history of his own was rendered only the more probable from the fact that he knew something of the history of his forefathers, though, indeed, there are some men who seem to have no other. It was strange, however, to think of that man working away at a trade in the very house in which such ancestors had eaten and drunk, and married and given in marriage. The house and family had declined together—in outward appearance at least; for it was quite possible both might have risen in the moral and spiritual scale in proportion as they sank in the social one. And if any of my readers are at first inclined to think that this could hardly be, seeing that the man was little, if anything, better than an infidel, I would just like to hold one minute's conversation with them on that subject. A man may be on the way to the truth, just in virtue of his doubting. I will tell you what Lord Bacon says, and of all writers of English I delight in him: "So it is in contemplation: if a man will begin with certainties, he shall end in doubts; but if he will be content to begin with doubts, he shall end in certainties." Now I could not tell the kind or character of this man's doubt; but it was evidently real and not affected doubt; and that was much in his favour. And I could see that he was a thinking man; just one of the sort I thought I should get on with in time, because he was honest—notwithstanding that unpleasant smile of his, which did irritate me a little, and partly piqued me into the determination to get the better of the man, if I possibly could, by making friends with him. At all events, here was another strange parishioner. And who could it be that he was like?

CHAPTER V. VISITORS FROM THE HALL.

When I came near my own gate, I saw that it was open; and when I came in sight of my own door, I found a carriage standing before it, and a footman ringing the bell. It was an old-fashioned carriage, with two white horses in it, yet whiter by age than by nature. They looked as if no coachman could get more than three miles an hour out of them, they were so fat and knuckle-kneed. But my attention could not rest long on the horses, and I reached the door just as my housekeeper was pronouncing me absent. There were two ladies in the carriage, one old and one young.

"Ah, here is Mr. Walton!" said the old lady, in a serene voice, with a clear hardness in its tone; and I held out my hand to aid her descent. She had pulled off her glove to get a card out of her card-case, and so put the tips of two old fingers, worn very smooth, as if polished with feeling what things were like, upon the palm of my hand. I then offered my hand to her companion, a girl apparently about fourteen, who took a hearty hold of it, and jumped down beside her with a smile. As I followed them into the house, I took their card from the housekeeper's hand, and read, Mrs Oldcastle and Miss Gladwyn.

I confess here to my reader, that these are not really the names I read on the card. I made these up this minute. But the names of the persons of humble position in my story are their real names. And my reason for making the difference will be plain enough. You can never find out my friend Old Rogers; you might find out the people who called on me in their carriage with the ancient white horses.

When they were seated in the drawing-room, I said to the old lady—

"I remember seeing you in church on Sunday morning. It is very kind of you to call so soon."

"You will always see me in church," she returned, with a stiff bow, and an expansion of deadness on her face, which I interpreted into an assertion of dignity, resulting from the implied possibility that I might have passed her over in my congregation, or might have forgotten her after not passing her over.

"Except when you have a headache, grannie," said Miss Gladwyn, with an arch look first at her grandmother, and then at me. "Grannie has bad headaches sometimes."

The deadness melted a little from Mrs Oldcastle's face, as she turned with half a smile to her grandchild, and said—

"Yes, Pet. But you know that cannot be an interesting fact to Mr. Walton."

"I beg your pardon, Mrs. Oldcastle," I said. "A clergyman ought to know something, and the more the better, of the troubles of his flock. Sympathy is one of the first demands he ought to be able to meet—I know what a headache is."

The former expression, or rather non-expression, returned; this time unaccompanied by a bow.

"I trust, Mr. Walton, I TRUST I am above any morbid necessity for sympathy. But, as you say, amongst the poor of your flock,—it IS very desirable that a clergyman should be able to sympathise."

"It's quite true what grannie says, Mr. Walton, though you mightn't think it. When she has a headache, she shuts herself up in her own room, and doesn't even let me come near her—nobody but Sarah; and how she can prefer her to me, I'm sure I don't know."

And here the girl pretended to pout, but with a sparkle in her bright gray eye.

"The subject is not interesting to me, Pet. Pray, Mr. Walton, is it a point of conscience with you to wear the surplice when you preach?"

"Not in the least," I answered. "I think I like it rather better on the whole. But that's not why I wear it."

"Never mind grannie, Mr. Walton. I think the surplice is lovely. I'm sure it's much liker the way we shall be dressed in heaven, though I don't think I shall ever get there, if I must read the good books grannie reads."

"I don't know that it is necessary to read any good books but the good book," I said.

"There, grannie!" exclaimed Miss Gladwyn, triumphantly. "I'm so glad I've got Mr Walton on my side!"

"Mr Walton is not so old as I am, my dear, and has much to learn yet."

I could not help feeling a little annoyed, (which was very foolish, I know,) and saying to myself, "If it's to make me like you, I had rather not learn any more;" but I said nothing aloud, of course.

"Have you got a headache to-day, grannie?"

"No, Pet. Be quiet. I wish to ask Mr Walton WHY he wears the surplice."

"Simply," I replied, "because I was told the people had been accustomed to it under my predecessor."

"But that can be no good reason for doing what is not right—that people have been accustomed to it."

"But I don't allow that it's not right. I think it is a matter of no consequence whatever. If I find that the people don't like it, I will give it up with pleasure."

"You ought to have principles of your own, Mr Walton."

"I hope I have. And one of them is, not to make mountains of molehills; for a molehill is not a mountain. A man ought to have too much to do in obeying his conscience and keeping his soul's garments clean, to mind whether he wears black or white when telling his flock that God loves them, and that they will never be happy till they believe it."

"They may believe that too soon."

"I don't think any one can believe the truth too soon."

A pause followed, during which it became evident to me that Miss Gladwyn saw fun in the whole affair, and was enjoying it thoroughly. Mrs Oldcastle's face, on the contrary, was illegible. She resumed in a measured still voice, which she meant to be meek, I daresay, but which was really authoritative—

"I am sorry, Mr Walton, that your principles are so loose and unsettled. You will see my honesty in saying so when you find that, objecting to the surplice, as I do, on Protestant grounds, I yet warn you against making any change because you may discover that your parishioners are against it. You have no idea, Mr Walton, what inroads Radicalism, as they call it, has been making in this neighbourhood. It is quite dreadful. Everybody, down to the poorest, claiming a right to think for himself, and set his betters right! There's one worse than any of the rest—but he's no better than an atheist—a carpenter of the name of Weir, always talking to his neighbours against the proprietors and the magistrates, and the clergy too, Mr Walton, and the game-laws; and what not? And if you once show them that you are afraid of them by going a step out of your way for THEIR opinion about anything, there will be no end to it; for, the beginning of strife is like the letting out of water, as you know. I should know nothing about it, but that, my daughter's maid—I came to hear of it through her—a decent girl of the name of Rogers, and born of decent parents, but unfortunately attached to the son of one of your churchwardens, who has put him into that mill on the river you can almost see from here."

"Who put him in the mill?"

"His own father, to whom it belongs."

"Well, it seems to me a very good match for her."

"Yes, indeed, and for him too. But his foolish father thinks the match below him, as if there was any difference between the positions of people in that rank of life! Every one seems striving to tread on the heels of every one else, instead of being content with the station to which God has called them. I am content with mine. I had nothing to do with putting myself there. Why should they not be content with theirs? They need to be taught Christian humility and respect for their superiors. That's the virtue most wanted at present. The poor have to look up to the rich"—

"That's right, grannie! And the rich have to look down on the poor."

"No, my dear. I did not say that. The rich have to be KIND to the poor."

"But, grannie, why did you marry Mr Oldcastle?"

"What does the child mean?"

"Uncle Stoddart says you refused ever so many offers when you were a girl."

"Uncle Stoddart has no business to be talking about such things to a chit like you," returned the grandmother smiling, however, at the charge, which so far certainly contained no reproach.

"And grandpapa was the ugliest and the richest of them all—wasn't he, grannie? and Colonel Markham the handsomest and the poorest?"

A flush of anger crimsoned the old lady's pale face. It looked dead no longer.

"Hold your tongue," she said. "You are rude."

And Miss Gladwyn did hold her tongue, but nothing else, for she was laughing all over.

The relation between these two was evidently a very odd one. It was clear

47

that Miss Gladwyn was a spoiled child, though I could not help thinking her very nicely spoiled, as far as I saw; and that the old lady persisted in regarding her as a cub, although her claws had grown quite long enough to be dangerous. Certainly, if things went on thus, it was pretty clear which of them would soon have the upper hand, for grannie was vulnerable, and Pet was not.

It really began to look as if there were none but characters in my parish. I began to think it must be the strangest parish in England, and to wonder that I had never heard of it before. "Surely it must be in some story-book at least!" I said to myself.

But her grand-daughter's tiger-cat-play drove the old lady nearer to me. She rose and held out her hand, saying, with some kindness—

"Take my advice, my dear Mr Walton, and don't make too much of your poor, or they'll soon be too much for you to manage.—Come, Pet: it's time to go home to lunch.—And for the surplice, take your own way and wear it. I shan't say anything more about it."

"I will do what I can see to be right in the matter," I answered as gently as I could; for I did not want to quarrel with her, although I thought her both presumptuous and rude.

"I'm on your side, Mr Walton," said the girl, with a sweet comical smile, as she squeezed my hand once more.

I led them to the carriage, and it was with a feeling of relief that I saw it drive off.

The old lady certainly was not pleasant. She had a white smooth face over which the skin was drawn tight, gray hair, and rather lurid hazel eyes. I felt a repugnance to her that was hardly to be accounted for by her arrogance to me, or by her superciliousness to the poor; although either would have accounted for much of it. For I confess that I have not yet learned to bear presumption and rudeness with all the patience and forgiveness with which I ought by this time to be able to meet them. And as to the poor, I am afraid I was always in some danger of being a partizan of theirs against the rich; and that a clergyman ought never to be. And indeed the poor rich have more need of the care of the clergyman than the others, seeing it is hardly that the rich shall enter into the kingdom of heaven, and the poor have all the advantage over them in that respect.

"Still," I said to myself, "there must be some good in the woman—she cannot be altogether so hard as she looks, else how should that child dare to take the liberties of a kitten with her? She doesn't look to ME like one to make game of! However, I shall know a little more about her when I return her call, and I will do my best to keep on good terms with her."

I took down a volume of Plato to comfort me after the irritation which my nerves had undergone, and sat down in an easy-chair beside the open window of my study. And with Plato in my hand, and all that outside my window, I began to feel as if, after all, a man might be happy, even if a lady had refused him. And there I sat, without opening my favourite vellum-bound volume, gazing out on the happy world, whence a gentle wind came in, as if to bid me welcome with a kiss to all it had to give me. And then I thought of the wind that bloweth where it listeth, which is everywhere, and I quite forgot to open my Plato, and thanked God for the Life of life, whose story and whose words are in that best of books, and who explains everything to us, and makes us love Socrates and David and all good men ten times more; and who follows no law but the law of love, and no fashion but the will of God; for where did ever one read words less like moralising and more like simple earnestness of truth than all those of Jesus? And I prayed my God that He would make me able to speak good common heavenly sense to my people, and forgive me for feeling so cross and proud towards the unhappy old lady—for I was sure she was not happy—and make me into a rock which swallowed up the waves of wrong in its great caverns, and never threw them back to swell the commotion of the angry sea whence they came. Ah, what it would be actually to annihilate wrong in this way!—to be able to say, it shall not be wrong against me, so utterly do I forgive it! How much sooner, then, would the wrong-doer repent, and get rid of the wrong from his side also! But the painful fact will show itself, not less curious than painful, that it is more difficult to forgive small wrongs than great ones. Perhaps, however, the forgiveness of the great wrongs is not so true as it seems. For do we not think it is a fine thing to forgive such wrongs, and so do it rather for our own sakes than for the sake of the wrongdoer? It is dreadful not to be good, and to have bad ways inside one.

Such thoughts passed through my mind. And once more the great light went up on me with regard to my office, namely, that just because I was parson to the parish, I must not be THE PERSON to myself. And I prayed God to keep me from feeling STUNG and proud, however any one might behave to me; for all my value lay in being a sacrifice to Him and the people.

So when Mrs Pearson knocked at the door, and told me that a lady and gentleman had called, I shut my book which I had just opened, and kept down as well as I could the rising grumble of the inhospitable Englishman, who is apt to be forgetful to entertain strangers, at least in the parlour of his heart. And I cannot count it perfect hospitality to be friendly and plentiful towards those whom you have invited to your house—what thank has a man in that?—while you are cold and forbidding to those who have not that claim on your attention. That is not to be perfect as our Father in heaven is perfect. By all means tell people, when you are busy about something that must be done, that you cannot spare the time for them except they want you upon something of yet more pressing necessity; but TELL them, and do not get rid of them by the use of the instrument commonly called THE COLD SHOULDER. It is a wicked instrument that, and ought to have fallen out of use by this time.

I went and received Mr and Miss Boulderstone, and was at least thus far rewarded—that the EERIE feeling, as the Scotch would call it, which I had about my parish, as containing none but CHARACTERS, and therefore not being CANNIE, was entirely removed. At least there was a wholesome leaven in it of honest stupidity. Please, kind reader, do not fancy I am sneering. I declare to you I think a sneer the worst thing God has not made. A curse is nothing in wickedness to it, it seems to me. I do mean that honest stupidity I respect heartily, and do assert my conviction that I do not know how England at least would get on without it. But I do not mean the stupidity that sets up for teaching itself to its neighbour, thinking itself wisdom all the time. That

50

I do not respect.

Mr and Miss Boulderstone left me a little fatigued, but in no way sore or grumbling. They only sent me back with additional zest to my Plato, of which I enjoyed a hearty page or two before any one else arrived. The only other visitors I had that day were an old surgeon in the navy, who since his retirement had practised for many years in the neighbourhood, and was still at the call of any one who did not think him too old-fashioned—for even here the fashions, though decidedly elderly young ladies by the time they arrived, held their sway none the less imperiously—and Mr Brownrigg, the churchwarden. More of Dr Duncan by and by.

Except Mr and Miss Boulderstone, I had not yet seen any common people. They were all decidedly uncommon, and, as regarded most of them, I could not think I should have any difficulty in preaching to them. For, whatever place a man may give to preaching in the ritual of the church—indeed it does not properly belong to the ritual at all—it is yet the part of the so-called service with which his personality has most to do. To the influences of the other parts he has to submit himself, ever turning the openings of his soul towards them, that he may not be a mere praying-machine; but with the sermon it is otherwise. That he produces. For that he is responsible. And therefore, I say, it was a great comfort to me to find myself amongst a people from which my spirit neither shrunk in the act of preaching, nor with regard to which it was likely to feel that it was beating itself against a stone wall. There was some good in preaching to a man like Weir or Old Rogers. Whether there was any good in preaching to a woman like Mrs Oldcastle I did not know.

The evening I thought I might give to my books, and thus end my first Monday in my parish; but, as I said, Mr Brownrigg, the churchwarden, called and stayed a whole weary hour, talking about matters quite uninteresting to any who may hereafter peruse what I am now writing. Really he was not an interesting man: short, broad, stout, red-faced, with an immense amount of mental inertia, discharging itself in constant lingual activity about little nothings. Indeed, when there was no new nothing to be had, the old nothing would do over again to make a fresh fuss about. But if you attempted to convey a thought into his mind which involved the moving round half a degree from where he stood, and looking at the matter from a point even so far new, you found him utterly, totally impenetrable, as pachydermatous as any rhinoceros or behemoth. One other corporeal fact I could not help observing, was, that his cheeks rose at once from the collar of his green coat, his neck being invisible, from the hollow between it and the jaw being filled up to a level. The conformation was just what he himself delighted to contemplate in his pigs, to which his resemblance was greatly increased by unwearied endeavours to keep himself close shaved.—I could not help feeling anxious about his son and Jane Rogers.—He gave a quantity of gossip about various people, evidently anxious that I should regard them as he regarded them; but in all he said concerning them I could scarcely detect one point of significance as to character or history. I was very glad indeed when the waddling of hands—for it was the perfect imbecility of hand-shaking—was over, and he was safely out of the gate. He had kept me standing on the steps for full five minutes, and I did not feel safe from him till I was once more in my study with the door shut.

I am not going to try my reader's patience with anything of a more detailed account of my introduction to my various parishioners. I shall mention them only as they come up in the course of my story. Before many days had passed I had found out my poor, who, I thought, must be somewhere, seeing the Lord had said we should have them with us always. There was a workhouse in the village, but there were not a great many in it; for the poor were kindly enough handled who belonged to the place, and were not too severely compelled to go into the house; though, I believe, in this house they would have been more comfortable than they were in their own houses.

I cannot imagine a much greater misfortune for a man, not to say a clergyman, than not to know, or knowing, not to minister to any of the poor. And I did not feel that I knew in the least where I was until I had found out and conversed with almost the whole of mine.

After I had done so, I began to think it better to return Mrs Oldcastle's visit, though I felt greatly disinclined to encounter that tight-skinned nose again, and that mouth whose smile had no light in it, except when it responded to some nonsense of her grand-daughter's.

CHAPTER VI. OLDCASTLE HALL.

About noon, on a lovely autumn day, I set out for Oldcastle Hall. The keenness of the air had melted away with the heat of the sun, yet still the air was fresh and invigorating. Can any one tell me why it is that, when the earth is renewing her youth in the spring, man should feel feeble and low-spirited, and gaze with bowed head, though pleased heart, on the crocuses; whereas, on the contrary, in the autumn, when nature is dying for the winter, he feels strong and hopeful, holds his head erect, and walks with a vigorous step, though the flaunting dahlias discourage him greatly? I do not ask for the physical causes: those I might be able to find out for myself; but I ask, Where is the rightness and fitness in the thing? Should not man and nature go together in this world which was made for man—not for science, but for man? Perhaps I have some glimmerings of where the answer lies. Perhaps "I see a cherub that sees it." And in many of our questions we have to be content with such an approximation to an answer as this. And for my part I am content with this. With less, I am not content.

Whatever that answer may be, I walked over the old Gothic bridge with a heart strong enough to meet Mrs Oldcastle without flinching. I might have to quarrel with her—I could not tell: she certainly was neither safe nor wholesome. But this I was sure of, that I would not quarrel with her without being quite certain that I ought. I wish it were NEVER one's duty to quarrel with anybody: I do so hate it. But not to do it sometimes is to smile in the devil's face, and that no one ought to do. However, I had not to quarrel this time.

The woods on the other side of the river from my house, towards which I was now walking, were of the most sombre rich colour—sombre and rich, like a life that has laid up treasure in heaven, locked in a casket of sorrow. I came nearer and nearer to them through the village, and approached the great iron gate with the antediluvian monsters on the top of its stone pillars. And awful monsters they were—are still! I see the tail of one of them at this very moment. But they let me through very quietly, notwithstanding their evil looks. I thought they were saying to each other across the top of the gate, "Never mind; he'll catch it soon enough." But, as I said, I did not catch it that day; and I could not have caught it that day; it was too lovely a day to catch any hurt even from that most hurtful of all beings under the sun, an unwomanly woman.

I wandered up the long winding road, through the woods which I had remarked flanking the meadow on my first walk up the river. These woods smelt so sweetly—their dead and dying leaves departing in sweet odours—that they quite made up for the absence of the flowers. And the wind—no, there was no wind—there was only a memory of wind that woke now and then in the bosom of the wood, shook down a few leaves, like the thoughts that flutter away in sighs, and then was still again.

I am getting old, as I told you, my friends. (See there, you seem my friends already. Do not despise an old man because he cannot help loving people he never saw or even heard of.) I say I am getting old—(is it BUT or THEREFORE? I do not know which)—but, therefore, I shall never forget that one autumn day in those grandly fading woods.

Up the slope of the hillside they rose like one great rainbow-billow of foliage—bright yellow, red-rusty and bright fading green, all kinds and shades of brown and purple. Multitudes of leaves lay on the sides of the path, so many that I betook myself to my old childish amusement of walking in them without lifting my feet, driving whole armies of them with ocean-like rustling before me. I did not do so as I came back. I walked in the middle of the way then, and I remember stepping over many single leaves, in a kind of mechanico-merciful way, as if they had been living creatures—as indeed who can tell but they are, only they must be pretty nearly dead when they are on the ground.

At length the road brought me up to the house. It did not look such a large house as I have since found it to be. And it certainly was not an interesting house from the outside, though its surroundings of green grass and trees would make any whole beautiful. Indeed the house itself tried hard to look ugly, not quite succeeding, only because of the kind foiling of its efforts by the Virginia creepers and ivy, which, as if ashamed of its staring countenance, did all they could to spread their hands over it and hide it. But there was one charming group of old chimneys, belonging to some portion behind, which indicated a very different, namely, a very much older, face upon the house once—a face that had passed away to give place to this. Once inside, I found there were more remains of the olden time than I had expected. I was led up one of those grand square oak staircases, which look like a portion of the house to be dwelt in, and not like a ladder for getting from one part of the habitable regions to another. On the top was a fine expanse of landing, another hall, in fact, from which I was led towards the back of the house by a narrow passage, and shown into a small dark drawing-room with a deep stone-mullioned window, wainscoted in oak simply carved and panelled. Several doors around indicated communication with other parts of the house. Here I found Mrs Oldcastle, reading what I judged to be one of the cheap and gaudy religious books of the present day. She rose and RECEIVED me, and having motioned me to a seat, began to talk about the parish. You would have perceived at once from her tone that she recognised no other bond of connexion between us but the parish.

"I hear you have been most kind in visiting the poor, Mr Walton. You must take care that they don't take advantage of your kindness, though. I assure you, you will find some of them very grasping indeed. And you need not expect that they will give you the least credit for good intentions."

"I have seen nothing yet to make me uneasy on that score. But certainly my testimony is of no weight yet."

"Mine is. I have proved them. The poor of this neighbourhood are very deficient in gratitude."

"Yes, grannie,——"

I started. But there was no interruption, such as I have made to indicate my surprise; although, when I looked half round in the direction whence the voice came, the words that followed were all rippled with a sweet laugh of amusement.

"Yes, grannie, you are right. You remember how old dame Hope wouldn't take the money you offered her, and dropped such a disdainful courtesy. It

55

was SO greedy of her, wasn't it?"

"I am sorry to hear of any disdainful reception of kindness," I said.

"Yes, and she had the coolness, within a fortnight, to send up to me and ask if I would be kind enough to lend her half-a-crown for a few weeks."

"And then it was your turn, grannie! You sent her five shillings, didn't you?—Oh no; I'm wrong. That was the other woman."

"Indeed, I did not send her anything but a rebuke. I told her that it would be a very wrong thing in me to contribute to the support of such an evil spirit of unthankfulness as she indulged in. When she came to see her conduct in its true light, and confessed that she had behaved very abominably, I would see what I could do for her."

"And meantime she was served out, wasn't she? With her sick boy at home, and nothing to give him?" said Miss Gladwyn.

"She made her own bed, and had to lie on it."

"Don't you think a little kindness might have had more effect in bringing her to see that she was wrong."

"Grannie doesn't believe in kindness, except to me—dear old grannie! She spoils me. I'm sure I shall be ungrateful some day; and then she'll begin to read me long lectures, and prick me with all manner of headless pins. But I won't stand it, I can tell you, grannie! I'm too much spoiled for that."

Mrs Oldcastle was silent—why, I could not tell, except it was that she knew she had no chance of quieting the girl in any other way.

I may mention here, lest I should have no opportunity afterwards, that I inquired of dame Hope as to her version of the story, and found that there had been a great misunderstanding, as I had suspected. She was really in no want at the time, and did not feel that it would be quite honourable to take the money when she did not need it—(some poor people ARE capable of such reasoning)—and so had refused it, not without a feeling at the same time that it was more pleasant to refuse than to accept from such a giver; some stray sparkle of which feeling, discovered by the keen eye of Miss Gladwyn, may have given that appearance of disdain to her courtesy to which the girl alluded. When, however, her boy in service was brought home ill, she had sent to ask for what she now required, on the very ground that it had been offered to her before. The misunderstanding had arisen from the total incapacity of Mrs Oldcastle to enter sympathetically into the feelings of one as superior to herself in character as she was inferior in worldly condition.

But to return to Oldcastle Hall.

I wished to change the subject, knowing that blind defence is of no use. One must have definite points for defence, if one has not a thorough understanding of the character in question; and I had neither.

"This is a beautiful old house," I said. "There must be strange places about it."

Mrs Oldcastle had not time to reply, or at least did not reply, before Miss Gladwyn said—

"Oh, Mr Walton, have you looked out of the window yet? You don't know what a lovely place this is, if you haven't."

And as she spoke she emerged from a recess in the room, a kind of dark alcove, where she had been amusing herself with what I took to be some sort of puzzle, but which I found afterwards to be the bit and curb-chain of her pony's bridle which she was polishing up to her own bright mind, because the stable-boy had not pleased her in the matter, and she wanted both to get them brilliant and to shame the lad for the future. I followed her to the window, where I was indeed as much surprised and pleased as she could have wished.

"There!" she said, holding back one of the dingy heavy curtains with her small childish hand.

And there, indeed, I saw an astonishment. It did not lie in the lovely sweeps of hill and hollow stretching away to the horizon, richly wooded, and—though I saw none of them—sprinkled, certainly with sweet villages full of human thoughts, loves, and hopes; the astonishment did not lie in this—

though all this was really much more beautiful to the higher imagination—but in the fact that, at the first glance, I had a vision properly belonging to a rugged or mountainous country. For I had approached the house by a gentle slope, which certainly was long and winding, but had occasioned no feeling in my mind that I had reached any considerable height. And I had come up that one beautiful staircase; no more; and yet now, when I looked from this window, I found myself on the edge of a precipice—not a very deep one, certainly, yet with all the effect of many a deeper. For below the house on this side lay a great hollow, with steep sides, up which, as far as they could reach, the trees were climbing. The sides were not all so steep as the one on which the house stood, but they were all rocky and steep, with here and there slopes of green grass. And down in the bottom, in the centre of the hollow, lay a pool of water. I knew it only by its slaty shimmer through the fading green of the tree-tops between me and it.

"There!" again exclaimed Miss Gladwyn; "isn't that beautiful? But you haven't seen the most beautiful thing yet. Grannie, where's—ah! there she is! There's auntie! Don't you see her down there, by the side of the pond? That pond is a hundred feet deep. If auntie were to fall in she would be drowned before you could jump down to get her out. Can you swim?"

Before I had time to answer, she was off again.

"Don't you see auntie down there?"

"No, I don't see her. I have been trying very hard, but I can't."

"Well, I daresay you can't. Nobody, I think, has got eyes but myself. Do you see a big stone by the edge of the pond, with another stone on the top of it, like a big potato with a little one grown out of it?"

"No."

"Well, auntie is under the trees on the opposite side from that stone. Do you see her yet?"

"No."

"Then you must come down with me, and I will introduce you to her.

She's much the prettiest thing here. Much prettier than grannie."

Here she looked over her shoulder at grannie, who, instead of being angry, as, from what I had seen on our former interview, I feared she would be, only said, without even looking up from the little blue-boarded book she was again reading—

"You are a saucy child."

Whereupon Miss Gladwyn laughed merrily.

"Come along," she said, and, seizing me by the hand, led me out of the room, down a back-staircase, across a piece of grass, and then down a stair in the face of the rock, towards the pond below. The stair went in zigzags, and, although rough, was protected by an iron balustrade, without which, indeed, it would have been very dangerous.

"Isn't your grandmamma afraid to let you run up and down here, Miss Gladwyn?" I said.

"Me!" she exclaimed, apparently in the utmost surprise. "That WOULD be fun! For, you know, if she tried to hinder me—but she knows it's no use; I taught her that long ago—let me see, how long: oh! I don't know—I should think it must be ten years at least. I ran away, and they thought I had drowned myself in the pond. And I saw them, all the time, poking with a long stick in the pond, which, if I had been drowned there, never could have brought me up, for it is a hundred feet deep, I am sure. How I hurt my sides trying to keep from screaming with laughter! I fancied I heard one say to the other, 'We must wait till she swells and floats.'"

"Dear me! what a peculiar child!" I said to myself.

And yet somehow, whatever she said—even when she was most rude to her grandmother—she was never offensive. No one could have helped feeling all the time that she was a little lady.—I thought I would venture a question with her. I stood still at a turn of the zigzag, and looked down into the hollow, still a good way below us, where I could now distinguish the form, on the opposite side of the pond, of a woman seated at the foot of a tree, and stooping forward over a book.

"May I ask you a question, Miss Gladwyn?"

"Yes, twenty, if you like; but I won't answer one of them till you give up calling me Miss Gladwyn. We can't be friends, you know, so long as you do that."

"What am I to call you, then? I never heard you called by any other name than Pet, and that would hardly do, would it?"

"Oh, just fancy if you called me Pet before grannie! That's grannie's name for me, and nobody dares to use it but grannie—not even auntie; for, between you and me, auntie is afraid of grannie; I can't think why. I never was afraid of anybody—except, yes, a little afraid of old Sarah. She used to be my nurse, you know; and grandmamma and everybody is afraid of her, and that's just why I never do one thing she wants me to do. It would never do to give in to being afraid of her, you know.—There's auntie, you see, down there, just where I told you before."

"Oh yes! I see her now.—What does your aunt call you, then?"

"Why, what you must call me—my own name, of course."

"What is that?"

"Judy."

She said it in a tone which seemed to indicate surprise that I should not know her name—perhaps read it off her face, as one ought to know a flower's name by looking at it. But she added instantly, glancing up in my face most comically—

"I wish yours was Punch."

"Why, Judy?"

"It would be such fun, you know."

"Well, it would be odd, I must confess. What is your aunt's name?"

"Oh, such a funny name!—much funnier than Judy: Ethelwyn. It sounds as if it ought to mean something, doesn't it?"

"Yes. It is an Anglo-Saxon word, without doubt."

"What does it mean?"

"I'm not sure about that. I will try to find out when I go home—if you would like to know."

"Yes, that I should. I should like to know everything about auntie Ethelwyn. Isn't it pretty?"

"So pretty that I should like to know something more about Aunt Ethelwyn. What is her other name?"

"Why, Ethelwyn Oldcastle, to be sure. What else could it be?"

"Why, you know, for anything I knew, Judy, it might have been Gladwyn. She might have been your father's sister."

"Might she? I never thought of that. Oh, I suppose that is because I never think about my father. And now I do think of it, I wonder why nobody ever mentions him to me, or my mother either. But I often think auntie must be thinking about my mother. Something in her eyes, when they are sadder than usual, seems to remind me of my mother."

"You remember your mother, then?"

"No, I don't think I ever saw her. But I've answered plenty of questions, haven't I? I assure you, if you want to get me on to the Catechism, I don't know a word of it. Come along."

I laughed.

"What!" she said, pulling me by the hand, "you a clergyman, and laugh at the Catechism! I didn't know that."

"I'm not laughing at the Catechism, Judy. I'm only laughing at the idea of putting Catechism questions to you."

"You KNOW I didn't mean it," she said, with some indignation.

"I know now," I answered. "But you haven't let me put the only question I wanted to put."

"What is it?"

"How old are you?"

"Twelve. Come along."

And away we went down the rest of the stair.

When we reached the bottom, a winding path led us through the trees to the side of the pond, along which we passed to get to the other side.

And then all at once the thought struck me—why was it that I had never seen this auntie, with the lovely name, at church? Was she going to turn out another strange parishioner?

There she sat, intent on her book. As we drew near she looked up and rose, but did not come forward.

"Aunt Winnie, here's Mr. Walton," said Judy.

I lifted my hat and held out my hand. Before our hands met, however, a tremendous splash reached my ears from the pond. I started round. Judy had vanished. I had my coat half off, and was rushing to the pool, when Miss Oldcastle stopped me, her face unmoved, except by a smile, saying, "It's only one of that frolicsome child's tricks, Mr Walton. It is well for you that I was here, though. Nothing would have delighted her more than to have you in the water too."

"But," I said, bewildered, and not half comprehending, "where is she?"

"There," returned Miss Oldcastle, pointing to the pool, in the middle of which arose a heaving and bubbling, presently yielding passage to the laughing face of Judy.

"Why don't you help me out, Mr Walton? You said you could swim."

"No, I did not," I answered coolly. "You talked so fast, you did not give me time to say so."

"It's very cold," she returned.

"Come out, Judy dear," said her aunt. "Run home and change your clothes. There's a dear."

Judy swam to the opposite side, scrambled out, and was off like a spaniel through the trees and up the stairs, dripping and raining as she went.

"You must be very much astonished at the little creature, Mr Walton."

"I find her very interesting. Quite a study."

"There never was a child so spoiled, and never a child on whom it took less effect to hurt her. I suppose such things do happen sometimes. She is really a good girl; though mamma, who has done all the spoiling, will not allow me to say she is good."

Here followed a pause, for, Judy disposed of, what should I say next? And the moment her mind turned from Judy, I saw a certain stillness—not a cloud, but the shadow of a cloud—come over Miss Oldcastle's face, as if she, too, found herself uncomfortable, and did not know what to say next. I tried to get a glance at the book in her hand, for I should know something about her at once if I could only see what she was reading. She never came to church, and I wanted to arrive at some notion of the source of her spiritual life; for that she had such, a single glance at her face was enough to convince me. This, I mean, made me even anxious to see what the book was. But I could only discover that it was an old book in very shabby binding, not in the least like the books that young ladies generally have in their hands.

And now my readers will possibly be thinking it odd that I have never yet said a word about what either Judy or Miss Oldcastle was like. If there is one thing I feel more inadequate to than another, in taking upon me to relate—it is to describe a lady. But I will try the girl first.

Judy was rosy, gray-eyed, auburn-haired, sweet-mouthed. She had confidence in her chin, assertion in her nose, defiance in her eyebrows, honesty and friendliness over all her face. No one, evidently, could have a warmer friend; and to an enemy she would be dangerous no longer than a fit of passion might last. There was nothing acrid in her; and the reason, I presume, was, that she had never yet hurt her conscience. That is a very different thing from saying she had never done wrong, you know. She was not tall, even for her age, and just a little too plump for the immediate suggestion of grace. Yet every motion of the child would have been graceful, except for the fact that impulse was always predominant, giving a certain jerkiness, like the hopping of a bird, instead of the gliding of one motion into another, such as you might see in the same bird on the wing.

There is one of the ladies.

But the other—how shall I attempt to describe her?

The first thing I felt was, that she was a lady-woman. And to feel that is almost to fall in love at first sight. And out of this whole, the first thing you distinguished would be the grace over all. She was rather slender, rather tall, rather dark-haired, and quite blue-eyed. But I assure you it was not upon that occasion that I found out the colour of her eyes. I was so taken with her whole that I knew nothing about her parts. Yet she was blue-eyed, indicating northern extraction—some centuries back perhaps. That blue was the blue of the sea that had sunk through the eyes of some sea-rover's wife and settled in those of her child, to be born when the voyage was over. It had been dyed so deep INGRAYNE, as Spenser would say, that it had never been worn from the souls of the race since, and so was every now and then shining like heaven out at some of its eyes. Her features were what is called regular. They were delicate and brave.—After the grace, the dignity was the next thing you came to discover. And the only thing you would not have liked, you would have discovered last. For when the shine of the courtesy with which she received me had faded away a certain look of negative haughtiness, of withdrawal, if not of repulsion, took its place, a look of consciousness of her own high breeding—a pride, not of life, but of circumstance of life, which disappointed me in the midst of so much that was very lovely. Her voice was sweet, and I could have fancied a tinge of sadness in it, to which impression her slowness of speech, without any drawl in it, contributed. But I am not doing well as an artist in describing her so fully before my reader has become in the least degree interested in her. I was seeing her, and no words can make him see her.

Fearing lest some such fancy as had possessed Judy should be moving in her mind, namely, that I was, if not exactly going to put her through her Catechism, yet going in some way or other to act the clergyman, I hastened to speak.

"This is a most romantic spot, Miss Oldcastle," I said; "and as surprising as it is romantic. I could hardly believe my eyes when I looked out of the window and saw it first."

"Your surprise was the more natural that the place itself is not properly natural, as you must have discovered."

This was rather a remarkable speech for a young lady to make. I answered—

"I only know that such a chasm is the last thing I should have expected to find in this gently undulating country. That it is artificial I was no more prepared to hear than I was to see the place itself."

"It looks pretty, but it has not a very poetic origin," she returned. "It is nothing but the quarry out of which the old house at the top of it was built."

"I must venture to differ from you entirely in the aspect such an origin assumes to me," I said. "It seems to me a more poetic origin than any convulsion of nature whatever would have been; for, look you," I said—being as a young man too much inclined to the didactic, "for, look you," I said—and she did look at me—"from that buried mass of rock has arisen this living house with its histories of ages and generations; and"—

Here I saw a change pass upon her face: it grew almost pallid. But her large blue eyes were still fixed on mine.

"And it seems to me," I went on, "that such a chasm made by the uplifting of a house therefrom, is therefore in itself more poetic than if it were even the mouth of an extinct volcano. For, grand as the motions and deeds of Nature are, terrible as is the idea of the fiery heart of the earth breaking out in convulsions, yet here is something greater; for human will, human thought, human hands in human labour and effort, have all been employed to build

65

this house, making not only the house beautiful, but the place whence it came beautiful too. It stands on the edge of what Shelley would call its 'antenatal tomb'—now beautiful enough to be its mother—filled from generation to generation "—

Her face had grown still paler, and her lips moved as if she would speak; but no sound came from them. I had gone on, thinking it best to take no notice of her paleness; but now I could not help expressing concern.

"I am afraid you feel ill, Miss Oldcastle."

"Not at all," she answered, more quickly than she had yet spoken.

"This place must be damp," I said. "I fear you have taken cold."

She drew herself up a little haughtily, thinking, no doubt, that after her denial I was improperly pressing the point. So I drew back to the subject of our conversation.

"But I can hardly think," I said, "that all this mass of stone could be required to build the house, large as it is. A house is not solid, you know."

"No," she answered. "The original building was more of a castle, with walls and battlements. I can show you the foundations of them still; and the picture, too, of what the place used to be. We are not what we were then. Many a cottage, too, has been built out of this old quarry. Not a stone has been taken from it for the last fifty years, though. Just let me show you one thing, Mr. Walton, and then I must leave you."

"Do not let me detain you a moment. I will go at once," I said; "though, if you would allow me, I should be more at ease if I might see you safe at the top of the stair first."

She smiled.

"Indeed, I am not ill," she answered; "but I have duties to attend to. Just let me show you this, and then you shall go with me back to mamma."

She led the way to the edge of the pond and looked into it. I followed, and gazed down into its depths, till my sight was lost in them. I could see no bottom to the rocky shaft.

"There is a strong spring down there," she said. "Is it not a dreadful place? Such a depth!"

"Yes," I answered; "but it has not the horror of dirty water; it is as clear as crystal. How does the surplus escape?"

"On the opposite side of the hill you came up there is a well, with a strong stream from it into the river."

"I almost wonder at your choosing such a place to read in. I should hardly like to be so near this pond," said I, laughing.

"Judy has taken all that away. Nothing in nature, and everything out of it, is strange to Judy, poor child! But just look down a little way into the water on this side. Do you see anything?"

"Nothing," I answered.

"Look again, against the wall of the pond," she said.

"I see a kind of arch or opening in the side," I answered.

"That is what I wanted you to see. Now, do you see a little barred window, there, in the face of the rock, through the trees?"

"I cannot say I do," I replied.

"No. Except you know where it is—and even then—it is not so easy to find it. I find it by certain trees."

"What is it?"

"It is the window of a little room in the rock, from which a stair leads down through the rock to a sloping passage. That is the end of it you see under the water."

"Provided, no doubt," I said, "in case of siege, to procure water."

"Most likely; but not, therefore, confined to that purpose. There are more dreadful stories than I can bear to think of"—-

Here she paused abruptly, and began anew "——As if that house had brought death and doom out of the earth with it. There was an old burial-ground here before the Hall was built."

"Have you ever been down the stair you speak of?" I asked.

"Only part of the way," she answered. "But Judy knows every step of it. If it were not that the door at the top is locked, she would have dived through that archway now, and been in her own room in half the time. The child does not know what fear means."

We now moved away from the pond, towards the side of the quarry and the open-air stair-case, which I thought must be considerably more pleasant than the other. I confess I longed to see the gleam of that water at the bottom of the dark sloping passage, though.

Miss Oldcastle accompanied me to the room where I had left her mother, and took her leave with merely a bow of farewell. I saw the old lady glance sharply from her to me as if she were jealous of what we might have been talking about.

"Grannie, are you afraid Mr. Walton has been saying pretty things to Aunt Winnie? I assure you he is not of that sort. He doesn't understand that kind of thing. But he would have jumped into the pond after me and got his death of cold if auntie would have let him. It WAS cold. I think I see you dripping now, Mr Walton."

There she was in her dark corner, coiled up on a couch, and laughing heartily; but all as if she had done nothing extraordinary. And, indeed, estimated either by her own notions or practices, what she had done was not in the least extraordinary.

Disinclined to stay any longer, I shook hands with the grandmother, with a certain invincible sense of slime, and with the grandchild with a feeling of mischievous health, as if the girl might soon corrupt the clergyman into a partnership in pranks as well as in friendship. She fallowed me out of the room, and danced before me down the oak staircase, clearing the portion from the first landing at a bound. Then she turned and waited for me, who came very deliberately, feeling the unsure contact of sole and wax. As soon as I reached her, she said, in a half-whisper, reaching up towards me on tiptoe—

"Isn't she a beauty?"

"Who? your grandmamma?" I returned.

She gave me a little push, her face glowing with fun. But I did not expect she would take her revenge as she did. "Yes, of course," she answered, quite gravely. "Isn't she a beauty?"

And then, seeing that she had put me hors de combat, she burst into loud laughter, and, opening the hall-door for me, let me go without another word.

I went home very quietly, and, as I said, stepping with curious care—of which, of course, I did not think at the time—over the yellow and brown leaves that lay in the middle of the road.

CHAPTER VII. THE BISHOP'S BASIN.

I went home very quietly, as I say, thinking about the strange elements that not only combine to make life, but must be combined in our idea of life, before we can form a true theory about it. Now-a-days, the vulgar notion of what is life-like in any annals is to be realised by sternly excluding everything but the commonplace; and the means, at least, are often attained, with this much of the end as well—that the appearance life bears to vulgar minds is represented with a wonderful degree of success. But I believe that this is, at least, quite as unreal a mode of representing life as the other extreme, wherein the unlikely, the romantic, and the uncommon predominate. I doubt whether there is a single history—if one could only get at the whole of it—in which there is not a considerable admixture of the unlikely become fact, including a few strange coincidences; of the uncommon, which, although striking at first, has grown common from familiarity with its presence as our own; with even, at least, some one more or less rosy touch of what we call the romantic. My own conviction is, that the poetry is far the deepest in us, and that the prose is only broken-down poetry; and likewise that to this our lives correspond. The poetic region is the true one, and just, THEREFORE, the incredible one to the lower order of mind; for although every mind is capable of the truth, or rather capable of becoming capable of the truth, there may lie ages between its capacity and the truth. As you will hear some people read poetry so that no mortal could tell it was poetry, so do some people read their own lives and those of others.

I fell into these reflections from comparing in my own mind my former experiences in visiting my parishioners with those of that day. True, I had never sat down to talk with one of them without finding that that man or that woman had actually a HISTORY, the most marvellous and important fact to a human being; nay, I had found something more or less remarkable in every one of their histories, so that I was more than barely interested in each of them. And as I made more acquaintance with them, (for I had not been in the position, or the disposition either, before I came to Marshmallows, necessary to the gathering of such experiences,) I came to the conclusion— not that I had got into an extraordinary parish of characters—but that every parish must be more or less extraordinary from the same cause. Why did I not use to see such people about me before? Surely I had undergone a change of some sort. Could it be, that the trouble I had been going through of late, had opened the eyes of my mind to the understanding, or rather the simple SEEING, of my fellow-men?

But the people among whom I had been to-day belonged rather to such as might be put into a romantic story. Certainly I could not see much that was romantic in the old lady; and yet, those eyes and that tight-skinned face—what might they not be capable of in the working out of a story? And then the place they lived in! Why, it would hardly come into my ideas of a nineteenth-century country parish at all. I was tempted to try to persuade myself that all that had happened, since I rose to look out of the window in the old house, had been but a dream. For how could that wooded dell have come there after all? It was much too large for a quarry. And that madcap girl—she never flung herself into the pond!—it could not be. And what could the book have been that the lady with the sea-blue eyes was reading? Was that a real book at all? No. Yes. Of course it was. But what was it? What had that to do with the matter? It might turn out to be a very commonplace book after all. No; for commonplace books are generally new, or at least in fine bindings. And here was a shabby little old book, such as, if it had been commonplace, would not have been likely to be the companion of a young lady at the bottom of a quarry—

> *"A savage place, as holy and enchanted*
>
> *As e'er beneath a waning moon was haunted*
>
> *By woman wailing for her demon lover."*

I know all this will sound ridiculous, especially that quotation from Kubla Khan coming after the close of the preceding sentence; but it is only so much the more like the jumble of thoughts that made a chaos of my mind as I went home. And then for that terrible pool, and subterranean passage, and all that—what had it all to do with this broad daylight, and these dying autumn leaves? No doubt there had been such places. No doubt there were such places somewhere yet. No doubt this was one of them. But, somehow or other, it would not come in well. I had no intention of GOING IN FOR—that is the phrase now—going in for the romantic. I would take the impression off by going to see Weir the carpenter's old father. Whether my plan was successful or not, I shall leave my reader to judge.

I found Weir busy as usual, but not with a coffin this time. He was working at a window-sash. "Just like life," I thought—tritely perhaps. "The other day he was closing up in the outer darkness, and now he is letting in the light."

"It's a long time since you was here last, sir," he said, but without a smile.

Did he mean a reproach? If so, I was more glad of that reproach than I would have been of the warmest welcome, even from Old Rogers. The fact was that, having a good deal to attend to besides, and willing at the same time to let the man feel that he was in no danger of being bored by my visits, I had not made use even of my reserve in the shape of a visit to his father.

"Well," I answered, "I wanted to know something about all my people, before I paid a second visit to any of them."

"All right, sir. Don't suppose I meant to complain. Only to let you know you was welcome, sir."

"I've just come from my first visit to Oldcastle Hall. And, to tell the truth, for I don't like pretences, my visit to-day was not so much to you as to your father, whom, perhaps, I ought to have called upon before, only I was afraid of seeming to intrude upon you, seeing we don't exactly think the same way about some things," I added—with a smile, I know, which was none the less genuine that I remember it yet.

And what makes me remember it yet? It is the smile that lighted up his face in response to mine. For it was more than I looked for. And his answer helped to fix the smile in my memory.

"You made me think, sir, that perhaps, after all, we were much of the same way of thinking, only perhaps you was a long way ahead of me."

Now the man was not right in saying that we were much of the same way of THINKING; for our opinions could hardly do more than come within sight of each other; but what he meant was right enough. For I was certain, from the first, that the man had a regard for the downright, honest way of things, and I hoped that I too had such a regard. How much of selfishness and of pride in one's own judgment might be mixed up with it, both in his case and mine, I had been too often taken in—by myself, I mean—to be at all careful to discriminate, provided there was a proportion of real honesty along with it, which, I felt sure, would ultimately eliminate the other. For in the moral nest, it is not as with the sparrow and the cuckoo. The right, the original inhabitant is the stronger; and, however unlikely at any given point in the history it may be, the sparrow will grow strong enough to heave the intruding cuckoo overboard. So I was pleased that the man should do me the honour of thinking I was right as far as he could see, which is the greatest honour one man can do another; for it is setting him on his own steed, as the eastern tyrants used to do. And I was delighted to think that the road lay open for further and more real communion between us in time to come.

"Well," I answered, "I think we shall understand each other perfectly before long. But now I must see your father, if it is convenient and agreeable."

"My father will be delighted to see you, I know, sir. He can't get so far as the church on Sundays; but you'll find him much more to your mind than me. He's been putting ever so many questions to me about the new parson, wanting me to try whether I couldn't get more out of you than the old parson. That's the way we talk about you, you see, sir. You'll understand. And I've never told him that I'd been to church since you came—I suppose from a bit of pride, because I had so long lefused to go; but I don't doubt some of the neighbours have told him, for he never speaks about it now. And I know he's been looking out for you; and I fancy he's begun to wonder that the parson was going to see everybody but him. It WILL be a pleasure to the old man, sir, for he don't see a great many to talk to; and he's fond of a bit of gossip, is the old man, sir."

So saying, Weir led the way through the shop into a lobby behind, and thence up what must have been a back-stair of the old house, into a large room over the workshop. There were bits of old carving about the walls of the room yet, but, as in the shop below, all had been whitewashed. At one end stood a bed with chintz curtains and a warm-looking counterpane of rich faded embroidery. There was a bit of carpet by the bedside, and another bit in front of the fire; and there the old man sat, on one side, in a high-backed not very easy-looking chair. With a great effort he managed to rise as I approached him, notwithstanding my entreaties that he would not move. He looked much older when on his feet, for he was bent nearly double, in which posture the marvel was how he could walk at all. For he did totter a few steps to meet me, without even the aid of a stick, and, holding out a thin, shaking hand, welcomed me with an air of breeding rarely to be met with in his station in society. But the chief part of this polish sprung from the inbred kindliness of his nature, which was manifest in the expression of his noble old countenance. Age is such a different thing in different natures! One man seems to grow more and more selfish as he grows older; and in another the slow fire of time seems only to consume, with fine, imperceptible gradations, the yet lingering selfishness in him, letting the light of the kingdom, which the Lord says is within, shine out more and more, as the husk grows thin and is ready to fall off, that the man, like the seed sown, may pierce the earth of this world, and rise into the pure air and wind and dew of the second life.

The face of a loving old man is always to me like a morning moon, reflecting the yet unrisen sun of the other world, yet fading before its approaching light, until, when it does rise, it pales and withers away from our gaze, absorbed in the source of its own beauty. This old man, you may see, took my fancy wonderfully, for even at this distance of time, when I am old myself, the recollection of his beautiful old face makes me feel as if I could write poetry about him.

"I'm blithe to see ye, sir," said he. "Sit ye down, sir."

And, turning, he pointed to his own easy-chair; and I then saw his profile. It was delicate as that of Dante, which in form it marvellously resembled. But all the sternness which Dante's evil times had generated in his prophetic face was in this old man's replaced by a sweetness of hope that was lovely to behold.

"No, Mr Weir," I said, "I cannot take your chair. The Bible tells us to rise up before the aged, not to turn them out of their seats."

"It would do me good to see you sitting in my cheer, sir. The pains that my son Tom there takes to keep it up as long as the old man may want it! It's a good thing I bred him to the joiner's trade, sir. Sit ye down, sir. The cheer'll hold ye, though I warrant it won't last that long after I be gone home. Sit ye down, sir."

Thus entreated, I hesitated no longer, but took the old man's seat. His son brought another chair for him, and he sat down opposite the fire and close to me. Thomas then went back to his work, leaving us alone.

"Ye've had some speech wi' my son Tom," said the old man, the moment he was gone, leaning a little towards me. "It's main kind o' you, sir, to take up kindly wi' poor folks like us."

"You don't say it's kind of a person to do what he likes best," I answered. "Besides, it's my duty to know all my people."

"Oh yes, sir, I know that. But there's a thousand ways ov doin' the same thing. I ha' seen folks, parsons and others, 'at made a great show ov bein' friendly to the poor, ye know, sir; and all the time you could see, or if you couldn't see you could tell without seein', that they didn't much regard them in their hearts; but it was a sort of accomplishment to be able to talk to the poor, like, after their own fashion. But the minute an ould man sees you, sir, he believes that you MEAN it, sir, whatever it is. For an ould man somehow comes to know things like a child. They call it a second childhood, don't they, sir? And there are some things worth growin' a child again to get a hould ov again."

"I only hope what you say may be true—about me, I mean."

"Take my word for it, sir. You have no idea how that boy of mine, Tom there, did hate all the clergy till you come. Not that he's anyway favourable to them yet, only he'll say nothin' again' you, sir. He's got an unfortunate gift o' seein' all the faults first, sir; and when a man is that way given, the faults always hides the other side, so that there's nothing but faults to be seen."

"But I find Thomas quite open to reason."

"That's because you understand him, sir, and know how to give him head. He tould me of the talk you had with him. You don't bait him. You don't say, 'You must come along wi' me,' but you turns and goes along wi' him. He's not a bad fellow at all, is Tom; but he will have the reason for everythink. Now I never did want the reason for everything. I was content to be tould a many things. But Tom, you see, he was born with a sore bit in him somewheres, I don't rightly know wheres; and I don't think he rightly knows what's the matter with him himself."

"I dare say you have a guess though, by this time, Mr. Weir," I said; "and I think I have a guess too."

"Well, sir, if he'd only give in, I think he would be far happier. But he can't see his way clear."

"You must give him time, you know. The fact is, he doesn't feel at home yet.' And how can he, so long as he doesn't know his own Father?"

"I'm not sure that I rightly understand you," said the old man, looking bewildered and curious.

"I mean," I answered, "that till a man knows that he is one of God's family, living in God's house, with God up-stairs, as it were, while he is at his work or his play in a nursery below-stairs, he can't feel comfortable. For a man could not be made that should stand alone, like some of the beasts. A man must feel a head over him, because he's not enough to satisfy himself, you know. Thomas just wants faith; that is, he wants to feel that there is a loving Father over him, who is doing things all well and right, if we could only understand them, though it really does not look like it sometimes."

"Ah, sir, I might have understood you well enough, if my poor old head hadn't been started on a wrong track. For I fancied for the moment that you were just putting your finger upon the sore place in Tom's mind. There's no use in keeping family misfortunes from a friend like you, sir. That boy has known his father all his life; but I was nearly half his age before I knew mine."

"Strange!" I said, involuntarily almost.

"Yes, sir; strange you may well say. A strange story it is. The Lord help my mother! I beg yer pardon, sir. I'm no Catholic. But that prayer will come of itself sometimes. As if it could be of any use now! God forgive me!"

"Don't you be afraid, Mr Weir, as if God was ready to take offence at what comes naturally, as you say. An ejaculation of love is not likely to offend Him who is so grand that He is always meek and lowly of heart, and whose love is such that ours is a mere faint light—'a little glooming light much like a shade'—as one of our own poets says, beside it."

"Thank you, Mr Walton. That's a real comfortable word, sir. And I am heart-sure it's true, sir. God be praised for evermore! He IS good, sir; as I have known in my poor time, sir. I don't believe there ever was one that just lifted his eyes and looked up'ards, instead of looking down to the ground, that didn't get some comfort, to go on with, as it were—the ready—money of comfort, as it were—though it might be none to put in the bank, sir."

"That's true enough," I said. "Then your father and mother—?"

And here I hesitated.

76

"Were never married, sir," said the old man promptly, as if he would relieve me from an embarrassing position. "I couldn't help it. And I'm no less the child of my Father in heaven for it. For if He hadn't made me, I couldn't ha' been their son, you know, sir. So that He had more to do wi' the makin' o' me than they had; though mayhap, if He had His way all out, I might ha' been the son o' somebody else. But, now that things be so, I wouldn't have liked that at all, sir; and bein' once born so, I would not have e'er another couple of parents in all England, sir, though I ne'er knew one o' them. And I do love my mother. And I'm so sorry for my father that I love him too, sir. And if I could only get my boy Tom to think as I do, I would die like a psalm-tune on an organ, sir."

"But it seems to me strange," I said, "that your son should think so much of what is so far gone by. Surely he would not want another father than you, now. He is used to his position in life. And there can be nothing cast up to him about his birth or descent."

"That's all very true, sir, and no doubt it would be as you say. But there has been other things to keep his mind upon the old affair. Indeed, sir, we have had the same misfortune all over again among the young people. And I mustn't say anything more about it; only my boy Tom has a sore heart."

I knew at once to what he alluded; for I could not have been about in my parish all this time without learning that the strange handsome woman in the little shop was the daughter of Thomas Weir, and that she was neither wife nor widow. And it now occurred to me for the first time that it was a likeness to her little boy that had affected me so pleasantly when I first saw Thomas, his grandfather. The likeness to his great-grandfather, which I saw plainly enough, was what made the other fact clear to me. And at the same moment I began to be haunted with a flickering sense of a third likeness which I could not in the least fix or identify.

"Perhaps," I said, "he may find some good come out of that too."

"Well, who knows, sir?"

"I think," I said, "that if we do evil that good may come, the good we looked for will never come thereby. But once evil is done, we may humbly look to Him who bringeth good out of evil, and wait. Is your granddaughter Catherine in bad health? She looks so delicate!"

"She always had an uncommon look. But what she looks like now, I don't know. I hear no complaints; but she has never crossed this door since we got her set up in that shop. She never conies near her father or her sister, though she lets them, leastways her sister, go and see her. I'm afraid Tom has been raythee unmerciful, with her. And if ever he put a bad name upon her in her hearing, I know, from what that lass used to be as a young one, that she wouldn't be likely to forget it, and as little likely to get over it herself, or pass it over to another, even her own father. I don't believe they do more nor nod to one another when they meet in the village. It's well even if they do that much. It's my belief there's some people made so hard that they never can forgive anythink."

"How did she get into the trouble? Who is the father of her child?"

"Nay, that no one knows for certain; though there be suspicions, and one of them, no doubt, correct. But, I believe, fire wouldn't drive his name out at her mouth. I know my lass. When she says a thing, she 'll stick to it."

I asked no more questions. But, after a short pause, the old man went on.

"I shan't soon forget the night I first heard about my father and mother. That was a night! The wind was roaring like a mad beast about the house;— not this house, sir, but the great house over the way."

"You don't mean Oldcastle Hall?" I said.

"'Deed I do, sir," returned the old man, "This house here belonged to the same family at one time; though when I was born it was another branch of the family, second cousins or something, that lived in it. But even then it was something on to the downhill road, I believe."

"But," I said, fearing my question might have turned the old man aside from a story worth hearing, "never mind all that now, if you please. I am anxious to hear all about that night. Do go on. You were saying the wind was blowing about the old house."

"Eh, sir, it was roaring!-roaring as if it was mad with rage! And every now and then it would come down the chimley like out of a gun, and blow the smoke and a'most the fire into the middle of the housekeeper's room. For the housekeeper had been giving me my supper. I called her auntie, then; and didn't know a bit that she wasn't my aunt really. I was at that time a kind of a under-gamekeeper upon the place, and slept over the stable. But I fared of the best, for I was a favourite with the old woman—I suppose because I had given her plenty of trouble in my time. That's always the way, sir.—Well, as I was a-saying, when the wind stopped for a moment, down came the rain with a noise that sounded like a regiment of cavalry on the turnpike road t'other side of the hill. And then up the wind got again, and swept the rain away, and took it all in its own hand again, and went on roaring worse than ever. 'You 'll be wet afore you get across the yard, Samuel,' said auntie, looking very prim in her long white apron, as she sat on the other side of the little round table before the fire, sipping a drop of hot rum and water, which she always had before she went to bed. 'You'll be wet to the skin, Samuel,' she said. 'Never mind,' says I. 'I'm not salt, nor yet sugar; and I'll be going, auntie, for you'll be wanting your bed.'-'Sit ye still,' said she. 'I don't want my bed yet.' And there she sat, sipping at her rum and water; and there I sat, o' the other side, drinking the last of a pint of October, she had gotten me from the cellar—for I had been out in the wind all day. 'It was just such a night as this,' said she, and then stopped again.—But I'm wearying you, sir, with my long story."

"Not in the least," I answered. "Quite the contrary. Pray tell it out your own way. You won't tire me, I assure you."

So the old man went on.

"' It was just such a night as this,' she began again—'leastways it was snow and not rain that was coming down, as if the Almighty was a-going to spend all His winter-stock at oncet.'—'What happened such a night, auntie?' I said. 'Ah, my lad!' said she, 'ye may well ask what happened. None has a better right. You happened. That's all.'—'Oh, that's all, is it, auntie?' I said, and laughed. 'Nay, nay, Samuel,' said she, quite solemn, 'what is there to laugh at, then? I assure you, you was anything but welcome.'—'And why wasn't I welcome?' I said. 'I couldn't help it, you know. I'm very sorry to hear I intruded,' I said, still making game of it, you see; for I always did like a joke. 'Well,' she said, 'you certainly wasn't wanted. But I don't blame you, Samuel, and I hope you won't blame me.'—'What do you mean, auntie?' I mean this, that it's my fault, if so be that fault it is, that you're sitting there now, and not lying, in less bulk by a good deal, at the bottom of the Bishop's Basin.' That's what they call a deep pond at the foot of the old house, sir; though why or wherefore, I'm sure I don't know. 'Most extraordinary, auntie!' I said, feeling very queer, and as if I really had no business to be there. 'Never you mind, my dear,' says she; 'there you are, and you can take care of yourself now as well as anybody.'—'But who wanted to drown me?' 'Are you sure you can forgive him, if I tell you?'—'Sure enough, suppose he was sitting where you be now,' I answered. 'It was, I make no doubt, though I can't prove it,—I am morally certain it was your own father.' I felt the skin go creepin' together upon my head, and I couldn't speak. 'Yes, it was, child; and it's time you knew all about it. Why, you don't know who your own father was!'—'No more I do,' I said; 'and I never cared to ask, somehow. I thought it was all right, I suppose. But I wonder now that I never did.'—'Indeed you did many a time, when you was a mere boy, like; but I suppose, as you never was answered, you give it up for a bad job, and forgot all about it, like a wise man. You always was a wise child, Samuel.' So the old lady always said, sir. And I was willing to believe she was right, if I could. 'But now,' said she, 'it's time you knew all about it.—Poor Miss Wallis!—I'm no aunt of yours, my boy, though I love you nearly as well, I think, as if I was; for dearly did I love your mother. She was a beauty, and better than she was beautiful, whatever folks may say. The only wrong thing, I'm certain, that she ever did, was to trust your father too much. But I must see and give you the story right through from beginning to end.— Miss Wallis, as I came to know from her own lips, was the daughter of a country attorney, who had a good practice, and was likely to leave her well off. Her mother died when she was a little girl. It's not easy getting on without a mother, my boy. So she wasn't taught much of the best sort, I reckon. When her father died early, and she was left atone, the only thing she could do was to take a governess's place, and she came to us. She never got on well with the children, for they were young and self willed and rude, and would not learn to do as they were bid. I never knew one o' them shut the door when they went out of this room. And, from having had all her own way at home, with plenty of servants, and money to spend, it was a sore change to her. But she was a sweet creature, that she was. She did look sorely tried when Master Freddy would get on the back of her chair, and Miss Gusta would lie down on the rug, and never stir for all she could say to them, but only laugh at her.—To be sure!' And then auntie would take a sip at her rum and water, and sit considering old times like a static. And I sat as if all my head was one great ear, and I never spoke a word. And auntie began again. 'The way I came to know so much about her was this. Nobody, you see, took any notice or care of her. For the children were kept away with her in the old house, and my lady wasn't one to take trouble about anybody till once she stood in her way, and then she would just shove her aside or crush her like a spider, and ha' done with her.'—They have always been a proud and a fierce race, the Oldcastles, sir," said Weir, taking up the speech in his own person, "and there's been a deal o' breedin in-and-in amongst them, and that has kept up the worst of them. The men took to the women of their own sort somehow, you see. The lady up at the old Hall now is a Crowfoot. I'll just tell you one thing the gardener told me about her years ago, sir. She had a fancy for hyacinths in her rooms in the spring, and she Had some particular fine ones; and a lady of her acquaintance begged for some of them. And what do you think she did? She couldn't refuse them, and she couldn't bear any one to have them as good as she. And so she sent the hyacinth-roots—but she boiled 'em first. The gardener told me himself, sir.—'And so, when the poor thing,' said auntie, 'was taken with a dreadful cold, which was no wonder if you saw the state of the window in the room she had to sleep in, and which I got old Jones to set to rights and paid him for it out of my own pocket, else he wouldn't ha' done it at all, for the family wasn't too much in the way or the means either of paying their debts—well, there she was, and nobody minding her, and of course it fell to me to look after her. It would have made your heart bleed to see the poor thing flung all of a heap on her bed, blue with cold and coughing. "My dear!" I said; and she burst out crying, and from that moment there was confidence

81

between us. I made her as warm and as comfortable as I could, but I had to nurse her for a fortnight before she was able to do anything again. She didn't shirk her work though, poor thing. It was a heartsore to me to see the poor young thing, with her sweet eyes and her pale face, talking away to those children, that were more like wild cats than human beings. She might as well have talked to wild cats, I'm sure. But I don't think she was ever so miserable again as she must have been before her illness; for she used often to come and see me of an evening, and she would sit there where you are sitting now for an hour at a time, without speaking, her thin white hands lying folded in her lap, and her eyes fixed on the fire. I used to wonder what she could be thinking about, and I had made up my mind she was not long for this world; when all at once it was announced that Miss Oldcastle, who had been to school for some time, was coming home; and then we began to see a great deal of company, and for month after month the house was more or less filled with visitors, so that my time was constantly taken up, and I saw much less of poor Miss Wallis than I had seen before. But when we did meet on some of the back stairs, or when she came to my room for a few minutes before going to bed, we were just as good friends as ever. And I used to say, "I wish this scurry was over, my dear, that we might have our old times again." And she would smile and say something sweet. But I was surprised to see that her health began to come back—at least so it seemed to me, for her eyes grew brighter and a flush came upon her pale face, and though the children were as tiresome as ever, she didn't seem to mind it so much. But indeed she had not very much to do with them out of school hours now; for when the spring came on, they would be out and about the place with their sister or one of their brothers; and indeed, out of doors it would have been impossible for Miss Wallis to do anything with them. Some of the visitors would take to them too, for they behaved so badly to nobody as to Miss Wallis, and indeed they were clever children, and could be engaging enough when they pleased.—But then I had a blow, Samuel. It was a lovely spring night, just after the sun was down, and I wanted a drop of milk fresh from the cow for something that I was making for dinner the next day; so I went through the kitchen-garden and through the belt of young larches to go to the shippen. But when I got among the trees, who should I see at the other end of the path that went along, but Miss

Wallis walking arm-in-arm with Captain Crowfoot, who was just home from India, where he had been with Lord Clive. The captain was a man about two or three and thirty, a relation of the family, and the son of Sir Giles Crowfoot'— who lived then in this old house, sir, and had but that one son, my father, you see, sir.—'And it did give me a turn,' said my aunt, 'to see her walking with him, for I felt as sure as judgment that no good could come of it. For the captain had not the best of characters—that is, when people talked about him in chimney corners, and such like, though he was a great favourite with everybody that knew nothing about him. He was a fine, manly, handsome fellow, with a smile that, as people said, no woman could resist, though I'm sure it would have given me no trouble to resist it, whatever they may mean by that, for I saw that that same smile was the falsest thing of all the false things about him. All the time he was smiling, you would have thought he was looking at himself in a glass. He was said to have gathered a power of money in India, somehow or other. But I don't know, only I don't think he would have been the favourite he was with my lady if he hadn't. And reports were about, too, of the ways and means by which he had made the money; some said by robbing the poor heathen creatures; and some said it was only that his brother officers didn't approve of his speculating as he did in horses and other things. I don't know whether officers are so particular. At all events, this was a fact, for it was one of his own servants that told me, not thinking any harm or any shame of it. He had quarrelled with a young ensign in the regiment. On which side the wrong was, I don't know. But he first thrashed him most unmercifully, and then called him out, as they say. And when the poor fellow appeared, he could scarcely see out of his eyes, and certainly couldn't take anything like an aim. And he shot him dead,—did Captain Crowfoot.'—Think of hearing that about one's own father, sir! But I never said a word, for I hadn't a word to say.—'Think of that, Samuel,' said my aunt, 'else you won't believe what I am going to tell you. And you won't even then, I dare say. But I must tell you, nevertheless and notwithstanding.— Well, I felt as if the earth was sinking away from under the feet of me, and I stood and stared at them. And they came on, never seeing me, and actually went close past me and never saw me; at least, if he saw me he took no notice, for I don't suppose that the angel with the flaming sword would have put him out. But for her, I know she didn't see me, for her face was down, burning and smiling at once.'—I'm an old man now, sir, and I never saw my mother; but I can't tell you the story without feeling as if my heart would break for the poor young lady.—'I went back to my room,' said my aunt, 'with my empty jug in my hand, and I sat down as if I had had a stroke, and I never moved till it was pitch dark and my fire out. It was a marvel to me afterwards that nobody came near me, for everybody was calling after me at that time. And it was days before I caught a glimpse of Miss Wallis again, at least to speak to her. At last, one night she came to my room; and without a moment of parley, I said to her, "Oh, my dear! what was that wretch saying to you?"—"What wretch?" says she, quite sharp like. "Why, Captain Crowfoot," says I, "to be sure."—"What have you to say against Captain Crowfoot?" says she, quite scornful like. So I tumbled out all I had against him in one breath. She turned awful pale, and she shook from head to foot, but she was able for all that to say, "Indian servants are known liars, Mrs Prendergast," says she, "and I don't believe one word of it all. But I'll ask him, the next time I see him."—"Do so, my dear," I said, not fearing for myself, for I knew he would not make any fuss that might bring the thing out into the air, and hoping that it might lead to a quarrel between them. And the next time I met her, Samuel—it was in the gallery that takes to the west turret—she passed me with a nod just, and a blush instead of a smile on her sweet face. And I didn't blame her, Samuel; but I knew that that villain had gotten a hold of her. And so I could only cry, and that I did. Things went on like this for some months. The captain came and went, stopping a week at a time. Then he stopped for a whole month, and this was in the first of the summer; and then he said he was ordered abroad again, and went away. But he didn't go abroad. He came again in the autumn for the shooting, and began to make up to Miss Oldcastle, who had grown a line young woman by that time. And then Miss Wallis began to pine. The captain went away again. Before long I was certain that if ever young creature was in a consumption, she was; but she never said a word to me. How ever the poor thing got on with her work, I can't think, but she grew weaker and weaker. I took the best care of her she would let me, and contrived that she should have her meals in her own room; but something was between her and me that she never spoke a word about herself, and never alluded to the captain. By and by came the news that the captain and Miss Oldcastle were to be married in the spring. And Miss Wallis took to her bed after that; and my lady said she had never been of much use, and wanted to send her away. But Miss Oldcastle, who was far superior to any of the rest in her disposition, spoke up for her. She had been to ask me about her, and I told her the poor thing must go to a hospital if she was sent away, for she had ne'er a home to go to. And then she went to see the governess, poor thing! and spoke very kindly to her; but never a word would Miss Wallis answer; she only stared at her with great, big, wild-like eyes. And Miss Oldcastle thought she was out of her mind, and spoke of an asylum. But I said she hadn't long to live, and if she would get my lady her mother to consent to take no notice, I would take all the care and trouble of her. And she promised, and the poor thing was left alone. I began to think myself her mind must be going, for not a word would she speak, even to me, though every moment I could spare I was up with her in her room. Only I was forced to be careful not to be out of the way when my lady wanted me, for that would have tied me more. At length one day, as I was settling her pillow for her, she all at once threw her arms about my neck, and burst into a terrible fit of crying. She sobbed and panted for breath so dreadfully, that I put my arms round her and lifted her up to give her relief; and when I laid her down again, I whispered in her ear, "I know now, my dear. I'll do all I can for you." She caught hold of my hand and held it to her lips, and then to her bosom, and cried again, but more quietly, and all was right between us once more. It was well for her, poor thing, that she could go to her bed. And I said to myself, "Nobody need ever know about it; and nobody ever shall if I can help it." To tell the truth, my hope was that she would die before there was any need for further concealment. "But people in that condition seldom die, they say, till all is over; and so she lived on and on, though plainly getting weaker and weaker.—At the captain's next visit, the wedding-day was fixed. And after that a circumstance came about that made me uneasy. A Hindoo servant—the captain called him his NIGGER always— had been constantly in attendance upon him. I never could abide the snake-look of the fellow, nor the noiseless way he went about the house. But this time the captain had a Hindoo woman with him as well. He said that his man had fallen in with her in London; that he had known her before; that she had come home as nurse with an English family, and it would be very nice for his wife to take her back with her to India, if she could only give her house room, and make her useful till after the wedding. This was easily arranged, and he went away to return in three weeks, when the wedding was to take place. Meantime poor Emily grew fast worse, and how she held out with that terrible cough of hers I never could understand—and spitting blood, too, every other hour or so, though not very much. And now, to my great trouble, with the preparations for the wedding, I could see yet less of her than before; and when Miss Oldcastle sent the Hindoo to ask me if she might not sit in the room with the poor girl, I did not know how to object, though I did not at all like her being there. I felt a great mistrust of the woman somehow or other. I never did like blacks, and I never shall. So she went, and sat by her, and waited on her very kindly—at least poor Emily said so. I called her Emily because she had begged me, that she might feel as if her mother were with her, and she was a child again. I had tried before to find out from her when greater care would be necessary, but she couldn't tell me anything. I doubted even if she understood me. I longed to have the wedding over that I might get rid of the black woman, and have time to take her place, and get everything prepared. The captain arrived, and his man with him. And twice I came upon the two blacks in close conversation.—Well, the wedding-day came. The people went to church; and while they were there a terrible storm of wind and snow came on, such that the horses would hardly face it. The captain was going to take his bride home to his father, Sir Giles's; but, short as the distance was, before the time came the storm got so dreadful that no one could think of leaving the house that night. The wind blew for all the world just as it blows this night, only it was snow in its mouth, and not rain. Carriage and horses and all would have been blown off the road for certain. It did blow, to be sure! After dinner was over and the ladies were gone to the drawing-room, and the gentlemen had been sitting over their wine for some time, the butler, William Weir—an honest man, whose wife lived at the lodge—came to my room looking scared. "Lawks, William!" says I,' said my aunt, sir, '"whatever is the matter with you?"—"Well, Mrs Prendergast!" says he, and said no more. "Lawks, William," says I, "speak out."—"Well," says he, "Mrs Prendergast, it's a strange wedding, it is! There's the ladies all alone in the withdrawing-room, and there's the gentlemen calling for more wine, and cursing and swearing that it's awful to hear. It's my belief that swords will be drawn afore long."—"Tut!" says I, "William, it will come the sooner if you don't give them what they want. Go and get it as fast as you can."—"I don't a'most like goin' down them stairs alone, in sich a night, ma'am," says he. "Would you mind coming with me?"—"Dear me, William," says I, "a pretty story to tell your wife"—she was my own half-sister, and younger than me— "a pretty story to tell your wife, that you wanted an old body like me to go and take care of you in your own cellar," says I. "But I'll go with you, if you like; for, to tell the truth, it's a terrible night." And so down we went, and brought up six bottles more of the best port. And I really didn't wonder, when I was down there, and heard the dull roar of the wind against the rock below, that William didn't much like to go alone.—When he went back with the wine, the captain said, "William, what kept you so long? Mr Centlivre says that you were afraid to go down into the cellar." Now, wasn't that odd, for it was a real fact? Before William could reply, Sir Giles said, "A man might well be afraid to go anywhere alone in a night like this." Whereupon the captain cried, with an oath, that he would go down the underground stair, and into every vault on the way, for the wager of a guinea. And there the matter, according to William, dropped, for the fresh wine was put on the table. But after they had drunk the most of it—the captain, according to William, drinking less than usual—it was brought up again, he couldn't tell by which of them. And in five minutes after, they were all at my door, demanding the key of the room at the top of the stair. I was just going up to see poor Emily when I heard the noise of their unsteady feet coming along the passage to my door; and I gave the captain the key at once, wishing with all my heart he might get a good fright for his pains. He took a jug with him, too, to bring some water up from the well, as a proof he had been down. The rest of the gentlemen went with him into the little cellar-room; but they wouldn't stop there till he came up again, they said it was so cold. They all came into my room, where they talked as gentlemen wouldn't do if the wine hadn't got uppermost. It was some time before the captain returned. It's a good way down and back. When he came in at last, he looked as if he had got the fright I wished him, he had such a scared look. The candle in his lantern was out, and there was no water in the jug. "There's your guinea, Centlivre," says he, throwing it on the table. "You needn't ask me any questions, for I won't answer one of them."—"Captain," says I, as he turned to leave the room, and the other gentlemen rose to follow him, "I'll just hang up the key again."—" By all means," says he. "Where is it, then?" says I. He started and made as if he searched his pockets all over for it. "I must have dropped it," says he; "but it's of no consequence; you can send William to look for it in the morning. It can't be lost, you know."—"Very well, captain," said I. But I didn't like being without the key, because of course he hadn't locked the door, and that part of the house has a bad name, and no wonder. It wasn't exactly pleasant to have the door left open. All this time I couldn't get to see how Emily was. As often as I looked from my window, I saw her light in the old west turret out there, Samuel. You know the room where the bed is still. The rain and the wind will be blowing right through it to-night. That's the bed you was born upon, Samuel.'—It's all gone now, sir, turret and all, like a good deal more about the old place; but there's a story about that turret afterwards, only I mustn't try to tell you two things at once.—'Now I had told the Indian woman that if anything happened, if she was worse, or wanted to see me, she must put the candle on the right side of the window, and I should always be looking out, and would come directly, whoever might wait. For I was expecting you some time soon, and nobody knew anything about when you might come. But there the blind continued drawn down as before. So I thought all was going on right. And what with the storm keeping Sir Giles and so many more that would have gone home that night, there was no end of work, and some contrivance necessary, I can tell you, to get them all bedded for the night, for we were nothing too well provided with blankets and linen in the house. There was always more room than money in it. So it was past twelve o'clock before I had a minute to myself, and that was only after they had all gone to bed—the bride and bridegroom in the crimson chamber, of course. Well, at last I crept quietly into Emily's room. I ought to have told you that I had not let her know anything about the wedding being that day, and had enjoined the heathen woman not to say a word; for I thought she might as well die without hearing about it. But I believe the vile wretch did tell her. When I opened the room-door, there was no light there. I spoke, but no one answered.

I had my own candle in my hand, but it had been blown out as I came up the stair. I turned and ran along the corridor to reach the main stair, which was the nearest way to my room, when all at once I heard such a shriek from the crimson chamber as I never heard in my life. It made me all creep like worms. And in a moment doors and doors were opened, and lights came out, everybody looking terrified; and what with drink, and horror, and sleep, some of the gentlemen were awful to look upon. And the door of the crimson chamber opened too, and the captain appeared in his dressing-gown, bawling out to know what was the matter; though I'm certain, to this day, the cry did come from that room, and that he knew more about it than any one else did. As soon as I got a light, however, which I did from Sir Giles's candle, I left them to settle it amongst them, and ran back to the west turret. When I entered the room, there was my dear girl lying white and motionless. There could be no doubt a baby had been born, but no baby was to be seen. I rushed to the bed; but though she was still warm, your poor mother was quite dead. There was no use in thinking about helping her; but what could have become of the child? As if by a light in my mind, I saw it all. I rushed down to my room, got my lantern, and, without waiting to be afraid, ran to the underground stairs, where I actually found the door standing open. I had not gone down more than three turnings, when I thought I heard a cry, and I sped faster still. And just about half-way down, there lay a bundle in a blanket. And how ever you got over the state I found you in, Samuel, I can't think. But I caught you up as you was, and ran to my own room with you; and I locked the door, and there being a kettle on the fire, and some conveniences in the place, I did the best for you I could. For the breath wasn't out of you, though it well might have been. And then I laid you before the fire, and by that time you had begun to cry a little, to my great pleasure, and then I got a blanket off my bed, and wrapt you up in it; and, the storm being abated by this time, made the best of my way with you through the snow to the lodge, where William's wife lived. It was not so far off then as it is now. But in the midst of my trouble the silly body did make me laugh when he opened the door to me, and saw the bundle in my arms. "Mrs Prendergast," says he, "I didn't expect it of you."—"Hold your tongue," I said. "You would never have talked such nonsense if you had had the grace to have any of your own," says I. And with that I into the bedroom and shut the door, and left him out there in his shirt. My sister and I soon got everything arranged, for there was no time to lose. And before morning I had all made tidy, and your poor mother lying as sweet a corpse as ever angel saw. And no one could say a word against her. And it's my belief that that villain made her believe somehow or other that she was as good as married to him. She was buried down there in the churchyard, close by the vestry-door,' said my aunt, sir; and all of our family have been buried there ever since, my son Tom's wife among them, sir."

"But what was that cry in the house?" I asked, "And what became of the black woman?"

"The woman was never seen again in our quarter; and what the cry was my aunt never would say. She seemed to know though; notwithstanding, as she said, that Captain and Mrs Crowfoot denied all knowledge of it. But the lady looked dreadful, she said, and never was well again, and died at the birth of her first child. That was the present Mrs Oldcastle's father, sir."

"But why should the woman have left you on the stair, instead of drowning you in the well at the bottom?"

"My aunt evidently thought there was some mystery about that as well as the other, for she had no doubt about the woman's intention. But all she would ever say concerning it was, 'The key was never found, Samuel. You see I had to get a new one made.' And she pointed to where it hung on the wall. 'But that doesn't look new now,' she would say. 'The lock was very hard to fit again.' And so you see, sir, I was brought up as her nephew, though people were surprised, no doubt, that William Weir's wife should have a child, and nobody know she was expecting.—Well, with all the reports of the captain's money, none of it showed in this old place, which from that day began, as it were, to crumble away. There's been little repair done upon it since then. If it hadn't been a well-built place to begin with, it wouldn't be standing now, sir. But it's a very different place, I can tell you. Why, all behind was a garden with terraces, and fruit trees, and gay flowers, to no end. I remember it as well as yesterday; nay, a great deal better, for the matter of that. For I don't remember yesterday at all, sir."

I have tried a little to tell the story as he told it. But I am aware that I have succeeded very badly; for I am not like my friend in London, who, I verily believe, could give you an exact representation of any dialect he ever heard. I wish I had been able to give a little more of the form of the old man's speech; all I have been able to do is to show a difference from my own way of telling a story. But in the main, I think, I have reported it correctly. I believe if the old man was correct in representing his aunt's account, the story is very little altered between us.

But why should I tell such a story at all?

I am willing to allow, at once, that I have very likely given it more room than it deserves in these poor Annals of mine; but the reason why I tell it at all is simply this, that, as it came from the old man's lips, it interested me greatly. It certainly did not produce the effect I had hoped to gain from an interview with him, namely, A REDUCTION TO THE COMMON AND PRESENT. For all this ancient tale tended to keep up the sense of distance between my day's experience at the Hall and the work I had to do amongst my cottagers and trades-people. Indeed, it came very strangely upon that experience.

"But surely you did not believe such an extravagant tale? The old man was in his dotage, to begin with."

Had the old man been in his dotage, which he was not, my answer would have been a more triumphant one. For when was dotage consistently and imaginatively inventive? But why should I not believe the story? There are people who can never believe anything that is not (I do not say merely in accordance with their own character, but) in accordance with the particular mood they may happen to be in at the time it is presented to them. They know nothing of human nature beyond their own immediate preference at the moment for port or sherry, for vice or virtue. To tell me there could not be a man so lost to shame, if to rectitude, as Captain Crowfoot, is simply to talk nonsense. Nay, gentle reader, if you—and let me suppose I address a lady—if you will give yourself up for thirty years to doing just whatever your lowest self and not your best self may like, I will warrant you capable, by the end of that time, of child murder at least. I do not think the descent to Avernus is always easy; but it is always possible. Many and many such a story was fact in old times; and human nature being the same still, though under different restraints, equally horrible things are constantly in progress towards the windows of the newspapers.

"But the whole tale has such a melodramatic air!"

That argument simply amounts to this: that, because such subjects are capable of being employed with great dramatic effect, and of being at the same time very badly represented, therefore they cannot take place in real life. But ask any physician of your acquaintance, whether a story is unlikely simply because it involves terrible things such as do not occur every day. The fact is, that such things, occurring monthly or yearly only, are more easily hidden away out of sight. Indeed we can have no sense of security for ourselves except in the knowledge that we are striving up and away, and therefore cannot be sinking nearer to the region of such awful possibilities.

Yet, as I said before, I am afraid I have given it too large a space in my narrative. Only it so forcibly reminded me at the time of the expression I could not understand upon Miss Oldcastle's face, and since then has been so often recalled by circumstances and events, that I felt impelled to record it in full. And now I have done with it.

I left the old man with thanks for the kind reception he had given me, and walked home, revolving many things with which I shall not detain the attention of my reader. Indeed my thoughts were confused and troubled, and would ill bear analysis or record. I shut myself up in my study, and tried to read a sermon of Jeremy Taylor. But it would not do. I fell fast asleep over it at last, and woke refreshed.

CHAPTER VIII. WHAT I PREACHED.

During the suffering which accompanied the disappointment at which I have already hinted, I did not think it inconsistent with the manly spirit in which I was resolved to endure it, to seek consolation from such a source as the New Testament—if mayhap consolation for such a trouble was to be found there. Whereupon, a little to my surprise, I discovered that I could not read the Epistles at all. For I did not then care an atom for the theological discussions in which I had been interested before, and for the sake of which I had read those epistles. Now that I was in trouble, what to me was that philosophical theology staring me in the face from out the sacred page? Ah! reader, do not misunderstand me. All reading of the Book is not reading of the Word. And many that are first shall be last and the last first. I know NOW that it was Jesus Christ and not theology that filled the hearts of the men that wrote those epistles—Jesus Christ, the living, loving God-Man, whom I found—not in the Epistles, but in the Gospels. The Gospels contain what the apostles preached—the Epistles what they wrote after the preaching. And until we understand the Gospel, the good news of Jesus Christ our brother-king—until we understand Him, until we have His Spirit, promised so freely to them that ask it—all the Epistles, the words of men who were full of Him, and wrote out of that fulness, who loved Him so utterly that by that very love they were lifted into the air of pure reason and right, and would die for Him, and did die for Him, without two thoughts about it, in the very simplicity of NO CHOICE—the Letters, I say, of such men are to us a sealed book. Until we love the Lord so as to do what He tells us, we have no right to have an opinion about what one of those men meant; for all they wrote is about things beyond us. The simplest woman who tries not to judge her neighbour, or not to be anxious for the morrow, will better know what is best to know, than the best-read bishop without that one simple outgoing of his highest nature in the effort to do the will of Him who thus spoke.

But I have, as is too common with me, been led away by my feelings from the path to the object before me. What I wanted to say was this: that, although I could make nothing of the epistles, could see no possibility of consolation for my distress springing from them, I found it altogether different when I tried the Gospel once more. Indeed, it then took such a hold of me as it had never taken before. Only that is simply saying nothing. I found out that I had known nothing at all about it; that I had only a certain surface-knowledge, which tended rather to ignorance, because it fostered the delusion that I did know. Know that man, Christ Jesus! Ah! Lord, I would go through fire and water to sit the last at Thy table in Thy kingdom; but dare I say now I KNOW Thee!—But Thou art the Gospel, for Thou art the Way, the

Truth, and the Life; and I have found Thee the Gospel. For I found, as I read, that Thy very presence in my thoughts, not as the theologians show Thee, but as Thou showedst Thyself to them who report Thee to us, smoothed the troubled waters of my spirit, so that, even while the storm lasted, I was able to walk upon them to go to Thee. And when those waters became clear, I most rejoiced in their clearness because they mirrored Thy form—because Thou wert there to my vision—the one Ideal, the perfect man, the God perfected as king of men by working out His Godhood in the work of man; revealing that God and man are one; that to serve God, a man must be partaker of the Divine nature; that for a man's work to be done thoroughly, God must come and do it first Himself; that to help men, He must be what He is—man in God, God in man—visibly before their eyes, or to the hearing of their ears. So much I saw.

And therefore, when I was once more in a position to help my fellows, what could I want to give them but that which was the very bread and water of life to me—the Saviour himself? And how was I to do this?—By trying to represent the man in all the simplicity of His life, of His sayings and doings, of His refusals to say or do.—I took the story from the beginning, and told them about the Baby; trying to make the fathers and mothers, and all whose love for children supplied the lack of fatherhood and motherhood, feel that it was a real baby-boy. And I followed the life on and on, trying to show them how He felt, as far as one might dare to touch such sacred things, when He did so and so, or said so and so; and what His relation to His father and mother and brothers and sisters was, and to the different kinds of people who came about Him. And I tried to show them what His sayings meant, as far as I understood them myself, and where I could not understand them I just told them so, and said I hoped for more light by and by to enable me to understand them; telling them that that hope was a sharp goad to my resolution, driving me on to do my duty, because I knew that only as I did my duty would light go up in my heart, making me wise to understand the precious words of my Lord. And I told them that if they would try to do their duty, they would find more understanding from that than from any explanation I could give them.

And so I went on from Sunday to Sunday. And the number of people

94

that slept grew less and less, until, at last, it was reduced to the churchwarden, Mr Brownrigg, and an old washerwoman, who, poor thing, stood so much all the week, that sitting down with her was like going to bed, and she never could do it, as she told me, without going to sleep. I, therefore, called upon her every Monday morning, and had five minutes' chat with her as she stood at her wash-tub, wishing to make up to her for her drowsiness; and thinking that if I could once get her interested in anything, she might be able to keep awake a little while at the beginning of the sermon; for she gave me no chance of interesting her on Sundays—going fast asleep the moment I stood up to preach. I never got so far as that, however; and the only fact that showed me I had made any impression upon her, beyond the pleasure she always manifested when I appeared on the Monday, was, that, whereas all my linen had been very badly washed at first, a decided improvement took place after a while, beginning with my surplice and bands, and gradually extending itself to my shirts and handkerchiefs; till at last even Mrs Pearson was unable to find any fault with the poor old sleepy woman's work. For Mr Brownrigg, I am not sure that the sense of any one sentence I ever uttered, down to the day of his death, entered into his brain—I dare not say his mind or heart. With regard to him, and millions besides, I am more than happy to obey my Lord's command, and not judge.

But it was not long either before my congregations began to improve, whatever might be the cause. I could not help hoping that it was really because they liked to hear the Gospel, that is, the good news about Christ himself. And I always made use of the knowledge I had of my individual hearers, to say what I thought would do them good. Not that I ever preached AT anybody; I only sought to explain the principles of things in which I knew action of some sort was demanded from them. For I remembered how our Lord's sermon against covetousness, with the parable of the rich man with the little barn, had for its occasion the request of a man that our Lord would interfere to make his brother share with him; which He declining to do, yet gave both brothers a lesson such as, if they wished to do what was right, would help them to see clearly what was the right thing to do in this and every such matter. Clear the mind's eye, by washing away the covetousness, and the whole nature would be full of light, and the right walk would speedily follow.

Before long, likewise, I was as sure of seeing the pale face of Thomas Weir perched, like that of a man beheaded for treason, upon the apex of the gablet of the old tomb, as I was of hearing the wonderful playing of that husky old organ, of which I have spoken once before. I continued to pay him a visit every now and then; and I assure you, never was the attempt to be thoroughly honest towards a man better understood or more appreciated than my attempt was by the ATHEISTICAL carpenter. The man was no more an atheist than David was when he saw the wicked spreading like a green bay-tree, and was troubled at the sight. He only wanted to see a God in whom he could trust. And if I succeeded at all in making him hope that there might be such a God, it is to me one of the most precious seals of my ministry.

But it was now getting very near Christmas, and there was one person whom I had never yet seen at church: that was Catherine Weir. I thought, at first, it could hardly be that she shrunk from being seen; for how then could she have taken to keeping a shop, where she must be at the beck of every one? I had several times gone and bought tobacco of her since that first occasion; and I had told my housekeeper to buy whatever she could from her, instead of going to the larger shop in the place; at which Mrs Pearson had grumbled a good deal, saying how could the things be so good out of a poky shop like that? But I told her I did not care if the things were not quite as good; for it would be of more consequence to Catherine to have the custom, than it would be to me to have the one lump of sugar I put in my tea of a morning one shade or even two shades whiter. So I had contrived to keep up a kind of connexion with her, although I saw that any attempt at conversation was so distasteful to her, that it must do harm until something should have brought about a change in her feelings; though what feeling wanted changing, I could not at first tell. I came to the conclusion that she had been wronged grievously, and that this wrong operating on a nature similar to her father's, had drawn all her mind to brood over it. The world itself, the whole order of her life, everything about her, would seem then to have wronged her; and to speak to her of religion would only rouse her scorn, and make her feel as if God himself, if there were a God, had wronged her too. Evidently, likewise, she had that peculiarity of strong, undeveloped natures, of being unable, once possessed by one set of thoughts, to get rid of it again, or to see anything except in the shadow of those thoughts. I had no doubt, however, at last, that she was ashamed of her position in the eyes of society, although a hitherto indomitable pride had upheld her to face it so far as was necessary to secure her independence; both of which—pride and shame—prevented her from appearing where it was unnecessary, and especially in church. I could do nothing more than wait for a favourable opportunity. I could invent no way of reaching her yet; for I had soon found that kindness to her boy was regarded rather in the light of an insult to her. I should have been greatly puzzled to account for his being such a sweet little fellow, had I not known that he was a great deal with his aunt and grandfather. A more attentive and devout worshipper was not in the congregation than that little boy.

Before going on to speak of another of the most remarkable of my parishioners, whom I have just once mentioned I believe already, I should like to say that on three several occasions before Christmas I had seen Judy look grave. She was always quite well-behaved in church, though restless, as one might expect. But on these occasions she was not only attentive, but grave, as if she felt something or other. I will not mention what subjects I was upon at those times, because the mention of them would not, in the minds of my readers, at all harmonise with the only notion of Judy they can yet by possibility have.

For Mrs Oldcastle, I never saw her change countenance or even expression at anything—I mean in church.

CHAPTER IX. THE ORGANIST.

On the afternoon of my second Sunday at Marshmallows, I was standing in the churchyard, casting a long shadow in the light of the declining sun. I was reading the inscription upon an old headstone, for I thought everybody was gone; when I heard a door open, and shut again before I could turn. I saw at once that it must have been a little door in the tower, almost concealed from where I stood by a deep buttress. I had never seen the door open, and I had never inquired anything about it, supposing it led merely into the tower.

After a moment it opened again, and, to my surprise, out came, stooping his tall form to get his gray head clear of the low archway, a man whom no one could pass without looking after him. Tall, and strongly built, he had the carriage of a military man, without an atom of that sternness which one generally finds in the faces of those accustomed to command. He had a large face, with large regular features, and large clear gray eyes, all of which united to express an exceeding placidity or repose. It shone with intelligence—a mild intelligence—no way suggestive of profundity, although of geniality. Indeed, there was a little too much expression. The face seemed to express ALL that lay beneath it.

I was not satisfied with the countenance; and yet it looked quite good. It was somehow a too well-ordered face. It was quite Greek in its outline; and marvellously well kept and smooth, considering that the beard, to which razors were utterly strange, and which descended half-way down his breast, would have been as white as snow except for a slight yellowish tinge. His eyebrows were still very dark, only just touched with the frost of winter. His hair, too, as I saw when he lifted his hat, was still wonderfully dark for the condition of his beard.—It flashed into my mind, that this must be the organist who played so remarkably. Somehow I had not happened yet to inquire about him. But there was a stateliness in this man amounting almost to consciousness of dignity; and I was a little bewildered. His clothes were all of black, very neat and clean, but old-fashioned and threadbare. They bore signs of use, but more signs of time and careful keeping. I would have spoken to him, but something in the manner in which he bowed to me as he passed, prevented me, and I let him go unaccosted.

The sexton coming out directly after, and proceeding to lock the door, I was struck by the action. "What IS he locking the door for?" I said to myself. But I said nothing to him, because I had not answered the question myself yet.

"Who is that gentleman," I asked, "who came out just now?"

"That is Mr Stoddart, sir," he answered.

I thought I had heard the name in the neighbourhood before.

"Is it he who plays the organ?" I asked.

"That he do, sir. He's played our organ for the last ten year, ever since he come to live at the Hall."

"What Hall?"

"Why the Hall, to be sure,—Oldcastle Hall, you know."

And then it dawned on my recollection that I had heard Judy mention her uncle Stoddart. But how could he be her uncle?

"Is he a relation of the family?" I asked.

"He's a brother-in-law, I believe, of the old lady, sir, but how ever he come to live there I don't know. It's no such binding connexion, you know, sir. He's been in the milintairy line, I believe, sir, in the Ingies, or somewheres."

I do not think I shall have any more strange parishioners to present to my readers; at least I do not remember any more just at this moment. And this one, as the reader will see, I positively could not keep out.

A military man from India! a brother-in-law of Mrs Oldcastle, choosing to live with her! an entrancing performer upon an old, asthmatic, dry-throated church organ! taking no trouble to make the clergyman's acquaintance, and passing him in the churchyard with a courteous bow, although his face was full of kindliness, if not of kindness! I could not help thinking all this strange. And yet—will the reader cease to accord me credit when I assert it?—although I had quite intended to inquire after him when I left the vicarage to go to the Hall, and had even thought of him when sitting with Mrs Oldcastle, I never thought of him again after going with Judy, and left the house without having made a single inquiry after him. Nor did I think of him again till just as I was passing under the outstretched neck of one of those serpivolants on the gate; and what made me think of him then, I cannot in the least imagine; but I resolved at once that I would call upon him the following week, lest he should think that the fact of his having omitted to call upon me had been the occasion of such an apparently pointed omission on my part. For I had long ago determined to be no further guided by the rules of society than as they might aid in bringing about true neighbourliness, and if possible friendliness and friendship. Wherever they might interfere with these, I would disregard them—as far on the other hand as the disregard of them might tend to bring about the results I desired.

When, carrying out this resolution, I rang the doorbell at the Hall, and inquired whether Mr Stoddart was at home, the butler stared; and, as I simply continued gazing in return, and waiting, he answered at length, with some hesitation, as if he were picking and choosing his words:

"Mr Stoddart never calls upon any one, sir."

"I am not complaining of Mr Stoddart," I answered, wishing to put the man at his ease.

"But nobody calls upon Mr Stoddart," he returned.

"That's very unkind of somebody, surely," I said.

"But he doesn't want anybody to call upon him, sir."

"Ah! that's another matter. I didn't know that. Of course, nobody has a right to intrude upon anybody. However, as I happen to have come without knowing his dislike to being visited, perhaps you will take him my card, and say that if it is not disagreeable to him, I should like exceedingly to thank him in person for his sermon on the organ last Sunday."

He had played an exquisite voluntary in the morning.

"Give my message exactly, if you please," I said, as I followed the man into the hall.

"I will try, sir," he answered. "But won't you come up-stairs to mistress's room, sir, while I take this to Mr Stoddart?"

"No, I thank you," I answered. "I came to call upon Mr Stoddart only, and I will wait the result of you mission here in the hall."

The man withdrew, and I sat down on a bench, and amused myself with looking at the portraits about me. I learned afterwards that they had hung, till some thirty years before, in a long gallery connecting the main part of the house with that portion to which the turret referred to so often in Old Weir's story was attached. One particularly pleased me. It was the portrait of a young woman—very lovely—but with an expression both sad and— scared, I think, would be the readiest word to communicate what I mean. It was indubitably, indeed remarkably, like Miss Oldcastle. And I learned afterwards that it was the portrait of Mrs Oldcastle's grandmother, that very Mrs Crowfoot mentioned in Weir's story. It had been taken about six months after her marriage, and about as many before her death.

The butler returned, with the request that I would follow him. He led me up the grand staircase, through a passage at right angles to that which led to the old lady's room, up a narrow circular staircase at the end of the passage, across a landing, then up a straight steep narrow stair, upon which two people could not pass without turning sideways and then squeezing. At the top of this I found myself in a small cylindrical lobby, papered in blocks of stone. There was no door to be seen. It was lighted by a conical skylight. My conductor gave a push against the wall. Certain blocks yielded, and others came forward. In fact a door revolved on central pivots, and we were admitted to a chamber crowded with books from floor to ceiling, arranged with wonderful neatness and solidity. From the centre of the ceiling, whence hung a globular lamp, radiated what I took to be a number of strong beams supporting a floor above; for our ancestors put the ceiling above the beams, instead of below them, as we do, and gained in space if they lost in quietness. But I soon found out my mistake. Those radiating beams were in reality book-shelves. For on each side of those I passed under I could see the gilded backs of books standing closely ranged together. I had never seen the connivance before, nor, I presume, was it to be seen anywhere else.

"How does Mr Stoddart reach those books?" I asked my conductor.

"I don't exactly know, sir," whispered the butler. "His own man could tell you, I dare say. But he has a holiday to-day; and I do not think he would explain it either; for he says his master allows no interference with his contrivances. I believe, however, he does not use a ladder."

There was no one in the room, and I saw no entrance but that by which we had entered. The next moment, however, a nest of shelves revolved in front of me, and there Mr Stoddart stood with outstretched hand.

"You have found me at last, Mr Walton, and I am glad to see you," he said.

He led me into an inner room, much larger than the one I had passed through.

"I am glad," I replied, "that I did not know, till the butler told me, your unwillingness to be intruded upon; for I fear, had I known it, I should have been yet longer a stranger to you."

"You are no stranger to me. I have heard you read prayers, and I have heard you preach."

"And I have heard you play; so you are no stranger to me either."

"Well, before we say another word," said Mr Stoddart, "I must just say one word about this report of my unsociable disposition.—I encourage it; but am very glad to see you, notwithstanding.—Do sit down."

I obeyed, and waited for the rest of his word.

"I was so bored with visits after I came, visits which were to me utterly uninteresting, that I was only too glad when the unusual nature of some of my pursuits gave rise to the rumour that I was mad. The more people say I am mad, the better pleased I am, so long as they are satisfied with my own mode of shutting myself up, and do not attempt to carry out any fancies of their own in regard to my personal freedom."

Upon this followed some desultory conversation, during which I took some observations of the room. Like the outer room, it was full of books from floor to ceiling. But the ceiling was divided into compartments, harmoniously coloured.

"What a number of books you have!" I observed.

"Not a great many," he answered. "But I think there is hardly one of them with which I have not some kind of personal acquaintance. I think I could almost find you any one you wanted in the dark, or in the twilight at least, which would allow me to distinguish whether the top edge was gilt, red, marbled, or uncut. I have bound a couple of hundred or so of them myself. I don't think you could tell the work from a tradesman's. I'll give you a guinea for the poor-box if you pick out three of my binding consecutively."

I accepted the challenge; for although I could not bind a book, I considered myself to have a keen eye for the outside finish. After looking over the backs of a great many, I took one down, examined a little further, and presented it.

"You are right. Now try again."

Again I was successful, although I doubted.

"And now for the last," he said.

Once more I was right.

"There is your guinea," said he, a little mortified.

"No," I answered. "I do not feel at liberty to take it, because, to tell the truth, the last was a mere guess, nothing more."

Mr Stoddart looked relieved.

"You are more honest than most of your profession," he said. "But I am far more pleased to offer you the guinea upon the smallest doubt of your having won it."

"I have no claim upon it."

"What! Couldn't you swallow a small scruple like that for the sake of the poor even? Well, I don't believe YOU could.—Oblige me by taking this guinea for some one or other of your poor people. But I AM glad you weren't sure of that last book. I am indeed."

I took the guinea, and put it in my purse.

"But," he resumed, "you won't do, Mr Walton. You're not fit for your profession. You won't tell a lie for God's sake. You won't dodge about a little to

103

keep all right between Jove and his weary parishioners. You won't cheat a little for the sake of the poor! You wouldn't even bamboozle a little at a bazaar!"

"I should not like to boast of my principles," I answered; "for the moment one does so, they become as the apples of Sodom. But assuredly I would not favour a fiction to keep a world out of hell. The hell that a lie would keep any man out of is doubtless the very best place for him to go to. It is truth, yes, The Truth that saves the world."

"You are right, I daresay. You are more sure about it than I am though."

"Let us agree where we can," I said, "first of all; and that will make us able to disagree, where we must, without quarrelling."

"Good," he said—"Would you like to see my work shop?"

"Very much, indeed," I answered, heartily.

"Do you take any pleasure in applied mechanics?"

"I used to do so as a boy. But of course I have little time now for anything of the sort."

"Ah! of course."

He pushed a compartment of books. It yielded, and we entered a small closet. In another moment I found myself leaving the floor, and in yet a moment we were on the floor of an upper room.

"What a nice way of getting up-stairs!" I said.

"There is no other way of getting to this room," answered Mr Stoddart. "I built it myself; and there was no room for stairs. This is my shop. In my library I only read my favourite books. Here I read anything I want to read; write anything I want to write; bind my books; invent machines; and amuse myself generally. Take a chair."

I obeyed, and began to look about me.

The room had many books in detached book-cases. There were various benches against the walls between,—one a bookbinder's; another a carpenter's;

a third had a turning-lathe; a fourth had an iron vice fixed on it, and was evidently used for working in metal. Besides these, for it was a large room, there were several tables with chemical apparatus upon them, Florence-flasks, retorts, sand-baths, and such like; while in a corner stood a furnace.

"What an accumulation of ways and means you have about you!" I said; "and all, apparently, to different ends."

"All to the same end, if my object were understood."

"I presume I must ask no questions as to that object?"

"It would take time to explain. I have theories of education. I think a man has to educate himself into harmony. Therefore he must open every possible window by which the influences of the All may come in upon him. I do not think any man complete without a perfect development of his mechanical faculties, for instance, and I encourage them to develop themselves into such windows."

"I do not object to your theory, provided you do not put it forward as a perfect scheme of human life. If you did, I should have some questions to ask you about it, lest I should misunderstand you."

He smiled what I took for a self-satisfied smile. There was nothing offensive in it, but it left me without anything to reply to. No embarrassment followed, however, for a rustling motion in the room the same instant attracted my attention, and I saw, to my surprise, and I must confess, a little to my confusion, Miss Oldcastle. She was seated in a corner, reading from a quarto lying upon her knees.

"Oh! you didn't know my niece was here? To tell the truth, I forgot her when I brought you up, else I would have introduced you."

"That is not necessary, uncle," said Miss Oldcastle, closing her book.

I was by her instantly. She slipped the quarto from her knee, and took my offered hand.

"Are you fond of old books?" I said, not having anything better to say.

"Some old books," she answered.

"May I ask what book you were reading?"

"I will answer you—under protest," she said, with a smile.

"I withdraw the question at once," I returned.

"I will answer it notwithstanding. It is a volume of Jacob Behmen."

"Do you understand him?"

"Yes. Don't you?"

"Well, I have made but little attempt," I answered. "Indeed, it was only as I passed through London last that I bought his works; and I am sorry to find that one of the plates is missing from my copy."

"Which plate is it? It is not very easy, I understand, to procure a perfect copy. One of my uncle's copies has no two volumes bound alike. Each must have belonged to a different set."

"I can't tell you what the plate is. But there are only three of those very curious unfolding ones in my third volume, and there should be four."

"I do not think so. Indeed, I am sure you are wrong."

"I am glad to hear it—though to be glad that the world does not possess what I thought I only was deprived of, is selfishness, cover it over as one may with the fiction of a perfect copy."

"I don't know," she returned, without any response to what I said. "I should always like things perfect myself."

"Doubtless," I answered; and thought it better to try another direction.

"How is Mrs Oldcastle?" I asked, feeling in its turn the reproach of hypocrisy; for though I could have suffered, I hope, in my person and goods and reputation, to make that woman other than she was, I could not say that I cared one atom whether she was in health or not. Possibly I should have preferred the latter member of the alternative; for the suffering of the lower nature is as a fire that drives the higher nature upwards. So I felt rather hypocritical when I asked Miss Oldcastle after her.

"Quite well, thank you," she answered, in a tone of indifference, which implied either that she saw through me, or shared in my indifference. I could not tell which.

"And how is Miss Judy?" I inquired.

"A little savage, as usual."

"Not the worse for her wetting, I hope."

"Oh! dear no. There never was health to equal that child's. It belongs to her savage nature."

"I wish some of us were more of savages, then," I returned; for I saw signs of exhaustion in her eyes which moved my sympathy.

"You don't mean me, Mr Walton, I hope. For if you do, I assure you your interest is quite thrown away. Uncle will tell you I am as strong as an elephant."

But here came a slight elevation of her person; and a shadow at the same moment passed over her face. I saw that she felt she ought not to have allowed herself to become the subject of conversation.

Meantime her uncle was busy at one of his benches filing away at a piece of brass fixed in the vice. He had thick gloves on. And, indeed, it had puzzled me before to think how he could have so many kinds of work, and yet keep his hands so smooth and white as they were. I could not help thinking the results could hardly be of the most useful description if they were all accomplished without some loss of whiteness and smoothness in the process. Even the feet that keep the garments clean must be washed themselves in the end.

When I glanced away from Miss Oldcastle in the embarrassment produced by the repulsion of her last manner, I saw Judy in the room. At the same moment Miss Oldcastle rose.

"What is the matter, Judy?" she said.

"Grannie wants you," said Judy.

Miss Oldcastle left the room, and Judy turned to me. "How do you do, Mr Walton?" she said.

"Quite well, thank you, Judy," I answered. "Your uncle admits you to his workshop, then?"

"Yes, indeed. He would feel rather dull, sometimes, without me. Wouldn't you, Uncle Stoddart?"

"Just as the horses in the field would feel dull without the gad-fly, Judy," said Mr Stoddart, laughing.

Judy, however, did not choose to receive the laugh as a scholium explanatory of the remark, and was gone in a moment, leaving Mr Stoddart and myself alone. I must say he looked a little troubled at the precipitate retreat of the damsel; but he recovered himself with a smile, and said to me,

"I wonder what speech I shall make next to drive you away, Mr Walton."

"I am not so easily got rid of, Mr Stoddart," I answered. "And as for taking offence, I don't like it, and therefore I never take it. But tell me what you are doing now."

"I have been working for some time at an attempt after a perpetual motion, but, I must confess, more from a metaphysical or logical point of view than a mechanical one."

Here he took a drawing from a shelf, explanatory of his plan.

"You see," he said, "here is a top made of platinum, the heaviest of metals, except iridium—which it would be impossible to procure enough of, and which would be difficult to work into the proper shape. It is surrounded you will observe, by an air-tight receiver, communicating by this tube with a powerful air-pump. The plate upon which the point of the top rests and revolves is a diamond; and I ought to have mentioned that the peg of the top is a diamond likewise. This is, of course, for the sake of reducing the friction. By this apparatus communicating with the top, through the receiver, I set the top in motion—after exhausting the air as far as possible. Still there is the difficulty of the friction of the diamond point upon the diamond plate, which must ultimately occasion repose. To obviate this, I have constructed here, underneath, a small steam-engine which shall cause the diamond plate to revolve at precisely the same rate of speed as the top itself. This, of course, will prevent all friction."

"Not that with the unavoidable remnant of air, however," I ventured to suggest.

"That is just my weak point," he answered. "But that will be so very small!"

"Yes; but enough to deprive the top of PERPETUAL motion."

"But suppose I could get over that difficulty, would the contrivance have a right to the name of a perpetual motion? For you observe that the steam-engine below would not be the cause of the motion. That comes from above, here, and is withdrawn, finally withdrawn."

"I understand perfectly," I answered. "At least, I think I do. But I return the question to you: Is a motion which, although not caused, is ENABLED by another motion, worthy of the name of a perpetual motion; seeing the perpetuity of motion has not to do merely with time, but with the indwelling of self-generative power—renewing itself constantly with the process of exhaustion?"

He threw down his file on the bench.

"I fear you are right," he said. "But you will allow it would have made a very pretty machine."

"Pretty, I will allow," I answered, "as distinguished from beautiful. For I can never dissociate beauty from use."

"You say that! with all the poetic things you say in your sermons! For I am a sharp listener, and none the less such that you do not see me. I have a loophole for seeing you. And I flatter myself, therefore, I am the only person in the congregation on a level with you in respect of balancing advantages. I

109

cannot contradict you, and you cannot address me."

"Do you mean, then, that whatever is poetical is useless?" I asked.

"Do you assert that whatever is useful is beautiful?" he retorted.

"A full reply to your question would need a ream of paper and a quarter of quills," I answered; "but I think I may venture so far as to say that whatever subserves a noble end must in itself be beautiful."

"Then a gallows must be beautiful because it subserves the noble end of ridding the world of malefactors?" he returned, promptly.

I had to think for a moment before I could reply.

"I do not see anything noble in the end," I answered.

"If the machine got rid of malefaction, it would, indeed, have a noble end. But if it only compels it to move on, as a constable does—from this world into another—I do not, I say, see anything so noble in that end. The gallows cannot be beautiful."

"Ah, I see. You don't approve of capital punishments."

"I do not say that. An inevitable necessity is something very different from a noble end. To cure the diseased mind is the noblest of ends; to make the sinner forsake his ways, and the unrighteous man his thoughts, the loftiest of designs; but to punish him for being wrong, however necessary it may be for others, cannot, if dissociated from the object of bringing good out of evil, be called in any sense a NOBLE end. I think now, however, it would be but fair in you to give me some answer to my question. Do you think the poetic useless?"

"I think it is very like my machine. It may exercise the faculties without subserving any immediate progress."

"It is so difficult to get out of the region of the poetic, that I cannot think it other than useful: it is so widespread. The useless could hardly be so nearly universal. But I should like to ask you another question: What is the immediate effect of anything poetic upon your mind?"

"Pleasure," he answered.

"And is pleasure good or bad?"

"Sometimes the one, sometimes the other."

"In itself?"

"I should say so."

"I should not."

"Are you not, then, by your very profession, more or less an enemy of pleasure?"

"On the contrary, I believe that pleasure is good, and does good, and urges to good. CARE is the evil thing."

"Strange doctrine for a clergyman."

"Now, do not misunderstand me, Mr Stoddart. That might not hurt you, but it would distress me. Pleasure, obtained by wrong, is poison and horror. But it is not the pleasure that hurts, it is the wrong that is in it that hurts; the pleasure hurts only as it leads to more wrong. I almost think myself, that if you could make everybody happy, half the evil would vanish from the earth."

"But you believe in God?"

"I hope in God I do."

"How can you then think that He would not destroy evil at such a cheap and pleasant rate."

"Because He wants to destroy ALL the evil, not the half of it; and destroy it so that it shall not grow again; which it would be sure to do very soon if it had no antidote but happiness. As soon as men got used to happiness, they would begin to sin again, and so lose it all. But care is distrust. I wonder now if ever there was a man who did his duty, and TOOK NO THOUGHT. I wish I could get the testimony of such a man. Has anybody actually tried the plan?"

But here I saw that I was not taking Mr Stoddart with me (as the old phrase was). The reason I supposed to be, that he had never been troubled with much care. But there remained the question, whether he trusted in God or the Bank?

I went back to the original question.

"But I should be very sorry you should think, that to give pleasure was my object in saying poetic things in the pulpit. If I do so, it is because true things come to me in their natural garments of poetic forms. What you call the POETIC is only the outer beauty that belongs to all inner or spiritual beauty—just as a lovely face—mind, I say LOVELY, not PRETTY, not HANDSOME—is the outward and visible presence of a lovely mind. Therefore, saying I cannot dissociate beauty from use, I am free to say as many poetic things—though, mind, I don't claim them: you attribute them to me—as shall be of the highest use, namely, to embody and reveal the true. But a machine has material use for its end. The most grotesque machine I ever saw that DID something, I felt to be in its own kind beautiful; as God called many fierce and grotesque things good when He made the world—good for their good end. But your machine does nothing more than raise the metaphysical doubt and question, whether it can with propriety be called a perpetual motion or not?"

To this Mr Stoddart making no reply, I take the opportunity of the break in our conversation to say to my readers, that I know there was no satisfactory following out of an argument on either side in the passage of words I have just given. Even the closest reasoner finds it next to impossible to attend to all the suggestions in his own mind, not one of which he is willing to lose, to attend at the same time to everything his antagonist says or suggests, that he may do him justice, and to keep an even course towards his goal—each having the opposite goal in view. In fact, an argument, however simply conducted and honourable, must just resemble a game at football; the unfortunate question being the ball, and the numerous and sometimes conflicting thoughts which arise in each mind forming the two parties whose energies are spent in a succession of kicks. In fact, I don't like argument, and I don't care for the victory. If I had my way, I would never argue at all. I would spend my energy in setting forth what I believe—as like itself as I could represent it, and so leave it to work its own way, which, if it be the right way, it must work in the right mind,—for Wisdom is justified of her children; while no one who loves the truth can be other than anxious, that if he has spoken the evil thing it may return to him void: that is a defeat he may well pray for. To succeed in the wrong is the most dreadful punishment to a man who, in the main, is honest. But I beg to assure my reader I could write a long treatise on the matter between Mr Stoddart and myself; therefore, if he is not yet interested in such questions, let him be thankful to me for considering such a treatise out of place here. I will only say in brief, that I believe with all my heart that the true is the beautiful, and that nothing evil can be other than ugly. If it seems not so, it is in virtue of some good mingled with the evil, and not in the smallest degree in virtue of the evil.

I thought it was time for me to take my leave. But I could not bear to run away with the last word, as it were: so I said,

"You put plenty of poetry yourself into that voluntary you played last Sunday. I am so much obliged to you for it!"

"Oh! that fugue. You liked it, did you?"

"More than I can tell you."

"I am very glad."

"Do you know those two lines of Milton in which he describes such a performance on the organ?"

"No. Can you repeat them?"

"'His volant touch, Instinct through all proportions, low and high, Fled and pursued transverse the resonant fugue.'"

"That is wonderfully fine. Thank you. That is better than my fugue by a good deal. You have cancelled the obligation."

"Do you think doing a good turn again is cancelling an obligation? I don't think an obligation can ever be RETURNED in the sense of being got rid of. But I am being hypercritical."

"Not at all.—Shall I tell you what I was thinking of while playing that fugue?"

"I should like much to hear."

"I had been thinking, while you were preaching, of the many fancies men had worshipped for the truth; now following this, now following that; ever believing they were on the point of laying hold upon her, and going down to the grave empty-handed as they came."

"And empty-hearted, too?" I asked; but he went on without heeding me.

"And I saw a vision of multitudes following, following where nothing was to be seen, with arms outstretched in all directions, some clasping vacancy to their bosoms, some reaching on tiptoe over the heads of their neighbours, and some with hanging heads, and hands clasped behind their backs, retiring hopeless from the chase."

"Strange!" I said; "for I felt so full of hope while you played, that I never doubted it was hope you meant to express."

"So I do not doubt I did; for the multitude was full of hope, vain hope, to lay hold upon the truth. And you, being full of the main expression, and in sympathy with it, did not heed the undertones of disappointment, or the sighs of those who turned their backs on the chase. Just so it is in life."

"I am no musician," I returned, "to give you a musical counter to your picture. But I see a grave man tilling the ground in peace, and the form of Truth standing behind him, and folding her wings closer and closer over and around him as he works on at his day's labour."

"Very pretty," said Mr Stoddart, and said no more.

"Suppose," I went on, "that a person knows that he has not laid hold on the truth, is that sufficient ground for his making any further assertion than that he has not found it?"

"No. But if he has tried hard and has not found ANYTHING that

114

he can say is true, he cannot help thinking that most likely there is no such thing."

"Suppose," I said, "that nobody has found the truth, is that sufficient ground for saying that nobody ever will find it? or that there is no such thing as truth to be found? Are the ages so nearly done that no chance yet remains? Surely if God has made us to desire the truth, He has got some truth to cast into the gulf of that desire. Shall God create hunger and no food? But possibly a man may be looking the wrong way for it. You may be using the microscope, when you ought to open both eyes and lift up your head. Or a man may be finding some truth which is feeding his soul, when he does not think he is finding any. You know the Fairy Queen. Think how long the Redcross Knight travelled with the Lady Truth—Una, you know—without learning to believe in her; and how much longer still without ever seeing her face. For my part, may God give me strength to follow till I die. Only I will venture to say this, that it is not by any agony of the intellect that I expect to discover her."

Mr Stoddart sat drumming silently with his fingers, a half-smile on his face, and his eyes raised at an angle of forty-five degrees. I felt that the enthusiasm with which I had spoken was thrown away upon him. But I was not going to be ashamed therefore. I would put some faith in his best nature.

"But does not," he said, gently lowering his eyes upon mine after a moment's pause—"does not your choice of a profession imply that you have not to give chase to a fleeting phantom? Do you not profess to have, and hold, and therefore teach the truth?"

"I profess only to have caught glimpses of her white garments,—those, I mean, of the abstract truth of which you speak. But I have seen that which is eternally beyond her: the ideal in the real, the living truth, not the truth that I can THINK, but the truth that thinks itself, that thinks me, that God has thought, yea, that God is, the truth BEING true to itself and to God and to man—Christ Jesus, my Lord, who knows, and feels, and does the truth. I have seen Him, and I am both content and unsatisfied. For in Him are hid all the treasures of wisdom and knowledge. Thomas a Kempis says:

115

'Cui aeternum Verbum loquitur, ille a multis opinionibus expeditur.'" (He to whom the eternal Word speaks, is set free from a press of opinions.)

I rose, and held out my hand to Mr Stoddart. He rose likewise, and took it kindly, conducted me to the room below, and ringing the bell, committed me to the care of the butler.

As I approached the gate, I met Jane Rogers coming back from the village. I stopped and spoke to her. Her eyes were very red.

"Nothing amiss at home, Jane?" I said.

"No, sir, thank you," answered Jane, and burst out crying.

"What is the matter, then? Is your——"

"Nothing's the matter with nobody, sir."

"Something is the matter with you."

"Yes, sir. But I'm quite well."

"I don't want to pry into your affairs; but if you think I can be of any use to you, mind you come to me."

"Thank you kindly, sir," said Jane; and, dropping a courtesy, walked on with her basket.

I went to her parents' cottage. As I came near the mill, the young miller was standing in the door with his eyes fixed on the ground, while the mill went on hopping behind him. But when he caught sight of me, he turned, and went in, as if he had not seen me.

"Has he been behaving ill to Jane?" thought I. As he evidently wished to avoid me, I passed the mill without looking in at the door, as I was in the habit of doing, and went on to the cottage, where I lifted the latch, and walked in. Both the old people were there, and both looked troubled, though they welcomed me none the less kindly.

"I met Jane," I said, "and she looked unhappy; so I came on to hear what was the matter."

116

"You oughtn't to be troubled with our small affairs," said Mrs. Rogers.

"If the parson wants to know, why, the parson must be told," said Old Rogers, smiling cheerily, as if he, at least, would be relieved by telling me.

"I don't want to know," I said, "if you don't want to tell me. But can I be of any use?"

"I don't think you can, sir,—leastways, I'm afraid not," said the old woman.

"I am sorry to say, sir, that Master Brownrigg and his son has come to words about our Jane; and it's not agreeable to have folk's daughter quarrelled over in that way," said Old Rogers. "What'll be the upshot on it, I don't know, but it looks bad now. For the father he tells the son that if ever he hear of him saying one word to our Jane, out of the mill he goes, as sure as his name's Dick. Now, it's rather a good chance, I think, to see what the young fellow's made of, sir. So I tells my old 'oman here; and so I told Jane. But neither on 'em seems to see the comfort of it somehow. But the New Testament do say a man shall leave father and mother, and cleave to his wife."

"But she ain't his wife yet," said Mrs Rogers to her husband, whose drift was not yet evident.

"No more she can be, 'cept he leaves his father for her."

"And what'll become of them then, without the mill?"

"You and me never had no mill, old 'oman," said Rogers; "yet here we be, very nearly ripe now,—ain't us, wife?"

"Medlar-like, Old Rogers, I doubt,—rotten before we're ripe," replied his wife, quoting a more humorous than refined proverb.

"Nay, nay, old 'oman. Don't 'e say so. The Lord won't let us rot before we're ripe, anyhow. That I be sure on."

"But, anyhow, it's all very well to talk. Thou knows how to talk, Rogers. But how will it be when the children comes, and no mill?"

"To grind 'em in, old 'oman?"

117

Mrs Rogers turned to me, who was listening with real interest, and much amusement.

"I wish you would speak a word to Old Rogers, sir. He never will speak as he's spoken to. He's always over merry, or over serious. He either takes me up short with a sermon, or he laughs me out of countenance that I don't know where to look."

Now I was pretty sure that Rogers's conduct was simple consistency, and that the difficulty arose from his always acting upon one or two of the plainest principles of truth and right; whereas his wife, good woman—for the bad, old leaven of the Pharisees could not rise much in her somehow—was always reminding him of certain precepts of behaviour to the oblivion of principles. "A bird in the hand," &c.—"Marry in haste," &c.—"When want comes in at the door love flies out at the window," were amongst her favourite sayings; although not one of them was supported by her own experience. For instance, she had married in haste herself, and never, I believe, had once thought of repenting of it, although she had had far more than the requisite leisure for doing so. And many was the time that want had come in at her door, and the first thing it always did was to clip the wings of Love, and make him less flighty, and more tender and serviceable. So I could not even pretend to read her husband a lecture.

"He's a curious man, Old Rogers," I said. "But as far as I can see, he's in the right, in the main. Isn't he now?"

"Oh, yes, I daresay. I think he's always right about the rights of the thing, you know. But a body may go too far that way. It won't do to starve, sir."

Strange confusion—or, ought I not rather to say?—ordinary and commonplace confusion of ideas!

"I don't think," I said, "any one can go too far in the right way."

"That's just what I want my old 'oman to see, and I can't get it into her, sir. If a thing's right, it's right, and if a thing's wrong, why, wrong it is. The helm must either be to starboard or port, sir."

118

"But why talk of starving?" I said. "Can't Dick work? Who could think of starting that nonsense?"

"Why, my old 'oman here. She wants 'em to give it up, and wait for better times. The fact is, she don't want to lose the girl."

"But she hasn't got her at home now."

"She can have her when she wants her, though—leastways after a bit of warning. Whereas, if she was married, and the consequences a follerin' at her heels, like a man-o'-war with her convoy, she would find she was chartered for another port, she would."

"Well, you see, sir, Rogers and me's not so young as we once was, and we're likely to be growing older every day. And if there's a difficulty in the way of Jane's marriage, why, I take it as a Godsend."

"How would you have liked such a Godsend, Mrs Rogers, when you were going to be married to your sailor here? What would you have done?"

"Why, whatever he liked to be sure. But then, you see, Dick's not my Rogers."

"But your daughter thinks about him much in the same way as you did about this dear old man here when he was young."

"Young people may be in the wrong, I see nothing in Dick Brownrigg."

"But young people may be right sometimes, and old people may be wrong sometimes."

"I can't be wrong about Rogers."

"No, but you may be wrong about Dick."

"Don't you trouble yourself about my old 'oman, sir. She allus was awk'ard in stays, but she never missed them yet. When she's said her say, round she comes in the wind like a bird, sir."

"There's a good old man to stick up for your old wife! Still, I say, they may as well wait a bit. It would be a pity to anger the old gentleman."

119

"What does the young man say to it?"

"Why, he says, like a man, he can work for her as well's the mill, and he's ready, if she is."

"I am very glad to hear such a good account of him. I shall look in, and have a little chat with him. I always liked the look of him. Good morning, Mrs. Rogers."

"I 'll see you across the stream, sir," said the old man, following me out of the house.

"You see, sir," he resumed, as soon as we were outside, "I'm always afeard of taking things out of the Lord's hands. It's the right way, surely, that when a man loves a woman, and has told her so, he should act like a man, and do as is right. And isn't that the Lord's way? And can't He give them what's good for them. Mayhap they won't love each other the less in the end if Dick has a little bit of the hard work that many a man that the Lord loved none the less has had before him. I wouldn't like to anger the old gentleman, as my wife says; but if I was Dick, I know what I would do. But don't 'e think hard of my wife, sir, for I believe there's a bit of pride in it. She's afeard of bein' supposed to catch at Richard Brownrigg, because he's above us, you know, sir. And I can't altogether blame her, only we ain't got to do with the look o' things, but with the things themselves."

"I understand you quite, and I'm very much of your mind. You can trust me to have a little chat with him, can't you?"

"That I can, sir."

Here we had come to the boundary of his garden—the busy stream that ran away, as if it was scared at the labour it had been compelled to go through, and was now making the best of its speed back to its mother-ocean, to tell sad tales of a world where every little brook must do some work ere it gets back to its rest. I bade him good day, jumped across it, and went into the mill, where Richard was tying the mouth of a sack, as gloomily as the brothers of Joseph must have tied their sacks after his silver cup had been found.

"Why did you turn away from me, as I passed half-an-hour ago,

Richard?" I said, cheerily.

"I beg your pardon, sir. I didn't think you saw me."

"But supposing I hadn't?—But I won't tease you. I know all about it. Can I do anything for you?"

"No, sir. You can't move my father. It's no use talking to him. He never hears a word anybody says. He never hears a word you say o' Sundays, sir. He won't even believe the Mark Lane Express about the price of corn. It's no use talking to him, sir."

"You wouldn't mind if I were to try?"

"No, sir. You can't make matters worse. No more can you make them any better, sir."

"I don't say I shall talk to him; but I may try it, if I find a fitting opportunity."

"He's always worse—more obstinate, that is, when he's in a good temper. So you may choose your opportunity wrong. But it's all the same. It can make no difference."

"What are you going to do, then?"

"I would let him do his worst. But Jane doesn't like to go against her mother. I'm sure I can't think how she should side with my father against both of us. He never laid her under any such obligation, I'm sure."

"There may be more ways than one of accounting for that. You must mind, however, and not be too hard upon your father. You're quite right in holding fast to the girl; but mind that vexation does not make you unjust."

"I wish my mother were alive. She was the only one that ever could manage him. How she contrived to do it nobody could think; but manage him she did, somehow or other. There's not a husk of use in talking to HIM."

"I daresay he prides himself on not being moved by talk. But has he ever had a chance of knowing Jane—of seeing what kind of a girl she is?"

"He's seen her over and over."

"But seeing isn't always believing."

"It certainly isn't with him."

"If he could only know her! But don't you be too hard upon him. And don't do anything in a hurry. Give him a little time, you know. Mrs Rogers won't interfere between you and Jane, I am pretty sure. But don't push matters till we see. Good-bye."

"Good-bye, and thank you kindly, sir.—Ain't I to see Jane in the meantime?"

"If I were you, I would make no difference. See her as often as you used, which I suppose was as often as you could. I don't think, I say, that her mother will interfere. Her father is all on your side."

I called on Mr Brownrigg; but, as his son had forewarned me, I could make nothing of him. He didn't see, when the mill was his property, and Dick was his son, why he shouldn't have his way with them. And he was going to have his way with them. His son might marry any lady in the land; and he wasn't going to throw himself away that way.

I will not weary my readers with the conversation we had together. All my missiles of argument were lost as it were in a bank of mud, the weight and resistance of which they only increased. My experience in the attempt, however, did a little to reconcile me to his going to sleep in church; for I saw that it could make little difference whether he was asleep or awake. He, and not Mr. Stoddart in his organ sentry-box, was the only person whom it was absolutely impossible to preach to. You might preach AT him; but TO him?—no.

CHAPTER X. MY CHRISTMAS PARTY.

As Christmas Day drew nearer and nearer, my heart glowed with the more gladness; and the question came more and more pressingly—Could I not do something to make it more really a holiday of the Church for my parishioners? That most of them would have a little more enjoyment on it than they had had all the year through, I had ground to hope; but I wanted to connect this gladness—in their minds, I mean, for who could dissever them in fact?—with its source, the love of God, that love manifested unto men in the birth of the Human Babe, the Son of Man. But I would not interfere with the Christmas Day at home. I resolved to invite as many of my parishioners as would come, to spend Christmas Eve at the Vicarage.

I therefore had a notice to that purport affixed to the church door; and resolved to send out no personal invitations whatever, so that I might not give offence by accidental omission. The only person thrown into perplexity by this mode of proceeding was Mrs. Pearson.

"How many am I to provide for, sir?" she said, with an injured air.

"For as many as you ever saw in church at one time," I said. "And if there should be too much, why so much the better. It can go to make Christmas Day the merrier at some of the poorer houses."

She looked discomposed, for she was not of an easy temper. But she never ACTED from her temper; she only LOOKED or SPOKE from it.

"I shall want help," she said, at length.

"As much as you like, Mrs. Pearson. I can trust you entirely."

Her face brightened; and the end showed that I had not trusted her amiss.

I was a little anxious about the result of the invitation—partly as indicating the amount of confidence my people placed in me. But although no one said a word to me about it beforehand except Old Rogers, as soon as the hour arrived, the people began to come. And the first I welcomed was Mr. Brownrigg.

I had had all the rooms on the ground-floor prepared for their reception. Tables of provision were set out in every one of them. My visitors had tea or coffee, with plenty of bread and butter, when they arrived; and the more solid supplies were reserved for a later part of the evening. I soon found myself with enough to do. But before long, I had a very efficient staff. For after having had occasion, once or twice, to mention something of my plans for the evening, I found my labours gradually diminish, and yet everything seemed to go right; the fact being that good Mr Boulderstone, in one part, had cast himself into the middle of the flood, and stood there immovable both in face and person, turning its waters into the right channel, namely, towards the barn, which I had fitted up for their reception in a body; while in another quarter, namely, in the barn, Dr Duncan was doing his best, and that was simply something first-rate, to entertain the people till all should be ready. From a kind of instinct these gentlemen had taken upon them to be my staff, almost without knowing it, and very grateful I was. I found, too, that they soon gathered some of the young and more active spirits about them, whom they employed in various ways for the good of the community.

When I came in and saw the goodly assemblage, for I had been busy receiving them in the house, I could not help rejoicing that my predecessor had been so fond of farming that he had rented land in the neighbourhood of the vicarage, and built this large barn, of which I could make a hall to entertain my friends. The night was frosty—the stars shining brilliantly overhead—so that, especially for country people, there was little danger in the short passage to be made to it from the house. But, if necessary, I resolved to have a covered-way built before next time. For how can a man be THE PERSON of a parish, if he never entertains his parishioners? And really, though it was lighted only with candles round the walls, and I had not been able to do much for the decoration of the place, I thought it looked very well, and my heart was glad that Christmas Eve—just as if the Babe had been coming again to us that same night. And is He not always coming to us afresh in every childlike feeling that awakes in the hearts of His people?

I walked about amongst them, greeting them, and greeted everywhere in turn with kind smiles and hearty shakes of the hand. As often as I paused in my communications for a moment, it was amusing to watch Mr. Boulderstone's honest, though awkward endeavours to be at ease with his inferiors; but Dr Duncan was just a sight worth seeing. Very tall and very stately, he was talking now to this old man, now to that young woman, and every face glistened towards which he turned. There was no condescension about him. He was as polite and courteous to one as to another, and the smile that every now and then lighted up his old face, was genuine and sympathetic. No one could have known by his behaviour that he was not at court. And I thought—Surely even the contact with such a man will do something to refine the taste of my people. I felt more certain than ever that a free mingling of all classes would do more than anything else towards binding us all into a wise patriotic nation; would tend to keep down that foolish emulation which makes one class ape another from afar, like Ben Jonson's Fungoso, "still lighting short a suit;" would refine the roughness of the rude, and enable the polished to see with what safety his just share in public matters might be committed into the hands of the honest workman. If we could once leave it to each other to give what honour is due; knowing that honour demanded is as worthless as insult undeserved is hurtless! What has one to do to honour himself? That is and can be no honour. When one has learned to seek the honour that cometh from God only, he will take the withholding of the honour that comes from men very quietly indeed.

The only thing that disappointed me was, that there was no one there to represent Oldcastle Hall. But how could I have everything a success at once!—And Catherine Weir was likewise absent.

After we had spent a while in pleasant talk, and when I thought nearly all were with us, I got up on a chair at the end of the barn, and said:—

"Kind friends,—I am very grateful to you for honouring my invitation as you have done. Permit me to hope that this meeting will be the first of many, and that from it may grow the yearly custom in this parish of gathering in love and friendship upon Christmas Eve. When God comes to man, man looks round for his neighbour. When man departed from God in the Garden of Eden, the only man in the world ceased to be the friend of the only woman in the world; and, instead of seeking to bear her burden, became her accuser to God, in whom he saw only the Judge, unable to perceive that the Infinite love of the Father had come to punish him in tenderness and grace. But when God in Jesus comes back to men, brothers and sisters spread forth their arms to embrace each other, and so to embrace Him. This is, when He is born again in our souls. For, dear friends, what we all need is just to become little children like Him; to cease to be careful about many things, and trust in Him, seeking only that He should rule, and that we should be made good like Him. What else is meant by 'Seek ye first the kingdom of God and his righteousness, and all these things shall be added unto you?' Instead of doing so, we seek the things God has promised to look after for us, and refuse to seek the thing He wants us to seek—a thing that cannot be given us, except we seek it. We profess to think Jesus the grandest and most glorious of men, and yet hardly care to be like Him; and so when we are offered His Spirit, that is, His very nature within us, for the asking, we will hardly take the trouble to ask for it. But to-night, at least, let all unkind thoughts, all hard judgments of one another, all selfish desires after our own way, be put from us, that we may welcome the Babe into our very bosoms; that when He comes amongst us—for is He not like a child still, meek and lowly of heart?—He may not be troubled to find that we are quarrelsome, and selfish, and unjust."

I came down from the chair, and Mr Brownrigg being the nearest of my guests, and wide awake, for he had been standing, and had indeed been listening to every word according to his ability, I shook hands with him. And positively there was some meaning in the grasp with which he returned mine.

I am not going to record all the proceedings of the evening; but I think it may be interesting to my readers to know something of how we spent it. First of all, we sang a hymn about the Nativity. And then I read an extract from a book of travels, describing the interior of an Eastern cottage, probably much resembling the inn in which our Lord was born, the stable being scarcely divided fron the rest of the house. For I felt that to open the inner eyes even of the brain, enabling people to SEE in some measure the reality of the old lovely story, to help them to have what the Scotch philosophers call a true CONCEPTION of the external conditions and circumstances of the events, might help to open the yet deeper spiritual eyes which alone can see the meaning and truth dwelling in and giving shape to the outward facts. And the extract was listened to with all the attention I could wish, except, at first, from some youngsters at the further end of the barn, who became, however, perfectly still as I proceeded.

After this followed conversation, during which I talked a good deal to

Jane Rogers, paying her particular attention indeed, with the hope of a chance of bringing old Mr Brownrigg and her together in some way.

"How is your mistress, Jane?" I said.

"Quite well, sir, thank you. I only wish she was here."

"I wish she were. But perhaps she will come next year."

"I think she will. I am almost sure she would have liked to come to-night; for I heard her say"——

"I beg your pardon, Jane, for interrupting you; but I would rather not be told anything you may have happened to overhear," I said, in a low voice.

"Oh, sir!" returned Jane, blushing a dark crimson; "it wasn't anything particular."

"Still, if it was anything on which a wrong conjecture might be built"—I wanted to soften it to her—"it is better that one should not be told it. Thank you for your kind intention, though. And now, Jane," I said, "will you do me a favour?"

"That I will, sir, if I can."

"Sing that Christmas carol I heard you sing last night to your mother."

"I didn't know any one was listening, sir."

"I know you did not. I came to the door with your father, and we stood and listened."

She looked very frightened. But I would not have asked her had I not known that she could sing like a bird.

"I am afraid I shall make a fool of myself," she said.

"We should all be willing to run that risk for the sake of others," I answered.

"I will try then, sir."

So she sang, and her clear voice soon silenced the speech all round.

"Babe Jesus lay on Mary's lap;
　　The sun shone in His hair:
　And so it was she saw, mayhap,
　　The crown already there.

"For she sang: 'Sleep on, my little King!
　　Bad Herod dares not come;
　Before Thee, sleeping, holy thing,
　　Wild winds would soon be dumb.

"'I kiss Thy hands, I kiss Thy feet,
　　My King, so long desired;
　Thy hands shall never be soil'd, my sweet,
　　Thy feet shall never be tired.

"'For Thou art the King of men, my son;
　　Thy crown I see it plain;
　And men shall worship Thee, every one,
　　And cry, Glory! Amen."

"Babe Jesus open'd His eyes so wide!
　　At Mary look'd her Lord.
　And Mary stinted her song and sigh'd.
　　Babe Jesus said never a word."

When Jane had done singing, I asked her where she had learned the carol; and she answered,—

"My mistress gave it me. There was a picture to it of the Baby on his mother's knee."

"I never saw it," I said. "Where did you get the tune?"

"I thought it would go with a tune I knew; and I tried it, and it did. But I was not fit to sing to you, sir."

"You must have quite a gift of song, Jane!" I said.

"My father and mother can both sing."

Mr Brownrigg was seated on the other side of me, and had apparently listened with some interest. His face was ten degrees less stupid than it usually was. I fancied I saw even a glimmer of some satisfaction in it. I turned to Old Rogers.

"Sing us a song, Old Rogers," I said.

"I'm no canary at that, sir; and besides, my singing days be over. I advise you to ask Dr. Duncan there. He CAN sing."

I rose and said to the assembly:

"My friends, if I did not think God was pleased to see us enjoying ourselves, I should have no heart for it myself. I am going to ask our dear friend Dr. Duncan to give us a song.—If you please, Dr. Duncan."

"I am very nearly too old," said the doctor; "but I will try."

His voice was certainly a little feeble; but the song was not much the worse for it. And a more suitable one for all the company he could hardly have pitched upon.

> *"There is a plough that has no share,*
>
> *But a coulter that parteth keen and fair.*
>
> *But the furrows they rise*
>
> *To a terrible size,*
>
> *Or ever the plough hath touch'd them there.*

'Gainst horses and plough in wrath they shake:

The horses are fierce; but the plough will break.

"And the seed that is dropt in those furrows of fear,

Will lift to the sun neither blade nor ear.

Down it drops plumb,

Where no spring times come;

And here there needeth no harrowing gear:

Wheat nor poppy nor any leaf

Will cover this naked ground of grief.

"But a harvest-day will come at last

When the watery winter all is past;

The waves so gray

Will be shorn away

By the angels' sickles keen and fast;

And the buried harvest of the sea

Stored in the barns of eternity."

Genuine applause followed the good doctor's song. I turned to Miss Boulderstone, from whom I had borrowed a piano, and asked her to play a country dance for us. But first I said—not getting up on a chair this time:—

"Some people think it is not proper for a clergyman to dance. I mean to assert my freedom from any such law. If our Lord chose to represent, in His parable of the Prodigal Son, the joy in Heaven over a repentant sinner by the figure of 'music and dancing,' I will hearken to Him rather than to men, be they as good as they may."

For I had long thought that the way to make indifferent things bad, was for good people not to do them.

And so saying, I stepped up to Jane Rogers, and asked her to dance with me. She blushed so dreadfully that, for a moment, I was almost sorry I had asked her. But she put her hand in mine at once; and if she was a little clumsy, she yet danced very naturally, and I had the satisfaction of feeling that I had an honest girl near me, who I knew was friendly to me in her heart.

But to see the faces of the people! While I had been talking, Old Rogers had been drinking in every word. To him it was milk and strong meat in one. But now his face shone with a father's gratification besides. And Richard's face was glowing too. Even old Brownrigg looked with a curious interest upon us, I thought.

Meantime Dr Duncan was dancing with one of his own patients, old Mrs Trotter, to whose wants he ministered far more from his table than his surgery. I have known that man, hearing of a case of want from his servant, send the fowl he was about to dine upon, untouched, to those whose necessity was greater than his.

And Mr Boulderstone had taken out old Mrs Rogers; and young Brownrigg had taken Mary Weir. Thomas Weir did not dance at all, but looked on kindly.

"Why don't you dance, Old Rogers?" I said, as I placed his daughter in a seat beside him.

"Did your honour ever see an elephant go up the futtock-shrouds?"

"No. I never did."

"I thought you must, sir, to ask me why I don't dance. You won't take my fun ill, sir? I'm an old man-o'-war's man, you know, sir."

"I should have thought, Rogers, that you would have known better by this time, than make such an apology to ME."

"God bless you, sir. An old man's safe with you—or a young lass, either, sir," he added, turning with a smile to his daughter.

I turned, and addressed Mr Boulderstone.

"I am greatly obliged to you, Mr Boulderstone, for the help you have given me this evening. I've seen you talking to everybody, just as if you had to entertain them all."

"I hope I haven't taken too much upon me. But the fact is, somehow or other, I don't know how, I got into the spirit of it."

"You got into the spirit of it because you wanted to help me, and I thank you heartily."

"Well, I thought it wasn't a time to mind one's peas and cues exactly. And really it's wonderful how one gets on without them. I hate formality myself."

The dear fellow was the most formal man I had ever met.

"Why don't you dance, Mr Brownrigg?"

"Who'd care to dance with me, sir? I don't care to dance with an old woman; and a young woman won't care to dance with me."

"I'll find you a partner, if you will put yourself in my hands."

"I don't mind trusting myself to you, sir."

So I led him to Jane Rogers. She stood up in respectful awe before the master of her destiny. There were signs of calcitration in the churchwarden, when he perceived whither I was leading him. But when he saw the girl stand trembling before him, whether it was that he was flattered by the signs of his own power, accepting them as homage, or that his hard heart actually softened a little, I cannot tell, but, after just a perceptible hesitation, he said:

"Come along, my lass, and let's have a hop together."

She obeyed very sweetly.

"Don't be too shy," I whispered to her as she passed me.

And the churchwarden danced very heartily with the lady's-maid.

I then asked him to take her into the house, and give her something to eat in return for her song. He yielded somewhat awkwardly, and what passed between them I do not know. But when they returned, she seemed less frightened at him than when she heard me make the proposal. And when the company was parting, I heard him take leave of her with the words—

"Give us a kiss, my girl, and let bygones be bygones."

Which kiss I heard with delight. For had I not been a peacemaker in this matter? And had I not then a right to feel blessed?—But the understanding was brought about simply by making the people meet—compelling them, as it were, to know something of each other really. Hitherto this girl had been a mere name, or phantom at best, to her lover's father; and it was easy for him to treat her as such, that is, as a mere fancy of his son's. The idea of her had passed through his mind; but with what vividness any idea, notion, or conception could be present to him, my readers must judge from my description of him. So that obstinacy was a ridiculously easy accomplishment to him. For he never had any notion of the matter to which he was opposed— only of that which he favoured. It is very easy indeed for such people to stick to their point.

But I took care that we should have dancing in moderation. It would not do for people either to get weary with recreation, or excited with what was not worthy of producing such an effect. Indeed we had only six country dances during the evening. That was all. And between the dances I read two or three of Wordsworth's ballads to them, and they listened even with more interest than I had been able to hope for. The fact was, that the happy and free hearted mood they were in "enabled the judgment." I wish one knew always by what musical spell to produce the right mood for receiving and reflecting a matter as it really is. Every true poem carries this spell with it in its own music, which it sends out before it as a harbinger, or properly a HERBERGER, to prepare a harbour or lodging for it. But then it needs a quiet mood first of all, to let this music be listened to.

For I thought with myself, if I could get them to like poetry and beautiful things in words, it would not only do them good, but help them to see what is in the Bible, and therefore to love it more. For I never could believe that a man who did not find God in other places as well as in the Bible ever found Him there at all. And I always thought, that to find God in other books enabled us to see clearly that he was MORE in the Bible than in any other book, or all other books put together.

After supper we had a little more singing. And to my satisfaction nothing came to my eyes or ears, during the whole evening, that was undignified or ill-bred. Of course, I knew that many of them must have two behaviours, and that now they were on their good behaviour. But I thought the oftener such were put on their good behaviour, giving them the opportunity of finding out how nice it was, the better. It might make them ashamed of the other at last.

There were many little bits of conversation I overheard, which I should like to give my readers; but I cannot dwell longer upon this part of my Annals. Especially I should have enjoyed recording one piece of talk, in which Old Rogers was evidently trying to move a more directly religious feeling in the mind of Dr Duncan. I thought I could see that THE difficulty with the noble old gentleman was one of expression. But after all the old foremast-man was a seer of the Kingdom; and the other, with all his refinement, and education, and goodness too, was but a child in it.

Before we parted, I gave to each of my guests a sheet of Christmas Carols, gathered from the older portions of our literature. For most of the modern hymns are to my mind neither milk nor meat—mere wretched imitations. There were a few curious words and idioms in these, but I thought it better to leave them as they were; for they might set them inquiring, and give me an opportunity of interesting them further, some time or other, in the history of a word; for, in their ups and downs of fortune, words fare very much like human beings.

And here is my sheet of Carols:—

AN HYMNE OF HEAVENLY LOVE.

O blessed Well of Love! O Floure of Grace!

O glorious Morning-Starre! O Lampe of Light!

Most lively image of thy Father's face,

Eternal King of Glorie, Lord of Might,

Meeke Lambe of God, before all worlds behight,

How can we Thee requite for all this good?

Or what can prize that Thy most precious blood?

Yet nought Thou ask'st in lieu of all this love,

But love of us, for guerdon of Thy paine:

Ay me! what can us lesse than that behove?

Had He required life of us againe,

Had it beene wrong to ask His owne with gaine?

He gave us life, He it restored lost;

Then life were least, that us so little cost.

But He our life hath left unto us free,

Free that was thrall, and blessed that was bann'd;

Ne ought demaunds but that we loving bee,

As He himselfe hath lov'd us afore-hand,

And bound therto with an eternall band,

Him first to love that us so dearely bought,

And next our brethren, to His image wrought.

Him first to love great right and reason is,

Who first to us our life and being gave,

And after, when we fared had amisse,

Us wretches from the second death did save;
And last, the food of life, which now we have,
Even He Himselfe, in His dear sacrament,
To feede our hungry soules, unto us lent.

Then next, to love our brethren, that were made
Of that selfe mould, and that self Maker's hand,
That we, and to the same againe shall fade,
Where they shall have like heritage of land,
However here on higher steps we stand,
Which also were with self-same price redeemed
That we, however of us light esteemed.

Then rouze thy selfe, O Earth! out of thy soyle,
In which thou wallowest like to filthy swyne,
And doest thy mynd in durty pleasures moyle,
Unmindfull of that dearest Lord of thyne;
Lift up to Him thy heavie clouded eyne,
That thou this soveraine bountie mayst behold,
And read, through love, His mercies manifold.

Beginne from first, where He encradled was
In simple cratch, wrapt in a wad of hay,
Betweene the toylfull oxe and humble asse,
And in what rags, and in how base array,

The glory of our heavenly riches lay,

When Him the silly shepheards came to see,

Whom greatest princes sought on lowest knee.

From thence reade on the storie of His life,

His humble carriage, His unfaulty wayes,

His cancred foes, His fights, His toyle, His strife,

His paines, His povertie, His sharpe assayes,

Through which He past His miserable dayes,

Offending none, and doing good to all,

Yet being malist both by great and small.

With all thy hart, with all thy soule and mind,

Thou must Him love, and His beheasts embrace;

All other loves, with which the world doth blind

Weake fancies, and stirre up affections base,

Thou must renounce and utterly displace,

And give thy selfe unto Him full and free,

That full and freely gave Himselfe to thee.

Then shall thy ravisht soul inspired bee

With heavenly thoughts farre above humane skil,

And thy bright radiant eyes shall plainly see

Th' idee of His pure glorie present still

Before thy face, that all thy spirits shall fill

With sweet enragement of celestial love,

Kindled through sight of those faire things above.

Spencer

NEW PRINCE, NEW POMP.

Behold a silly tender Babe,

  In freezing winter night,

In homely manger trembling lies;

  Alas! a piteous sight.

The inns are full, no man will yield

  This little Pilgrim bed;

But forced He is with silly beasts

  In crib to shroud His head.

Despise Him not for lying there,

  First what He is inquire;

An orient pearl is often found

  In depth of dirty mire.

Weigh not His crib, His wooden dish,

  Nor beast that by Him feed;

Weigh not his mother's poor attire,

  Nor Joseph's simple weed.

This stable is a Prince's court,

The crib His chair of state;
The beasts are parcel of His pomp,
  The wooden dish His plate.

The persons in that poor attire
  His royal liveries wear;
The Prince himself is come from heaven—
  This pomp is praised there.

With joy approach, O Christian wight!
  Do homage to thy King;
And highly praise this humble pomp
  Which He from heaven doth bring.

SOUTHWELL.

A DIALOGUE BETWEEN THREE SHEPHERDS.

1. Where is this blessed Babe
   That hath made
  All the world so full of joy
    And expectation;
   That glorious Boy
    That crowns each nation
  With a triumphant wreath of blessedness?

2. Where should He be but in the throng,

And among

His angel-ministers, that sing

And take wing

Just as may echo to His voice,

And rejoice,

When wing and tongue and all

May so procure their happiness?

3. But He hath other waiters now.

A poor cow,

An ox and mule stand and behold,

And wonder

That a stable should enfold

Him that can thunder.

Chorus. O what a gracious God have we!

How good! How great! Even as our misery.

Jeremy Taylor.

A SONG OF PRAISE FOR THE BIRTH OF CHRIST.

Away, dark thoughts; awake, my joy;

Awake, my glory; sing;

Sing songs to celebrate the birth

Of Jacob's God and King.

O happy night, that brought forth light,

Which makes the blind to see!
The day spring from on high came down
To cheer and visit thee.

The wakeful shepherds, near their flocks,
Were watchful for the morn;
But better news from heaven was brought,
Your Saviour Christ is born.
In Bethlem-town the infant lies,
Within a place obscure,
O little Bethlem, poor in walls,
But rich in furniture!

Since heaven is now come down to earth,
Hither the angels fly!
Hark, how the heavenly choir doth sing
Glory to God on High!
The news is spread, the church is glad,
SIMEON, o'ercome with joy,
Sings with the infant in his arms,
NOW LET THY SERVANT DIE.

Wise men from far beheld the star,
Which was their faithful guide,
Until it pointed forth the Babe,

141

And Him they glorified.

Do heaven and earth rejoice and sing—

Shall we our Christ deny?

He's born for us, and we for Him:

GLORY TO GOD ON HIGH.

JOHN MASON.

CHAPTER XI. SERMON ON GOD AND MAMMON.

I never asked questions about the private affairs of any of my parishioners, except of themselves individually upon occasion of their asking me for advice, and some consequent necessity for knowing more than they told me. Hence, I believe, they became the more willing that I should know. But I heard a good many things from others, notwithstanding, for I could not be constantly closing the lips of the communicative as I had done those of Jane Rogers. And amongst other things, I learned that Miss Oldcastle went most Sundays to the neighbouring town of Addicehead to church. Now I had often heard of the ability of the rector, and although I had never met him, was prepared to find him a cultivated, if not an original man. Still, if I must be honest, which I hope I must, I confess that I heard the news with a pang, in analysing which I discovered the chief component to be jealousy. It was no use asking myself why I should be jealous: there the ugly thing was. So I went and told God I was ashamed, and begged Him to deliver me from the evil, because His was the kingdom and the power and the glory. And He took my part against myself, for He waits to be gracious. Perhaps the reader may, however, suspect a deeper cause for this feeling (to which I would rather not give the true name again) than a merely professional one.

But there was one stray sheep of my flock that appeared in church for the first time on the morning of Christmas Day—Catherine Weir. She did not sit beside her father, but in the most shadowy corner of the church—near the organ loft, however. She could have seen her father if she had looked up, but she kept her eyes down the whole time, and never even lifted them to me.

The spot on one cheek was much brighter than that on the other, and made her look very ill.

I prayed to our God to grant me the honour of speaking a true word to them all; which honour I thought I was right in asking, because the Lord reproached the Pharisees for not seeking the honour that cometh from God. Perhaps I may have put a wrong interpretation on the passage. It is, however, a joy to think that He will not give you a stone, even if you should take it for a loaf, and ask for it as such. Nor is He, like the scribes, lying in wait to catch poor erring men in their words or their prayers, however mistaken they may be.

I took my text from the Sermon on the Mount. And as the magazine for which these Annals were first written was intended chiefly for Sunday reading, I wrote my sermon just as if I were preaching it to my unseen readers as I spoke it to my present parishioners. And here it is now:

The Gospel according to St Matthew, the sixth chapter, and part of the twenty-fourth and twenty-fifth verses:—

"'YE CANNOT SERVE GOD AND MAMMON. THEREFORE I SAY TO YOU, TAKE NO THOUGHT FOR YOUR LIFE.'

"When the Child whose birth we celebrate with glad hearts this day, grew up to be a man, He said this. Did He mean it?—He never said what He did not mean. Did He mean it wholly?—He meant it far beyond what the words could convey. He meant it altogether and entirely. When people do not understand what the Lord says, when it seems to them that His advice is impracticable, instead of searching deeper for a meaning which will be evidently true and wise, they comfort themselves by thinking He could not have meant it altogether, and so leave it. Or they think that if He did mean it, He could not expect them to carry it out. And in the fact that they could not do it perfectly if they were to try, they take refuge from the duty of trying to do it at all; or, oftener, they do not think about it at all as anything that in the least concerns them. The Son of our Father in heaven may have become a child, may have led the one life which belongs to every man to lead, may have suffered because we are sinners, may have died for our sakes, doing the will

143

of His Father in heaven, and yet we have nothing to do with the words He spoke out of the midst of His true, perfect knowledge, feeling, and action! Is it not strange that it should be so? Let it not be so with us this day. Let us seek to find out what our Lord means, that we may do it; trying and failing and trying again—verily to be victorious at last—what matter WHEN, so long as we are trying, and so coming nearer to our end!

"MAMMON, you know, means RICHES. Now, riches are meant to be the slave—not even the servant of man, and not to be the master. If a man serve his own servant, or, in a word, any one who has no just claim to be his master, he is a slave. But here he serves his own slave. On the other hand, to serve God, the source of our being, our own glorious Father, is freedom; in fact, is the only way to get rid of all bondage. So you see plainly enough that a man cannot serve God and Mammon. For how can a slave of his own slave be the servant of the God of freedom, of Him who can have no one to serve Him but a free man? His service is freedom. Do not, I pray you, make any confusion between service and slavery. To serve is the highest, noblest calling in creation. For even the Son of man came not to be ministered unto, but to minister, yea, with Himself.

"But how can a man SERVE riches? Why, when he says to riches, 'Ye are my good.' When he feels he cannot be happy without them. When he puts forth the energies of his nature to get them. When he schemes and dreams and lies awake about them. When he will not give to his neighbour for fear of becoming poor himself. When he wants to have more, and to know he has more, than he can need. When he wants to leave money behind him, not for the sake of his children or relatives, but for the name of the wealth. When he leaves his money, not to those who NEED it, even of his relations, but to those who are rich like himself, making them yet more of slaves to the overgrown monster they worship for his size. When he honours those who have money because they have money, irrespective of their character; or when he honours in a rich man what he would not honour in a poor man. Then is he the slave of Mammon. Still more is he Mammon's slave when his devotion to his god makes him oppressive to those over whom his wealth gives him power; or when he becomes unjust in order to add to his stores.—How will it be with such a man when on a sudden he finds that the world has vanished, and he is alone with God? There lies the body in which he used to live, whose poor necessities first made money of value to him, but with which itself and its fictitious value are both left behind. He cannot now even try to bribe God with a cheque. The angels will not bow down to him because his property, as set forth in his will, takes five or six figures to express its amount It makes no difference to them that he has lost it, though; for they never respected him. And the poor souls of Hades, who envied him the wealth they had lost before, rise up as one man to welcome him, not for love of him—no worshipper of Mammon loves another—but rejoicing in the mischief that has befallen him, and saying, 'Art thou also become one of us?' And Lazarus in Abraham's bosom, however sorry he may be for him, however grateful he may feel to him for the broken victuals and the penny, cannot with one drop of the water of Paradise cool that man's parched tongue.

"Alas, poor Dives! poor server of Mammon, whose vile god can pretend to deliver him no longer! Or rather, for the blockish god never pretended anything—it was the man's own doing—Alas for the Mammon-worshipper! he can no longer deceive himself in his riches. And so even in hell he is something nobler than he was on earth; for he worships his riches no longer. He cannot. He curses them.

"Terrible things to say on Christmas Day! But if Christmas Day teaches us anything, it teaches us to worship God and not Mammon; to worship spirit and not matter; to worship love and not power.

"Do I now hear any of my friends saying in their hearts: Let the rich take that! It does not apply to us. We are poor enough? Ah, my friends, I have known a light-hearted, liberal rich man lose his riches, and be liberal and light-hearted still. I knew a rich lady once, in giving a large gift of money to a poor man, say apologetically, 'I hope it is no disgrace in me to be rich, as it is none in you to be poor.' It is not the being rich that is wrong, but the serving of riches, instead of making them serve your neighbour and yourself—your neighbour for this life, yourself for the everlasting habitations. God knows it is hard for the rich man to enter into the kingdom of heaven; but the rich man does sometimes enter in; for God hath made it possible. And the greater

145

the victory, when it is the rich man that overcometh the world. It is easier for the poor man to enter into the kingdom, yet many of the poor have failed to enter in, and the greater is the disgrace of their defeat. For the poor have more done for them, as far as outward things go, in the way of salvation than the rich, and have a beatitude all to themselves besides. For in the making of this world as a school of salvation, the poor, as the necessary majority, have been more regarded than the rich. Do not think, my poor friend, that God will let you off. He lets nobody off. You, too, must pay the uttermost farthing. He loves you too well to let you serve Mammon a whit more than your rich neighbour. 'Serve Mammon!' do you say? 'How can I serve Mammon? I have no Mammon to serve.'—Would you like to have riches a moment sooner than God gives them? Would you serve Mammon if you had him?—'Who can tell?' do you answer? 'Leave those questions till I am tried.' But is there no bitterness in the tone of that response? Does it not mean, 'It will be a long time before I have a chance of trying THAT?'—But I am not driven to such questions for the chance of convicting some of you of Mammon-worship. Let us look to the text. Read it again.

"'YE CANNOT SERVE GOD AND MAMMON. THEREFORE I SAY UNTO YOU, TAKE NO THOUGHT FOR YOUR LIFE.'

"Why are you to take no thought? Because you cannot serve God and Mammon. Is taking thought, then, a serving of Mammon? Clearly.—Where are you now, poor man? Brooding over the frost? Will it harden the ground, so that the God of the sparrows cannot find food for His sons? Where are you now, poor woman? Sleepless over the empty cupboard and to-morrow's dinner? 'It is because we have no bread?' do you answer? Have you forgotten the five loaves among the five thousand, and the fragments that were left? Or do you know nothing of your Father in heaven, who clothes the lilies and feeds the birds? O ye of little faith? O ye poor-spirited Mammon-worshippers! who worship him not even because he has given you anything, but in the hope that he may some future day benignantly regard you. But I may be too hard upon you. I know well that our Father sees a great difference between the man who is anxious about his children's dinner, or even about his own, and the man who is only anxious to add another ten thousand to his much

146

goods laid up for many years. But you ought to find it easy to trust in God for such a matter as your daily bread, whereas no man can by any possibility trust in God for ten thousand pounds. The former need is a God-ordained necessity; the latter desire a man-devised appetite at best—possibly swinish greed. Tell me, do you long to be rich? Then you worship Mammon. Tell me, do you think you would feel safer if you had money in the bank? Then you are Mammon-worshippers; for you would trust the barn of the rich man rather than the God who makes the corn to grow. Do you say—'What shall we eat? and what shall we drink? and wherewithal shall we be clothedl?' Are ye thus of doubtful mind?—Then you are Mammon-worshippers. "But how is the work of the world to be done if we take no thought?—We are nowhere told not to take thought. We MUST take thought. The question is—What are we to take or not to take thought about? By some who do not know God, little work would be done if they were not driven by anxiety of some kind. But you, friends, are you content to go with the nations of the earth, or do you seek a better way—THE way that the Father of nations would have you walk in?

"WHAT then are we to take thought about? Why, about our work. What are we not to take thought about? Why, about our life. The one is our business: the other is God's. But you turn it the other way. You take no thought of earnestness about the doing of your duty; but you take thought of care lest God should not fulfil His part in the goings on of the world. A man's business is just to do his duty: God takes upon Himself the feeding and the clothing. Will the work of the world be neglected if a man thinks of his work, his duty, God's will to be done, instead of what he is to eat, what he is to drink, and wherewithal he is to be clothed? And remember all the needs of the world come back to these three. You will allow, I think, that the work of the world will be only so much the better done; that the very means of procuring the raiment or the food will be the more thoroughly used. What, then, is the only region on which the doubt can settle? Why, God. He alone remains to be doubted. Shall it be so with you? Shall the Son of man, the baby now born, and for ever with us, find no faith in you? Ah, my poor friend, who canst not trust in God—I was going to say you DESERVE—but what do I know of you to condemn and judge you?—I was going to say, you deserve to be treated like the child who frets and complains because his mother holds him on her knee and feeds him mouthful by mouthful with her own loving hand. I meant—you deserve to have your own way for a while; to be set down, and told to help yourself, and see what it will come to; to have your mother open the cupboard door for you, and leave you alone to your pleasures. Alas! poor child! When the sweets begin to pall, and the twilight begins to come duskily into the chamber, and you look about all at once and see no mother, how will your cupboard comfort you then? Ask it for a smile, for a stroke of the gentle hand, for a word of love. All the full-fed Mammon can give you is what your mother would have given you without the consequent loathing, with the light of her countenance upon it all, and the arm of her love around you.—And this is what God does sometimes, I think, with the Mammon-worshippers amongst the poor. He says to them, Take your Mammon, and see what he is worth. Ah, friends, the children of God can never be happy serving other than Him. The prodigal might fill his belly with riotous living or with the husks that the swine ate. It was all one, so long as he was not with his father. His soul was wretched. So would you be if you had wealth, for I fear you would only be worse Mammon-worshippers than now, and might well have to thank God for the misery of any swine-trough that could bring you to your senses.

"But we do see people die of starvation sometimes,—Yes. But if you did your work in God's name, and left the rest to Him, that would not trouble you. You would say, If it be God's will that I should starve, I can starve as well as another. And your mind would be at ease. "Thou wilt keep him in perfect peace whose mind is stayed upon Thee, because he trusteth in Thee." Of that I am sure. It may be good for you to go hungry and bare-foot; but it must be utter death to have no faith in God. It is not, however, in God's way of things that the man who does his work shall not live by it. We do not know why here and there a man may be left to die of hunger, but I do believe that they who wait upon the Lord shall not lack any good. What it may be good to deprive a man of till he knows and acknowledges whence it comes, it may be still better to give him when he has learned that every good and every perfect gift is from above, and cometh down from the Father of lights.

"I SHOULD like to know a man who just minded his duty and troubled himself about nothing; who did his own work and did not interfere with God's. How nobly he would work—working not for reward, but because it was the will of God! How happily he would receive his food and clothing, receiving them as the gifts of God! What peace would be his! What a sober gaiety! How hearty and infectious his laughter! What a friend he would be! How sweet his sympathy! And his mind would be so clear he would understand everything His eye being single, his whole body would be full of light. No fear of his ever doing a mean thing. He would die in a ditch, rather. It is this fear of want that makes men do mean things. They are afraid to part with their precious lord—Mammon. He gives no safety against such a fear. One of the richest men in England is haunted with the dread of the workhouse. This man whom I should like to know, would be sure that God would have him liberal, and he would be what God would have him. Riches are not in the least necessary to that. Witness our Lord's admiration of the poor widow with her great farthing.

"But I think I hear my troubled friend who does not love money, and yet cannot trust in God out and out, though she fain would,—I think I hear her say, "I believe I could trust Him for myself, or at least I should be ready to dare the worst for His sake; but my children—it is the thought of my children that is too much for me." Ah, woman! she whom the Saviour praised so pleasedly, was one who trusted Him for her daughter. What an honour she had! "Be it unto thee even as thou wilt." Do you think you love your children better than He who made them? Is not your love what it is because He put it into your heart first? Have not you often been cross with them? Sometimes unjust to them? Whence came the returning love that rose from unknown depths in your being, and swept away the anger and the injustice! You did not create that love. Probably you were not good enough to send for it by prayer. But it came. God sent it. He makes you love your children; be sorry when you have been cross with them; ashamed when you have been unjust to them; and yet you won't trust Him to give them food and clothes! Depend upon it, if He ever refuses to give them food and clothes, and you knew all about it, the why and the wherefore, you would not dare to give them food or clothes either. He loves them a thousand times better than you do—be sure of that—and feels for their sufferings too, when He cannot give them just what He would like

149

to give them—cannot for their good, I mean.

"But as your mistrust will go further, I can go further to meet it. You will say, 'Ah! yes'—in your feeling, I mean, not in words,—you will say, 'Ah! yes—food and clothing of a sort! Enough to keep life in and too much cold out! But I want my children to have plenty of GOOD food, and NICE clothes.'

"Faithless mother! Consider the birds of the air. They have so much that at least they can sing! Consider the lilies—they were red lilies, those. Would you not trust Him who delights in glorious colours—more at least than you, or He would never have created them and made us to delight in them? I do not say that your children shall be clothed in scarlet and fine linen; but if not, it is not because God despises scarlet and fine linen or does not love your children. He loves them, I say, too much to give them everything all at once. But He would make them such that they may have everything without being the worse, and with being the better for it. And if you cannot trust Him yet, it begins to be a shame, I think.

"It has been well said that no man ever sank under the burden of the day. It is when to-morrow's burden is added to the burden of to-day, that the weight is more than a man can bear. Never load yourselves so, my friends. If you find yourselves so loaded, at least remember this: it is your own doing, not God's. He begs you to leave the future to Him, and mind the present. What more or what else could He do to take the burden off you? Nothing else would do it. Money in the bank wouldn't do it. He cannot do to-morrow's business for you beforehand to save you from fear about it. That would derange everything. What else is there but to tell you to trust in Him, irrespective of the fact that nothing else but such trust can put our heart at peace, from the very nature of our relation to Him as well as the fact that we need these things. We think that we come nearer to God than the lower animals do by our foresight. But there is another side to it. We are like to Him with whom there is no past or future, with whom a day is as a thousand years, and a thousand years as one day, when we live with large bright spiritual eyes, doing our work in the great present, leaving both past and future to Him to whom they are ever present, and fearing nothing, because He is in our future, as much as He is in our past, as much as, and far more than, we can feel Him to be in our present. Partakers thus of the divine nature, resting in that perfect All-in-all in whom our nature is eternal too, we walk without fear, full of hope and courage and strength to do His will, waiting for the endless good which He is always giving as fast as He can get us able to take it in. Would not this be to be more of gods than Satan promised to Eve? To live carelessly-divine, duty-doing, fearless, loving, self-forgetting lives—is not that more than to know both good and evil—lives in which the good, like Aaron's rod, has swallowed up the evil, and turned it into good? For pain and hunger are evils, but if faith in God swallows them up, do they not so turn into good? I say they do. And I am glad to believe that I am not alone in my parish in this conviction. I have never been too hungry, but I have had trouble which I would gladly have exchanged for hunger and cold and weariness. Some of you have known hunger and cold and weariness. Do you not join with me to say: It is well, and better than well—whatever helps us to know the love of Him who is our God?

"But there HAS BEEN just one man who has acted thus. And it is His Spirit in our hearts that makes us desire to know or to be another such—who would do the will of God for God, and let God do God's will for Him. For His will is all. And this man is the baby whose birth we celebrate this day. Was this a condition to choose—that of a baby—by one who thought it part of a man's high calling to take care of the morrow? Did He not thus cast the whole matter at once upon the hands and heart of His Father? Sufficient unto the baby's day is the need thereof; he toils not, neither does he spin, and yet he if fed and clothed, and loved, and rejoiced in. Do you remind me that sometimes even his mother forgets him—a mother, most likely, to whose self-indulgence or weakness the child owes his birth as hers? Ah! but he is not therefore forgotten, however like things it may look to our half-seeing eyes, by his Father in heaven. One of the highest benefits we can reap from understanding the way of God with ourselves is, that we become able thus to trust Him for others with whom we do not understand His ways.

"But let us look at what will be more easily shown—how, namely, He did the will of His Father, and took no thought for the morrow after He became a man. Remember how He forsook His trade when the time came for Him to preach. Preaching was not a profession then. There were no monasteries, or vicarages, or stipends, then. Yet witness for the Father the garment woven throughout; the ministering of women; the purse in common! Hard-working men and rich ladies were ready to help Him, and did help Him with all that He needed.—Did He then never want? Yes; once at least—for a little while only.

"He was a-hungered in the wilderness. 'Make bread,' said Satan. 'No,' said our Lord.—He could starve; but He could not eat bread that His Father did not give Him, even though He could make it Himself. He had come hither to be tried. But when the victory was secure, lo! the angels brought Him food from His Father.—Which was better? To feed Himself, or be fed by His Father? Judg? yourselves, jinxious people, He sought the kingdom of God and His righteousness, and the bread was added unto Him.

"And this gives me occasion to remark that the same truth holds with regard to any portion of the future as well as the morrow. It is a principle, not a command, or an encouragement, or a promise merely. In respect of it there is no difference between next day and next year, next hour and next century. You will see at once the absurdity of taking no thought for the morrow, and taking thought for next year. But do you see likewise that it is equally reasonable to trust God for the next moment, and equally unreasonable not to trust Him? The Lord was hungry and needed food now, though He could still go without for a while. He left it to His Father. And so He told His disciples to do when they were called to answer before judges and rulers. 'Take no thought. It shall be given you what ye shall say.' You have a disagreeable duty to do at twelve o'clock. Do not blacken nine and ten and eleven, and all between, with the colour of twelve. Do the work of each, and reap your reward in peace. So when the dreaded moment in the future becomes the present, you shall meet it walking in the light, and that light will overcome its darkness. How often do men who have made up their minds what to say and do under certain expected circumstances, forget the words and reverse the actions! The best preparation is the present well seen to, the last duty done. For this will keep the eye so clear and the body so full of light that the right action will be perceived at once, the right words will rush from the heart to the lips, and the man, full of the Spirit of God because he cares for nothing but the will of God, will trample on the evil thing in love, and be sent, it may be, in a chariot of fire to the presence of his Father, or stand unmoved amid the cruel mockings of the men he loves.

"Do you feel inclined to say in your hearts: 'It was easy for Him to take no thought, for He had the matter in His own hands?' But observe, there is nothing very noble in a man's taking no thought except it be from faith. If there were no God to take thought for us, we should have no right to blame any one for taking thought. You may fancy the Lord had His own power to fall back upon. But that would have been to Him just the one dreadful thing. That His Father should forget Him!—no power in Himself could make up for that. He feared nothing for Himself; and never once employed His divine power to save Him from His human fate. Let God do that for Him if He saw fit. He did not come into the world to take care of Himself. That would not be in any way divine. To fall back on Himself, God failing Him—how could that make it easy for Him to avoid care? The very idea would be torture. That would be to declare heaven void, and the world without a God. He would not even pray to His Father for what He knew He should have if He did ask it. He would just wait His will.

"But see how the fact of His own power adds tenfold significance to the fact that He trusted in God. We see that this power would not serve His need—His need not being to be fed and clothed, but to be one with the Father, to be fed by His hand, clothed by His care. This was what the Lord wanted—and we need, alas! too often without wanting it. He never once, I repeat, used His power for Himself. That was not his business. He did not care about it. His life was of no value to Him but as His Father cared for it. God would mind all that was necessary for Him, and He would mind the work His Father had given Him to do. And, my friends, this is just the one secret of a blessed life, the one thing every man comes into this world to learn. With what authority it comes to us from the lips of Him who knew all about it, and ever did as He said!

"Now you see that He took no thought for the morrow. And, in the name of the holy child Jesus, I call upon you, this Christmas day, to cast care

153

to the winds, and trust in God; to receive the message of peace and good-will to men; to yield yourselves to the Spirit of God, that you may be taught what He wants you to know; to remember that the one gift promised without reserve to those who ask it—the one gift worth having—the gift which makes all other gifts a thousand-fold in value, is the gift of the Holy Spirit, the spirit of the child Jesus, who will take of the things of Jesus, and show them to you—make you understand them, that is—so that you shall see them to be true, and love Him with all your heart and soul, and your neighbour as yourselves."

And here, having finished my sermon, I will give my reader some lines with which he may not be acquainted, from a writer of the Elizabethan time. I had meant to introduce them into my sermon, but I was so carried away with my subject that I forgot them. For I always preached extempore, which phrase I beg my reader will not misinterpret as meaning ON THE SPUR OF THE MOMENT, OF WITHOUT THE DUE PREPARATION OF MUCH THOUGHT.

> "O man! thou image of thy Maker's good,
>
> What canst thou fear, when breathed into thy blood
>
> His Spirit is that built thee? What dull sense
>
> Makes thee suspect, in need, that Providence
>
> Who made the morning, and who placed the light
>
> Guide to thy labours; who called up the night,
>
> And bid her fall upon thee like sweet showers,
>
> In hollow murmurs, to lock up thy powers;
>
> Who gave thee knowledge; who so trusted thee
>
> To let thee grow so near Himself, the Tree?
>
> Must He then be distrusted? Shall His frame
>
> Discourse with Him why thus and thus I am?

He made the Angels thine, thy fellows all;

Nay even thy servants, when devotions call.

Oh! canst thou be so stupid then, so dim,

To seek a saving* influence, and lose Him?

Can stars protect thee? Or can poverty,

Which is the light to heaven, put out His eye!

He is my star; in Him all truth I find,

All influence, all fate. And when my mind

Is furnished with His fulness, my poor story

Shall outlive all their age, and all their glory.

The hand of danger cannot fall amiss,

When I know what, and in whose power, it is,

Nor want, the curse of man, shall make me groan:

A holy hermit is a mind alone.

* * * *

Affliction, when I know it, is but this,

A deep alloy whereby man tougher is

To bear the hammer; and the deeper still,

We still arise more image of His will;

Sickness, an humorous cloud 'twixt us and light;

And death, at longest, but another night."

[Many, in those days, believed in astrology.]

I had more than ordinary attention during my discourse, at one point in which I saw the down-bent head of Catherine Weir sink yet lower upon her hands. After a moment, however, she sat more erect than before, though she never lifted her eyes to meet mine. I need not assure my reader that she was not present to my mind when I spoke the words that so far had moved her. Indeed, had I thought of her, I could not have spoken them.

As I came out of the church, my people crowded about me with outstretched hands and good wishes. One woman, the aged wife of a more aged labourer, who could not get near me, called from the outskirts of the little crowd—

"May the Lord come and see ye every day, sir. And may ye never know the hunger and cold as me and Tomkins has come through."

"Amen to the first of your blessing, Mrs Tomkins, and hearty thanks to you. But I daren't say AMEN to the other part of it, after what I've been preaching, you know."

"But there'll be no harm if I say it for ye, sir?"

"No, for God will give me what is good, even if your kind heart should pray against it."

"Ah, sir, ye don't know what it is to be hungry AND cold."

"Neither shall you any more, if I can help it."

"God bless ye, sir. But we're pretty tidy just in the meantime."

I walked home, as usual on Sunday mornings, by the road. It was a lovely day. The sun shone so warm that you could not help thinking of what he would be able to do before long—draw primroses and buttercups out of the earth by force of sweet persuasive influences. But in the shadows lay fine webs and laces of ice, so delicately lovely that one could not but be glad of the cold that made the water able to please itself by taking such graceful forms. And I wondered over again for the hundredth time what could be the principle which, in the wildest, most lawless, fantastically chaotic, apparently capricious work of nature, always kept it beautiful. The beauty of holiness must be at the heart of it somehow, I thought. Because our God is so free from stain, so loving, so unselfish, so good, so altogether what He wants us to be, so holy, therefore all His works declare Him in beauty; His fingers can touch nothing but to mould it into loveliness; and even the play of His elements is in grace and tenderness of form.

And then I thought how the sun, at the farthest point from us, had begun to come back towards us; looked upon us with a hopeful smile; was like the Lord when He visited His people as a little one of themselves, to grow upon the earth till it should blossom as the rose in the light of His presence. "Ah! Lord," I said, in my heart, "draw near unto Thy people. It is spring-time with Thy world, but yet we have cold winds and bitter hail, and pinched voices forbidding them that follow Thee and follow not with us. Draw nearer, Sun of Righteousness, and make the trees bourgeon, and the flowers blossom, and the voices grow mellow and glad, so that all shall join in praising Thee, and find thereby that harmony is better than unison. Let it be summer, O Lord, if it ever may be summer in this court of the Gentiles. But Thou hast told us that Thy kingdom cometh within us, and so Thy joy must come within us too. Draw nigh then, Lord, to those to whom Thou wilt draw nigh; and others beholding their welfare will seek to share therein too, and seeing their good works will glorify their Father in heaven."

So I walked home, hoping in my Saviour, and wondering to think how pleasant I had found it to be His poor servant to this people. Already the doubts which had filled my mind on that first evening of gloom, doubts as to whether I had any right to the priest's office, had utterly vanished, slain by the effort to perform the priest's duty. I never thought about the matter now.—And how can doubt ever be fully met but by action? Try your theory; try your hypothesis; or if it is not worth trying, give it up, pull it down. And I hoped that if ever a cloud should come over me again, however dark and dismal it might be, I might be able, notwithstanding, to rejoice that the sun was shining on others though not on me, and to say with all my heart to my Father in heaven, "Thy will be done."

When I reached my own study, I sat down by a blazing fire, and poured myself out a glass of wine; for I had to go out again to see some of my poor friends, and wanted some luncheon first.—It is a great thing to have the greetings of the universe presented in fire and food. Let me, if I may, be ever welcomed to my room in winter by a glowing hearth, in summer by a vase of flowers; if I may not, let me then think how nice they would be, and bury myself in my work. I do not think that the road to contentment lies in despising what we have not got. Let us acknowledge all good, all delight that the world holds, and be content without it. But this we can never be except by possessing the one thing, without which I do not merely say no man ought to be content, but no man CAN be content—the Spirit of the Father.

If any young people read my little chronicle, will they not be inclined to say, "The vicar has already given us in this chapter hardly anything but a long sermon; and it is too bad of him to go on preaching in his study after we saw him safe out of the pulpit"? Ah, well! just one word, and I drop the preaching for a while. My word is this: I may speak long-windedly, and even inconsiderately as regards my young readers; what I say may fail utterly to convey what I mean; I may be actually stupid sometimes, and not have a suspicion of it; but what I mean is true; and if you do not know it to be true yet, some of you at least suspect it to be true, and some of you hope it is true; and when you all see it as I mean it and as you can take it, you will rejoice with a gladness you know nothing about now There, I have done for a little while. I won't pledge myself for more, I assure you. For to speak about such things is the greatest delight of my age, as it was of my early manhood, next to that of loving God and my neighbour. For as these are THE two commandments of life, so they are in themselves THE pleasures of life. But there I am at it again. I beg your pardon now, for I have already inadvertently broken my promise.

I had allowed myself a half-hour before the fire with my glass of wine and piece of bread, and I soon fell into a dreamy state called REVERIE, which I fear not a few mistake for THINKING, because it is the nearest approach they ever make to it. And in this reverie I kept staring about my book-shelves. I am an old man now, and you do not know my name; and if you should ever find it out, I shall very soon hide it under some daisies, I hope, and so escape; and therefore, I am going to be egotistic in the most unpardonable manner. I am going to tell you one of my faults, for it continues, I fear, to be one of my faults still, as it certainly was at the period of which I am now writing. I am very fond of books. Do not mistake me. I do not mean that I love reading. I hope I do. That is no fault—a virtue rather than a fault. But, as the old meaning of the word FOND was FOOLISH, I use that word: I am foolishly fond of the bodies of books as distinguished from their souls, or thought-element. I do not say I love their bodies as DIVIDED from their souls; I do not say I should let a book stand upon my shelves for which I felt no respect, except indeed it happened to be useful to me in some inferior way. But I delight in seeing books about me, books even of which there seems to be no prospect that I shall have time to read a single chapter before I lay this old head down for the last time. Nay, more: I confess that if they are nicely bound, so as to glow and shine in such a fire-light as that by which I was then sitting, I like them ever so much the better. Nay, more yet—and this comes very near to showing myself worse than I thought I was when I began to tell you my fault: there are books upon my shelves which certainly at least would not occupy the place of honour they do occupy, had not some previous owner dressed them far beyond their worth, making modern apples of Sodom of them. Yet there I let them stay, because they are pleasant to the eye, although certainly not things to be desired to make one wise. I could say a great deal more about the matter, pro and con, but it would be worse than a sermon, I fear. For I suspect that by the time books, which ought to be loved for the truth that is in them, of one sort or another, come to be loved as articles of furniture, the mind has gone through a process more than analogous to that which the miser's mind goes through—namely, that of passing from the respect of money because of what it can do, to the love of money because it is money. I have not yet reached the furniture stage, and I do not think I ever shall. I would rather burn them all. Meantime, I think one safeguard is to encourage one's friends to borrow one's books—not to offer individual books, which is much the same as OFFERING advice. That will probably take some of the shine off them, and put a few thumb-marks in them, which both are very wholesome towards the arresting of the furniture declension. For my part, thumb-marks I find very obnoxious—far more so than the spoiling of the binding.—I know that some of my readers, who have had sad experience of the sort, will be saying in themselves, "He might have mentioned a surer antidote resulting from this measure, than either rubbed Russia or dirty GLOVE-marks even—that of utter disappearance and irreparable loss." But no; that has seldom happened to me—because I trust my pocketbook, and never my memory, with the names of those to whom the individual books are committed.—There, then, is a little bit of practical advice in both directions for young book-lovers.

Again I am reminded that I am getting old. What digressions!

Gazing about on my treasures, the thought suddenly struck me that I had never done as I had promised Judy; had never found out what her aunt's name meant in Anglo-Saxon. I would do so now. I got down my dictionary, and soon discovered that Ethelwyn meant Home-joy, or Inheritance.

"A lovely meaning," I said to myself.

And then I went off into another reverie, with the composition of which I shall not trouble my reader; and with the mention of which I had, perhaps, no right to occupy the fragment of his time spent in reading it, seeing I did not intend to tell him how it was made up. I will tell him something else instead.

Several families had asked me to take my Christmas dinner with them; but, not liking to be thus limited, I had answered each that I would not, if they would excuse me, but would look in some time or other in the course of the evening.

When my half-hour was out, I got up and filled my pockets with little presents for my poor people, and set out to find them in their own homes.

I was variously received, but unvaryingly with kindness; and my little presents were accepted, at least in most instances, with a gratitude which made me ashamed of them and of myself too for a few moments. Mrs. Tomkins looked as if she had never seen so much tea together before, though there was only a couple of pounds of it; and her husband received a pair of warm trousers none the less cordially that they were not quite new, the fact being that I found I did not myself need such warm clothing this winter as I had needed the last. I did not dare to offer Catherine Weir anything, but I gave her little boy a box of water-colours—in remembrance of the first time I saw him, though I said nothing about that. His mother did not thank me. She told little Gerard to do so, however, and that was something. And, indeed, the boy's sweetness would have been enough for both.

Gerard—an unusual name in England; specially not to be looked for in the class to which she belonged.

When I reached Old Rogers's cottage, whither I carried a few yards of ribbon, bought by myself, I assure my lady friends, with the special object that the colour should be bright enough for her taste, and pure enough of its kind for mine, as an offering to the good dame, and a small hymn-book, in which were some hymns of my own making, for the good man—

But do forgive me, friends, for actually describing my paltry presents. I can dare to assure you it comes from a talking old man's love of detail, and from no admiration of such small givings as those. You see I trust you, and I want to stand well with you. I never could be indifferent to what people thought of me; though I have had to fight hard to act as freely as if I were indifferent, especially when upon occasion I found myself approved of. It is more difficult to walk straight then, than when men are all against you.—As I have already broken a sentence, which will not be past setting for a while yet, I may as well go on to say here, lest any one should remark that a clergyman ought not to show off his virtues, nor yet teach his people bad habits by making them look out for presents—that my income not only seemed to me disproportioned to the amount of labour necessary in the parish, but certainly was larger than I required to spend upon myself; and the miserly passion for books I contrived to keep a good deal in check; for I had no fancy for gliding devil-wards for the sake of a few books after all. So there was no great virtue—was there?—in easing my heart by giving a few of the good things people give their children to my poor friends, whose kind reception of them gave me as much pleasure as the gifts gave them. They valued the kindness in the gift, and to look out for kindness will not make people greedy.

When I reached the cottage, I found not merely Jane there with her father and mother, which was natural on Christmas Day, seeing there seemed to be no company at the Hall, but my little Judy as well, sitting in the old woman's arm-chair, (not that she Used it much, but it was called hers,) and looking as much at home as—as she did in the pond.

"Why, Judy!" I exclaimed, "you here?"

"Yes. Why not, Mr Walton?" she returned, holding out her hand without rising, for the chair was such a large one, and she was set so far back in it that the easier way was not to rise, which, seeing she was not greatly overburdened with reverence, was not, I presume, a cause of much annoyance to the little damsel.

"I know no reason why I shouldn't see a Sandwich Islander here. Yet I might express surprise if I did find one, might I not?"

Judy pretended to pout, and muttered something about comparing her to a cannibal. But Jane took up the explanation.

"Mistress had to go off to London with her mother to-day, sir, quite unexpected, on some banking business, I fancy, from what I—I beg your pardon, sir. They're gone anyhow, whatever the reason may be; and so I came to see my father and mother, and Miss Judy would come with me."

"She's very welcome," said Mrs Rogers.

"How could I stay up there with nobody but Jacob, and that old wolf Sarah? I wouldn't be left alone with her for the world. She'd have me in the Bishop's Pool before you came back, Janey dear."

"That wouldn't matter much to you, would it, Judy?" I said.

"She's a white wolf, that old Sarah, I know?" was all her answer.

"But what will the old lady say when she finds you brought the young lady here?" asked Mrs Rogers.

"I didn't bring her, mother. She would come."

"Besides, she'll never know it," said Judy.

I did not see that it was my part to read Judy a lecture here, though

162

perhaps I might have done so if I had had more influence over her than I had. I wanted to gain some influence over her, and knew that the way to render my desire impossible of fulfilment would be, to find fault with what in her was a very small affair, whatever it might be in one who had been properly brought up. Besides, a clergyman is not a moral policeman. So I took no notice of the impropriety.

"Had they actually to go away on the morning of Christmas Day?" I said.

"They went anyhow, whether they had to do it or not, sir," answered Jane.

"Aunt Ethelwyn didn't want to go till to-morrow," said Judy. "She said something about coming to church this morning. But grannie said they must go at once. It was very cross of old grannie. Think what a Christmas Day to me without auntie, and with Sarah! But I don't mean to go home till it's quite dark. I mean to stop here with dear Old Rogers—that I do." The latch was gently lifted, and in came young Brownrigg. So I thought it was time to leave my best Christmas wishes and take myself away. Old Rogers came with me to the mill-stream as usual.

"It 'mazes me, sir," he said, "a gentleman o' your age and bringin' up to know all that you tould us this mornin'. It 'ud be no wonder now for a man like me, come to be the shock o' corn fully ripe—leastways yallow and white enough outside if there bean't much more than milk inside it yet,—it 'ud be no mystery for a man like me who'd been brought up hard, and tossed about well-nigh all the world over—why, there's scarce a wave on the Atlantic but knows Old Rogers!"

He made the parenthesis with a laugh, and began anew.

"It 'ud be a shame of a man like me not to know all as you said this mornin', sir—leastways I don't mean able to say it right off as you do, sir; but not to know it, after the Almighty had been at such pains to beat it into my hard head just to trust in Him and fear nothing and nobody—captain, bosun, devil, sunk rock, or breakers ahead; but just to mind Him and stand by halliard, brace, or wheel, or hang on by the leeward earing for that matter. For, you see, what does it signify whether I go to the bottom or not, so long as I didn't skulk? or rather," and here the old man took off his hat and looked up, "so long as the Great Captain has His way, and things is done to His mind? But how ever a man like you, goin' to the college, and readin' books, and warm o' nights, and never, by your own confession this blessed mornin', sir, knowin' what it was to be downright hungry, how ever you come to know all those things, is just past my comprehension, except by a double portion o' the Spirit, sir. And that's the way I account for it, sir."

Although I knew enough about a ship to understand the old man, I am not sure that I have properly represented his sea-phrase. But that is of small consequence, so long as I give his meaning. And a meaning can occasionally be even better CONVEYED by less accurate words.

"I will try to tell you how I come to know about these things as I do," I returned. "How my knowledge may stand the test of further and severer trials remains to be seen. But if I should fail any time, old friend, and neither trust in God nor do my duty, what I have said to you remains true all the same."

"That it do, sir, whoever may come short."

"And more than that: failure does not necessarily prove any one to be a hypocrite of no faith. He may be still a man of little faith."

"Surely, surely, sir. I remember once that my faith broke down—just for one moment, sir. And then the Lord gave me my way lest I should blaspheme Him in thy wicked heart."

"How was that, Rogers?"

"A scream came from the quarter-deck, and then the cry: 'Child overboard!' There was but one child, the captain's, aboard. I was sitting just aft the foremast, herring-boning a split in a spare jib. I sprang to the bulwark, and there, sure enough, was the child, going fast astern, but pretty high in the water. How it happened I can't think to this day, sir, but I suppose my needle, in the hurry, had got into my jacket, so as to skewer it to my jersey, for we were far south of the line at the time, sir, and it was cold. However that may be, as soon as I was overboard, which you may be sure didn't want the time I take tellin' of it, I found that I ought to ha' pulled my jacket off afore I gave the bulwark the last kick. So I rose on the water, and began to pull it over my head—for it was wide, and that was the easiest way, I thought, in the water. But when I had got it right over my head, there it stuck. And there was I, blind as a Dutchman in a fog, and in as strait a jacket as ever poor wretch in Bedlam, for I could only just wag my flippers. Mr Walton, I believe I swore— the Lord forgive me!—but it was trying. And what was far worse, for one moment I disbelieved in Him; and I do say that's worse than swearing—in a hurry I mean. And that moment something went, the jacket was off, and there was I feelin' as if every stroke I took was as wide as the mainyard. I had no time to repent, only to thank God. And wasn't it more than I deserved, sir? Ah! He can rebuke a man for unbelief by giving him the desire of his heart. And that's a better rebuke than tying him up to the gratings."

"And did you save the child?"

"Oh yes, sir."

"And wasn't the captain pleased?"

"I believe he was, sir. He gave me a glass o' grog, sir. But you was a sayin' of something, sir, when I interrupted of you."

"I am very glad you did interrupt me."

"I'm not though, sir. I Ve lost summat I 'll never hear more."

"No, you shan't lose it. I was going to tell you how I think I came to understand a little about the things I was talking of to-day."

"That's it, sir; that's it. Well, sir, if you please?"

"You've heard of Sir Philip Sidney, haven't you, Old Rogers?"

"He was a great joker, wasn't he, sir?"

"No, no; you're thinking of Sydney Smith, Rogers."

"It may be, sir. I am an ignorant man."

"You are no more ignorant than you ought to be.—But it is time you should know him, for he was just one of your sort. I will come down some evening and tell you about him."

I may as well mention here that this led to week-evening lectures in the barn, which, with the help of Weir the carpenter, was changed into a comfortable room, with fixed seats all round it, and plenty of cane-chairs besides—for I always disliked forms in the middle of a room. The object of these lectures was to make the people acquainted with the true heroes of their own country—men great in themselves. And the kind of choice I made may be seen by those who know about both, from the fact that, while my first two lectures were on Philip Sidney, I did not give one whole lecture even to Walter Raleigh, grand fellow as he was. I wanted chiefly to set forth the men that could rule themselves, first of all, after a noble fashion. But I have not finished these lectures yet, for I never wished to confine them to the English heroes; I am going on still, old man as I am—not however without retracing passed ground sometimes, for a new generation has come up since I came here, and there is a new one behind coming up now which I may be honoured to present in its turn to some of this grand company—this cloud of witnesses to the truth in our own and other lands, some of whom subdued kingdoms, and others were tortured to death, for the same cause and with the same result.

"Meantime," I went on, "I only want to tell you one little thing he says in a letter to a younger brother whom he wanted to turn out as fine a fellow as possible. It is about horses, or rather, riding—for Sir Philip was the best horseman in Europe in his day, as, indeed, all things taken together, he seems to have really been the most accomplished man generally of his time in the world. Writing to this brother he says—"

I could not repeat the words exactly to Old Rogers, but I think it better to copy them exactly, in writing this account of our talk:

"At horsemanship, when you exercise it, read Crison Claudio, and a book that is called La Gloria del Cavallo, withal that you may join the thorough contemplation of it with the exercise; and so shall you profit more in a month than others in a year."

"I think I see what you mean, sir. I had got to learn it all without book, as it were, though you know I had my old Bible, that my mother gave me, and without that I should not have learned it at all."

"I only mean it comparatively, you know. You have had more of the practice, and I more of the theory. But if we had not both had both, we should neither of us have known anything about the matter. I never was content without trying at least to understand things; and if they are practical things, and you try to practise them at the same time as far as you do understand them, there is no end to the way in which the one lights up the other. I suppose that is how, without your experience, I have more to say about such things than you could expect. You know besides that a small matter in which a principle is involved will reveal the principle, if attended to, just as well as a great one containing the same principle. The only difference, and that a most important one, is that, though I've got my clay and my straw together, and they stick pretty well as yet, my brick, after all, is not half so well baked as yours, old friend, and it may crumble away yet, though I hope not."

"I pray God to make both our bricks into stones of the New Jerusalem, sir. I think I understand you quite well. To know about a thing is of no use, except you do it. Besides, as I found out when I went to sea, you never can know a thing till you do do it, though I thought I had a tidy fancy about some things beforehand. It's better not to be quite sure that all your seams are caulked, and so to keep a look-out on the bilge-pump; isn't it, sir?"

During the most of this conversation, we were standing by the mill-water, half frozen over. The ice from both sides came towards the middle, leaving an empty space between, along which the dark water showed itself, hurrying away as if in fear of its life from the white death of the frost. The wheel stood motionless, and the drip from the thatch of the mill over it in the sun, had frozen in the shadow into icicles, which hung in long spikes from the spokes and the floats, making the wheel—soft green and mossy when it revolved in the gentle sun-mingled summer-water—look like its own gray skeleton now. The sun was getting low, and I should want all my time to see my other friends before dinner, for I would not willingly offend Mrs Pearson on Christmas Day by being late, especially as I guessed she was using

167

extraordinary skill to prepare me a more than comfortable meal.

"I must go, Old Rogers," I said; "but I will leave you something to think about till we meet again. Find out why our Lord was so much displeased with the disciples, whom He knew to be ignorant men, for not knowing what He meant when He warned them against the leaven of the Pharisees. I want to know what you think about it. You'll find the story told both in the sixteenth chapter of St Matthew and the eighth of St Mark."

"Well, sir, I'll try; that is, if you will tell me what you think about it afterwards, so as to put me right, if I'm wrong."

"Of course I will, if I can find out an explanation to satisfy me. But it is not at all clear to me now. In fact, I do not see the connecting links of our Lord's logic in the rebuke He gives them."

"How am I to find out then, sir—knowing nothing of logic at all?" said the old man, his rough worn face summered over with his child-like smile.

"There are many things which a little learning, while it cannot really hide them, may make you less ready to see all at once," I answered, shaking hands with Old Rogers, and then springing across the brook with my carpet-bag in my hand.

By the time I had got through the rest of my calls, the fogs were rising from the streams and the meadows to close in upon my first Christmas Day in my own parish. How much happier I was than when I came such a few months before! The only pang I felt that day was as I passed the monsters on the gate leading to Oldcastle Hall. Should I be honoured to help only the poor of the flock? Was I to do nothing for the rich, for whom it is, and has been, and doubtless will be so hard to enter into the kingdom of heaven? And it seemed to me at the moment that the world must be made for the poor: they had so much more done for them to enable them to inherit it than the rich had.—To these people at the Hall, I did not seem acceptable. I might in time do something with Judy, but the old lady was still so dreadfully repulsive to me that it troubled my conscience to feel how I disliked her. Mr Stoddart seemed nothing more than a dilettante in religion, as well as in the arts and sciences—music always excepted; while for Miss Oldcastle, I simply did not understand her yet. And she was so beautiful! I thought her more, beautiful every time I saw her. But I never appeared to make the least progress towards any real acquaintance with her thoughts and feelings.—It seemed to me, I say, for a moment, coming from the houses of the warm-hearted poor, as if the rich had not quite fair play, as it were—as if they were sent into the world chiefly for the sake of the cultivation of the virtues of the poor, and without much chance for the cultivation of their own. I knew better than this you know, my reader; but the thought came, as thoughts will come sometimes. It vanished the moment I sought to lay hands upon it, as if it knew quite well it had no business there. But certainly I did believe that it was more like the truth to say the world was made for the poor than to say that it was made for the rich. And therefore I longed the more to do something for these whom I considered the rich of my flock; for it was dreadful to think of their being poor inside instead of outside.

Perhaps my reader will say, and say with justice, that I ought to have been as anxious about poor Farmer Brownrigg as about the beautiful lady. But the farmer liai given me good reason to hope some progress in him after the way he had given in about Jane Rogers. Positively I had caught his eye during the sermon that very day. And, besides—but I will not be a hypocrite; and seeing I did not certainly take the same interest in Mr Brownrigg, I will at least be honest and confess it. As far as regards the discharge of my duties, I trust I should have behaved impartially had the necessity for any choice arisen. But my feelings were not quite under my own control. And we are nowhere, told to love everybody alike, only to love every one who comes within our reach as ourselves.

I wonder whether my old friend Dr Duncan was right. He had served on shore in Egypt under General Abercrombie, and had of course, after the fighting was over on each of the several occasions—the French being always repulsed—exercised his office amongst the wounded left on the field of battle.—"I do not know," he said, "whether I did right or not; but I always took the man I came to first—French or English."—I only know that my heart did not wait for the opinion of my head on the matter. I loved the old man the more that he did as he did. But as a question of casuistry, I am doubtful about its answer.

This digression is, I fear, unpardonable.

I made Mrs Pearson sit down with me to dinner, for Christmas Day was not one to dine alone upon. And I have ever since had my servants to dine with me on Christmas Day.

Then I went out again, and made another round of visits, coming in for a glass of wine at one table, an orange at another, and a hot chestnut at a third. Those whom I could not see that day, I saw on the following days between it and the new year. And so ended my Christmas holiday with my people.

But there is one little incident which I ought to relate before I close this chapter, and which I am ashamed of having so nearly forgotten.

When we had finished our dinner, and I was sitting alone drinking a class of claret before going out again, Mrs Pearson came in and told me that little Gerard Weir wanted to see me. I asked her to show him in; and the little fellow entered, looking very shy, and clinging first to the door and then to the wall.

"Come, my dear boy," I said, "and sit down by me."

He came directly and stood before me.

"Would you like a little wine and water?" I said; for unhappily there was no dessert, Mrs Pearson knowing that I never eat such things.

"No, thank you, sir; I never tasted wine."

"I did not press him to take it.

"Please, sir," he went on after a pause, putting his nand in his pocket, "mother gave me some goodies, and I kept them till I saw you come back, and here they are, sir."

Does any reader doubt what I did or said upon this?

I said, "Thank you, my darling," and I ate them up every one of them, that he might see me eat them before he left the house. And the dear child went off radiant.

If anybody cannot understand why I did so, I beg him to consider the matter. If then he cannot come to a conclusion concerning it, I doubt if any explanation of mine would greatly subserve his enlightenment. Meantime, I am forcibly restraining myself from yielding to the temptation to set forth my reasons, which would result in a half-hour's sermon on the Jewish dispensation, including the burnt offering, and the wave and heave offerings, with an application to the ignorant nurses and mothers of English babies, who do the best they can to make original sin an actual fact by training children down in the way they should not go.

CHAPTER XII. THE AVENUE.

It will not appear strange that I should linger so long upon the first few months of my association with a people who, now that I am an old man, look to me like my own children. For those who were then older than myself are now "old dwellers in those high countries" where there is no age, only wisdom; and I shall soon go to them. How glad I shall be to see my Old Rogers again, who, as he taught me upon earth, will teach me yet niore, I thank my God, in heaven! But I must not let the reverie which' always gathers about the feather-end of my pen the moment I take it up to write these recollections, interfere with the work before me.

After this Christmas-tide, I found myself in closer relationship to my parishioners. No doubt I was always in danger of giving unknown offence to those who were ready to fancy that I neglected them, and did not distribute my FAVOURS equally. But as I never took offence, the offence I gave was easily got rid of. A clergyman, of all men, should be slow to take offence, for if he does, he will never be free or strong to reprove sin. And it must sometimes be his duty to speak severely to those, especially the good, who are turning their faces the wrong way. It is of little use to reprove the sinner, but it is worth while sometimes to reprove those who have a regard for righteousness, however imperfect they may be. "Reprove not a scorner, lest he hate thee; rebuke a wise man, and he will love thee."

171

But I took great care about INTERFERING; though I would interfere upon request—not always, however, upon the side whence the request came, and more seldom still upon either side. The clergyman must never be a partisan. When our Lord was requested to act as umpire between two brothers, He refused. But He spoke and said, "Take heed, and beware of covetousness." Now, though the best of men is unworthy to loose the latchet of His shoe, yet the servant must be as his Master. Ah me! while I write it, I remember that the sinful woman might yet do as she would with His sacred feet. I bethink me: Desert may not touch His shoe-tie: Love may kiss His feet.

I visited, of course, at the Hall, as at the farmhouses in the country, and the cottages in the village. I did not come to like Mrs Oldcastle better. And there was one woman in the house whom I disliked still more: that Sarah whom Judy had called in my hearing a white wolf. Her face was yet whiter than that of her mistress, only it was not smooth like hers; for its whiteness came apparently from the small-pox, which had so thickened the skin that no blood, if she had any, could shine through. I seldom saw her—only, indeed, caught a glimpse of her now and then as I passed through the house.

Nor did I make much progress with Mr Stoddart. He had always something friendly to say, and often some theosophical theory to bring forward, which, I must add, never seemed to me to mean, or, at least, to reveal, anything. He was a great reader of mystical books, and yet the man's nature seemed cold. It was sunshiny, but not sunny. His intellect was rather a lambent flame than a genial warmth. He could make things, but he could not grow anything. And when I came to see that he had had more than any one else to do with the education of Miss Oldcastle, I understood her a little better, and saw that her so-called education had been in a great measure repression— of a negative sort, no doubt, but not therefore the less mischievous. For to teach speculation instead of devotion, mysticism instead of love, word instead of deed, is surely ruinously repressive to the nature that is meant for sunbright activity both of heart and hand. My chief perplexity continued to be how he could play the organ as he did.

My reader will think that I am always coming round to Miss Oldcastle; but if he does, I cannot help it. I began, I say, to understand her a little better.

She seemed to me always like one walking in a "watery sunbeam," without knowing that it was but the wintry pledge of a summer sun at hand. She took it, or was trying to take it, for THE sunlight; trying to make herself feel all the glory people said was in the light, instead of making haste towards the perfect day. I found afterwards that several things had combined to bring about this condition; and I know she will forgive me, should I, for the sake of others, endeavour to make it understood by and by.

I have not much more to tell my readers about this winter. As but of a whole changeful season only one day, or, it may be, but one moment in which the time seemed to burst into its own blossom, will cling to the memory; so of the various interviews with my friends, and the whole flow of the current of my life, during that winter, nothing more of nature or human nature occurs to me worth recording. I will pass on to the summer season as rapidly as I may, though the early spring will detain me with the relation of just a single incident.

I was on my way to the Hall to see Mr Stoddart. I wanted to ask him whether something could not be done beyond his exquisite playing to rouse the sense of music in my people. I believed that nothing helps you so much to feel as the taking of what share may, from the nature of the thing, be possible to you; because, for one reason, in order to feel, it is necessary that the mind should rest upon the matter, whatever it is. The poorest success, provided the attempt has been genuine, will enable one to enter into any art ten times better than before. Now I had, I confess, little hope of moving Mr Stoddart in the matter; but if I should succeed, I thought it would do himself more good to mingle with his humble fellows in the attempt to do them a trifle of good, than the opening of any number of intellectual windows towards the circumambient truth.

It was just beginning to grow dusk. The wind was blustering in gusts among the trees, swaying them suddenly and fiercely like a keen passion, now sweeping them all one way as if the multitude of tops would break loose and rush away like a wild river, and now subsiding as suddenly, and allowing them to recover themselves and stand upright, with tones and motions of indignant expostulation. There was just one cold bar of light in the west, and the east was one gray mass, while overhead the stars were twinkling. The grass and all the ground about the trees were very wet. The time seemed more dreary somehow than the winter. Rigour was past, and tenderness had not come. For the wind was cold without being keen, and bursting from the trees every now and then with a roar as of a sea breaking on distant sands, whirled about me as if it wanted me to go and join in its fierce play.

Suddenly I saw, to my amazement, in a walk that ran alongside of the avenue, Miss Oldcastle struggling against the wind, which blew straight down the path upon her. The cause of my amazement was twofold. First, I had supposed her with her mother in London, whither their journeys had been not infrequent since Christmas-tide; and next—why should she be fighting with the wind, so far from the house, with only a shawl drawn over her head?

The reader may wonder how I should know her in this attire in the dusk, and where there was not the smallest probability of finding her. Suffice it to say that I did recognise her at once; and passing between two great tree-trunks, and through an opening in some under-wood, was by her side in a moment. But the noise of the wind had prevented her from hearing my approach, and when I uttered her name, she started violently, and, turning, drew herself up very haughtily, in part, I presume, to hide her tremor.—She was always a little haughty with me, I must acknowledge. Could there have been anything in my address, however unconscious of it I was, that made her fear I was ready to become intrusive? Or might it not be that, hearing of my footing with my parishioners generally, she was prepared to resent any assumption of clerical familiarity with her; and so, in my behaviour, any poor innocent "bush was supposed a bear." For I need not tell my reader that nothing was farther from my intention, even with the lowliest of my flock, than to presume upon my position as clergyman. I think they all GAVE me the relation I occupied towards them personally.—But I had never seen her look so haughty as now. If I had been watching her very thoughts she could hardly have looked more indignant.

"I beg your pardon," I said, distressed; "I have startled you dreadfully."

"Not in the least," she replied, but without moving, and still with a curve in her form like the neck of a frayed horse.

I thought it better to leave apology, which was evidently disagreeable to her, and speak of indifferent things.

"I was on my way to call on Mr Stoddart," I said.

"You will find him at home, I believe."

"I fancied you and Mrs Oldcastle in London."

"We returned yesterday."

Still she stood as before. I made a movement in the direction of the house. She seemed as if she would walk in the opposite direction.

"May I not walk with you to the house?"

"I am not going in just yet."

"Are you protected enough for sucn a night?"

"I enjoy the wind."

I bowed and walked on; for what else could I do?

I cannot say that I enjoyed leaving her behind me in the gathering dark, the wind blowing her about with no more reverence than if she had been a bush of privet. Nor was it with a light heart that I bore her repulse as I slowly climbed the hill to the house. However, a little personal mortification is wholesome—though I cannot say either that I derived much consolation from the reflection.

Sarah opened the glass door, her black, glossy, restless eyes looking out of her white face from under gray eyebrows. I knew at once by her look beyond me that she had expected to find me accompanied by her young mistress. I did not volunteer any information, as my reader may suppose.

I found, as I had feared, that, although Mr. Stoddart seemed to listen with some interest to what I said, I could not bring him to the point of making any practical suggestion, or of responding to one made by me; and

I left him with the conviction that he would do nothing to help me. Yet during the whole of our interview he had not opposed a single word I said. He was like clay too much softened with water to keep the form into which it has been modelled. He would take SOME kind of form easily, and lose it yet more easily. I did not show all my dissatisfaction, however, for that would only have estranged us; and it is not required, nay, it may be wrong, to show all you feel or think: what is required of us is, not to show what we do not feel or think; for that is to be false.

I left the house in a gloomy mood. I know I ought to have looked up to God and said: "These things do not reach to Thee, my Father. Thou art ever the same; and I rise above my small as well as my great troubles by remembering Thy peace, and Thy unchangeable Godhood to me and all Thy creatures." But I did not come to myself all at once. The thought of God had not come, though it was pretty sure to come before I got home. I was brooding over the littleness of all I could do; and feeling that sickness which sometimes will overtake a man in the midst of the work he likes best, when the unpleasant parts of it crowd upon him, and his own efforts, especially those made from the will without sustaining impulse, come back upon him with a feeling of unreality, decay, and bitterness, as if he had been unnatural and untrue, and putting himself in false relations by false efforts for good. I know this all came from selfishness—thinking about myself instead of about God and my neighbour. But so it was.—And so I was walking down the avenue, where it was now very dark, with my head bent to the ground, when I in my turn started at the sound of a woman's voice, and looking up, saw by the starlight the dim form of Miss Oldcastle standing before me.

She spoke first.

"Mr Walton, I was very rude to you. I beg your pardon."

"Indeed, I did not think so. I only thought what a blundering awkward fellow I was to startle you as I did. You have to forgive me."

"I fancy"—and here I know she smiled, though how I know I do not know—"I fancy I have made that even," she said, pleasantly; "for you must confess I startled you now."

176

"You did; but it was in a very different way. I annoyed you with my rudeness. You only scattered a swarm of bats that kept flapping their skinny wings in my face."

"What do you mean? There are no bats at this time of the year."

"Not outside. In 'winter and rough weather' they creep inside, you know."

"Ah! I ought to understand you. But I did not think you were ever like that. I thought you were too good."

"I wish I were. I hope to be some day. I am not yet, anyhow. And I thank you for driving the bats away in the meantime."

"You make me the more ashamed of myself to think that perhaps my rudeness had a share in bringing them.—Yours is no doubt thankless labour sometimes."

She seemed to make the last remark just to prevent the conversation from returning to her as its subject. And now all the bright portions of my work came up before me.

"You are quite mistaken in that, Miss Oldcastle. On the contrary, the thanks I get are far more than commensurate with the labour. Of course one meets with a disappointment sometimes, but that is only when they don't know what you mean. And how should they know what you mean till they are different themselves?—You remember what Wordsworth says on this very subject in his poem of Simon Lee?"—

"I do not know anything of Wordsworth."

"'I've heard of hearts unkind, kind deeds With coldness still returning; Alas! the gratitude of men Hath oftener left me mourning.'"

"I do not quite see what he means."

"May I recommend you to think about it? You will be sure to find it out for yourself, and that will be ten times more satisfactory than if I were to explain it to you. And, besides, you will never forget it, if you do."

"Will you repeat the lines again?"

I did so.

All this time the wind had been still. Now it rose with a slow gush in the trees. Was it fancy? Or, as the wind moved the shrubbery, did I see a white face? And could it be the White Wolf, as Judy called her?

I spoke aloud:

"But it is cruel to keep you standing here in such a night. You must be a real lover of nature to walk in the dark wind."

"I like it. Good night."

So we parted. I gazed into the darkness after her, though she disappeared at the distance of a yard or two; and would have stood longer had I not still suspected the proximity of Judy's Wolf, which made me turn and go home, regardless now of Mr Stoddart's DOUGHINESS.

I met Miss Oldcastle several times before the summer, but her old manner remained, or rather had returned, for there had been nothing of it in the tone of her voice in that interview, if INTERVIEW it could be called where neither could see more than the other's outline.

CHAPTER XIII. YOUNG WEIR.

By slow degrees the summer bloomed. Green came instead of white; rainbows instead of icicles. The grounds about the Hall seemed the incarnation of a summer which had taken years to ripen to its perfection. The very grass seemed to have aged into perfect youth in that "haunt of ancient peace;" for surely nowhere else was such thick, delicate-bladed, delicate-coloured grass to be seen. Gnarled old trees of may stood like altars of smoking perfume, or each like one million-petalled flower of upheaved whiteness—or of tender rosiness, as if the snow which had covered it in winter had sunk in and gathered warmth from the life of the tree, and now crept out again to adorn the summer. The long loops of the laburnum hung heavy with gold towards the sod below; and the air was full of the fragrance of the young leaves of the limes. Down in the valley below, the daisies shone in all the meadows,

178

varied with the buttercup and the celandine; while in damp places grew large pimpernels, and along the sides of the river, the meadow-sweet stood amongst the reeds at the very edge of the water, breathing out the odours of dreamful sleep. The clumsy pollards were each one mass of undivided green. The mill wheel had regained its knotty look, with its moss and its dip and drip, as it yielded to the slow water, which would have let it alone, but that there was no other way out of the land to the sea.

I used now to wander about in the fields and woods, with a book in my hand, at which I often did not look the whole day, and which yet I liked to have with me. And I seemed somehow to come back with most upon those days in which I did not read. In this manner I prepared almost all my sermons that summer. But, although I prepared them thus in the open country, I had another custom, which perhaps may appear strange to some, before I preached them. This was, to spend the Saturday evening, not in my study, but in the church. This custom of mine was known to the sexton and his wife, and the church was always clean and ready for me after about mid-day, so that I could be alone there as soon as I pleased. It would take more space than my limits will afford to explain thoroughly why I liked to do this. But I will venture to attempt a partial explanation in a few words.

This fine old church in which I was honoured to lead the prayers of my people, was not the expression of the religious feeling of my time. There was a gloom about it—a sacred gloom, I know, and I loved it; but such gloom as was not in my feeling when I talked to my flock. I honoured the place; I rejoiced in its history; I delighted to think that even by the temples made with hands outlasting these bodies of ours, we were in a sense united to those who in them had before us lifted up holy hands without wrath or doubting; and with many more who, like us, had lifted up at least prayerful hands without hatred or despair. The place soothed me, tuned me to a solemn mood—one of self-denial, and gentle gladness in all sober things. But, had I been an architect, and had I had to build a church—I do not in the least know how I should have built it—I am certain it would have been very different from this. Else I should be a mere imitator, like all the church-architects I know anything about in the present day. For I always found the open air the most genial influence upon me for the production of religious feeling and thought. I had been led to try whether it might not be so with me by the fact that our Lord seemed so much to delight in the open air, and late in the day as well as early in the morning would climb the mountain to be alone with His Father. I found that it helped to give a reality to everything that I thought about, if I only contemplated it under the high untroubled blue, with the lowly green beneath my feet, and the wind blowing on me to remind me of the Spirit that once moved on the face of the waters, bringing order out of disorder and light out of darkness, and was now seeking every day a fuller entrance into my heart, that there He might work the one will of the Father in heaven.

My reader will see then that there was, as it were, not so much a discord, as a lack of harmony between the surroundings wherein my thoughts took form, or, to use a homelier phrase, my sermon was studied, and the surroundings wherein I had to put these forms into the garments of words, or preach that sermon. I therefore sought to bridge over this difference (if I understood music, I am sure I could find an expression exactly fitted to my meaning),—to find an easy passage between the open-air mood and the church mood, so as to be able to bring into the church as much of the fresh air, and the tree-music, and the colour-harmony, and the gladness over all, as might be possible; and, in order to this, I thought all my sermon over again in the afternoon sun as it shone slantingly through the stained window over Lord Eagleye's tomb, and in the failing light thereafter and the gathering dusk of the twilight, pacing up and down the solemn old place, hanging my thoughts here on a crocket, there on a corbel; now on the gable-point over which Weir's face would gaze next morning, and now on the aspiring peaks of the organ. I thus made the place a cell of thought and prayer. And when the next day came, I found the forms around me so interwoven with the forms of my thought, that I felt almost like one of the old monks who had built the place, so little did I find any check to my thought or utterance from its unfitness for the expression of my individual modernism. But not one atom the more did I incline to the evil fancy that God was more in the past than in the present; that He is more within the walls of the church, than in the unwalled sky and earth; or seek to turn backwards one step from a living Now to an entombed and consecrated Past.

180

One lovely Saturday, I had been out all the morning. I had not walked far, for I had sat in the various places longer than I had walked, my path lying through fields and copses, crossing a country road only now and then. I had my Greek Testament with me, and I read when I sat, and thought when I walked. I remember well enough that I was going to preach about the cloud of witnesses, and explain to my people that this did not mean persons looking at, witnessing our behaviour—not so could any addition be made to the awfulness of the fact that the eye of God was upon us—but witnesses to the truth, people who did what God wanted them to do, come of it what might, whether a crown or a rack, scoffs or applause; to behold whose witnessing might well rouse all that was human and divine in us to chose our part with them and their Lord.—When I came home, I had an early dinner, and then betook myself to my Saturday's resort.—I had never had a room large enough to satisfy me before. Now my study was to my mind.

All through the slowly-fading afternoon, the autumn of the day, when the colours are richest and the shadows long and lengthening, I paced my solemn old-thoughted church. Sometimes I went up into the pulpit and sat there, looking on the ancient walls which had grown up under men's hands that men might be helped to pray by the visible symbol of unity which the walls gave, and that the voice of the Spirit of God might be heard exhorting men to forsake the evil and choose the good. And I thought how many witnesses to the truth had knelt in those ancient pews. For as the great church is made up of numberless communities, so is the great shining orb of witness-bearers made up of millions of lesser orbs. All men and women of true heart bear individual testimony to the truth of God, saying, "I have trusted and found Him faithful." And the feeble light of the glowworm is yet light, pure, and good, and with a loveliness of its own. "So, O Lord," I said, "let my light shine before men." And I felt no fear of vanity in such a prayer, for I knew that the glory to come of it is to God only—"that men may glorify their Father in heaven." And I knew that when we seek glory for ourselves, the light goes out, and the Horror that dwells in darkness breathes cold upon our spirits. And I remember that just as I thought thus, my eye was caught first by a yellow light that gilded the apex of the font-cover, which had been wrought like a flame or a bursting blossom: it was so old and worn, I never could tell which; and then by a red light all over a white marble tablet in the wall—the red of life on the cold hue of the grave. And this red light did not come from any work of man's device, but from the great window of the west, which little Gerard Weir wanted to help God to paint. I must have been in a happy mood that Saturday afternoon, for everything pleased me and made me happier; and all the church-forms about me blended and harmonised graciously with the throne and footstool of God which I saw through the windows. And I lingered on till the night had come; till the church only gloomed about me, and had no shine; and then I found my spirit burning up the clearer, as a lamp which has been flaming all the day with light unseen becomes a glory in the room when the sun is gone down.

At length I felt tired, and would go home. Yet I lingered for a few moments in the vestry, thinking what hymns would harmonize best with the things I wanted to make my people think about. It was now almost quite dark out of doors—at least as dark as it would be.

Suddenly through the gloom I thought I heard a moan and a sob. I sat upright in my chair and listened. But I heard nothing more, and concluded I had deceived myself. After a few moments, I rose to go home and have some tea, and turn my mind rather away from than towards the subject of witness-bearing any more for that night, lest I should burn the fuel of it out before I came to warm the people with it, and should have to blow its embers instead of flashing its light and heat upon them in gladness. So I left the church by my vestry-door, which I closed behind me, and took my way along the path through the clustering group of graves.

Again I heard a sob. This time I was sure of it. And there lay something dark upon one of the grassy mounds. I approached it, but it did not move. I spoke.

"Can I be of any use to you?" I said.

"No," returned an almost inaudible voice.

Though I did not know whose was the grave, I knew that no one had been buried there very lately, and if the grief were for the loss of the dead, it was more than probably aroused to fresh vigour by recent misfortune.

I stooped, and taking the figure by the arm, said, "Come with me, and let us see what can be done for you."

I then saw that it was a youth—perhaps scarcely more than a boy. And as soon as I saw that, I knew that his grief could hardly be incurable. He returned no answer, but rose at once to his feet, and submitted to be led away. I took him the shortest road to my house through the shrubbery, brought him into the study, made him sit down in my easy-chair, and rang for lights and wine; for the dew had been falling heavily, and his clothes were quite dank. But when the wine came, he refused to take any.

"But you want it," I said.

"No, sir, I don't, indeed."

"Take some for my sake, then."

"I would rather not, sir."

"Why?"

"I promised my father a year ago, when I left home that I would not drink anything stronger than water. [sic] And I can't break my promise now."

"Where is your home?"

"In the village, sir."

"That wasn't your father's grave I found you upon, was it?"

"No, sir. It was my mother's."

"Then your father is still alive?"

"Yes, sir. You know him very well—Thomas Weir."

"Ah! He told me he had a son in London. Are you that son?"

"Yes, sir," answered the youth, swallowing a rising sob.

"Then what is the matter? Your father is a good friend of mine, and

183

would tell you-you might trust me."

"I don't doubt it, sir. But you won't believe me any more than my father."

By this time I had perused his person, his dress, and his countenance. He was of middle size, but evidently not full grown. His dress was very decent. His face was pale and thin, and revealed a likeness to his father. He had blue eyes that looked full at me, and, as far as I could judge, betokened, along with the whole of his expression, an honest and sensitive nature. I found him very attractive, and was therefore the more emboldened to press for the knowledge of his story.

"I cannot promise to believe whatever you say; but almost I could. And if you tell me the truth, I like you too much already to be in great danger of doubting you, for you know the truth has a force of its own."

"I thought so till to-night," he answered. "But if my father would not believe me, how can I expect you to do so, sir?"

"Your father may have been too much troubled by your story to be able to do it justice. It is not a bit like your father to be unfair."

"No, sir. And so much the less chance of your believing me."

Somehow his talk prepossessed me still more in his favour. There was a certain refinement in it, a quality of dialogue which indicated thought, as I judged; and I became more and more certain that, whatever I might have to think of it when told, he would yet tell me the truth.

"Come, try me," I said.

"I will, sir. But I must begin at the beginning."

"Begin where you like. I have nothing more to do to-night, and you may take what time you please. But I will ring for tea first; for I dare say you have not made any promise about that."

A faint smile flickered on his face. He was evidently beginning to feel a little more comfortable.

"When did you arrive from London?" I asked.

"About two hours ago, I suppose."

"Bring tea, Mrs Pearson, and that cold chicken and ham, and plenty of toast. We are both hungry."

Mrs Pearson gave a questioning look at the lad, and departed to do her duty.

When she returned with the tray, I saw by the unconsciously eager way in which he looked at the eatables, that he had had nothing for some time; and so, even after we were left alone, I would not let him say a word till he had made a good meal. It was delightful to see how he ate. Few troubles will destroy a growing lad's hunger; and indeed it has always been to me a marvel how the feelings and the appetites affect each other. I have known grief actually make people, and not sensual people at all, quite hungry. At last I thought I had better not offer him any more.

After the tea-things had been taken away, I put the candles out; and the moon, which had risen, nearly full, while we were at tea, shone into the room. I had thought that he might possibly find it easier to tell his story in the moonlight, which, if there were any shame in the recital, would not, by too much revelation, reduce him to the despair of Macbeth, when, feeling that he could contemplate his deed, but not his deed and himself together, he exclaimed,

"To know my deed, 'twere best not know myself."

So, sitting by the window in the moonlight, he told his tale. The moon lighted up his pale face as he told it, and gave rather a wild expression to his eyes, eager to find faith in me.—I have not much of the dramatic in me, I know; and I am rather a flat teller of stories on that account. I shall not, therefore, seeing there is no necessity for it, attempt to give the tale in his own words. But, indeed, when I think of it, they did not differ so much from the form of my own, for he had, I presume, lost his provincialisms, and being, as I found afterwards, a reader of the best books that came in his way, had not caught up many cockneyisms instead.

He had filled a place in the employment of Messrs——& Co., large silk-mercers, linen-drapers, etc., etc., in London; for all the trades are mingled now. His work at first was to accompany one of the carts which delivered the purchases of the day; but, I presume because he showed himself to be a smart lad, they took him at length into the shop to wait behind the counter. This he did not like so much, but, as it was considered a rise in life, made no objection to the change.

He seemed to himself to get on pretty well. He soon learned all the marks on the goods intended to be understood by the shopmen, and within a few months believed that he was found generally useful. He had as yet had no distinct department allotted to him, but was moved from place to place, according as the local pressure of business might demand.

"I confess," he said, "that I was not always satisfied with what was going on about me. I mean I could not help doubting if everything was done on the square, as they say. But nothing came plainly in my way, and so I could honestly say it did not concern me. I took care to be straightforward for my part, and, knowing only the prices marked for the sale of the goods, I had nothing to do with anything else. But one day, while I was showing a lady some handkerchiefs which were marked as mouchoirs de Paris—I don't know if I pronounce it right, sir—she said she did not believe they were French cambric; and I, knowing nothing about it, said nothing. But, happening to look up while we both stood silent, the lady examining the handkerchiefs, and I doing nothing till she should have made up her mind, I caught sight of the eyes of the shop-walker, as they call the man who shows customers where to go for what they want, and sees that they are attended to. He is a fat man, dressed in black, with a great gold chain, which they say in the shop is only copper gilt. But that doesn't matter, only it would be the liker himself. He was standing staring at me. I could not tell what to make of it; but from that day I often caught him watching me, as if I had been a customer suspected of shop-lifting. Still I only thought he was very disagreeable, and tried to forget him.

"One day—the day before yesterday—two ladies, an old lady and a young one, came into the shop, and wanted to look at some shawls. It was dinner-time, and most of the men were in the house at their dinner. The shop-walker sent me to them, and then, I do believe, though I did not see him, stood behind a pillar to watch me, as he had been in the way of doing more openly. I thought I had seen the ladies before, and though I could not then tell where, I am now almost sure they were Mrs and Miss Oldcastle, of the Hall. They wanted to buy a cashmere for the young lady. I showed them some. They wanted better. I brought the best we had, inquiring, that I might make no mistake. They asked the price. I told them. They said they were not good enough, and wanted to see some more. I told them they were the best we had. They looked at them again; said they were sorry, but the shawls were not good enough, and left the shop without buying anything. I proceeded to take the shawls up-stairs again, and, as I went, passed the shop walker, whom I had not observed while I was attending to the ladies. 'YOU're for no good, young man!' he said with a nasty sneer. 'What do you mean by that, Mr B.?' I asked, for his sneer made me angry. 'You 'll know before to-morrow,' he answered, and walked away. That same evening, as we were shutting up shop, I was sent for to the principal's room. The moment I entered, he said, 'You won't suit us, young man, I find. You had better pack up your box to-night, and be off to-morrow. There's your quarter's salary.' 'What have I done?' I asked in astonishment, and yet with a vague suspicion of the matter. 'It's not what you've done, but what you don't do,' he answered. 'Do you think we can afford to keep you here and pay you wages to send people away from the shop without buying? If you do, you're mistaken, that's all. You may go.' 'But what could I do?' I said. 'I suppose that spy, B——,'—I believe I said so, sir. 'Now, now, young man, none of your sauce!' said Mr——. 'Honest people don't think about spies.' 'I thought it was for honesty you were getting rid of me,' I said. Mr——rose to his feet, his lips white, and pointed to the door. 'Take your money and be off. And mind you don't refer to me for a character. After such impudence I couldn't in conscience give you one.' Then, calming down a little when he saw I turned to go, 'You had better take to your hands again, for your head will never keep you. There, be off!' he said, pushing the money towards me, and turning his back to me. I could not touch it. 'Keep the money, Mr——,' I said. 'It'll make up for what you've lost by me.' And I left the room at once without waiting for an answer.

"While I was packing my box, one of my chums came in, and I told him all about it. He is rather a good fellow that, sir; but he laughed, and

187

said, 'What a fool you are, Weir! YOU'll never make your daily bread, and you needn't think it. If you knew what I know, you'd have known better. And it's very odd it was about shawls, too. I'll tell you. As you're going away, you won't let it out. Mr——' (that was the same who had just turned me away) 'was serving some ladies himself, for he wasn't above being in the shop, like his partner. They wanted the best Indian shawl they could get. None of those he showed them were good enough, for the ladies really didn't know one from another. They always go by the price you ask, and Mr——knew that well enough. He had sent me up-stairs for the shawls, and as I brought them he said, "These are the best imported, madam." There were three ladies; and one shook her head, and another shook her head, and they all shook their heads. And then Mr——was sorry, I believe you, that he had said they were the best. But you won't catch him in a trap! He's too old a fox for that.' I'm telling you, sir, what Johnson told me. 'He looked close down at the shawls, as if he were short-sighted, though he could see as far as any man. "I beg your pardon, ladies," said he, "you're right. I am quite wrong. What a stupid blunder to make! And yet they did deceive me. Here, Johnson, take these shawls away. How could you be so stupid? I will fetch the thing you want myself, ladies." So I went with him. He chose out three or four shawls, of the nicest patterns, from the very same lot, marked in the very same way, folded them differently, and gave them to me to carry down. "Now, ladies, here they are!" he said. "These are quite a different thing, as you will see; and, indeed, they cost half as much again." In five minutes they had bought two of them, and paid just half as much more than he had asked for them the first time. That's Mr——! and that's what you should have done if you had wanted to keep your place.'—But I assure you, sir, I could not help being glad to be out of it."

"But there is nothing in all this to be miserable about," I said. "You did your duty."

"It would be all right, sir, if father believed me. I don't want to be idle, I'm sure."

"Does your father think you do?"

"I don't know what he thinks. He won't speak to me. I told my story—as much of it as he would let me, at least—but he wouldn't listen to me. He only said he knew better than that. I couldn't bear it. He always was rather hard upon us. I'm sure if you hadn't been so kind to me, sir, I don't know what I should have done by this time. I haven't another friend in the world."

"Yes, you have. Your Father in heaven is your friend."

"I don't know that, sir. I'm not good enough."

"That's quite true. But you would never have done your duty if He had not been with you."

"DO you think so, sir?" he returned, eagerly.

"Indeed, I do. Everything good comes from the Father of lights. Every one that walks in any glimmering of light walks so far in HIS light. For there is no light—only darkness—comes from below. And man apart from God can generate no light. He's not meant to be separated from God, you see. And only think then what light He can give you if you will turn to Him and ask for it. What He has given you should make you long for more; for what you have is not enough—ah! far from it."

"I think I understand. But I didn't feel good at all in the matter. I didn't see any other way of doing."

"So much the better. We ought never to feel good. We are but unprofitable servants at best. There is no merit in doing your duty; only you would have been a poor wretched creature not to do as you did. And now, instead of making yourself miserable over the consequences of it, you ought to bear them like a man, with courage and hope, thanking God that He has made you suffer for righteousness' sake, and denied you the success and the praise of cheating. I will go to your father at once, and find out what he is thinking about it. For no doubt Mr——has written to him with his version of the story. Perhaps he will be more inclined to believe you when he finds that I believe you."

"Oh, thank you, sir!" cried the lad, and jumped up from his seat to go with me.

"No," I said; "you had better stay where you are. I shall be able to speak more freely if you are not present. Here is a book to amuse yourself with. I do not think I shall be long gone."

But I was longer gone than I thought I should be.

When I reached the carpenter's house, I found, to my surprise, that he was still at work. By the light of a single tallow candle placed beside him on the bench, he was ploughing away at a groove. His pale face, of which the lines were unusually sharp, as I might have expected after what had occurred, was the sole object that reflected the light of the candle to my eyes as I entered the gloomy place. He looked up, but without even greeting me, dropped his face again and went on with his work.

"What!" I said, cheerily,—for I believed that, like Gideon's pitcher, I held dark within me the light that would discomfit his Midianites, which consciousness may well make the pitcher cheery inside, even while the light as yet is all its own—worthless, till it break out upon the world, and cease to illuminate only glazed pitcher-sides—"What!" I said, "working so late?"

"Yes, sir."

"It is not usual with you, I know."

"It's all a humbug!" he said fiercely, but coldly notwithstanding, as he stood erect from his work, and turned his white face full on me—of which, however, the eyes drooped—"It's all a humbug; and I don't mean to be humbugged any more."

"Am I a humbug?" I returned, not quite taken by surprise.

"I don't say that. Don't make a personal thing of it, sir. You're taken in, I believe, like the rest of us. Tell me that a God governs the world! What have I done, to be used like this?"

I thought with myself how I could retort for his young son: "What has he done to be used like this?" But that was not my way, though it might work well enough in some hands. Some men are called to be prophets. I could only "stand and wait."

190

"It would be wrong in me to pretend ignorance," I said, "of what you mean. I know all about it."

"Do you? He has been to you, has he? But you don't know all about it, sir. The impudence of the young rascal!"

He paused for a moment.

"A man like me!" he resumed, becoming eloquent in his indignation, and, as I thought afterwards, entirely justifying what Wordsworth says about the language of the so-called uneducated,—"A man like me, who was as proud of his honour as any aristocrat in the country—prouder than any of them would grant me the right to be!"

"Too proud of it, I think—not too careful of it," I said. But I was thankful he did not heed me, for the speech would only have irritated him. He went on.

"Me to be treated like this! One child a ..."

Here came a terrible break in his speech. But he tried again.

"And the other a ..."

Instead of finishing the sentence, however, he drove his plough fiercely through the groove, splitting off some inches of the wall of it at the end.

"If any one has treated you so," I said, "it must be the devil, not God."

"But if there was a God, he could have prevented it all."

"Mind what I said to you once before: He hasn't done yet. And there is another enemy in His way as bad as the devil—I mean our SELVES. When people want to walk their own way without God, God lets them try it. And then the devil gets a hold of them. But God won't let him keep them. As soon as they are 'wearied in the greatness of their way,' they begin to look about for a Saviour. And then they find God ready to pardon, ready to help, not breaking the bruised reed—leading them to his own self manifest—with whom no man can fear any longer, Jesus Christ, the righteous lover of men— their elder brother—what we call BIG BROTHER, you know—one to help them and take their part against the devil, the world, and the flesh, and all the rest of the wicked powers. So you see God is tender—just like the prodigal son's father—only with this difference, that God has millions of prodigals, and never gets tired of going out to meet them and welcome them back, every one as if he were the only prodigal son He had ever had. There's a father indeed! Have you been such a father to your son?"

"The prodigal didn't come with a pack of lies. He told his father the truth, bad as it was."

"How do you know that your son didn't tell you the truth? All the young men that go from home don't do as the prodigal did. Why should you not believe what he tells you?"

"I'm not one to reckon without my host. Here's my bill."

And so saying, he handed me a letter. I took it and read:—

"SIR,—It has become our painful duty to inform you that your son has this day been discharged from the employment of Messrs—-and Co., his conduct not being such as to justify the confidence hitherto reposed in him. It would have been contrary to the interests of the establishment to continue him longer behind the counter, although we are not prepared to urge anything against him beyond the fact that he has shown himself absolutely indifferent to the interests of his employers. We trust that the chief blame will be found to lie with certain connexions of a kind easy to be formed in large cities, and that the loss of his situation may be punishment sufficient, if not for justice, yet to make him consider his ways and be wise. We enclose his quarter's salary, which the young man rejected with insult, and,

"*We remain, &c.,*

"*—and Co.*"

"And," I exclaimed, "this is what you found your judgment of your own son upon! You reject him unheard, and take the word of a stranger! I don't wonder you cannot believe in your Father when you behave so to your son. I don't say your conclusion is false, though I don't believe it. But I do say the grounds you go upon are anything but sufficient."

"You don't mean to tell me that a man of Mr——'s standing, who has one of the largest shops in London, and whose brother is Mayor of Addicehead, would slander a poor lad like that!"

"Oh you mammon-worshipper!" I cried. "Because a man has one of the largest shops in London, and his brother is Mayor of Addicehead, you take his testimony and refuse your son's! I did not know the boy till this evening; but I call upon you to bring back to your memory all that you have known of him from his childhood, and then ask yourself whether there is not, at least, as much probability of his having remained honest as of the master of a great London shop being infallible in his conclusions—at which conclusions, whatever they be, I confess no man can wonder, after seeing how readily his father listens to his defamation."

I spoke with warmth. Before I had done, the pale face of the carpenter was red as fire; for he had been acting contrary to all his own theories of human equality, and that in a shameful manner. Still, whether convinced or not, he would not give in. He only drove away at his work, which he was utterly destroying. His mouth was closed so tight, he looked as if he had his jaw locked; and his eyes gleamed over the ruined board with a light which seemed to me to have more of obstinacy in it than contrition.

"Ah, Thomas!" I said, taking up the speech once more, "if God had behaved to us as you have behaved to your boy—be he innocent, be he guilty—there's not a man or woman of all our lost race would have returned to Him from the time of Adam till now. I don't wonder that you find it difficult to believe in Him."

And with those words I left the shop, determined to overwhelm the unbeliever with proof, and put him to shame before his own soul, whence, I thought, would come even more good to him than to his son. For there was a great deal of self-satisfaction mixed up with the man's honesty, and the sooner that had a blow the better—it might prove a death-blow in the long run. It was pride that lay at the root of his hardness. He visited the daughter's fault upon the son. His daughter had disgraced him; and he was ready to flash into wrath with his son upon any imputation which recalled to him the torture he had undergone when his daughter's dishonour came first to the light. Her he had never forgiven, and now his pride flung his son out after her upon the first suspicion. His imagination had filled up all the blanks in the wicked insinuations of Mr——. He concluded that he had taken money to spend in the worst company, and had so disgraced him beyond forgiveness. His pride paralysed his love. He thought more about himself than about his children. His own shame outweighed in his estimation the sadness of their guilt. It was a less matter that they should be guilty, than that he, their father, should be disgraced.

Thinking over all this, and forgetting how late it was, I found myself half-way up the avenue of the Hall. I wanted to find out whether young Weir's fancy that the ladies he had failed in serving, or rather whom he had really served with honesty, were Mrs and Miss Oldcastle, was correct. What a point it would be if it was! I should not then be satisfied except I could prevail on Miss Oldcastle to accompany me to Thomas Weir, and shame the faithlessness out of him. So eager was I after certainty, that it was not till I stood before the house that I saw clearly the impropriety of attempting anything further that night. One light only was burning in the whole front, and that was on the first floor.

Glancing up at it, I knew not why, as I turned to go down the hill again, I saw a corner of the blind drawn aside and a face peeping out—whose, I could not tell. This was uncomfortable—for what could be taking me there at such a time? But I walked steadily away, certain I could not escape recognition, and determining to refer to this ill-considered visit when I called the next day. I would not put it off till Monday, I was resolved.

I lingered on the bridge as I went home. Not a light was to be seen in the village, except one over Catherine Weir's shop. There were not many restless souls in my parish—not so many as there ought to be. Yet gladly would I see the troubled in peace—not a moment, though, before their troubles should have brought them where the weary and heavy-laden can alone find rest to their souls—finding the Father's peace in the Son—the Father himself reconciling them to Himself.

How still the night was! My soul hung, as it were, suspended in stillness; for the whole sphere of heaven seemed to be about me, the stars above shining as clear below in the mirror of the all but motionless water. It was a pure type of the "rest that remaineth"—rest, the one immovable centre wherein lie all the stores of might, whence issue all forces, all influences of making and moulding. "And, indeed," I said to myself, "after all the noise, uproar, and strife that there is on the earth, after all the tempests, earthquakes, and volcanic outbursts, there is yet more of peace than of tumult in the world. How many nights like this glide away in loveliness, when deep sleep hath fallen upon men, and they know neither how still their own repose, nor how beautiful the sleep of nature! Ah, what must the stillness of the kingdom be? When the heavenly day's work is done, with what a gentle wing will the night come down! But I bethink me, the rest there, as here, will be the presence of God; and if we have Him with us, the battle-field itself will be—if not quiet, yet as full of peace as this night of stars." So I spoke to myself, and went home.

I had little immediate comfort to give my young guest, but I had plenty of hope. I told him he must stay in the house to-morrow; for it would be better to have the reconciliation with his father over before he appeared in public. So the next day neither Weir was at church.

As soon as the afternoon service was over, I went once more to the Hall, and was shown into the drawing-room—a great faded room, in which the prevailing colour was a dingy gold, hence called the yellow drawing-room when the house had more than one. It looked down upon the lawn, which, although little expense was now laid out on any of the ornamental adjuncts of the Hall, was still kept very nice. There sat Mrs Oldcastle reading, with her face to the house. A little way farther on, Miss Oldcastle sat, with a book on her knee, but her gaze fixed on the wide-spread landscape before her, of which, however, she seemed to be as inobservant as of her book. I caught glimpses of Judy flitting hither and thither among the trees, never a moment in one place.

Fearful of having an interview with the old lady alone, which was not likely to lead to what I wanted, I stepped from a window which was open, out upon the terrace, and thence down the steps to the lawn below. The servant had just informed Mrs Oldcastle of my visit when I came near. She drew herself up in her chair, and evidently chose to regard my approach as an intrusion.

"I did not expect a visit from you to-day, Mr Walton, you will allow me to say."

"I am doing Sunday work," I answered. "Will you kindly tell me whether you were in London on Thursday last? But stay, allow me to ask Miss Oldcastle to join us."

Without waiting for answer, I went to Miss Oldcastle, and begged her to come and listen to something in which I wanted her help. She rose courteously though without cordiality, and accompanied me to her mother, who sat with perfect rigidity, watching us.

"Again let me ask," I said, "if you were in London on Thursday."

Though I addressed the old lady, the answer came from her daughter.

"Yes, we were."

"Were you in——& Co.'s, in——Street?"

But now before Miss Oldcastle could reply, her mother interposed.

"Are we charged with shoplifting, Mr Walton? Really, one is not accustomed to such cross-questioning—except from a lawyer."

"Have patience with me for a moment," I returned. "I am not going to be mysterious for more than two or three questions. Please tell me whether you were in that shop or not."

"I believe we were," said the mother.

"Yes, certainly," said the daughter.

"Did you buy anything?"

"No. We—" Miss Oldcastle began.

"Not a word more," I exclaimed eagerly. "Come with me at once."

"What DO you mean, Mr Walton?" said the mother, with a sort of cold indignation, while the daughter looked surprised, but said nothing.

"I beg your pardon for my impetuosity; but much is in your power at this moment. The son of one of my parishioners has come home in trouble. His father, Thomas Weir—"

"Ah!" said Mrs Oldcastle, in a tone considerably at strife with refinement. But I took no notice.

"His father will not believe his story. The lad thinks you were the ladies in serving whom he got into trouble. I am so confident he tells the truth, that I want Miss Oldcastle to be so kind as to accompany me to Weir's house—"

"Really, Mr Walton, I am astonished at your making such a request!" exclaimed Mrs Oldcastle, with suitable emphasis on every salient syllable, while her white face flushed with anger. "To ask Miss Oldcastle to accompany you to the dwelling of the ringleader of all the canaille of the neighbourhood!"

"It is for the sake of justice," I interposed.

"That is no concern of ours. Let them fight it out between them, I am sure any trouble that comes of it is no more than they all deserve. A low family—men and women of them."

"I assure you, I think very differently."

"I daresay you do."

"But neither your opinion nor mine has anything to do with the matter."

Here I turned to Miss Oldcastle and went on—

"It is a chance which seldom occurs in one's life, Miss Oldcastle—a chance of setting wrong right by a word; and as a minister of the gospel of truth and love, I beg you to assist me with your presence to that end."

I would have spoken more strongly, but I knew that her word given to me would be enough without her presence. At the same time, I felt not only that there would be a propriety in her taking a personal interest in the matter, but that it would do her good, and tend to create a favour towards each other in some of my flock between whom at present there seemed to be nothing in common.

But at my last words, Mrs Oldcastle rose to her feet no longer red—now whiter than her usual whiteness with passion.

"You dare to persist! You take advantage of your profession to persist in dragging my daughter into a vile dispute between mechanics of the lowest class—against the positive command of her only parent! Have you no respect for her position in society?—for her sex? MISTER WALTON, you act in a manner unworthy of your cloth."

I had stood looking in her eyes with as much self-possession as I could muster. And I believe I should have borne it all quietly, but for that last word.

If there is one epithet I hate more than another, it is that execrable word CLOTH—used for the office of a clergyman. I have no time to set forth its offence now. If my reader cannot feel it, I do not care to make him feel it. Only I am sorry to say it overcame my temper.

"Madam," I said, "I owe nothing to my tailor. But I owe God my whole being, and my neighbour all I can do for him. 'He that loveth not his brother is a murderer,' or murderess, as the case may be."

At that word MURDERESS, her face became livid, and she turned away without reply. By this time her daughter was half way to the house. She followed her. And here was I left to go home, with the full knowledge that, partly from trying to gain too much, and partly from losing my temper, I had at best but a mangled and unsatisfactory testimony to carry back to Thomas Weir. Of course I walked away—round the end of the house and down the avenue; and the farther I went the more mortified I grew. It was not merely the shame of losing my temper, though that was a shame—and with a woman too, merely because she used a common epithet!—but I saw that it must appear very strange to the carpenter that I was not able to give a more explicit account of some sort, what I had learned not being in the least decisive in the matter. It only amounted to this, that Mrs and Miss Oldcastle were in the shop on the very day on which Weir was dismissed. It proved that so much of what he had told me was correct—nothing more. And if I tried to better the matter by explaining how I had offended them, would it not deepen the very hatred I had hoped to overcome? In fact, I stood convicted before the tribunal of my own conscience of having lost all the certain good of my attempt, in part at least from the foolish desire to produce a conviction OF Weir rather than IN Weir, which should be triumphant after a melodramatic fashion, and—must I confess it?—should PUNISH him for not believing in his son when I did; forgetting in my miserable selfishness that not to believe in his son was an unspeakably worse punishment in itself than any conviction or consequent shame brought about by the most overwhelming of stage-effects. I assure my reader, I felt humiliated.

Now I think humiliation is a very different condition of mind from humility. Humiliation no man can desire: it is shame and torture. Humility is the true, right condition of humanity—peaceful, divine. And yet a man may gladly welcome humiliation when it comes, if he finds that with fierce shock and rude revulsion it has turned him right round, with his face away from pride, whither he was travelling, and towards humility, however far away upon the horizon's verge she may sit waiting for him. To me, however, there came a gentle and not therefore less effective dissolution of the bonds both of pride and humiliation; and before Weir and I met, I was nearly as anxious to heal his wounded spirit, as I was to work justice for his son.

I was walking slowly, with burning cheek and downcast eyes, the one of conflict, the other of shame and defeat, away from the great house, which seemed to be staring after me down the avenue with all its window-eyes, when suddenly my deliverance came. At a somewhat sharp turn, where the avenue changed into a winding road, Miss Oldcastle stood waiting for me, the glow of haste upon her cheek, and the firmness of resolution upon her lips. Once more I was startled by her sudden presence, but she did not smile.

"Mr Walton, what do you want me to do? I would not willing refuse, if it is, as you say, really my duty to go with you."

"I cannot be positive about that," I answered. "I think I put it too strongly. But it would be a considerable advantage, I think, if you WOULD go with me and let me ask you a few questions in the presence of Thomas Weir. It will have more effect if I am able to tell him that I have only learned as yet that you were in the shop on that day, and refer him to you for the rest."

"I will go."

"A thousand thanks. But how did you manage to—?"

Here I stopped, not knowing how to finish the question.

"You are surprised that I came, notwithstanding mamma's objection to my going?"

"I confess I am. I should not have been surprised at Judy's doing so, now."

She was silent for a moment.

"Do you think obedience to parents is to last for ever? The honour is, of course. But I am surely old enough to be right in following my conscience at least."

"You mistake me. That is not the difficulty at all. Of course you ought to do what is right against the highest authority on earth, which I take to be just the parental. What I am surprised at is your courage."

"Not because of its degree, only that it is mine!"

And she sighed.—She was quite right, and I did not know what to answer. But she resumed.

"I know I am cowardly. But if I cannot dare, I can bear. Is it not strange?—With my mother looking at me, I dare not say a word, dare hardly move against her will. And it is not always a good will. I cannot honour my mother as I would. But the moment her eyes are off me, I can do anything, knowing the consequences perfectly, and just as regardless of them; for, as I tell you, Mr Walton, I can endure; and you do not know what that might COME to mean with my mother. Once she kept me shut up in my room, and sent me only bread and water, for a whole week to the very hour. Not that I minded that much, but it will let you know a little of my position in my own home. That is why I walked away before her. I saw what was coming."

And Miss Oldcastle drew herself up with more expression of pride than I had yet seen in her, revealing to me that perhaps I had hitherto quite misunderstood the source of her apparent haughtiness. I could not reply for indignation. My silence must have been the cause of what she said next.

"Ah! you think I have no right to speak so about my own mother! Well! well! But indeed I would not have done so a month ago."

"If I am silent, Miss Oldcastle, it is that my sympathy is too strong for me. There are mothers and mothers. And for a mother not to be a mother is too dreadful."

She made no reply. I resumed.

"It will seem cruel, perhaps;—certainly in saying it, I lay myself open to the rejoinder that talk is SO easy;—still I shall feel more honest when I have said it: the only thing I feel should be altered in your conduct—forgive me— is that you should DARE your mother. Do not think, for it is an unfortunate phrase, that my meaning is a vulgar one. If it were, I should at least know better than to utter it to you. What I mean is, that you ought to be able to be and do the same before your mother's eyes, that you are and do when she is out of sight. I mean that you should look in your mother's eyes, and do what is RIGHT."

"I KNOW that—know it WELL." (She emphasized the words as I do.) "But you do not know what a spell she casts upon me; how impossible it is to do as you say."

"Difficult, I allow. Impossible, not. You will never be free till you do so."

"You are too hard upon me. Besides, though you will scarcely be able to believe it now, I DO honour her, and cannot help feeling that by doing as I do, I avoid irreverence, impertinence, rudeness—whichever is the right word for what I mean."

"I understand you perfectly. But the truth is more than propriety of behaviour, even to a parent; and indeed has in it a deeper reverence, or the germ of it at least, than any adherence to the mere code of respect. If you once did as I want you to do, you would find that in reality you both revered and loved your mother more than you do now."

"You may be right. But I am certain you speak without any real idea of the difficulty."

"That may be. And yet what I say remains just as true."

"How could I meet VIOLENCE, for instance?"

"Impossible!"

She returned no reply. We walked in silence for some minutes. At length she said,

"My mother's self-will amounts to madness, I do believe. I have yet to learn where she would stop of herself."

"All self-will is madness," I returned—stupidly enough For what is the use of making general remarks when you have a terrible concrete before you? "To want one's own way just and only because it is one's own way is the height of madness."

"Perhaps. But when madness has to be encountered as if it were sense, it makes it no easier to know that it is madness."

"Does your uncle give you no help?"

"He! Poor man! He is as frightened at her as I am. He dares not even go away. He did not know what he was coming to when he came to Oldcastle Hall. Dear uncle! I owe him a great deal. But for any help of that sort, he is of no more use than a child. I believe mamma looks upon him as half an idiot. He can do anything or everything but help one to live, to BE anything. Oh me! I AM so tired!"

And the PROUD lady, as I had thought her, perhaps not incorrectly, burst out crying.

What was I to do? I did not know in the least. What I said, I do not even now know. But by this time we were at the gate, and as soon as we had passed the guardian monstrosities, we found the open road an effectual antidote to tears. When we came within sight of the old house where Weir lived, Miss Oldcastle became again a little curious as to what I required of her.

"Trust me," I said. "There is nothing mysterious about it. Only I prefer the truth to come out fresh in the ears of the man most concerned."

"I do trust you," she answered. And we knocked at the house-door.

Thomas Weir himself opened the door, with a candle in his hand. He looked very much astonished to see his lady-visitor. He asked us, politely enough, to walk up-stairs, and ushered us into the large room I have already described. There sat the old man, as I had first seen him, by the side of the fire. He received us with more than politeness—with courtesy; and I could not help glancing at Miss Oldcastle to see what impression this family of "low, free-thinking republicans" made upon her. It was easy to discover that the impression was of favourable surprise. But I was as much surprised at her behaviour as she was at theirs. Not a haughty tone was to be heard in her voice; not a haughty movement to be seen in her form. She accepted the chair offered her, and sat down, perfectly at home, by the fireside, only that she turned towards me, waiting for what explanation I might think proper to give.

Before I had time to speak, however, old Mr Weir broke the silence.

"I've been telling Tom, sir, as I've told him many a time afore, as how he's a deal too hard with his children."

"Father!" interrupted Thomas, angrily.

"Have patience a bit, my boy," persisted the old man, turning again towards me.—"Now, sir, he won't even hear young Tom's side of the story; and I say that boy won't tell him no lie if he's the same boy he went away."

"I tell you, father," again began Thomas; but this time I interposed, to prevent useless talk beforehand.

"Thomas," I said, "listen to me. I have heard your son's side of the story.

Because of something he said I went to Miss Oldcastle, and asked her whether she was in his late master's shop last Thursday. That is all I have asked her, and all she has told me is that she was. I know no more than you what she is going to reply to my questions now, but I have no doubt her answers will correspond to your son's story."

I then put my questions to Miss Oldcastle, whose answers amounted to this:—That they had wanted to buy a shawl; that they had seen none good enough; that they had left the shop without buying anything; and that they had been waited upon by a young man, who, while perfectly polite and attentive to their wants, did not seem to have the ways or manners of a London shop-lad.

I then told them the story as young Tom had related it to me, and asked if his sister was not in the house and might not go to fetch him. But she was with her sister Catherine.

"I think, Mr Walton, if you have done with me, I ought to go home now," said Miss Oldcastle.

"Certainly," I answered. "I will take you home at once. I am greatly obliged to you for coming."

"Indeed, sir," said the old man, rising with difficulty, "we're obliged both to you and the lady more than we can tell. To take such a deal of trouble for us! But you see, sir, you're one of them as thinks a man's got his duty to do one way or another, whether he be clergyman or carpenter. God bless you, Miss. You're of the right sort, which you'll excuse an old man, Miss, as'll never see ye again till ye've got the wings as ye ought to have."

Miss Oldcastle smiled very sweetly, and answered nothing, but shook hands with them both, and bade them good-night. Weir could not speak a word; he could hardly even lift his eyes. But a red spot glowed on each of his pale cheeks, making him look very like his daughter Catherine, and I could see Miss Oldcastle wince and grow red too with the gripe he gave her hand. But she smiled again none the less sweetly.

"I will see Miss Oldcastle home, and then go back to my house and bring the boy with me," I said, as we left.

It was some time before either of us spoke. The sun was setting, the sky the earth and the air lovely with rosy light, and the world full of that peculiar calm which belongs to the evening of the day of rest. Surely the world ought to wake better on the morrow.

"Not very dangerous people, those, Miss Oldcastle?" I said, at last.

"I thank you very much for taking me to see them," she returned, cordially.

"You won't believe all you may happen to hear against the working people now?"

"I never did."

"There are ill-conditioned, cross-grained, low-minded, selfish, unbelieving people amongst them. God knows it. But there are ladies and gentlemen amongst them too."

"That old man is a gentleman."

"He is. And the only way to teach them all to be such, is to be such to them. The man who does not show himself a gentleman to the working people—why should I call them the poor? some of them are better off than many of the rich, for they can pay their debts, and do it—"

I had forgot the beginning of my sentence.

"You were saying that the man who does not show himself a gentleman to the poor—"

"Is no gentleman at all—only a gentle without the man; and if you consult my namesake old Izaak, you will find what that is."

"I will look. I know your way now. You won't tell me anything I can find out for myself."

"Is it not the best way?"

"Yes. Because, for one thing, you find out so much more than you look for."

"Certainly that has been my own experience."

"Are you a descendant of Izaak Walton?"

"No. I believe there are none. But I hope I have so much of his spirit that I can do two things like him."

"Tell me."

"Live in the country, though I was not brought up in it; and know a good man when I see him."

"I am very glad you asked me to go to-night."

"If people only knew their own brothers and sisters, the kingdom of heaven would not be far off."

I do not think Miss Oldcastle quite liked this, for she was silent thereafter; though I allow that her silence was not conclusive. And we had now come close to the house.

"I wish I could help you," I said.

"In what?"

"To bear what I fear is waiting you."

"I told you I was equal to that. It is where we are unequal that we want help. You may have to give it me some day—who knows?"

I left her most unwillingly in the porch, just as Sarah (the white wolf) had her hand on the door, rejoicing in my heart, however, over her last words.

My reader will not be surprised, after all this, if, before I get very much further with my story, I have to confess that I loved Miss Oldcastle.

When young Tom and I entered the room, his grandfather rose and tottered to meet him. His father made one step towards him and then hesitated. Of all conditions of the human mind, that of being ashamed of himself must have been the strangest to Thomas Weir. The man had never in his life, I believe, done anything mean or dishonest, and therefore he had had less frequent opportunities than most people of being ashamed of himself. Hence his fall had been from another pinnacle—that of pride. When a man thinks it such a fine thing to have done right, he might almost as well have done wrong, for it shows he considers right something EXTRA, not absolutely essential to human existence, not the life of a man. I call it Thomas Weir's fall; for surely to behave in an unfatherly manner to both daughter and son—the one sinful, and therefore needing the more tenderness—the other innocent, and therefore claiming justification—and to do so from pride, and hurt pride, was fall enough in one history, worse a great deal than many sins that go by harder names; for the world's judgment of wrong does not exactly correspond with the reality. And now if he was humbled in the one instance, there would be room to hope he might become humble in the other. But I had soon to see that, for a time, his pride, driven from its entrenchment against his son, only retreated, with all its forces, into the other against his daughter.

Before a moment had passed, justice overcame so far that he held out his hand and said:—

"Come, Tom, let by-gones be by-gones."

But I stepped between.

"Thomas Weir," I said, "I have too great a regard for you—and you know I dare not flatter you—to let you off this way, or rather leave you to think you have done your duty when you have not done the half of it. You have done your son a wrong, a great wrong. How can you claim to be a gentleman—I say nothing of being a Christian, for therein you make no claim—how, I say, can you claim to act like a gentleman, if, having done a man wrong—his being your own son has nothing to do with the matter one way or other, except that it ought to make you see your duty more easily—having done him wrong, why don't you beg his pardon, I say, like a man?"

He did not move a step. But young Tom stepped hurriedly forward, and catching his father's hand in both of his, cried out:

"My father shan't beg my pardon. I beg yours, father, for everything I ever did to displease you, but I WASN'T to blame in this. I wasn't, indeed."

"Tom, I beg your pardon," said the hard man, overcome at last. "And now, sir," he added, turning to me, "will you let by-gones be by-gones between my boy and me?"

There was just a touch of bitterness in his tone.

"With all my heart," I replied. "But I want just a word with you in the shop before I go."

"Certainly," he answered, stiffly; and I bade the old and the young man good night, and followed him down stairs.

"Thomas, my friend," I said, when we got into the shop, laying my hand on his shoulder, "will you after this say that God has dealt hardly with you? There's a son for any man God ever made to give thanks for on his knees! Thomas, you have a strong sense of fair play in your heart, and you GIVE fair play neither to your own son nor yet to God himself. You close your doors and brood over your own miseries, and the wrongs people have done you; whereas, if you would but open those doors, you might come out into the light of God's truth, and see that His heart is as clear as sunlight towards you. You won't believe this, and therefore naturally you can't quite believe that there is a God at all; for, indeed, a being that was not all light would be no God at all. If you would but let Him teach you, you would find your perplexities melt away like the snow in spring, till you could hardly believe you had ever felt them. No arguing will convince you of a God; but let Him once come in, and all argument will be tenfold useless to convince you that there is no God. Give God justice. Try Him as I have said.—Good night."

He did not return my farewell with a single word. But the grasp of his strong rough hand was more earnest and loving even than usual. I could not see his face, for it was almost dark; but, indeed, I felt that it was better I could not see it.

I went home as peaceful in my heart as the night whose curtains God had drawn about the earth that it might sleep till the morrow.

CHAPTER XIV. MY PUPIL.

Although I do happen to know how Miss Oldcastle fared that night after I left her, the painful record is not essential to my story. Besides, I have hitherto recorded only those things "quorum pars magna"—or minima, as the case may be—"fui." There is one exception, old Weir's story, for the introduction of which my reader cannot yet see the artistic reason. For whether a story be real in fact, or only real in meaning, there must always be an idea, or artistic model in the brain, after which it is fashioned: in the latter case one of invention, in the former case one of choice.

In the middle of the following week I was returning from a visit I had paid to Tomkins and his wife, when I met, in the only street of the village, my good and honoured friend Dr Duncan. Of course I saw him often—and I beg my reader to remember that this is no diary, but only a gathering together of some of the more remarkable facts of my history, admitting of being ideally grouped—but this time I recall distinctly because the interview bore upon many things.

"Well, Dr Duncan," I said, "busy as usual fighting the devil."

"Ah, my dear Mr Walton," returned the doctor—and a kind word from him went a long way into my heart—"I know what you mean. You fight the devil from the inside, and I fight him from the outside. My chance is a poor one."

"It would be, perhaps, if you were confined to outside remedies. But what an opportunity your profession gives you of attacking the enemy from the inside as well! And you have this advantage over us, that no man can say it belongs to your profession to say such things, and THEREFORE disregard them."

"Ah, Mr Walton, I have too great a respect for your profession to dare to interfere with it. The doctor in 'Macbeth,' you know, could

'not minister to a mind diseased,

Pluck from the memory a rooted sorrow,

Raze out the written troubles of the brain,

And with some sweet oblivious antidote

Cleanse the stuff'd bosom of that perilous stuff

Which weighs upon the heart.'"

"What a memory you have! But you don't think I can do that any more than you?"

"You know the best medicine to give, anyhow. I wish I always did. But you see we have no theriaca now."

"Well, we have. For the Lord says, 'Come unto me, and I will give you rest.'"

"There! I told you! That will meet all diseases."

"Strangely now, there comes into my mind a line of Chaucer, with which I will make a small return for your quotation from Shakespeare; you have mentioned theriaca; and I, without thinking of this line, quoted our Lord's words. Chaucer brings the two together, for the word triacle is merely a corruption of theriaca, the unfailing cure for every thing.

'Crist, which that is to every harm triacle.'"

"That is delightful: I thank you. And that is in Chaucer?"

"Yes. In the Man-of-Law's Tale."

"Shall I tell you how I was able to quote so correctly from Shakespeare? I have just come from referring to the passage. And I mention that because I want to tell you what made me think of the passage. I had been to see poor Catherine Weir. I think she is not long for this world. She has a bad cough, and I fear her lungs are going."

"I am concerned to hear that. I considered her very delicate, and am not surprised. But I wish, I do wish, I had got a little hold of her before, that I might be of some use to her now. Is she in immediate danger, do you think?"

"No. I do not think so. But I have no expectation of her recovery.

Very likely she will just live through the winter and die in the spring. Those patients so often go as the flowers come! All her coughing, poor woman, will not cleanse her stuffed bosom. The perilous stuff weighs on her heart, as Shakespeare says, as well as on her lungs."

"Ah, dear! What is it, doctor, that weighs upon her heart? Is it shame, or what is it? for she is so uncommunicative that I hardly know anything at all about her yet."

"I cannot tell. She has the faculty of silence."

"But do not think I complain that she has not made me her confessor. I only mean that if she would talk at all, one would have a chance of knowing something of the state of her mind, and so might give her some help."

"Perhaps she will break down all at once, and open her mind to you. I have not told her she is dying. I think a medical man ought at least to be quite sure before he dares to say such a thing. I have known a long life injured, to human view at least, by the medical verdict in youth of ever imminent death."

"Certainly one has no right to say what God is going to do with any one till he knows it beyond a doubt. Illness has its own peculiar mission, independent of any association with coming death, and may often work better when mingled with the hope of life. I mean we must take care of presumption when we measure God's plans by our theories. But could you not suggest something, Doctor Duncan, to guide me in trying to do my duty by her?"

"I cannot. You see you don't know what she is THINKING; and till you know that, I presume you will agree with me that all is an aim in the dark. How can I prescribe, without SOME diagnosis? It is just one of those few cases in which one would like to have the authority of the Catholic priests to urge confession with. I do not think anything will save her life, as we say, but you have taught some of us to think of the life that belongs to the spirit as THE life; and I do believe confession would do everything for that."

"Yes, if made to God. But I will grant that communication of one's sorrows or even sins to a wise brother of mankind may help to a deeper confession to the Father in heaven. But I have no wish for AUTHORITY in the matter. Let us see whether the Spirit of God working in her may not be quite as powerful for a final illumination of her being as the fiat confessio of a priest. I have no confidence in FORCING in the moral or spiritual garden. A hothouse development must necessarily be a sickly one, rendering the plant unfit for the normal life of the open air. Wait. We must not hurry things. She will perhaps come to me of herself before long. But I will call and inquire after her."

We parted; and I went at once to Catherine Weir's shop. She received me much as usual, which was hardly to be called receiving at all. Perhaps there was a doubtful shadow, not of more cordiality, but of less repulsion in it. Her eyes were full of a stony brilliance, and the flame of the fire that was consuming her glowed upon her cheeks more brightly, I thought, than ever; but that might be fancy, occasioned by what the doctor had said about her. Her hand trembled, but her demeanour was perfectly calm.

"I am sorry to hear you are complaining, Miss Weir," I said.

"I suppose Dr Duncan told you so, sir. But I am quite well. I did not send for him. He called of himself, and wanted to persuade me I was ill."

I understood that she felt injured by his interference.

"You should attend to his advice, though. He is a prudent man, and not in the least given to alarming people without cause."

She returned no answer. So I tried another subject.

"What a fine fellow your brother is!"

"Yes; he grows very much."

"Has your father found another place for him yet?"

"I don't know. My father never tells me about any of his doings."

"But don't you go and talk to him, sometimes?"

"No. He does not care to see me."

"I am going there now: will you come with me?"

"Thank you. I never go where I am not wanted."

"But it is not right that father and daughter should live as you do. Suppose he may not have been so kind to you as he ought, you should not cherish resentment against him for it. That only makes matters worse, you know."

"I never said to human being that he had been unkind to me."

"And yet you let every person in the village know it."

"How?"

Her eye had no longer the stony glitter. It flashed now.

"You are never seen together. You scarcely speak when you meet. Neither of you crosses the other's threshold."

"It is not my fault."

"It is not ALL your fault, I know. But do you think you can go to a heaven at last where you will be able to keep apart from each other, he in his house and you in your house, without any sign that it was through this father on earth that you were born into the world which the Father in heaven redeemed by the gift of His own Son?"

She was silent; and, after a pause, I went on.

"I believe, in my heart, that you love your father. I could not believe otherwise of you. And you will never be happy till you have made it up with him. Have you done him no wrong?"

At these words, her face turned white—with anger, I could see—all but those spots on her cheek-bones, which shone out in dreadful contrast to the deathly paleness of the rest of her face. Then the returning blood surged violently from her heart, and the red spots were lost in one crimson glow. She opened her lips to speak, but apparently changing her mind, turned and walked haughtily out of the shop and closed the door behind her.

I waited, hoping she would recover herself and return; but, after ten minutes had passed, I thought it better to go away.

As I had told her, I was going to her father's shop.

There I was received very differently. There was a certain softness in the manner of the carpenter which I had not observed before, with the same heartiness in the shake of his hand which had accompanied my last leave-taking. I had purposely allowed ten days to elapse before I called again, to give time for the unpleasant feelings associated with my interference to vanish. And now I had something in my mind about young Tom.

"Have you got anything for your boy yet, Thomas?"

"Not yet, sir. There's time enough. I don't want to part with him just yet. There he is, taking his turn at what's going. Tom!"

And from the farther end of the large shop, where I had not observed him, now approached young Tom, in a canvas jacket, looking quite like a workman.

"Well, Tom, I am glad to find you can turn your hand to anything."

"I must be a stupid, sir, if I couldn't handle my father's tools," returned the lad.

"I don't know that quite. I am not just prepared to admit it for my own sake. My father is a lawyer, and I never could read a chapter in one of his books—his tools, you know."

"Perhaps you never tried, sir."

"Indeed, I did; and no doubt I could have done it if I had made up my mind to it. But I never felt inclined to finish the page. And that reminds me why I called to-day. Thomas, I know that lad of yours is fond of reading. Can you spare him from his work for an hour or so before breakfast?"

"To-morrow, sir?"

"To-morrow, and to-morrow, and to-morrow," I answered; "and there's

Shakespeare for you."

"Of course, sir, whatever you wish," said Thomas, with a perplexed look, in which pleasure seemed to long for confirmation, and to be, till that came, afraid to put its "native semblance on."

"I want to give him some direction in his reading. When a man is fond of any tools, and can use them, it is worth while showing him how to use them better."

"Oh, thank you, sir!" exclaimed Tom, his face beaming with delight.

"That IS kind of you, sir! Tom, you're a made man!" cried the father.

"So," I went on, "if you will let him come to me for an hour every morning, till he gets another place, say from eight to nine, I will see what I can do for him."

Tom's face was as red with delight as his sister's had been with anger. And I left the shop somewhat consoled for the pain I had given Catherine, which grieved me without making me sorry that I had occasioned it.

I had intended to try to do something from the father's side towards a reconciliation with his daughter. But no sooner had I made up my proposal for Tom than I saw I had blocked up my own way towards my more important end. For I could not bear to seem to offer to bribe him even to allow me to do him good. Nor would he see that it was for his good and his daughter's—not at first. The first impression would be that I had a PROFESSIONAL end to gain, that the reconciling of father and daughter was a sort of parish business of mine, and that I had smoothed the way to it by offering a gift—an intellectual one, true, but not, therefore, the less a gift in the eyes of Thomas, who had a great respect for books. This was just what would irritate such a man, and I resolved to say nothing about it, but bide my time.

When Tom came, I asked him if he had read any of Wordsworth. For I always give people what I like myself, because that must be wherein I can best help them. I was anxious, too, to find out what he was capable of. And for this, anything that has more than a surface meaning will do. I had no doubt

215

about the lad's intellect, and now I wanted to see what there was deeper than the intellect in him.

He said he had not.

I therefore chose one of Wordsworth's sonnets, not one of his best by any means, but suitable for my purpose—the one entitled, "Composed during a Storm." This I gave him to read, telling him to let me know when he considered that he had mastered the meaning of it, and sat down to my own studies. I remember I was then reading the Anglo-Saxon Gospels. I think it was fully half-an-hour before Tom rose and gently approached my place. I had not been uneasy about the experiment after ten minutes had passed, and after that time was doubled, I felt certain of some measure of success. This may possibly puzzle my reader; but I will explain. It was clear that Tom did not understand the sonnet at first; and I was not in the least certain that he would come to understand it by any exertion of his intellect, without further experience. But what I was delighted to be made sure of was that Tom at least knew that he did not know. For that is the very next step to knowing. Indeed, it may be said to be a more valuable gift than the other, being of general application; for some quick people will understand many things very easily, but when they come to a thing that is beyond their present reach, will fancy they see a meaning in it, or invent one, or even—which is far worse— pronounce it nonsense; and, indeed, show themselves capable of any device for getting out of the difficulty, except seeing and confessing to themselves that they are not able to understand it. Possibly this sonnet might be beyond Tom now, but, at least, there was great hope that he saw, or believed, that there must be something beyond him in it. I only hoped that he would not fall upon some wrong interpretation, seeing he was brooding over it so long.

"Well, Tom," I said, "have you made it out?"

"I can't say I have, sir. I'm afraid I'm very stupid, for I've tried hard. I must just ask you to tell me what it means. But I must tell you one thing, sir: every time I read it over—twenty times, I daresay—I thought I was lying on my mother's grave, as I lay that terrible night; and then at the end there you were standing over me and saying, 'Can I do anything to help you?'"

I was struck with astonishment. For here, in a wonderful manner, I saw the imagination outrunning the intellect, and manifesting to the heart what the brain could not yet understand. It indicated undeveloped gifts of a far higher nature than those belonging to the mere power of understanding alone. For there was a hidden sympathy of the deepest kind between the life experience of the lad, and the embodiment of such life experience on the part of the poet. But he went on:

"I am sure, sir, I ought to have been at my prayers, then, but I wasn't; so I didn't deserve you to come. But don't you think God is sometimes better to us than we deserve?"

"He is just everything to us, Tom; and we don't and can't deserve anything. Now I will try to explain the sonnet to you."

I had always had an impulse to teach; not for the teaching's sake, for that, regarded as the attempt to fill skulls with knowledge, had always been to me a desolate dreariness; but the moment I saw a sign of hunger, an indication of readiness to receive, I was invariably seized with a kind of passion for giving. I now proceeded to explain the sonnet. Having done so, nearly as well as I could, Tom said:

"It is very strange, sir; but now that I have heard you say what the poem means, I feel as if I had known it all the time, though I could not say it."

Here at least was no common mind. The reader will not be surprised to hear that the hour before breakfast extended into two hours after breakfast as well. Nor did this take up too much of my time, for the lad was capable of doing a great deal for himself under the sense of help at hand. His father, so far from making any objection to the arrangement, was delighted with it. Nor do I believe that the lad did less work in the shop for it: I learned that he worked regularly till eight o'clock every night.

Now the good of the arrangement was this: I had the lad fresh in the morning, clear-headed, with no mists from the valley of labour to cloud the heights of understanding. From the exercise of the mind it was a pleasant and relieving change to turn to bodily exertion. I am certain that he both thought and worked better, because he both thought and worked. Every literary man ought to be MECHANICAL (to use a Shakespearean word) as well. But it would have been quite a different matter, if he had come to me after the labour of the day. He would not then have been able to think nearly so well. But LABOUR, SLEEP, THOUGHT, LABOUR AGAIN, seems to me to be the right order with those who, earning their bread by the sweat of the brow, would yet remember that man shall not live by bread alone. Were it possible that our mechanics could attend the institutions called by their name in the morning instead of the evening, perhaps we should not find them so ready to degenerate into places of mere amusement. I am not objecting to the amusement; only to cease to educate in order to amuse is to degenerate. Amusement is a good and sacred thing; but it is not on a par with education; and, indeed, if it does not in any way further the growth of the higher nature, it cannot be called good at all.

Having exercised him in the analysis of some of the best portions of our home literature,—I mean helped him to take them to pieces, that, putting them together again, he might see what kind of things they were—for who could understand a new machine, or find out what it was meant for, without either actually or in his mind taking it to pieces? (which pieces, however, let me remind my reader, are utterly useless, except in their relation to the whole)—I resolved to try something fresh with him.

At this point I had intended to give my readers a theory of mine about the teaching and learning of a language; and tell them how I had found the trial of it succeed in the case of Tom Weir. But I think this would be too much of a digression from the course of my narrative, and would, besides, be interesting to those only who had given a good deal of thought to subjects belonging to education. I will only say, therefore, that, by the end of three months, my pupil, without knowing any other Latin author, was able to read any part of the first book of the AEneid—to read it tolerably in measure, and to enjoy the poetry of it—and this not without a knowledge of the declensions and conjugations. As to the syntax, I made the sentences themselves teach him that. Now I know that, as an end, all this was of no great value; but as a beginning, it was invaluable, for it made and KEPT him hungry for more; whereas, in most modes of teaching, the beginnings are such that without the pressure of circumstances, no boy, especially after an interval of cessation, will return to them. Such is not Nature's mode, for the beginnings with her are as pleasant as the fruition, and that without being less thorough than they can be. The knowledge a child gains of the external world is the foundation upon which all his future philosophy is built. Every discovery he makes is fraught with pleasure—that is the secret of his progress, and the essence of my theory: that learning should, in each individual case, as in the first case, be DISCOVERY—bringing its own pleasure with it. Nor is this to be confounded with turning study into play. It is upon the moon itself that the infant speculates, after the moon itself—that he stretches out his eager hands—to find in after years that he still wants her, but that in science and poetry he has her a thousand-fold more than if she had been handed him down to suck.

So, after all, I have bored my reader with a shadow of my theory, instead of a description. After all, again, the description would have plagued him more, and that must be both his and my comfort.

So through the whole of that summer and the following winter, I went on teaching Tom Weir. He was a lad of uncommon ability, else he could not have effected what I say he had within his first three months of Latin, let my theory be not only perfect in itself, but true as well—true to human nature, I mean. And his father, though his own book-learning was but small, had enough of insight to perceive that his son was something out of the common, and that any possible advantage he might lose by remaining in Marshmallows was considerably more than counterbalanced by the instruction he got from the vicar. Hence, I believe, it was that not a word was said about another situation for Tom. And I was glad of it; for it seemed to me that the lad had abilities equal to any profession whatever.

CHAPTER XV. DR DUNCAN'S STORY.

On the next Sunday but one—which was surprising to me when I considered the manner of our last parting—Catherine Weir was in church, for the second time since I had come to the place. As it happened, only as Spenser says—

"It chanced—eternal God that chance did guide,"

—and why I say this, will appear afterwards—I had, in preaching upon, that is, in endeavouring to enforce the Lord's Prayer by making them think about the meaning of the words they were so familiar with, come to the petition, "Forgive us our debts, as we forgive our debtors;" with which I naturally connected the words of our Lord that follow: "For if ye forgive men their trespasses, your heavenly Father will also forgive you; but if ye forgive not men their trespasses, neither will your Father forgive your trespasses." I need not tell my reader more of what I said about this, than that I tried to show that even were it possible with God to forgive an unforgiving man, the man himself would not be able to believe for a moment that God did forgive him, and therefore could get no comfort or help or joy of any kind from the forgiveness; so essentially does hatred, or revenge, or contempt, or anything that separates us from man, separate us from God too. To the loving soul alone does the Father reveal Himself; for love alone can understand Him. It is the peace-makers who are His children.

This I said, thinking of no one more than another of my audience. But as I closed my sermon, I could not help fancying that Mrs Oldcastle looked at me with more than her usual fierceness. I forgot all about it, however, for I never seemed to myself to have any hold of, or relation to, that woman. I know I was wrong in being unable to feel my relation to her because I disliked her. But not till years after did I begin to understand how she felt, or recognize in myself a common humanity with her. A sin of my own made me understand her condition. I can hardly explain now; I will tell it when the time comes. When I called upon her next, after the interview last related, she behaved much as if she had forgotten all about it, which was not likely.

In the end of the week after the sermon to which I have alluded, I was passing the Hall-gate on my usual Saturday's walk, when Judy saw me from within, as she came out of the lodge. She was with me in a moment.

"Mr Walton," she said, "how could you preach at Grannie as you did last Sunday?"

"I did not preach at anybody, Judy."

"Oh, Mr Walton!"

"You know I didn't, Judy. You know that if I had, I would not say I had not."

"Yes, yes; I know that perfectly," she said, seriously. "But Grannie thinks you did."

"How do you know that?"

"By her face."

"That is all, is it?"

"You don't think Grannie would say so?"

"No. Nor yet that you could know by her face what she was thinking."

"Oh! can't I just? I can read her face—not so well as plain print; but, let me see, as well as what Uncle Stoddart calls black-letter, at least. I know she thought you were preaching at her; and her face said, 'I shan't forgive YOU, anyhow. I never forgive, and I won't for all your preaching.' That's what her face said."

"I am sure she would not say so, Judy," I said, really not knowing what to say.

"Oh, no; she would not say so. She would say, 'I always forgive, but I never forget.' That's a favourite saying of hers."

"But, Judy, don't you think it is rather hypocritical of you to say all this to me about your grandmother when she is so kind to you, and you seem such good friends with her?"

She looked up in my face with an expression of surprise.

"It is all TRUE, Mr Walton," she said.

"Perhaps. But you are saying it behind her back."

"I will go home and say it to her face directly."

She turned to go.

"No, no, Judy. I did not mean that," I said, taking her by the arm.

"I won't say you told me to do it. I thought there was no harm in telling you. Grannie is kind to me, and I am kind to her. But Grannie is afraid of my tongue, and I mean her to be afraid of it. It's the only way to keep her in order. Darling Aunt Winnie! it's all she's got to defend her. If you knew how she treats her sometimes, you would be cross with Grannie yourself, Mr Walton, for all your goodness and your white surplice."

And to my yet greater surprise, the wayward girl burst out crying, and, breaking away from me, ran through the gate, and out of sight amongst the trees, without once looking back.

I pursued my walk, my meditations somewhat discomposed by the recurring question:—Would she go home and tell her grandmother what she had said to me? And, if she did, would it not widen the breach upon the opposite side of which I seemed to see Ethelwyn stand, out of the reach of my help?

I walked quickly on to reach a stile by means of which I should soon leave the little world of Marshmallows quite behind me, and be alone with nature and my Greek Testament. Hearing the sound of horse-hoofs on the road from Addicehead, I glanced up from my pocket-book, in which I had been looking over the thoughts that had at various moments passed through my mind that week, in order to choose one (or more, if they would go together) to be brooded over to-day for my people's spiritual diet to-morrow—I say I glanced up from my pocket-book, and saw a young man, that is, if I could call myself young still, of distinguished appearance, approaching upon a good serviceable hack. He turned into my road and passed me. He was pale, with a dark moustache, and large dark eyes; sat his horse well and carelessly; had fine features of the type commonly considered Grecian, but thin, and expressive chiefly of conscious weariness. He wore a white hat with crape upon it, white gloves, and long, military-looking boots. All this I caught as he passed me; and I remember them, because, looking after him, I saw him stop at the lodge of the Hall, ring the bell, and then ride through the gate. I confess I did not quite like this; but I got over the feeling so far as to be able to turn to my

Testament when I had reached and crossed the stile.

I came home another way, after one of the most delightful days I had ever spent. Having reached the river in the course of my wandering, I came down the side of it towards Old Rogers's cottage, loitering and looking, quiet in heart and soul and mind, because I had committed my cares to Him who careth for us. The earth was round me—I was rooted, as it were, in it, but the air of a higher life was about me. I was swayed to and fro by the motions of a spiritual power; feelings and desires and hopes passed through me, passed away, and returned; and still my head rose into the truth, and the will of God was the regnant sunlight upon it. I might change my place and condition; new feelings might come forth, and old feelings retire into the lonely corners of my being; but still my heart should be glad and strong in the one changeless thing, in the truth that maketh free; still my head should rise into the sunlight of God, and I should know that because He lived I should live also, and because He was true I should remain true also, nor should any change pass upon me that should make me mourn the decadence of humanity. And then I found that I was gazing over the stump of an old pollard, on which I was leaning, down on a great bed of white water-lilies, that lay in the broad slow river, here broader and slower than in most places. The slanting yellow sunlight shone through the water down to the very roots anchored in the soil, and the water swathed their stems with coolness and freshness, and a universal sense, I doubt not, of watery presence and nurture. And there on their lovely heads, as they lay on the pillow of the water, shone the life-giving light of the summer sun, filling all the spaces between their outspread petals of living silver with its sea of radiance, and making them gleam with the whiteness which was born of them and the sun. And then came a hand on my shoulder, and, turning, I saw the gray head and the white smock of my old friend Rogers, and I was glad that he loved me enough not to be afraid of the parson and the gentleman.

"I've found it, sir, I do think," he said, his brown furrowed old face shining with a yet lovelier light than that which shone from the blossoms of the water-lilies, though, after what I had been thinking about them, it was no wonder that they seemed both to mean the same thing,—both to shine in the light of His countenance.

"Found what, Old Rogers?" I returned, raising myself, and laying my hand in return on his shoulder.

"Why He was displeased with the disciples for not knowing—"

"What He meant about the leaven of the Pharisees," I interrupted. "Yes, yes, of course. Tell me then."

"I will try, sir. It was all dark to me for days. For it appeared to me very nat'ral that, seeing they had no bread in the locker, and hearing tell of leaven which they weren't to eat, they should think it had summat to do with their having none of any sort. But He didn't seem to think it was right of them to fall into the blunder. For why then? A man can't be always right. He may be like myself, a foremast-man with no schoolin' but what the winds and the waves puts into him, and I'm thinkin' those fishermen the Lord took to so much were something o' that sort. 'How could they help it?' I said to myself, sir. And from that I came to ask myself, 'Could they have helped it?' If they couldn't, He wouldn't have been vexed with them. Mayhap they ought to ha' been able to help it. And all at once, sir, this mornin', it came to me. I don't know how, but it was give to me, anyhow. And I flung down my rake, and I ran in to the old woman, but she wasn't in the way, and so I went back to my work again. But when I saw you, sir, a readin' upon the lilies o' the field, leastways, the lilies o' the water, I couldn't help runnin' out to tell you. Isn't it a satisfaction, sir, when yer dead reckonin' runs ye right in betwixt the cheeks of the harbour? I see it all now."

"Well, I want to know, old Rogers. I'm not so old as you, and so I MAY live longer; and every time I read that passage, I should like to be able to say to myself, 'Old Rogers gave me this.'"

"I only hope I'm right, sir. It was just this: their heads was full of their dinner because they didn't know where it was to come from. But they ought to ha' known where it always come from. If their hearts had been full of the dinner He gave the five thousand hungry men and women and children, they wouldn't have been uncomfortable about not having a loaf. And so they wouldn't have been set upon the wrong tack when He spoke about the leaven of the Pharisees and Sadducees; and they would have known in a moment what He meant. And if I hadn't been too much of the same sort, I wouldn't have started saying it was but reasonable to be in the doldrums because they were at sea with no biscuit in the locker."

"You're right; you must be right, old Rogers. It's as plain as possible," I cried, rejoiced at the old man's insight. "Thank you. I'll preach about it to-morrow. I thought I had got my sermon in Foxborough Wood, but I was mistaken: you had got it."

But I was mistaken again. I had not got my sermon yet.

I walked with him to his cottage and left him, after a greeting with the "old woman." Passing then through the village, and seeing by the light of her candle the form of Catherine Weir behind her counter, I went in. I thought old Rogers's tobacco must be nearly gone, and I might safely buy some more. Catherine's manner was much the same as usual. But as she was weighing my purchase, she broke out all at once:

"It's no use your preaching at me, Mr Walton. I cannot, I WILL not forgive. I will do anything BUT forgive. And it's no use."

"It is not I that say it, Catherine. It is the Lord himself."

I saw no great use in protesting my innocence, yet I thought it better to add—

"And I was not preaching AT you. I was preaching to you, as much as to any one there, and no more."

Of this she took no notice, and I resumed:

"Just think of what HE says; not what I say."

"I can't help it. If He won't forgive me, I must go without it. I can't forgive."

I saw that good and evil were fighting in her, and felt that no words of mine could be of further avail at the moment. The words of our Lord had laid hold of her; that was enough for this time. Nor dared I ask her any questions. I had the feeling that it would hurt, not help. All I could venture to say, was:

"I won't trouble you with talk, Catherine. Our Lord wants to talk to you. It is not for me to interfere. But please to remember, if ever you think I can serve you in any way, you have only to send for me."

She murmured a mechanical thanks, and handed me my parcel. I paid for it, bade her good night, and left the shop.

"O Lord," I said in my heart, as I walked away, "what a labour Thou hast with us all! Shall we ever, some day, be all, and quite, good like Thee? Help me. Fill me with Thy light, that my work may all go to bring about the gladness of Thy kingdom—the holy household of us brothers and sisters—all Thy children."

And now I found that I wanted very much to see my friend Dr Duncan. He received me with his stately cordiality, and a smile that went farther than all his words of greeting.

"Come now, Mr Walton, I am just going to sit down to my dinner, and you must join me. I think there will be enough for us both. There is, I believe, a chicken a-piece for us, and we can make up with cheese and a glass of— would you believe it?—my own father's port. He was fond of port—the old man—though I never saw him with one glass more aboard than the registered tonnage. He always sat light on the water. Ah, dear me! I'm old myself now."

"But what am I to do with Mrs Pearson?" I said. "There's some chef-d'oeuvre of hers waiting for me by this time. She always treats me particularly well on Saturdays and Sundays."

"Ah! then, you must not stop with me. You will fare better at home."

"But I should much prefer stopping with you. Couldn't you send a message for me?"

"To be sure. My boy will run with it at once."

Now, what is the use of writing all this? I do not know. Only that even a tete-a-tete dinner with an old friend, now that I am an old man myself, has such a pearly halo about it in the mists of the past, that every little circumstance connected with it becomes interesting, though it may be quite unworthy of record. So, kind reader, let it stand.

We sat down to our dinner, so simple and so well-cooked that it was just what I liked. I wanted very much to tell my friend what had occurred in Catherine's shop, but I would not begin till we were safe from interruption; and so we chatted away concerning many things, he telling me about his seafaring life, and I telling him some of the few remarkable things that had happened to me in the course of my life-voyage. There is no man but has met with some remarkable things that other people would like to know, and which would seem stranger to them than they did at the time to the person to whom they happened.

At length I brought our conversation round to my interview with Catherine Weir.

"Can you understand," I said, "a woman finding it so hard to forgive her own father?"

"Are you sure it is her father?" he returned.

"Surely she has not this feeling towards more than one. That she has it towards her father, I know."

"I don't know," he answered. "I have known resentment preponderate over every other feeling and passion—in the mind of a woman too. I once heard of a good woman who cherished this feeling against a good man because of some distrustful words he had once addressed to herself. She had lived to a great age, and was expressing to her clergyman her desire that God would take her away: she had been waiting a long time. The clergyman—a very shrewd as well as devout man, and not without a touch of humour, said: 'Perhaps God doesn't mean to let you die till you've forgiven Mr——.' She was as if struck with a flash of thought, sat silent during the rest of his visit, and when the clergyman called the next day, he found Mr —— and her talking together very quietly over a cup of tea. And she hadn't long to wait after that,

227

I was told, but was gathered to her fathers—or went home to her children, whichever is the better phrase."

"I wish I had had your experience, Dr Duncan," I said.

"I have not had so much experience as a general practitioner, because I have been so long at sea. But I am satisfied that until a medical man knows a good deal more about his patient than most medical men give themselves the trouble to find out, his prescriptions will partake a good deal more than is necessary of haphazard.—As to this question of obstinate resentment, I know one case in which it is the ruling presence of a woman's life—the very light that is in her is resentment. I think her possessed myself."

"Tell me something about her."

"I will. But even to you I will mention no names. Not that I have her confidence in the least. But I think it is better not. I was called to attend a lady at a house where I had never yet been."

"Was it in——?" I began, but checked myself. Dr Duncan smiled and went on without remark. I could see that he told his story with great care, lest, I thought, he should let anything slip that might give a clue to the place or people.

"I was led up into an old-fashioned, richly-furnished room. A great wood-fire burned on the hearth. The bed was surrounded with heavy dark curtains, in which the shadowy remains of bright colours were just visible. In the bed lay one of the loveliest young creatures I had ever seen. And, one on each side, stood two of the most dreadful-looking women I had ever beheld. Still as death, while I examined my patient, they stood, with moveless faces, one as white as the other. Only the eyes of both of them were alive. One was evidently mistress, and the other servant. The latter looked more self-contained than the former, but less determined and possibly more cruel. That both could be unkind at least, was plain enough. There was trouble and signs of inward conflict in the eyes of the mistress. The maid gave no sign of any inside to her at all, but stood watching her mistress. A child's toy was lying in a corner of the room."

I may here interrupt my friend's story to tell my reader that I may be mingling some of my own conclusions with what the good man told me of his. For he will see well enough already that I had in a moment attached his description to persons I knew, and, as it turned out, correctly, though I could not be certain about it till the story had advanced a little beyond this early stage of its progress.

"I found the lady very weak and very feverish—a quick feeble pulse, now bounding, and now intermitting—and a restlessness in her eye which I felt contained the secret of her disorder. She kept glancing, as if involuntarily, towards the door, which would not open for all her looking, and I heard her once murmur to herself—for I was still quick of hearing then—'He won't come!' Perhaps I only saw her lips move to those words—I cannot be sure, but I am certain she said them in her heart. I prescribed for her as far as I could venture, but begged a word with her mother. She went with me into an adjoining room.

"'The lady is longing for something,' I said, not wishing to be so definite as I could have been.

"The mother made no reply. I saw her lips shut yet closer than before.

"'She is your daughter, is she not?'

"'Yes,'—very decidedly.

"'Could you not find out what she wishes?'

"'Perhaps I could guess.'

"'I do not think I can do her any good till she has what she wants.'

"'Is that your mode of prescribing, doctor?' she said, tartly.

"'Yes, certainly,' I answered—'in the present case. Is she married?'

"'Yes.'

"'Has she any children?'

"'One daughter.'

"'Let her see her, then.'

"'She does not care to see her.'

"'Where is her husband?'

"'Excuse me, doctor; I did not send for you to ask questions, but to give advice.'

"'And I came to ask questions, in order that I might give advice. Do you think a human being is like a clock, that can be taken to pieces, cleaned, and put together again?'

"'My daughter's condition is not a fit subject for jesting.'

"'Certainly not. Send for her husband, or the undertaker, whichever you please,' I said, forgetting my manners and my temper together, for I was more irritable then than I am now, and there was something so repulsive about the woman, that I felt as if I was talking to an evil creature that for her own ends, though what I could not tell, was tormenting the dying lady.

"'I understood you were a GENTLEMAN—of experience and breeding.'

"'I am not in the question, madam. It is your daughter.'

"'She shall take your prescription.'

"'She must see her husband if it be possible.'

"'It is not possible.'

"'Why?'

"'I say it is not possible, and that is enough. Good morning.'

"I could say no more at that time. I called the next day. She was just the same, only that I knew she wanted to speak to me, and dared not, because of the presence of the two women. Her troubled eyes seemed searching mine for pity and help, and I could not tell what to do for her. There are, indeed, as some one says, strongholds of injustice and wrong into which no law can enter to help.

"One afternoon, about a week after my first visit, I was sitting by her bedside, wondering what could be done to get her out of the clutches of these tormentors, who were, evidently to me, consuming her in the slow fire of her own affections, when I heard a faint noise, a rapid foot in the house so quiet before; heard doors open and shut, then a dull sound of conflict of some sort. Presently a quick step came up the oak-stair. The face of my patient flushed, and her eyes gleamed as if her soul would come out of them. Weak as she was she sat up in bed, almost without an effort, and the two women darted from the room, one after the other.

"'My husband!' said the girl—for indeed she was little more in age, turning her face, almost distorted with eagerness, towards me.

"'Yes, my dear,' I said, 'I know. But you must be as still as you can, else you will be very ill. Do keep quiet.'

"'I will, I will,' she gasped, stuffing her pocket-handkerchief actually into her mouth to prevent herself from screaming, as if that was what would hurt her. 'But go to him. They will murder him.'

"That moment I heard a cry, and what sounded like an articulate imprecation, but both from a woman's voice; and the next, a young man—as fine a fellow as I ever saw—dressed like a game-keeper, but evidently a gentleman, walked into the room with a quietness that strangely contrasted with the dreadful paleness of his face and with his disordered hair; while the two women followed, as red as he was white, and evidently in fierce wrath from a fruitless struggle with the powerful youth. He walked gently up to his wife, whose outstretched arms and face followed his face as he came round the bed to where she was at the other side, till arms, and face, and head, fell into his embrace.

"I had gone to the mother.

"'Let us have no scene now,' I said, 'or her blood will be on your head.'

"She took no notice of what I said, but stood silently glaring, not gazing,

231

at the pair. I feared an outburst, and had resolved, if it came, to carry her at once from the room, which I was quite able to do then, Mr Walton, though I don't look like it now. But in a moment more the young man, becoming uneasy at the motionlessness of his wife, lifted up her head, and glanced in her face. Seeing the look of terror in his, I hastened to him, and lifting her from him, laid her down—dead. Disease of the heart, I believe. The mother burst into a shriek—not of horror, or grief, or remorse, but of deadly hatred.

"'Look at your work!' she cried to him, as he stood gazing in stupor on the face of the girl. 'You said she was yours, not mine; take her. You may have her now you have killed her.'

"'He may have killed her; but you have MURDERED her, madam,' I said, as I took the man by the arm, and led him away, yielding like a child. But the moment I got him out of the house, he gave a groan, and, breaking away from me, rushed down a road leading from the back of the house towards the home-farm. I followed, but he had disappeared. I went on; but before I could reach the farm, I heard the gallop of a horse, and saw him tearing away at full speed along the London road. I never heard more of him, or of the story. Some women can be secret enough, I assure you."

I need not follow the rest of our conversation. I could hardly doubt whose was the story I had heard. It threw a light upon several things about which I had been perplexed. What a horror of darkness seemed to hang over that family! What deeds of wickedness! But the reason was clear: the horror came from within; selfishness, and fierceness of temper were its source— no unhappy DOOM. The worship of one's own will fumes out around the being an atmosphere of evil, an altogether abnormal condition of the moral firmament, out of which will break the very flames of hell. The consciousness of birth and of breeding, instead of stirring up to deeds of gentleness and "high emprise," becomes then but an incentive to violence and cruelty; and things which seem as if they could not happen in a civilized country and a polished age, are proved as possible as ever where the heart is unloving, the feelings unrefined, self the centre, and God nowhere in the man or woman's vision. The terrible things that one reads in old histories, or in modern newspapers, were done by human beings, not by demons.

I did not let my friend know that I knew all that he concealed; but I may as well tell my reader now, what I could not have told him then. I know all the story now, and, as no better place will come, as far as I can see, I will tell it at once, and briefly.

Dorothy—a wonderful name, THE GIFT OF GOD, to be so treated, faring in this, however, like many other of God's gifts—Dorothy Oldcastle was the eldest daughter of Jeremy and Sibyl Oldcastle, and the sister therefore of Ethelwyn. Her father, who was an easy-going man, entirely under the dominion of his wife, died when she was about fifteen, and her mother sent her to school, with especial recommendation to the care of a clergyman in the neighbourhood, whom Mrs Oldcastle knew; for, somehow—and the fact is not so unusual as to justify especial inquiry here—though she paid no attention to what our Lord or His apostles said, nor indeed seemed to care to ask herself if what she did was right, or what she accepted (I cannot say BELIEVED) was true, she had yet a certain (to me all but incomprehensible) leaning to the clergy. I think it belongs to the same kind of superstition which many of our own day are turning to. Offered the Spirit of God for the asking, offered it by the Lord himself, in the misery of their unbelief they betake themselves to necromancy instead, and raise the dead to ask their advice, AND FOLLOW IT, and will find some day that Satan had not forgotten how to dress like an angel of light. Nay, he can be more cunning with the demands of the time. We are clever: he will be cleverer. Why should he dress and not speak like an angel of light? Why should he not give good advice if that will help to withdraw people by degrees from regarding the source of all good? He knows well enough that good advice goes for little, but that what fills the heart and mind goes for much. What religion is there in being convinced of a future state? Is that to worship God? It is no more religion than the belief that the sun will rise to-morrow is religion. It may be a source of happiness to those who could not believe it before, but it is not religion. Where religion comes that will certainly be likewise, but the one is not the other. The devil can afford a kind of conviction of that. It costs him little. But to believe that the spirits of the departed are the mediators between God and us is essential paganism—to call it nothing worse; and a bad enough name too since Christ has come and we have heard and seen the only-begotten of the Father. Thus

233

the instinctive desire for the wonderful, the need we have of a revelation from above us, denied its proper food and nourishment, turns in its hunger to feed upon garbage. As a devout German says—I do not quote him quite correctly—"Where God rules not, demons will." Let us once see with our spiritual eyes the Wonderful, the Counsellor, and surely we shall not turn from Him to seek elsewhere the treasures of wisdom and knowledge.

Those who sympathize with my feeling in regard to this form of the materialism of our day, will forgive this divergence. I submit to the artistic blame of such as do not, and return to my story.

Dorothy was there three or four years. I said I would be brief. She and the clergyman's son fell in love with each other. The mother heard of it, and sent for her home. She had other views for her. Of course, in such eyes, a daughter's FANCY was, irrespective of its object altogether, a thing to be sneered at. But she found, to her fierce disdain, that she had not been able to keep all her beloved obstinacy to herself: she had transmitted a portion of it to her daughter. But in her it was combined with noble qualities, and, ceasing to be the evil thing it was in her mother, became an honourable firmness, rendering her able to withstand her mother's stormy importunities. Thus Nature had begun to right herself—the right in the daughter turning to meet and defy the wrong in the mother, and that in the same strength of character which the mother had misused for evil and selfish ends. And thus the bad breed was broken. She was and would be true to her lover. The consequent SCENES were dreadful. The spirit but not the will of the girl was all but broken. She felt that she could not sustain the strife long. By some means, unknown to my informant, her lover contrived to communicate with her. He had, through means of relations who had great influence with Government, procured a good appointment in India, whither he must sail within a month. The end was that she left her mother's house. Mr Gladwyn was waiting for her near, and conducted her to his father's, who had constantly refused to aid Mrs Oldcastle by interfering in the matter. They were married next day by the clergyman of a neighbouring parish. But almost immediately she was taken so ill, that it was impossible for her to accompany her husband, and she was compelled to remain behind at the rectory, hoping to join him the following year.

Before the time arrived, she gave birth to my little friend Judy; and her departure was again delayed by a return of her old complaint, probably the early stages of the disease of which she died. Then, just as she was about to set sail for India, news arrived that Mr Gladwyn had had a sunstroke, and would have leave of absence and come home as soon as he was able to be moved; so that instead of going out to join him, she must wait for him where she was. His mother had been dead for some time. His father, an elderly man of indolent habits, was found dead in his chair one Sunday morning soon after the news had arrived of the illness of his son, to whom he was deeply attached. And so the poor young creature was left alone with her child, without money, and in weak health. The old man left nothing behind him but his furniture and books. And nothing could be done in arranging his affairs till the arrival of his son, of whom the last accounts had been that he was slowly recovering. In the meantime his wife was in want of money, without a friend to whom she could apply. I presume that one of the few parishioners who visited at the rectory had written to acquaint Mrs Oldcastle with the condition in which her daughter was left, for, influenced by motives of which I dare not take upon me to conjecture an analysis, she wrote, offering her daughter all that she required in her old home. Whether she fore-intended her following conduct, or old habit returned with the return of her daughter, I cannot tell; but she had not been more than a few days in the house before she began to tyrannise over her, as in old times, and although Mrs Gladwyn's health, now always weak, was evidently failing in consequence, she either did not see the cause, or could not restrain her evil impulses. At length the news arrived of Mr Gladwyn's departure for home. Perhaps then for the first time the temptation entered her mind to take her revenge upon him, by making her daughter's illness a pretext for refusing him admission to her presence. She told her she should not see him till she was better, for that it would make her worse; persisted in her resolution after his arrival; and effected, by the help of Sarah, that he should not gain admittance to the house, keeping all the doors locked except one. It was only by the connivance of Ethelwyn, then a girl about fifteen, that he was admitted by the underground way, of which she unlocked the upper door for his entrance. She had then guided him as far as she dared, and directed him the rest of the way to his wife's room.

My reader will now understand how it came about in the process of writing these my recollections, that I have given such a long chapter chiefly to that one evening spent with my good friend, Dr Duncan; for he will see, as I have said, that what he told me opened up a good deal to me.

I had very little time for the privacy of the church that night. Dark as it was, however, I went in before I went home: I had the key of the vestry-door always in my pocket. I groped my way into the pulpit, and sat down in the darkness, and thought. Nor did my personal interest in Dr Duncan's story make me forget poor Catherine Weir and the terrible sore in her heart, the sore of unforgivingness. And I saw that of herself she would not, could not, forgive to all eternity; that all the pains of hell could not make her forgive, for that it was a divine glory to forgive, and must come from God. And thinking of Mrs Oldcastle, I saw that in ourselves we could be sure of no safety, not from the worst and vilest sins; for who could tell how he might not stupify himself by degrees, and by one action after another, each a little worse than the former, till the very fires of Sinai would not flash into eyes blinded with the incense arising to the golden calf of his worship? A man may come to worship a devil without knowing it. Only by being filled with a higher spirit than our own, which, having caused our spirits, is one with our spirits, and is in them the present life principle, are we or can we be safe from this eternal death of our being. This spirit was fighting the evil spirit in Catherine Weir: how was I to urge her to give ear to the good? If will would but side with God, the forces of self, deserted by their leader, must soon quit the field; and the woman—the kingdom within her no longer torn by conflicting forces—would sit quiet at the feet of the Master, reposing in that rest which He offered to those who could come to Him. Might she not be roused to utter one feeble cry to God for help? That would be one step towards the forgiveness of others. To ask something for herself would be a great advance in such a proud nature as hers. And to ask good heartily is the very next step to giving good heartily.

Many thoughts such as these passed through my mind, chiefly associated with her. For I could not think how to think about Mrs Oldcastle yet. And the old church gloomed about me all the time. And I kept lifting up my heart to the God who had cared to make me, and then drew me to be a preacher to my fellows, and had surely something to give me to say to them; for did He not choose so to work by the foolishness of preaching?—Might not my humble ignorance work His will, though my wrath could not work His righteousness? And I descended from the pulpit thinking with myself, "Let Him do as He will. Here I am. I will say what I see: let Him make it good."

And the next morning, I spoke about the words of our Lord:

"If ye then, being evil, know how to give good gifts to your children, how much more shall your heavenly Father give the Holy Spirit to them that ask Him!"

And I looked to see. And there Catherine Weir sat, looking me in the face.

There likewise sat Mrs Oldcastle, looking me in the face too.

And Judy sat there, also looking me in the face, as serious as man could wish grown woman to look.

CHAPTER XVI. THE ORGAN.

One little matter I forgot to mention as having been talked about between Dr Duncan and myself that same evening. I happened to refer to Old Rogers.

"What a fine old fellow that is!" said Dr Duncan.

"Indeed he is," I answered. "He is a great comfort and help to me. I don't think anybody but myself has an idea what there is in that old man."

"The people in the village don't quite like him, though, I find. He is too ready to be down upon them when he sees things going amiss. The fact is, they are afraid of him."

"Something as the Jews were afraid of John the Baptist, because he was an honest man, and spoke not merely his own mind, but the mind of God in it."

"Just so. I believe you're quite right. Do you know, the other day, happening to go into Weir's shop to get him to do a job for me, I found him and Old Rogers at close quarters in an argument? I could not well understand the drift of it, not having been present at the beginning, but I soon saw that, keen as Weir was, and far surpassing Rogers in correctness of speech, and precision as well, the old sailor carried too heavy metal for the carpenter. It evidently annoyed Weir; but such was the good humour of Rogers, that he could not, for very shame, lose his temper, the old man's smile again and again compelling a response on the thin cheeks of ihe other."

"I know how he would talk exactly," I returned. "He has a kind of loving banter with him, if you will allow me the expression, that is irresistible to any man with a heart in his bosom. I am very glad to hear there is anything like communion begun between them. Weir will get good from him."

"My man-of-all-work is going to leave me. I wonder if the old man would take his place?"

"I do not know whether he is fit for it. But of one thing you may be sure—if Old Rogers does not honestly believe he is fit for it, he will not take it. And he will tell you why, too."

"Of that, however, I think I may be a better judge than he. There is nothing to which a good sailor cannot turn his hand, whatever he may think himself. You see, Mr Walton, it is not like a routine trade. Things are never twice the same at sea. The sailor has a thousand chances of using his judgment, if he has any to use; and that Old Rogers has in no common degree. So I should have no fear of him. If he won't let me steer him, you must put your hand to the tiller for me."

"I will do what I can," I answered; "for nothing would please me more than to see him in your service. It would be much better for him, and his wife too, than living by uncertain jobs as he does now."

The result of it all was, that Old Rogers consented to try for a month; but when the end of the month came, nothing was said on either side, and the old man remained. And I could see several little new comforts about the cottage, in consequence of the regularity of his wages.

Now I must report another occurrence in regular sequence.

To my surprise, and, I must confess, not a little to my discomposure, when I rose in the reading-desk on the day after this dinner with Dr Duncan, I saw that the Hall-pew was full. Miss Oldcastle was there for the first time, and, by her side, the gentleman whom the day before I had encountered on horseback. He sat carelessly, easily, contentedly—indifferently; for, although I never that morning looked up from my Prayer-book, except involuntarily in the changes of posture, I could not help seeing that he was always behind the rest of the congregation, as if he had no idea of what was coming next, or did not care to conform. Gladly would I, that day, have shunned the necessity of preaching that was laid upon me. "But," I said to myself, "shall the work given me to do fare ill because of the perturbation of my spirit? No harm is done, though I suffer; but much harm if one tone fails of its force because I suffer." I therefore prayed God to help me; and feeling the right, because I felt the need, of looking to Him for aid, I cast my care upon Him, kept my thoughts strenuously away from that which discomposed me, and never turned my eyes towards the Hall-pew from the moment I entered the pulpit. And partly, I presume, from the freedom given by the sense of irresponsibility for the result, I being weak and God strong, I preached, I think, a better sermon than I had ever preached before. But when I got into the vestry I found that I could scarcely stand for trembling; and I must have looked ill, for when my attendant came in he got me a glass of wine without even asking me if I would have it, although it was not my custom to take any there. But there was one of my congregation that morning who suffered more than I did from the presence of one of those who filled the Hall-pew.

I recovered in a few moments from my weakness, but, altogether disinclined to face any of my congregation, went out at my vestry-door, and home through the shrubbery—a path I seldom used, because it had a separatist look about it. When I got to my study, I threw myself on a couch, and fell fast asleep. How often in trouble have I had to thank God for sleep as for one of His best gifts! And how often when I have awaked refreshed and calm, have I thought of poor Sir Philip Sidney, who, dying slowly and patiently in the prime of life and health, was sorely troubled in his mind to know how he had offended God, because, having prayed earnestly for sleep, no sleep came in answer to his cry!

I woke just in time for my afternoon service; and the inward peace in which I found my heart was to myself a marvel and a delight. I felt almost as if I was walking in a blessed dream come from a world of serener air than this of ours. I found, after I was already in the reading-desk, that I was a few minutes early; and while, with bowed head, I was simply living in the consciousness of the presence of a supreme quiet, the first low notes of the organ broke upon my stillness with the sense of a deeper delight. Never before had I felt, as I felt that afternoon, the triumph of contemplation in Handel's rendering of "I know that my Redeemer liveth." And I felt how through it all ran a cold silvery quiver of sadness, like the light in the east after the sun is gone down, which would have been pain, but for the golden glow of the west, which looks after the light of the world with a patient waiting.—Before the music ceased, it had crossed my mind that I had never before heard that organ utter itself in the language of Handel. But I had no time to think more about it just then, for I rose to read the words of our Lord, "I will arise and go to my Father."

There was no one in the Hall-pew; indeed it was a rare occurrence if any one was there in the afternoon.

But for all the quietness of my mind during that evening service, I felt ill before I went to bed, and awoke in the morning with a headache, which increased along with other signs of perturbation of the system, until I thought it better to send for Dr Duncan. I have not yet got so imbecile as to suppose that a history of the following six weeks would be interesting to my readers— for during so long did I suffer from low fever; and more weeks passed during which I was unable to meet my flock. Thanks to the care of Mr Brownrigg, a clever young man in priest's orders, who was living at Addicehead while waiting for a curacy, kindly undertook my duty for me, and thus relieved me from all anxiety about supplying my place.

CHAPTER XVII. THE CHURCH-RATE.

But I cannot express equal satisfaction in regard to everything that Mr Brownrigg took upon his own responsibility, as my reader will see. He, and another farmer, his neighbour, had been so often re-elected churchwardens, that at last they seemed to have gained a prescriptive right to the office, and the form of election fell into disuse; so much so, that after Mr Summer's death, which took place some year and a half before I became Vicar of Marshmallows, Mr Brownrigg continued to exercise the duty in his own single person, and nothing had as yet been said about the election of a colleague. So little seemed to fall to the duty of the churchwarden that I regarded the neglect as a trifle, and was remiss in setting it right. I had, therefore, to suffer, as was just. Indeed, Mr Brownrigg was not the man to have power in his hands unchecked.

I had so far recovered that I was able to rise about noon and go into my study, though I was very weak, and had not yet been out, when one morning Mrs Pearson came into the room and said,—

"Please, sir, here's young Thomas Weir in a great way about something, and insisting upon seeing you, if you possibly can."

I had as yet seen very few of my friends, except the Doctor, and those only for two or three minutes; but although I did not feel very fit for seeing anybody just then, I could not but yield to his desire, confident there must be a good reason for it, and so told Mrs Pearson to show him in.

"Oh, sir, I know you would be vexed if you hadn't been told," he exclaimed, "and I am sure you will not be angry with me for troubling you."

"What is the matter, Tom?" I said. "I assure you I shall not be angry with you."

"There's Farmer Brownrigg, at this very moment, taking away Mr Templeton's table because he won't pay the church-rate."

"What church-rate?" I cried, starting up from the sofa. "I never heard of a church-rate."

Now, before I go farther, it is necessary to explain some things. One day before I was taken ill, I had had a little talk with Mr Brownrigg about some repairs of the church which were necessary, and must be done before another winter. I confess I was rather pleased; for I wanted my people to feel that the church was their property, and that it was their privilege, if they could regard it as a blessing to have the church, to keep it in decent order and repair. So I said, in a by-the-by way, to my churchwarden, "We must call a vestry before long, and have this looked to." Now my predecessor had left everything of the kind to his churchwardens; and the inhabitants from their side had likewise left the whole affair to the churchwardens. But Mr Brownrigg, who, I must say, had taken more pains than might have been expected of him to make himself acquainted with the legalities of his office, did not fail to call a vestry, to which, as usual, no one had responded; whereupon he imposed a rate according to his own unaided judgment. This, I believe, he did during my illness, with the notion of pleasing me by the discovery that the repairs had been already effected according to my mind. Nor did any one of my congregation throw the least difficulty in the churchwarden's way.—And now I must refer to another circumstance in the history of my parish.

I think I have already alluded to the fact that there were Dissenters in Marshmallows. There was a little chapel down a lane leading from the main street of the village, in which there was service three times every Sunday. People came to it from many parts of the parish, amongst whom were the families of two or three farmers of substance, while the village and its neighbourhood contributed a portion of the poorest of the inhabitants. A year or two before I came, their minister died, and they had chosen another, a very worthy man, of considerable erudition, but of extreme views, as I heard, upon insignificant points, and moved by a great dislike to national churches and episcopacy. This, I say, is what I had made out about him from what I had heard; and my reader will very probably be inclined to ask, "But why, with principles such as yours, should you have only hearsay to go upon? Why did you not make the honest man's acquaintance? In such a small place, men should not keep each other at arm's length." And any reader who says so, will say right. All I have to suggest for myself is simply a certain shyness, for which I cannot entirely account, but which was partly made up of fear to intrude, or of being supposed to arrogate to myself the right of making advances, partly of a dread lest we should not be able to get on together, and so the attempt should result in something unpleasantly awkward. I daresay, likewise, that the natural SHELLINESS of the English had something to do with it. At all events, I had not made his acquaintance.

Mr Templeton, then, had refused, as a point of conscience, to pay the church-rate when the collector went round to demand it; had been summoned before a magistrate in consequence; had suffered a default; and, proceedings being pushed from the first in all the pride of Mr Brownrigg's legality, had on this very day been visited by the churchwarden, accompanied by a broker from the neighbouring town of Addicehead, and at the very time when I was hearing of the fact was suffering distraint of his goods. The porcine head of the churchwarden was not on his shoulders by accident, nor without significance.

But I did not wait to understand all this now. It was enough for me that Tom bore witness to the fact that at that moment proceedings were thus driven to extremity. I rang the bell for my boots, and, to the open-mouthed dismay of Mrs Pearson, left the vicarage leaning on Tom's arm. But such was the commotion in my mind, that I had become quite unconscious of illness or even feebleness. Hurrying on in more terror than I can well express lest I should be too late, I reached Mr Templeton's house just as a small mahogany table was being hoisted into a spring-cart which stood at the door. Breathless with haste, I was yet able to call out,—

"Put that table down directly."

At the same moment Mr Brownrigg appeared from within the door. He approached with the self-satisfied look of a man who has done his duty, and is proud of it. I think he had not heard me.

"You see I'm prompt, Mr Walton," he said. "But, bless my soul, how ill you look!"

Without answering him—for I was more angry with him than I ought to have been—I repeated—

"Put that table down, I tell you."

They did so.

"Now," I said, "carry it back into the house."

"Why, sir," interposed Mr Brownrigg, "it's all right."

"Yes," I said, "as right as the devil would have it."

"I assure you, sir, I have done everything according to law."

"I'm not so sure of that. I believe I had the right to be chairman at the vestry-meeting; but, instead of even letting me know, you took advantage of my illness to hurry on matters to this shameful and wicked excess."

I did the poor man wrong in this, for I believe he had hurried things really to please me. His face had lengthened considerably by this time, and its rubicund hue declined.

"I did not think you would stand upon ceremony about it, sir. You never seemed to care for business."

"If you talk about legality, so will I. Certainly YOU don't stand upon ceremony."

"I didn't expect you would turn against your own churchwarden in the execution of his duty, sir," he said in an offended tone. "It's bad enough to have a meetin'-house in the place, without one's own parson siding with t'other parson as won't pay a lawful church-rate."

"I would have paid the church-rate for the whole parish ten times over before such a thing should have happened. I feel so disgraced, I am ashamed to look Mr Templeton in the face. Carry that table into the house again, directly."

"It's my property, now," interposed the broker. "I've bought it of the churchwarden, and paid for it."

I turned to Mr Brownrigg.

"How much did he give you for it?" I asked.

"Twenty shillings," returned he, sulkily, "and it won't pay expenses."

"Twenty shillings!" I exclaimed; "for a table that cost three times as much at least!—What do you expect to sell it for?"

"That's my business," answered the broker.

I pulled out my purse, and threw a sovereign and a half on the table, saying—

"FIFTY PER CENT. will be, I think, profit enough even on such a transaction."

"I did not offer you the table," returned the broker. "I am not bound to sell except I please, and at my own price."

"Possibly. But I tell you the whole affair is illegal. And if you carry away that table, I shall see what the law will do for me. I assure you I will prosecute you myself. You take up that money, or I will. It will go to pay counsel, I give you my word, if you do not take it to quench strife."

I stretched out my hand. But the broker was before me. Without another word, he pocketed the money, jumped into his cart with his man, and drove off, leaving the churchwarden and the parson standing at the door of the dissenting minister with his mahogany table on the path between them.

"Now, Mr Brownrigg," I said, "lend me a hand to carry this table in again."

He yielded, not graciously,—that could not be expected,—but in silence.

"Oh! sir," interposed young Tom, who had stood by during the dispute, "let me take it. You're not able to lift it."

"Nonsense! Tom. Keep away," I said. "It is all the reparation I can make."

And so Mr Brownrigg and I blundered into the little parlour with our burden—not a great one, but I began to find myself failing.

Mr Templeton sat in a Windsor chair in the middle of the room. Evidently the table had been carried away from before him, leaving his position uncovered. The floor was strewed with the books which had lain upon it. He sat reading an old folio, as if nothing had happened. But when we entered he rose.

He was a man of middle size, about forty, with short black hair and overhanging bushy eyebrows. His mouth indicated great firmness, not unmingled with sweetness, and even with humour. He smiled as he rose, but looked embarrassed, glancing first at the table, then at me, and then at Mr Brownrigg, as if begging somebody to tell him what to say. But I did not leave him a moment in this perplexity.

"Mr Templeton," I said, quitting the table, and holding out my hand, "I beg your pardon for myself and my friend here, my churchwarden"—Mr Brownrigg gave a grunt—"that you should have been annoyed like this. I have—"

Mr Templeton interrupted me.

"I assure you it was a matter of conscience with me," he said. "On no other ground—"

"I know it, I know it," I said, interrupting him in my turn. "I beg your pardon; and I have done my best to make amends for it. Offences must come, you know, Mr Templeton; but I trust I have not incurred the woe that follows upon them by means of whom they come, for I knew nothing of it, and indeed was too ill—"

Here my strength left me altogether, and I sat down. The room began to whirl round me, and I remember nothing more till I knew that I was lying on a couch, with Mrs Templeton bathing my forehead, and Mr Templeton trying to get something into my mouth with a spoon.

Ashamed to find myself in such circumstances, I tried to rise; but Mr Templeton, laying his hand on mine, said—

"My dear sir, add to your kindness this day, by letting my wife and me minister to you."

Now, was not that a courteous speech? He went on—

"Mr Brownrigg has gone for Dr Duncan, and will be back in a few moments. I beg you will not exert yourself."

I yielded and lay still. Dr Duncan came. His carriage followed, and I was taken home. Before we started, I said to Mr Brownrigg—for I could not rest till I had said it—

"Mr Brownrigg, I spoke in heat when I came up to you, and I am sure I did you wrong. I am certain you had no improper motive in not making me acquainted with your proceedings. You meant no harm to me. But you did very wrong towards Mr Templeton. I will try to show you that when I am well again; but—"

"But you mustn't talk more now," said Dr Duncan.

So I shook hands with Mr Brownrigg, and we parted. I fear, from what I know of my churchwarden, that he went home with the conviction that he had done perfectly right; and that the parson had made an apology for interfering with a churchwarden who was doing his best to uphold the dignity of Church and State. But perhaps I may be doing him wrong again.

I went home to a week more of bed, and a lengthened process of recovery, during which many were the kind inquiries made after me by my friends, and amongst them by Mr Templeton.

And here I may as well sketch the result of that strange introduction to the dissenting minister.

After I was tolerably well again, I received a friendly letter from him one day, expostulating with me on the inconsistency of my remaining within the pale of the ESTABLISHED CHURCH. The gist of the letter lay in these words:—

"I confess it perplexes me to understand how to reconcile your Christian and friendly behaviour to one whom most of your brethren would consider as much beneath their notice as inferior to them in social position, with your remaining the minister of a Church in which such enormities as you employed your private influence to counteract in my case, are not only possible, but certainly lawful, and recognized by most of its members as likewise expedient."

To this I replied:—

"MY DEAR SIR,—I do not like writing letters, especially on subjects of importance. There are a thousand chances of misunderstanding. Whereas, in a personal interview, there is a possibility of controversy being hallowed by communion. Come and dine with me to-morrow, at any hour convenient to you, and make my apologies to Mrs Templeton for not inviting her with you, on the ground that we want to have a long talk with each other without the distracting influence which even her presence would unavoidably occasion.

"I am," &c. &c.

He accepted my invitation at once. During dinner we talked away, not upon indifferent, but upon the most interesting subjects—connected with the poor, and parish work, and the influence of the higher upon the lower classes of society. At length we sat down on opposite sides of the fire; and as soon as Mrs Pearson had shut the door, I said,—

"You ask me, Mr Templeton, in your very kind letter—" and here I put my hand in my pocket to find it.

"I asked you," interposed Mr Templeton, "how you could belong to a Church which authorizes things of which you yourself so heartily disapprove."

"And I answer you," I returned, "that just to such a Church our Lord belonged."

"I do not quite understand you."

"Our Lord belonged to the Jewish Church."

"But ours is His Church."

"Yes. But principles remain the same. I speak of Him as belonging to a Church. His conduct would be the same in the same circumstances, whatever Church He belonged to, because He would always do right. I want, if you will allow me, to show you the principle upon which He acted with regard to church-rates."

"Certainly. I beg your pardon for interrupting you."

"The Pharisees demanded a tribute, which, it is allowed, was for the support of the temple and its worship. Our Lord did not refuse to acknowledge their authority, notwithstanding the many ways in which they had degraded the religious observances of the Jewish Church. He acknowledged himself a child of the Church, but said that, as a child, He ought to have been left to contribute as He pleased to the support of its ordinances, and not to be compelled after such a fashion."

"There I have you," exclaimed Mr Templeton. "He said they were wrong to make the tribute, or church-rate, if it really was such, compulsory."

"I grant it: it is entirely wrong—a very unchristian proceeding. But our Lord did not therefore desert the Church, as you would have me do. HE PAID THE MONEY, lest He should offend. And not having it of His own, He had to ask His Father for it; or, what came to the same thing, make a servant of His Father, namely, a fish in the sea of Galilee, bring Him the money. And there I have YOU, Mr Templeton. It is wrong to compel, and wrong to refuse, the payment of a church-rate. I do not say equally wrong: it is much worse to compel than to refuse."

"You are very generous," returned Mr Templeton. "May I hope that you will do me the credit to believe that if I saw clearly that they were the same thing, I would not hesitate a moment to follow our Lord's example."

"I believe it perfectly. Therefore, however we may differ, we are in reality at no strife."

"But is there not this difference, that our Lord was, as you say, a child of the Jewish Church, which was indubitably established by God? Now, if I cannot conscientiously belong to the so-called English Church, why should I have to pay church-rate or tribute?"

"Shall I tell you the argument the English Church might then use? The Church might say, 'Then you are a stranger, and no child; therefore, like the kings of the earth, we MAY take tribute of you.' So you see it would come to this, that Dissenters alone should be COMPELLED to pay church-rates."

We both laughed at this pushing of the argument to illegitimate conclusions. Then I resumed:

"But the real argument is that not for such faults should we separate from each other; not for such faults, or any faults, so long as it is the repository of the truth, should you separate from the Church."

"I will yield the point when you can show me the same ground for believing the Church of England THE NATIONAL CHURCH, appointed such by God, that I can show you, and you know already, for receiving the Jewish Church as the appointment of God."

"That would involve a long argument, upon which, though I have little doubt upon the matter myself, I cannot say I am prepared to enter at this moment. Meantime, I would just ask you whether you are not sufficiently a child of the Church of England, having received from it a thousand influences for good, if in no other way, yet through your fathers, to find it no great hardship, and not very unreasonable, to pay a trifle to keep in repair one of the tabernacles in which our forefathers worshipped together, if, as I hope you will allow, in some imperfect measure God is worshipped, and the truth is preached in it?"

"Most willingly would I pay the money. I object simply because the rate is compulsory."

"And therein you have our Lord's example to the contrary."

A silence followed; for I had to deal with an honest man, who was thinking. I resumed:—

"A thousand difficulties will no doubt come up to be considered in the matter. Do not suppose I am anxious to convince you. I believe that our Father, our Elder Brother, and the Spirit that proceedeth from them, is teaching you, as I believe I too am being taught by the same. Why, then, should I be anxious to convince you of anything? Will you not in His good time come to see what He would have you see? I am relieved to speak my mind, knowing He would have us speak our minds to each other; but I do not want to proselytize. If you change your mind, you will probably do so on different grounds from any I give you, on grounds which show themselves in the course of your own search after the foundations of truth in regard perhaps to some other question altogether."

Again a silence followed. Then Mr Templeton spoke:—

"Don't think I am satisfied," he said, "because I don't choose to say anything more till I have thought about it. I think you are wrong in your conclusions about the Church, though surely you are right in thinking we ought to have patience with each other. And now tell me true, Mr Walton,— I'm a blunt kind of man, descended from an old Puritan, one of Cromwell's Ironsides, I believe, and I haven't been to a university like you, but I'm no fool either, I hope,—don't be offended at my question: wouldn't you be glad to see me out of your parish now?"

I began to speak, but he went on.

"Don't you regard me as an interloper now—one who has no right to speak because he does not belong to the Church?"

"God forbid!" I answered. "If a word of mine would make you leave my parish to-morrow, I dare not say it. I do not want to incur the rebuke of our Lord—for surely the words 'Forbid him not' involved some rebuke. Would it not be a fearful thing that one soul, because of a deed of mine, should receive a less portion of elevation or comfort in his journey towards his home? Are there not countless modes of saying the truth? You have some of them. I hope I have some. People will hear you who will not hear me. Preach to them in the name and love of God, Mr Templeton. Speak that you do know and testify that you have seen. You and I will help each other, in proportion as we serve the Master. I only say that in separating from us you are in effect, and by your conduct, saying to us, "Do not preach, for you follow not with us." I will not be guilty of the same towards you. Your fathers did the Church no end of good by leaving it. But it is time to unite now."

Once more followed a silence.

"If people could only meet, and look each other in the face," said Mr Templeton at length, "they might find there was not such a gulf between them as they had fancied."

And so we parted.

Now I do not write all this for the sake of the church-rate question. I write it to commemorate the spirit in which Mr Templeton met me. For it is of consequence that two men who love their Master should recognize each that the other does so, and thereupon, if not before, should cease to be estranged because of difference of opinion, which surely, inevitable as offence, does not involve the same denunciation of woe.

After this Mr Templeton and I found some opportunities of helping each other. And many a time ere his death we consulted together about things that befell. Once he came to me about a legal difficulty in connexion with the deed of trust of his chapel; and although I could not help him myself, I directed him to such help as was thorough and cost him nothing.

I need not say he never became a churchman, or that I never expected he would. All his memories of a religious childhood, all the sources of the influences which had refined and elevated him, were surrounded with other associations than those of the Church and her forms. The Church was his grandmother, not his mother, and he had not made any acquaintance with her till comparatively late in life.

But while I do not say that his intellectual objections to the Church were less strong than they had been, I am sure that his feelings were moderated, even changed towards her. And though this may seem of no consequence to one who loves the Church more than the brotherhood, it does not seem of little consequence to me who love the Church because of the brotherhood of which it is the type and the restorer.

It was long before another church-rate was levied in Marshmallows. And when the circumstance did take place, no one dreamed of calling on Mr Templeton for his share in it. But, having heard of it, he called himself upon the churchwarden—Mr Brownrigg still—and offered the money cheerfully. AND MR BROWRIGG REFUSED TO TAKE IT TILL HE HAD CONSULTED ME! I told him to call on Mr Templeton, and say he would be much obliged to him for his contribution, and give him a receipt for it.

CHAPTER XVIII. JUDY'S NEWS.

Perhaps my reader may be sufficiently interested in the person, who, having once begun to tell his story, may possibly have allowed his feelings, in concert with the comfortable confidence afforded by the mask of namelessness, to run away with his pen, and so have babbled of himself more than he ought—may be sufficiently interested, I say, in my mental condition, to cast a speculative thought upon the state of my mind, during my illness, with regard to Miss Oldcastle and the stranger who was her mother's guest at the Hall. Possibly, being by nature gifted, as I have certainly discovered, with more of hope than is usually mingled with the other elements composing the temperament of humanity, I did not suffer quite so much as some would have suffered during such an illness. But I have reason to fear that when I was light-headed from fever, which was a not uncommon occurrence, especially in the early mornings during the worst of my illness—when Mrs Pearson had to sit up with me, and sometimes an old woman of the village who was generally called in upon such occasions—I may have talked a good deal of nonsense about Miss Oldcastle. For I remember that I was haunted with visions of magnificent conventual ruins which I had discovered, and which, no one seeming to care about them but myself, I was left to wander through at my own lonely will. Would I could see with the waking eye such a grandeur of Gothic arches and "long-drawn aisles" as then arose upon my sick sense! Within was a labyrinth of passages in the walls, and "long-sounding corridors," and sudden galleries, whence I looked down into the great church aching with silence. Through these I was ever wandering, ever discovering new rooms, new galleries, new marvels of architecture; ever disappointed and ever dissatisfied, because I knew that in one room somewhere in the forgotten mysteries of the pile sat Ethelwyn reading, never lifting those sea-blue eyes of hers from the great volume on her knee, reading every word, slowly turning leaf after leaf; knew that she would sit there reading, till, one by one, every leaf in the huge volume was turned, and she came to the last and read it from top to bottom—down to the finis and the urn with a weeping willow over it; when she would close the book with a sigh, lay it down on the floor, rise and walk slowly away, and leave the glorious ruin dead to me as it had so long been to every one else; knew that if I did not find her before that terrible last

253

page was read, I should never find her at all; but have to go wandering alone all my life through those dreary galleries and corridors, with one hope only left—that I might yet before I died find the "palace-chamber far apart," and see the read and forsaken volume lying on the floor where she had left it, and the chair beside it upon which she had sat so long waiting for some one in vain.

And perhaps to words spoken under these impressions may partly be attributed the fact, which I knew nothing of till long afterwards, that the people of the village began to couple my name with that of Miss Oldcastle.

When all this vanished from me in the returning wave of health that spread through my weary brain, I was yet left anxious and thoughtful. There was no one from whom I could ask any information about the family at the Hall, so that I was just driven to the best thing—to try to cast my care upon Him who cared for my care. How often do we look upon God as our last and feeblest resource! We go to Him because we have nowhere else to go. And then we learn that the storms of life have driven us, not upon the rocks, but into the desired haven; that we have been compelled, as to the last remaining, so to the best, the only, the central help, the causing cause of all the helps to which we had turned aside as nearer and better.

One day when, having considerably recovered from my second attack, I was sitting reading in my study, who should be announced but my friend Judy!

"Oh, dear Mr Walton, I am so sorry you have been so ill!" exclaimed the impulsive girl, taking my hand in both of hers, and sitting down beside me. "I haven't had a chance of coming to see you before; though we've always managed—I mean auntie and I—to hear about you. I would have come to nurse you, but it was no use thinking of it."

I smiled as I thanked her.

"Ah! you think because I'm such a tom-boy, that I couldn't nurse you. I only wish I had had a chance of letting you see. I am so sorry for you!"

"But I'm nearly well now, Judy, and I have been taken good care of."

"By that frumpy old thing, Mrs Pearson, and—"

"Mrs Pearson is a very kind woman, and an excellent nurse," I said; but she would not heed me.

"And that awful old witch, Mother Goose. She was enough to give you bad dreams all night she sat by you."

"I didn't dream about Mother Goose, as you call her, Judy. I assure you. But now I want to hear how everybody is at the Hall."

"What, grannie, and the white wolf, and all?"

"As many as you please to tell me about."

"Well, grannie is gracious to everybody but auntie."

"Why isn't she gracious to auntie?"

"I don't know. I only guess."

"Is your visitor gone?"

"Yes, long ago. Do you know, I think grannie wants auntie to marry him, and auntie doesn't quite like it? But he's very nice. He's so funny! He 'll be back again soon, I daresay. I don't QUITE like him—not so well as you by a whole half, Mr Walton. I wish you would marry auntie; but that would never do. It would drive grannie out of her wits."

To stop the strange girl, and hide some confusion, I said:

"Now tell me about the rest of them."

"Sarah comes next. She's as white and as wolfy as ever. Mr Walton, I hate that woman. She walks like a cat. I am sure she is bad."

"Did you ever think, Judy, what an awful thing it is to be bad? If you did, I think you would be so sorry for her, you could not hate her."

At the same time, knowing what I knew now, and remembering that impressions can date from farther back than the memory can reach, I was not surprised to hear that Judy hated Sarah, though I could not believe that in

255

such a child the hatred was of the most deadly description.

"I am afraid I must go on hating in the meantime," said Judy. "I wish some one would marry auntie, and turn Sarah away. But that couldn't be, so long as grannie lives."

"How is Mr Stoddart?"

"There now! That's one of the things auntie said I was to be sure to tell you."

"Then your aunt knew you were coming to see me?"

"Oh, yes, I told her. Not grannie, you know.—You mustn't let it out."

"I shall be careful. How is Mr Stoddart, then?"

"Not well at all. He was taken ill before you, and has been in bed and by the fireside ever since. Auntie doesn't know what to do with him, he is so out of spirits."

"If to-morrow is fine, I shall go and see him."

"Thank you. I believe that's just what auntie wanted. He won't like it at first, I daresay. But he'll come to, and you'll do him good. You do everybody good you come near."

"I wish that were true, Judy. I fear it is not. What good did I ever do you, Judy?"

"Do me!" she exclaimed, apparently half angry at the question. "Don't you know I have been an altered character ever since I knew you?"

And here the odd creature laughed, leaving me in absolute ignorance of how to interpret her. But presently her eyes grew clearer, and I could see the slow film of a tear gathering.

"Mr Walton," she said, "I HAVE been trying not to be selfish. You have done me that much good."

"I am very glad, Judy. Don't forget who can do you ALL good. There is

One who can not only show you what is right, but can make you able to do and be what is right. You don't know how much you have got to learn yet, Judy; but there is that one Teacher ever ready to teach if you will only ask Him."

Judy did not answer, but sat looking fixedly at the carpet. She was thinking, though, I saw.

"Who has played the organ, Judy, since your uncle was taken ill?" I asked, at length.

"Why, auntie, to be sure. Didn't you hear?"

"No," I answered, turning almost sick at the idea of having been away from church for so many Sundays while she was giving voice and expression to the dear asthmatic old pipes. And I did feel very ready to murmur, like a spoilt child that had not had his way. Think of HER there, and me here!

"Then," I said to myself at last, "it must have been she that played I know that my Redeemer liveth, that last time I was in church! And instead of thanking God for that, here I am murmuring that He did not give me more! And this child has just been telling me that I have taught her to try not to be selfish. Certainly I should be ashamed of myself."

"When was your uncle taken ill?"

"I don't exactly remember. But you will come and see him to-morrow? And then we shall see you too. For we are always out and in of his room just now."

"I will come if Dr Duncan will let me. Perhaps he will take me in his carriage."

"No, no. Don't you come with him. Uncle can't bear doctors. He never was ill in his life before, and he behaves to Dr Duncan just as if he had made him ill. I wish I could send the carriage for you. But I can't, you know."

"Never mind, Judy. I shall manage somehow.—What is the name of the gentleman who was staying with you?"

"Don't you know? Captain George Everard. He would change his name to Oldcastle, you know."

What a foolish pain, like a spear-thrust, they sent through me—those words spoken in such a taken-for-granted way!

"He's a relation—on grannie's side mostly, I believe. But I never could understand the explanation. What makes it harder is, that all the husbands and wives in our family, for a hundred and fifty years, have been more or less of cousins, or half-cousins, or second or third cousins. Captain Everard has what grandmamma calls a neat little property of his own from his mother, some where in Northumberland; for he IS only a third son, one of a class grannie does not in general feel very friendly to, I assure you, Mr Walton. But his second brother is dead, and the eldest something the worse for the wear, as grannie says; so that the captain comes just within sight of the coronet of an old uncle who ought to have been dead long ago. Just the match for auntie!"

"But you say auntie doesn't like him."

"Oh! but you know that doesn't matter," returned Judy, with bitterness. "What will grannie care for that? It's nothing to anybody but auntie, and she must get used to it. Nobody makes anything of her."

It was only after she had gone that I thought how astounding it would have been to me to hear a girl of her age show such an acquaintance with worldliness and scheming, had I not been personally so much concerned about one of the objects of her remarks. She certainly was a strange girl. But strange as she was it was a satisfaction to think that the aunt had such a friend and ally in her wild niece. Evidently she had inherited her father's fearlessness; and if only it should turn out that she had likewise inherited her mother's firmness, she might render the best possible service to her aunt against the oppression of her wilful mother.

"How were you able to get here to-day?" I asked, as she rose to go.

"Grannie is in London, and the wolf is with her. Auntie wouldn't leave uncle."

"They have been a good deal in London of late, have they not?"

258

"Yes. They say it's about money of auntie's. But I don't understand. I think it's that grannie wants to make the captain marry her; for they sometimes see him when they go to London."

CHAPTER XIX. THE INVALID.

The following day being very fine, I walked to Oldcastle Hall; but I remember well how much slower I was forced to walk than I was willing. I found to my relief that Mrs Oldcastle had not yet returned. I was shown at once to Mr Stoddart's library. There I found the two ladies in attendance upon him. He was seated by a splendid fire, for the autumn days were now chilly on the shady side, in the most luxurious of easy chairs, with his furred feet buried in the long hair of the hearth-rug. He looked worn and peevish. All the placidity of his countenance had vanished. The smooth expanse of his forehead was drawn into fifty wrinkles, like a sea over which the fretting wind has been blowing all night. Nor was it only suffering that his face expressed. He looked like a man who strongly suspected that he was ill-used.

After salutation,—

"You are well off, Mr Stoddart," I said, "to have two such nurses."

"They are very kind," sighed the patient

"You would recommend Mrs Pearson and Mother Goose instead, would you not, Mr Walton?" said Judy, her gray eyes sparkling with fun.

"Judy, be quiet," said the invalid, languidly and yet sharply.

Judy reddened and was silent.

"I am sorry to find you so unwell," I said.

"Yes; I am very ill," he returned.

Aunt and niece rose and left the room quietly.

"Do you suffer much, Mr Stoddart?"

"Much weariness, worse than pain. I could welcome death."

"I do not think, from what Dr Duncan says of you, that there is reason

259

to apprehend more than a lingering illness," I said—to try him, I confess.

"I hope not indeed," he exclaimed angrily, sitting up in his chair. "What right has Dr Duncan to talk of me so?"

"To a friend, you know," I returned, apologetically, "who is much interested in your welfare."

"Yes, of course. So is the doctor. A sick man belongs to you both by prescription."

"For my part I would rather talk about religion to a whole man than a sick man. A sick man is not a WHOLE man. He is but part of a man, as it were, for the time, and it is not so easy to tell what he can take."

"Thank you. I am obliged to you for my new position in the social scale. Of the tailor species, I suppose."

I could not help wishing he were as far up as any man that does such needful honest work.

"My dear sir, I beg your pardon. I meant only a glance at the peculiar relation of the words WHOLE and HEAL."

"I do not find etymology interesting at present."

"Not seated in such a library as this?"

"No; I am ill."

Satisfied that, ill as he was, he might be better if he would, I resolved to make another trial.

"Do you remember how Ligarius, in Julius Caesar, discards his sickness?—

"'I am not sick, if Brutus have in hand Any exploit worthy the name of honour.'"

"I want to be well because I don't like to be ill. But what there is in this foggy, swampy world worth being well for, I'm sure I haven't found out yet."

"If you have not, it must be because you have never tried to find out. But I'm not going to attack you when you are not able to defend yourself. We shall find a better time for that. But can't I do something for you? Would you like me to read to you for half an hour?"

"No, thank you. The girls tire me out with reading to me. I hate the very sound of their voices."

"I have got to-day's Times in my pocket."

"I've heard all the news already."

"Then I think I shall only bore you if I stay."

He made me no answer. I rose. He just let me take his hand, and returned my good morning as if there was nothing good in the world, least of all this same morning.

I found the ladies in the outer room. Judy was on her knees on the floor occupied with a long row of books. How the books had got there I wondered; but soon learned the secret which I had in vain asked of the butler on my first visit—namely, how Mr Stoddart reached the volumes arranged immediately under the ceiling, in shelves, as my reader may remember, that looked like beams radiating from the centre. For Judy rose from the floor, and proceeded to put in motion a mechanical arrangement concealed in one of the divisions of the book-shelves along the wall; and I now saw that there were strong cords reaching from the ceiling, and attached to the shelf or rather long box sideways open which contained the books.

"Do take care, Judy," said Ethelwyn. "You know it is very venturous of you to let that shelf down, when uncle is as jealous of his books as a hen of her chickens. I oughtn't to have let you touch the cords."

"You couldn't help it, auntie, dear; for I had the shelf half-way down before you saw me," returned Judy, proceeding to raise the books to their usual position under the ceiling.

But in another moment, either from Judy's awkwardness, or from the gradual decay and final fracture of some cord, down came the whole shelf with a thundering noise, and the books were scattered hither and thither in confusion about the floor. Ethelwyn was gazing in dismay, and Judy had built up her face into a defiant look, when the door of the inner room opened and Mr Stoddart appeared. His brow was already flushed; but when he saw the condition of his idols, (for the lust of the eye had its full share in his regard for his books,) he broke out in a passion to which he could not have given way but for the weak state of his health.

"How DARE you?" he said, with terrible emphasis on the word DARE. "Judy, I beg you will not again show yourself in my apartment till I send for you."

"And then," said Judy, leaving the room, "I am not in the least likely to be otherwise engaged."

"I am very sorry, uncle," began Miss Oldcastle.

But Mr Stoddart had already retreated and banged the door behind him. So Miss Oldcastle and I were left standing together amid the ruins.

She glanced at me with a distressed look. I smiled. She smiled in return.

"I assure you," she said, "uncle is not a bit like himself."

"And I fear in trying to rouse him, I have done him no good,—only made him more irritable," I said. "But he will be sorry when he comes to himself, and so we must take the reversion of his repentance now, and think nothing more of the matter than if he had already said he was sorry. Besides, when books are in the case, I, for one, must not be too hard upon my unfortunate neighbour."

"Thank you, Mr Walton. I am so much obliged to you for taking my uncle's part. He has been very good to me; and that dear Judy is provoking sometimes. I am afraid I help to spoil her; but you would hardly believe how good she really is, and what a comfort she is to me—with all her waywardness."

"I think I understand Judy," I replied; "and I shall be more mistaken than I am willing to confess I have ever been before, if she does not turn out a very fine woman. The marvel to me is that with all the various influences amongst which she is placed here, she is not really, not seriously, spoiled after all. I assure you I have the greatest regard for, as well as confidence in, my friend Judy."

Ethelwyn—Miss Oldcastle, I should say—gave me such a pleased look that I was well recompensed—if justice should ever talk of recompense—for my defence of her niece.

"Will you come with me?" she said; "for I fear our talk may continue to annoy Mr Stoddart. His hearing is acute at all times, and has been excessively so since his illness."

"I am at your service," I returned, and followed her from the room.

"Are you still as fond of the old quarry as you used to be, Miss Oldcastle?" I said, as we caught a glimpse of it from the window of a long passage we were going through.

"I think I am. I go there most days. I have not been to-day, though. Would you like to go down?"

"Very much," I said.

"Ah! I forgot, though. You must not go; it is not a fit place for an invalid."

"I cannot call myself an invalid now."

"Your face, I am sorry to say, contradicts your words."

And she looked so kindly at me, that I almost broke out into thanks for the mere look.

"And indeed," she went on, "it is too damp down there, not to speak of the stairs."

By this time we had reached the little room in which I was received the first time I visited the Hall. There we found Judy.

"If you are not too tired already, I should like to show you my little study. It has, I think, a better view than any other room in the house," said Miss Oldcastle.

"I shall be delighted," I replied.

"Come, Judy," said her aunt.

"You don't want me, I am sure, auntie."

"I do, Judy, really. You mustn't be cross to us because uncle has been cross to you. Uncle is not well, you know, and isn't a bit like himself; and you know you should not have meddled with his machinery."

And Miss Oldcastle put her arm round Judy, and kissed her. Whereupon Judy jumped from her seat, threw her book down, and ran to one of the several doors that opened from the room. This disclosed a little staircase, almost like a ladder, only that it wound about, up which we climbed, and reached a charming little room, whose window looked down upon the Bishop's Basin, glimmering slaty through the tops of the trees between. It was panelled in small panels of dark oak, like the room below, but with more of carving. Consequently it was sombre, and its sombreness was unrelieved by any mirror. I gazed about me with a kind of awe. I would gladly have carried away the remembrance of everything and its shadow.—Just opposite the window was a small space of brightness formed by the backs of nicely-bound books. Seeing that these attracted my eye—

"Those are almost all gifts from my uncle," said Miss Oldcastle. "He is really very kind, and you will not think of him as you have seen him to-day ?"

"Indeed I will not," I replied.

My eye fell upon a small pianoforte.

"Do sit down," said Miss Oldcastle.—"You have been very ill, and I could do nothing for you who have been so kind to me."

She spoke as if she had wanted to say this.

"I only wish I had a chance of doing anything for you," I said, as I took a chair in the window. "But if I had done all I ever could hope to do, you have repaid me long ago, I think."

"How? I do not know what you mean, Mr Walton. I have never done you the least service."

"Tell me first, did you play the organ in church that afternoon when—after—before I was taken ill—I mean the same day you had—a friend with you in the pew in the morning?"

I daresay my voice was as irregular as my construction. I ventured just one glance. Her face was flushed. But she answered me at once.

"I did."

"Then I am in your debt more than you know or I can tell you."

"Why, if that is all, I have played the organ every Sunday since uncle was taken ill," she said, smiling.

"I know that now. And I am very glad I did not know it till I was better able to bear the disappointment. But it is only for what I heard that I mean now to acknowledge my obligation. Tell me, Miss Oldcastle,—what is the most precious gift one person can give another?"

She hesitated; and I, fearing to embarrass her, answered for her.

"It must be something imperishable,—something which in its own nature IS. If instead of a gem, or even of a flower, we could cast the gift of a lovely thought into the heart of a friend, that would be giving, as the angels, I suppose, must give. But you did more and better for me than that. I had been troubled all the morning; and you made me know that my Redeemer liveth. I did not know you were playing, mind, though I felt a difference. You gave me more trust in God; and what other gift so great could one give? I think that last impression, just as I was taken ill, must have helped me through my illness. Often when I was most oppressed, 'I know that my Redeemer liveth' would rise up in the troubled air of my mind, and sung by a voice which, though I never heard you sing, I never questioned to be yours."

She turned her face towards me: those sea-blue eyes were full of tears.

"I was troubled myself," she said, with a faltering voice, "when I sang—I mean played—that. I am so glad it did somebody good! I fear it did not do me much.—I will sing it to you now, if you like."

And she rose to get the music. But that instant Judy, who, I then found, had left the room, bounded into it, with the exclamation,—

"Auntie, auntie! here's grannie!"

Miss Oldcastle turned pale. I confess I felt embarrassed, as if I had been caught in something underhand.

"Is she come in?" asked Miss Oldcastle, trying to speak with indifference.

"She is just at the door,—must be getting out of the fly now. What SHALL we do?"

"What DO you mean, Judy?" said her aunt.

"Well you know, auntie, as well as I do, that grannie will look as black as a thunder-cloud to find Mr Walton here; and if she doesn't speak as loud, it will only be because she can't. I don't care for myself, but you know on whose head the storm will fall. Do, dear Mr Walton, come down the back-stair. Then she won't be a bit the wiser. I'll manage it all."

Here was a dilemma for me; either to bring suffering on her, to save whom I would have borne any pain, or to creep out of the house as if I were and ought to be ashamed of myself. I believe that had I been in any other relation to my fellows, I would have resolved at once to lay myself open to the peculiarly unpleasant reproach of sneaking out of the house, rather than that she should innocently suffer for my being innocently there. But I was a clergyman; and I felt, more than I had ever felt before, that therefore I could not risk ever the appearance of what was mean. Miss Oldcastle, however, did not leave it to me to settle the matter. All that I have just written had but flashed through my mind when she said:—

"Judy, for shame to propose such a thing to Mr Walton! I am very sorry that he may chance to have an unpleasant meeting with mamma; but we can't help it. Come, Judy, we will show Mr Walton out together."

"It wasn't for Mr Walton's sake," returned Judy, pouting. "You are very troublesome, auntie dear. Mr Walton, she is so hard to take care of! and she's worse since you came. I shall have to give her up some day. Do be generous, Mr Walton, and take my side—that is, auntie's."

"I am afraid, Judy, I must thank your aunt for taking the part of my duty against my inclination. But this kindness, at least," I said to Miss Oldcastle, "I can never hope to return."

It was a stupid speech, but I could not be annoyed that I had made it.

"All obligations are not burdens to be got rid of, are they?" she replied, with a sweet smile on such a pale troubled face, that I was more moved for her, deliberately handing her over to the torture for the truth's sake, than I care definitely to confess.

Thereupon, Miss Oldcastle led the way down the stairs, I followed, and Judy brought up the rear. The affair was not so bad as it might have been, inasmuch as, meeting the mistress of the house in no penetralia of the same, I insisted on going out alone, and met Mrs Oldcastle in the hall only. She held out no hand to greet me. I bowed, and said I was sorry to find Mr Stoddart so far from well.

"I fear he is far from well," she returned; "certainly in my opinion too ill to receive visitors."

So saying, she bowed and passed on. I turned and walked out, not ill-pleased, as my readers will believe, with my visit.

From that day I recovered rapidly, and the next Sunday had the pleasure of preaching to my flock; Mr Aikin, the gentleman already mentioned as doing duty for me, reading prayers. I took for my subject one of our Lord's miracles of healing, I forget which now, and tried to show my people that all healing and all kinds of healing come as certainly and only from His hand as those instances in which He put forth His bodily hand and touched the diseased, and told them to be whole.

And as they left the church the organ played, "Comfort ye, comfort ye, my people, saith your God."

I tried hard to prevent my new feelings from so filling my mind as to make me fail of my duty towards my flock. I said to myself, "Let me be the more gentle, the more honourable, the more tender, towards these my brothers and sisters, forasmuch as they are her brothers and sisters too." I wanted to do my work the better that I loved her.

Thus week after week passed, with little that I can remember worthy of record. I seldom saw Miss Oldcastle, and during this period never alone. True, she played the organ still, for Mr Stoddart continued too unwell to resume his ministry of sound, but I never made any attempt to see her as she came to or went from the organ-loft. I felt that I ought not, or at least that it was better not, lest an interview should trouble my mind, and so interfere with my work, which, if my calling meant anything real, was a consideration of vital import. But one thing I could not help noting—that she seemed, by some intuition, to know the music I liked best; and great help she often gave me by so uplifting my heart upon the billows of the organ-harmony, that my thinking became free and harmonious, and I spoke, as far as my own feeling was concerned, like one upheld on the unseen wings of ministering cherubim. How it might be to those who heard me, or what the value of the utterance in itself might be, I cannot tell. I only speak of my own feelings, I say.

Does my reader wonder why I did not yet make any further attempt to gain favour in the lady's eyes? He will see, if he will think for a moment. First of all, I could not venture until she had seen more of me; and how to enjoy more of her society while her mother was so unfriendly, both from instinctive dislike to me, and because of the offence I had given her more than once, I did not know; for I feared that to call oftener might only occasion measures upon her part to prevent me from seeing her daughter at all; and I could not tell how far such measures might expedite the event I most dreaded, or add to the discomfort to which Miss Oldcastle was already so much exposed. Meantime I heard nothing of Captain Everard; and the comfort that flowed from such a negative source was yet of a very positive character. At the same time—will my reader understand me?—I was in some measure deterred from making further advances by the doubt whether her favour for Captain Everard might not be greater than Judy had represented it. For I had always shrunk, I can hardly say with invincible dislike, for I had never tried to conquer it, from rivalry of every kind: it was, somehow, contrary to my nature. Besides, Miss Oldcastle was likely to be rich some day—apparently had money of her own even now; and was it a weakness? was it not a weakness?—I cannot tell—I writhed at the thought of being supposed to marry for money, and being made the object of such remarks as, "Ah! you see! That's the way with the clergy! They talk about poverty and faith, pretending to despise riches and to trust in God; but just put money in their way, and what chance will a poor girl have beside a rich one! It's all very well in the pulpit. It's their business to talk so. But does one of them believe what he says? or, at least, act upon it?" I think I may be a little excused for the sense of creeping cold that passed over me at the thought of such remarks as these, accompanied by compressed lips and down-drawn corners of the mouth, and reiterated nods of the head of KNOWINGNESS. But I mention this only as a repressing influence, to which I certainly should not have been such a fool as to yield, had I seen the way otherwise clear. For a man by showing how to use money, or rather simply by using money aright, may do more good than by refusing to possess it, if it comes to him in an entirely honourable way, that is, in such a case as mine, merely as an accident of his history. But I was glad to feel pretty sure that if I should be so blessed as to marry Miss Oldcastle—which at the time whereof I now write, seemed far too gorgeous a castle in the clouds ever to descend to the earth for me to enter it—the POOR of my own people would be those most likely to understand my position and feelings, and least likely to impute to me worldly motives, as paltry as they are vulgar, and altogether unworthy of a true man.

So the time went on. I called once or twice on Mr Stoddart, and found him, as I thought, better. But he would not allow that he was. Dr Duncan said he was better, and would be better still, if he would only believe it and exert himself.

He continued in the same strangely irritable humour.

CHAPTER XX. MOOD AND WILL.

Winter came apace. When we look towards winter from the last borders of autumn, it seems as if we could not encounter it, and as if it never would go over. So does threatened trouble of any kind seem to us as we look forward upon its miry ways from the last borders of the pleasant greensward on which we have hitherto been walking. But not only do both run their course, but each has its own alleviations, its own pleasures; and very marvellously does the healthy mind fit itself to the new circumstances; while to those who will bravely take up their burden and bear it, asking no more questions than just, "Is this my burden?" a thousand ministrations of nature and life will come with gentle comfortings. Across a dark verdureless field will blow a wind through the heart of the winter which will wake in the patient mind not a memory merely, but a prophecy of the spring, with a glimmer of crocus, or snow-drop, or primrose; and across the waste of tired endeavour will a gentle hope, coming he knows not whence, breathe springlike upon the heart of the man around whom life looks desolate and dreary. Well do I remember a friend of mine telling me once—he was then a labourer in the field of literature, who had not yet begun to earn his penny a day, though he worked hard—telling me how once, when a hope that had kept him active for months was suddenly quenched—a book refused on which he had spent a passion of labour—the weight of money that must be paid and could not be had, pressing him down like the coffin-lid that had lately covered the ONLY friend to whom he could have applied confidently for aid—telling me, I say, how he stood at the corner of a London street, with the rain, dripping black from the brim of his hat, the dreariest of atmospheres about him in the closing afternoon of the City, when the rich men were going home, and the poor men who worked for them were longing to follow; and how across this waste came energy and hope into his bosom, swelling thenceforth with courage to fight, and yield no ear to suggested failure. And the story would not be complete—though it is for the fact of the arrival of unexpected and apparently unfounded HOPE that I tell it—if I did not add, that, in the morning, his wife gave him a letter which their common trouble of yesterday had made her forget, and which had lain with its black border all night in the darkness unopened, waiting to tell him how the vanished friend had not forgotten him on her death-bed, but had left him enough to take him out of all those difficulties, and give him strength and time to do far better work than the book which had failed of birth.— Some of my readers may doubt whether I am more than "a wandering voice," but whatever I am, or may be thought to be, my friend's story is true.

And all this has come out of the winter that I, in the retrospect of my history, am looking forward to. It came, with its fogs, and dripping boughs, and sodden paths, and rotting leaves, and rains, and skies of weary gray; but also with its fierce red suns, shining aslant upon sheets of manna-like hoarfrost, and delicate ice-films over prisoned waters, and those white falling chaoses of perfect forms—called snow-storms—those confusions confounded of infinite symmetries.

And when the hard frost came, it brought a friend to my door. It was Mr Stoddart.

He entered my room with something of the countenance Naaman must have borne, after his flesh had come again like unto the flesh of a little child. He did not look ashamed, but his pale face looked humble and distressed. Its somewhat self-satisfied placidity had vanished, and instead of the diffused geniality which was its usual expression, it now showed traces of feeling as well as plain signs of suffering. I gave him as warm a welcome as I could, and having seated him comfortably by the fire, and found that he would take no refreshment, began to chat about the day's news, for I had just been reading the newspaper. But he showed no interest beyond what the merest politeness required. I would try something else.

"The cold weather, which makes so many invalids creep into bed, seems to have brought you out into the air, Mr Stoddart," I said.

"It has revived me, certainly."

"Indeed, one must believe that winter and cold are as beneficent, though not so genial, as summer and its warmth. Winter kills many a disease and many a noxious influence. And what is it to have the fresh green leaves of spring instead of the everlasting brown of some countries which have no winter!"

I talked thus, hoping to rouse him to conversation, and I was successful.

"I feel just as if I were coming out of a winter. Don't you think illness is

271

a kind of human winter?"

"Certainly—more or less stormy. With some a winter of snow and hail and piercing winds; with others of black frosts and creeping fogs, with now and then a glimmer of the sun."

"The last is more like mine. I feel as if I had been in a wet hole in the earth."

"And many a man," I went on, "the foliage of whose character had been turning brown and seared and dry, rattling rather than rustling in the faint hot wind of even fortunes, has come out of the winter of a weary illness with the fresh delicate buds of a new life bursting from the sun-dried bark."

"I wish it would be so with me. I know you mean me. But I don't feel my green leaves coming."

"Facts are not always indicated by feelings."

"Indeed, I hope not; nor yet feelings indicated by facts."

"I do not quite understand you."

"Well, Mr Walton, I will explain myself. I have come to tell you how sorry and ashamed I am that I behaved so badly to you every time you came to see me."

"Oh, nonsense!" I said. "It was your illness, not you."

"At least, my dear sir, the facts of my behaviour did not really represent my feelings towards you."

"I know that as well as you do. Don't say another word about it. You had the best excuse for being cross; I should have had none for being offended."

"It was only the outside of me."

"Yes, yes; I acknowledge it heartily."

"But that does not settle the matter between me and myself, Mr Walton; although, by your goodness, it settles it between me and you. It is humiliating to think that illness should so completely 'overcrow' me, that I am no more myself—lose my hold, in fact, of what I call ME—so that I am almost driven to doubt my personal identity."

"You are fond of theories, Mr Stoddart—perhaps a little too much so."

"Perhaps."

"Will you listen to one of mine?"

"With pleasure."

"It seems to me sometimes—I know it is a partial representation—as if life were a conflict between the inner force of the spirit, which lies in its faith in the unseen—and the outer force of the world, which lies in the pressure of everything it has to show us. The material, operating upon our senses, is always asserting its existence; and if our inner life is not equally vigorous, we shall be moved, urged, what is called actuated, from without, whereas all our activity ought to be from within. But sickness not only overwhelms the mind, but, vitiating all the channels of the senses, causes them to represent things as they are not, of which misrepresentations the presence, persistency, and iteration seduce the man to act from false suggestions instead of from what he knows and believes."

"Well, I understand all that. But what use am I to make of your theory?"

"I am delighted, Mr Stoddart, to hear you put the question. That is always the point.—The inward holy garrison, that of faith, which holds by the truth, by sacred facts, and not by appearances, must be strengthened and nourished and upheld, and so enabled to resist the onset of the powers without. A friend's remonstrance may appear an unkindness—a friend's jest an unfeelingness—a friend's visit an intrusion; nay, to come to higher things, during a mere headache it will appear as if there was no truth in the world, no reality but that of pain anywhere, and nothing to be desired but deliverance from it. But all such impressions caused from without—for, remember, the body and its innermost experiences are only OUTSIDE OF THE MAN—have to be met by the inner confidence of the spirit, resting in God and resisting every impulse to act according to that which APPEARS

TO IT instead of that which IT BELIEVES. Hence, Faith is thus allegorically represented: but I had better give you Spenser's description of her—Here is the 'Fairy Queen':—

> 'She was arrayed all in lily white,
>
> And in her right hand bore a cup of gold,
>
> With wine and water filled up to the height,
>
> In which a serpent did himself enfold,
>
> That horror made to all that did behold;
>
> But she no whit did change her constant mood.'

This serpent stands for the dire perplexity of things about us, at which yet Faith will not blench, acting according to what she believes, and not what shows itself to her by impression and appearance."

"I admit all that you say," returned Mr Stoddart. "But still the practical conclusion—which I understand to be, that the inward garrison must be fortified—is considerably incomplete unless we buttress it with the final HOW. How is it to be fortified? For,

> 'I have as much of this in art as you,
>
> But yet my nature could not bear it so.'

(You see I read Shakespeare as well as you, Mr Walton.) I daresay, from a certain inclination to take the opposite side, and a certain dislike to the dogmatism of the clergy—I speak generally—I may have appeared to you indifferent, but I assure you that I have laboured much to withdraw my mind from the influence of money, and ambition, and pleasure, and to turn it to the contemplation of spiritual things. Yet on the first attack of a depressing illness I cease to be a gentleman, I am rude to ladies who do their best and kindest to serve me, and I talk to the friend who comes to cheer and comfort me as if he were an idle vagrant who wanted to sell me a worthless book with the recommendation of the pretence that he wrote it himself. Now that I am in my right mind, I am ashamed of myself, ashamed that it should be possible for me to behave so, and humiliated yet besides that I have no ground of assurance that, should my illness return to-morrow, I should not behave in the same manner the day after. I want to be ALWAYS in my right mind. When I am not, I know I am not, and yet yield to the appearance of being."

"I understand perfectly what you mean, for I fancy I know a little more of illness than you do. Shall I tell you where I think the fault of your self-training lies?"

"That is just what I want. The things which it pleased me to contemplate when I was well, gave me no pleasure when I was ill. Nothing seemed the same."

"If we were always in a right mood, there would be no room for the exercise of the will. We should go by our mood and inclination only. But that is by the by.—Where you have been wrong is—that you have sought to influence your feelings only by thought and argument with yourself—and not also by contact with your fellows. Besides the ladies of whom you have spoken, I think you have hardly a friend in this neighbourhood but myself. One friend cannot afford you half experience enough to teach you the relations of life and of human needs. At best, under such circumstances, you can only have right theories: practice for realising them in yourself is nowhere. It is no more possible for a man in the present day to retire from his fellows into the cave of his religion, and thereby leave the world of his own faults and follies behind, than it was possible for the eremites of old to get close to God in virtue of declining the duties which their very birth of human father and mother laid upon them. I do not deny that you and the eremite may both come NEARER to God, in virtue of whatever is true in your desires and your worship; 'but if a man love not his brother whom he hath seen, how can he love God whom he hath not seen?'—which surely means to imply at least that to love our neighbour is a great help towards loving God. How this love is to come about without intercourse, I do not see. And how without this love we are to bear up from within against the thousand irritations to which, especially in sickness, our unavoidable relations with humanity will expose us, I cannot tell either."

"But," returned Mr Stoddart, "I had had a true regard for you, and some friendly communication with you. If human intercourse were what is required in my case, how should I fail just with respect to the only man with whom I had held such intercourse?"

"Because the relations in which you stood with me were those of the individual, not of the race. You like me, because I am fortunate enough to please you—to be a gentleman, I hope—to be a man of some education, and capable of understanding, or at least docile enough to try to understand, what you tell me of your plans and pursuits. But you do not feel any relation to me on the ground of my humanity—that God made me, and therefore I am your brother. It is not because we grow out of the same stem, but merely because my leaf is a little like your own that you draw to me. Our Lord took on Him the nature of man: you will only regard your individual attractions. Disturb your liking and your love vanishes."

"You are severe."

"I don't mean really vanishes, but disappears for the time. Yet you will confess you have to wait till, somehow, you know not how, it comes back again—of itself, as it were."

"Yes, I confess. To my sorrow, I find it so."

"Let me tell you the truth, Mr Stoddart. You seem to me to have been hitherto only a dilettante or amateur in spiritual matters. Do not imagine I mean a hypocrite. Very far from it. The word amateur itself suggests a real interest, though it may be of a superficial nature. But in religion one must be all there. You seem to me to have taken much interest in unusual forms of theory, and in mystical speculations, to which in themselves I make no objection. But to be content with those, instead of knowing God himself, or to substitute a general amateur friendship towards the race for the love of your neighbour, is a mockery which will always manifest itself to an honest mind like yours in such failure and disappointment in your own character as you are now lamenting, if not indeed in some mode far more alarming, because gross and terrible."

"Am I to understand you, then, that intercourse with one's neighbours ought to take the place of meditation?"

"By no means: but ought to go side by side with it, if you would have at once a healthy mind to judge and the means of either verifying your speculations or discovering their falsehood."

"But where am I to find such friends besides yourself with whom to hold spiritual communion?"

"It is the communion of spiritual deeds, deeds of justice, of mercy, of humility—the kind word, the cup of cold water, the visitation in sickness, the lending of money—not spiritual conference or talk, that I mean: the latter will come of itself where it is natural. You would soon find that it is not only to those whose spiritual windows are of the same shape as your own that you are neighbour: there is one poor man in my congregation who knows more—practically, I mean, too—of spirituality of mind than any of us. Perhaps you could not teach him much, but he could teach you. At all events, our neighbours are just those round about us. And the most ignorant man in a little place like Marshmallows, one like you with leisure ought to know and understand, and have some good influence upon: he is your brother whom you are bound to care for and elevate—I do not mean socially, but really, in himself—if it be possible. You ought at least to get into some simple human relation with him, as you would with the youngest and most ignorant of your brothers and sisters born of the same father and mother; approaching him, not with pompous lecturing or fault-finding, still less with that abomination called condescension, but with the humble service of the elder to the younger, in whatever he may be helped by you without injury to him. Never was there a more injurious mistake than that it is the business of the clergy only to have the care of souls."

"But that would be endless. It would leave me no time for myself."

"Would that be no time for yourself spent in leading a noble, Christian life; in verifying the words of our Lord by doing them; in building your house on the rock of action instead of the sands of theory; in widening your own being by entering into the nature, thoughts, feelings, even fancies of those around you? In such intercourse you would find health radiating into your own bosom; healing sympathies springing up in the most barren acquaintance; channels opened for the in-rush of truth into your own mind; and opportunities afforded for the exercise of that self-discipline, the lack of which led to the failures which you now bemoan. Soon then would you have cause to wonder how much some of your speculations had fallen into the background, simply because the truth, showing itself grandly true, had so filled and occupied your mind that it left no room for anxiety about such questions as, while secured in the interest all reality gives, were yet dwarfed by the side of it. Nothing, I repeat, so much as humble ministration to your neighbours, will help you to that perfect love of God which casteth out fear; nothing but the love of God—that God revealed in Christ—will make you able to love your neighbour aright; and the Spirit of God, which alone gives might for any good, will by these loves, which are life, strengthen you at last to believe in the light even in the midst of darkness; to hold the resolution formed in health when sickness has altered the appearance of everything around you; and to feel tenderly towards your fellow, even when you yourself are plunged in dejection or racked with pain.—But," I said, "I fear I have transgressed the bounds of all propriety by enlarging upon this matter as I have done. I can only say I have spoken in proportion to my feeling of its weight and truth."

"I thank you, heartily," returned Mr Stoddart, rising. "And I promise you at least to think over what you have been saying—I hope to be in my old place in the organ-loft next Sunday."

So he was. And Miss Oldcastle was in the pew with her mother. Nor did she go any more to Addicehead to church.

CHAPTER XXI. THE DEVIL IN THOMAS WEIR.

As the winter went on, it was sad to look on the evident though slow decline of Catherine Weir. It seemed as if the dead season was dragging her to its bosom, to lay her among the leaves of past summers. She was still to be found in the shop, or appeared in it as often as the bell suspended over the door rang to announce the entrance of a customer; but she was terribly worn, and her step indicated much weakness. Nor had the signs of restless trouble diminished as these tide-marks indicated ebbing strength. There was the same dry fierce fire in her eyes; the same forceful compression of her lips; the same evidences of brooding over some one absorbing thought or feeling. She seemed to me, and to Dr Duncan as well, to be dying of resentment. Would nobody do anything for her? I thought. Would not her father help her? He had got more gentle now; whence I had reason to hope that Christian principles and feelings had begun to rise and operate in him; while surely the influence of his son must, by this time, have done something not only to soften his character generally, but to appease the anger he had cherished towards the one ewe-lamb, against which, having wandered away into the desert place, he had closed and barred the door of the sheep-fold. I would go and see him, and try what could be done for her.

I may be forgiven here if I make the remark that I cannot help thinking that what measure of success I had already had with my people, was partly owing to this, that when I thought of a thing and had concluded it might do, I very seldom put off the consequent action. I found I was wrong sometimes, and that the particular action did no good; but thus movement was kept up in my operative nature, preventing it from sinking towards the inactivity to which I was but too much inclined. Besides, to find out what will not do, is a step towards finding out what will do. Moreover, an attempt in itself unsuccessful may set something or other in motion that will help.

My present attempt turned out one of my failures, though I cannot think that it would have been better left unmade.

A red rayless sun, which one might have imagined sullen and disconsolate because he could not make the dead earth smile into flowers, was looking through the frosty fog of the winter morning as I walked across the bridge to find Thomas Weir in his workshop. The poplars stood like goblin sentinels, with black heads, upon which the long hair stood on end, all along the dark cold river. Nature looked like a life out of which the love has vanished. I turned from it and hastened on.

Thomas was busy working with a spoke-sheave at the spoke of a cart-wheel. How curiously the smallest visual fact will sometimes keep its place in the memory, when it cannot with all earnestness of endeavour recall a thought—a far more important fact! That will come again only when its time comes first.

"A cold morning, Thomas," I called from the door.

"I can always keep myself warm, sir," returned Thomas, cheerfully.

"What are you doing, Tom?" I said, going up to him first.

"A little job for myself, sir. I'm making a few bookshelves."

"I want to have a little talk with your father. Just step out in a minute or so, and let me have half-an-hour."

"Yes, sir, certainly."

I then went to the other end of the shop, for, curiously, as it seemed to me, although father and son were on the best of terms, they always worked as far from each other as the shop would permit, and it was a very large room.

"It is not easy always to keep warm through and through, Thomas," I said.

I suppose my tone revealed to his quick perceptions that "more was meant than met the ear." He looked up from his work, his tool filled with an uncompleted shaving.

"And when the heart gets cold," I went on, "it is not easily warmed again. The fire's hard to light there, Thomas."

Still he looked at me, stooping over his work, apparently with a presentiment of what was coming.

"I fear there is no way of lighting it again, except the blacksmith's way."

"Hammering the iron till it is red-hot, you mean, sir?"

"I do. When a man's heart has grown cold, the blows of affliction must fall thick and heavy before the fire can be got that will light it.—When did you see your daughter Catherine, Thomas?"

His head dropped, and he began to work as if for bare life. Not a word came from the form now bent over his tool as if he had never lifted himself up since he first began in the morning. I could just see that his face was deadly pale, and his lips compressed like those of one of the violent who take the kingdom of heaven by force. But it was for no such agony of effort that his were thus closed. He went on working till the silence became so lengthened that it seemed settled into the endless. I felt embarrassed. To break a silence is sometimes as hard as to break a spell. What Thomas would have done or said if he had not had this safety-valve of bodily exertion, I cannot even imagine.

"Thomas," I said, at length, laying my hand on his shoulder, "you are not going to part company with me, I hope?"

"You drive a man too far, sir. I've given in more to you than ever I did to man, sir; and I don't know that I oughtn't to be ashamed of it. But you don't know where to stop. If we lived a thousand years you would be driving a man on to the last. And there's no good in that, sir. A man must be at peace somewhen."

"The question is, Thomas, whether I would be driving you ON or BACK. You and I too MUST go on or back. I want to go on myself, and to make you go on too. I don't want to be parted from you now or then."

"That's all very well, sir, and very kind, I don't doubt; but, as I said afore, a man must be at peace SOMEWHEN."

"That's what I want so much that I want you to go on. Peace! I trust in God we shall both have it one day, SOMEWHEN, as you say. Have you got this peace so plentifully now that you are satisfied as you are? You will never get it but by going on."

"I do not think there is any good got in stirring a puddle. Let by-gones be by-gones. You make a mistake, sir, in rousing an anger which I would willingly let sleep."

"Better a wakeful anger, and a wakeful conscience with it, than an anger sunk into indifference, and a sleeping dog of a conscience that will not bark. To have ceased to be angry is not one step nearer to your daughter. Better strike her, abuse her, with the chance of a kiss to follow. Ah, Thomas, you are

281

like Jonas with his gourd."

"I don't see what that has to do with it."

"I will tell you. You are fierce in wrath at the disgrace to your family. Your pride is up in arms. You don't care for the misery of your daughter, who, the more wrong she has done, is the more to be pitied by a father's heart. Your pride, I say, is all that you care about. The wrong your daughter has done, you care nothing about; or you would have taken her to your arms years ago, in the hope that the fervour of your love would drive the devil out of her and make her repent. I say it is not the wrong, but the disgrace you care for. The gourd of your pride is withered, and yet you will water it with your daughter's misery."

"Go out of my shop," he cried; "or I may say what I should be sorry for."

I turned at once and left him. I found young Tom round the corner, leaning against the wall, and reading his Virgil.

"Don't speak to your father, Tom," I said, "for a while. I've put him out of temper. He will be best left alone."

He looked frightened.

"There's no harm done, Tom, my boy. I've been talking to him about your sister. He must have time to think over what I have said to him."

"I see, sir; I see."

"Be as attentive to him as you can."

"I will, sir."

It was not alone resentment at my interference that had thus put the poor fellow beside himself, I was certain: I had called up all the old misery—set the wound bleeding again. Shame was once more wide awake and tearing at his heart. That HIS daughter should have done so! For she had been his pride. She had been the belle of the village, and very lovely; but having been apprenticed to a dressmaker in Addicehead, had, after being there about a year and a half, returned home, apparently in a decline. After the birth of her child, however, she had, to her own disappointment, and no doubt to that of her father as well, begun to recover. What a time of wretchedness it must have been to both of them until she left his house, one can imagine. Most likely the misery of the father vented itself in greater unkindness than he felt, which, sinking into the proud nature she had derived from him, roused such a resentment as rarely if ever can be thoroughly appeased until Death comes in to help the reconciliation. How often has an old love blazed up again under the blowing of his cold breath, and sent the spirit warm at heart into the regions of the unknown! She never would utter a word to reveal the name or condition of him by whom she had been wronged. To his child, as long as he drew his life from her, she behaved with strange alternations of dislike and passionate affection; after which season the latter began to diminish in violence, and the former to become more fixed, till at length, by the time I had made their acquaintance, her feelings seemed to have settled into what would have been indifference but for the constant reminder of her shame and her wrong together, which his very presence necessarily was.

They were not only the gossips of the village who judged that the fact of Addicehead's being a garrison town had something to do with the fate that had befallen her; a fate by which, in its very spring-time, when its flowers were loveliest, and hope was strongest for its summer, her life was changed into the dreary wind-swept, rain-sodden moor. The man who can ACCEPT such a sacrifice from a woman,—I say nothing of WILING it from her—is, in his meanness, selfishness, and dishonour, contemptible as the Pharisee who, with his long prayers, devours the widow's house. He leaves her desolate, while he walks off free. Would to God a man like the great-hearted, pure-bodied Milton, a man whom young men are compelled to respect, would in this our age, utter such a word as, making "mad the guilty," if such grace might be accorded them, would "appal the free," lest they too should fall into such a mire of selfish dishonour!

CHAPTER XXII. THE DEVIL IN CATHERINE WEIR.

About this time my father was taken ill, and several journeys to London followed. It is only as vicar that I am writing these memorials—for such they should be called, rather than ANNALS, though certainly the use of the latter word has of late become vague enough for all convenience—therefore I have said nothing about my home-relations; but I must just mention here that I had a half-sister, about half my own age, whose anxiety during my father's illness rendered my visits more frequent than perhaps they would have been from my own. But my sister was right in her anxiety. My father grew worse, and in December he died. I will not eulogize one so dear to me. That he was no common man will appear from the fact of his unconventionality and justice in leaving his property to my sister, saying in his will that he had done all I could require of him, in giving me a good education; and that, men having means in their power which women had not, it was unjust to the latter to make them, without a choice, dependent upon the former. After the funeral, my sister, feeling it impossible to remain in the house any longer, begged me to take her with me. So, after arranging affairs, we set out, and reached Marshmallows on New Year's Day.

My sister being so much younger than myself, her presence in my house made very little change in my habits. She came into my ways without any difficulty, so that I did not experience the least restraint from having to consider her. And I soon began to find her of considerable service among the poor and sick of my flock, the latter class being more numerous this winter on account of the greater severity of the weather.

I now began to note a change in the habits of Catherine Weir. As far as I remember, I had never up to this time seen her out of her own house, except in church, at which she had been a regular attendant for many weeks. Now, however, I began to meet her when and where I least expected—I do not say often, but so often as to make me believe she went wandering about frequently. It was always at night, however, and always in stormy weather. The marvel was, not that a sick woman could be there—for a sick woman may be able to do anything; but that she could do so more than once—that was the marvel. At the same time, I began to miss her from church.

Possibly my reader may wonder how I came to have the chance of meeting any one again and again at night and in stormy weather. I can relieve him from the difficulty. Odd as it will appear to some readers, I had naturally a predilection for rough weather. I think I enjoyed fighting with a storm in winter nearly as much as lying on the grass under a beech-tree in summer. Possibly this assertion may seem strange to one likewise who has remarked the ordinary peaceableness of my disposition. But he may have done me the justice to remark at the same time, that I have some considerable pleasure in fighting the devil, though none in fighting my fellow-man, even in the ordinary form of disputation in which it is not heart's blood, but soul's blood, that is so often shed. Indeed there are many controversies far more immoral, as to the manner in which they are conducted, than a brutal prize-fight. There is, however, a pleasure of its own in conflict; and I have always experienced a certain indescribable, though I believe not at all unusual exaltation, even in struggling with a well-set, thoroughly roused storm of wind and snow or rain. The sources of this by no means unusual delight, I will not stay to examine, indicating only that I believe the sources are deep.—I was now quite well, and had no reason to fear bad consequences from the indulgence of this surely innocent form of the love of strife.

But I find I must give another reason as well, if I would be thoroughly honest with my reader. The fact was, that as I had recovered strength, I had become more troubled and restless about Miss Oldcastle. I could not see how I was to make any progress towards her favour. There seemed a barrier as insurmountable as intangible between her and me. The will of one woman came between and parted us, and that will was as the magic line over which no effort of will or strength could enable the enchanted knight to make a single stride. And this consciousness of being fettered by insensible and infrangible bonds, this need of doing something with nothing tangible in the reach of the outstretched hand, so worked upon my mind, that it naturally sought relief, as often as the elemental strife arose, by mingling unconstrained with the tumult of the night.—Will my readers find it hard to believe that this disquietude of mind should gradually sink away as the hours of Saturday glided down into night, and the day of my best labour drew nigh? Or will they answer, "We believe it easily; for then you could at least see the lady, and that comforted you?" Whatever it was that quieted me, not the less have I to thank God for it.

All might have been so different. What a fearful thing would it have been for me to have found my mind so full of my own cares, that I was unable to do God's work and bear my neighbour's burden! But even then I would have cried to Him, and said, "I know Thee that Thou art NOT a hard master."

Now, however, that I have quite accounted, as I believe, by the peculiarity both of my disposition and circumstances, for unusual wanderings under conditions when most people consider themselves fortunate within doors, I must return to Catherine Weir, the eccentricity of whose late behaviour, being in the particulars discussed identical with that of mine, led to the necessity for the explanation of my habits given above.

One January afternoon, just as twilight was folding her gray cloak about her, and vanishing in the night, the wind blowing hard from the south-west, melting the snow under foot, and sorely disturbing the dignity of the one grand old cedar which stood before my study window, and now filled my room with the great sweeps of its moaning, I felt as if the elements were calling me, and rose to obey the summons. My sister was, by this time, so accustomed to my going out in all weathers, that she troubled me with no expostulation. My spirits began to rise the moment I was in the wind. Keen, and cold, and unsparing, it swept through the leafless branches around me, with a different hiss for every tree that bent, and swayed, and tossed in its torrent. I made my way to the gate and out upon the road, and then, turning to the right, away from the village, I sought a kind of common, open and treeless, the nearest approach to a moor that there was in the county, I believe, over which a wind like this would sweep unstayed by house, or shrub, or fence, the only shelter it afforded lying in the inequalities of its surface.

I had walked with my head bent low against the blast, for the better part of a mile, fighting for every step of the way, when, coming to a deep cut in the common, opening at right angles from the road, whence at some time or other a large quantity of sand had been carted, I turned into its defence to recover my breath, and listen to the noise of the wind in the fierce rush of its sea over the open channel of the common. And I remember I was thinking with myself: "If the air would only become faintly visible for a moment, what a sight it would be of waste grandeur with its thousands of billowing eddies, and self-involved, conflicting, and swallowing whirlpools from the sea-bottom of this common!" when, with my imagination resting on the fancied vision, I was startled by such a moan as seemed about to break into a storm of passionate cries, but was followed by the words:

"O God! I cannot bear it longer. Hast thou NO help for me?"

Instinctively almost I knew that Catherine Weir was beside me, though I could not see where she was. In a moment more, however, I thought I could distinguish through the darkness—imagination no doubt filling up the truth of its form—a figure crouching in such an attitude of abandoned despair as recalled one of Flaxman's outlines, the body bent forward over the drawn-up knees, and the face thus hidden even from the darkness. I could not help saying to myself, as I took a step or two towards her, "What is thy trouble to hers!"

I may here remark that I had come to the conclusion, from pondering over her case, that until a yet deeper and bitterer resentment than that which she bore to her father was removed, it would be of no use attacking the latter. For the former kept her in a state of hostility towards her whole race: with herself at war she had no gentle thoughts, no love for her kind; but ever

"She fed her wound with fresh-renewed bale"

from every hurt that she received from or imagined to be offered her by anything human. So I had resolved that the next time I had an opportunity of speaking to her, I would make an attempt to probe the evil to its root, though I had but little hope, I confess, of doing any good. And now when I heard her say, "Hast thou NO help for me?" I went near her with the words:

"God has, indeed, help for His own offspring. Has He not suffered that He might help? But you have not yet forgiven."

When I began to speak, she gave a slight start: she was far too miserable to be terrified at anything. Before I had finished, she stood erect on her feet, facing me with the whiteness of her face glimmering through the blackness of the night.

"I ask Him for peace," she said, "and He sends me more torment."

And I thought of Ahab when he said, "Hast thou found me, O mine enemy?"

"If we had what we asked for always, we should too often find it was not what we wanted, after all."

"You will not leave me alone," she said. "It is too bad."

Poor woman! It was well for her she could pray to God in her trouble; for she could scarcely endure a word from her fellow-man. She, despairing before God, was fierce as a tigress to her fellow-sinner who would stretch a hand to help her out of the mire, and set her beside him on the rock which he felt firm under his own feet.

"I will not leave you alone, Catherine," I said, feeling that I must at length assume another tone of speech with her who resisted gentleness. "Scorn my interference as you will," I said, "I have yet to give an account of you. And I have to fear lest my Master should require your blood at my hands. I did not follow you here, you may well believe me; but I have found you here, and I must speak."

All this time the wind was roaring overhead. But in the hollow was stillness, and I was so near her, that I could hear every word she said, although she spoke in a low compressed tone.

"Have you a right to persecute me," she said, "because I am unhappy?"

"I have a right, and, more than a right, I have a duty to aid your better self against your worse. You, I fear, are siding with your worse self."

"You judge me hard. I have had wrongs that—"

And here she stopped in a way that let me know she WOULD say no more.

"That you have had wrongs, and bitter wrongs, I do not for a moment doubt. And him who has done you most wrong, you will not forgive."

"No."

"No. Not even for the sake of Him who, hanging on the tree, after all

288

the bitterness of blows and whipping, and derision, and rudest gestures and taunts, even when the faintness of death was upon Him, cried to His Father to forgive their cruelty. He asks you to forgive the man who wronged you, and you will not—not even for Him! Oh, Catherine, Catherine!"

"It is very easy to talk, Mr Walton," she returned with forced but cool scorn.

"Tell me, then," I said, "have YOU nothing to repent of? Have YOU done no wrong in this same miserable matter?"

"I do not understand you, sir," she said, freezingly, petulantly, not sure, perhaps, or unwilling to believe, that I meant what I did mean.

I was fully resolved to be plain with her now.

"Catherine Weir," I said, "did not God give you a house to keep fair and pure for Him? Did you keep it such?"

"He told me lies," she cried fiercely, with a cry that seemed to pierce through the storm over our heads, up towards the everlasting justice. "He lied, and I trusted. For his sake I sinned, and he threw me from him."

"You gave him what was not yours to give. What right had you to cast your pearl before a swine? But dare you say it was ALL FOR HIS SAKE you did it? Was it ALL self-denial? Was there no self-indulgence?"

She made a broken gesture of lifting her hands to her head, let them drop by her side, and said nothing.

"You knew you were doing wrong. You felt it even more than he did. For God made you with a more delicate sense of purity, with a shrinking from the temptation, with a womanly foreboding of disgrace, to help you to hold the cup of your honour steady, which yet you dropped on the ground. Do not seek refuge in the cant about a woman's weakness. The strength of the woman is as needful to her womanhood as the strength of the man is to his manhood; and a woman is just as strong as she will be. And now, instead of humbling yourself before your Father in heaven, whom you have wronged more even than your father on earth, you rage over your injuries and cherish

289

hatred against him who wronged you. But I will go yet further, and show you, in God's name, that you wronged your seducer. For you were his keeper, as he was yours. What if he had found a noble-hearted girl who also trusted him entirely—just until she knew she ought not to listen to him a moment longer? who, when his love showed itself less than human, caring but for itself, rose in the royalty of her maidenhood, and looked him in the face? Would he not have been ashamed before her, and so before himself, seeing in the glass of her dignity his own contemptibleness? But instead of such a woman he found you, who let him do as he would. No redemption for him in you. And now he walks the earth the worse for you, defiled by your spoil, glorying in his poor victory over you, despising all women for your sake, unrepentant and proud, ruining others the easier that he has already ruined you."

"He does! he does!" she shrieked; "but I will have my revenge. I can and I will."

And, darting past me, she rushed out into the storm. I followed, and could just see that she took the way to the village. Her dim shape went down the wind before me into the darkness. I followed in the same direction, fast and faster, for the wind was behind me, and a vague fear which ever grew in my heart urged me to overtake her. What had I done? To what might I not have driven her? And although all I had said was true, and I had spoken from motives which, as far as I knew my own heart, I could not condemn, yet, as I sped after her, there came a reaction of feeling from the severity with which I had displayed her own case against her. "Ah! poor sister," I thought, "was it for me thus to reproach thee who had suffered already so fiercely? If the Spirit speaking in thy heart could not win thee, how should my words of hard accusation, true though they were, every one of them, rouse in thee anything but the wrath that springs from shame? Should I not have tried again, and yet again, to waken thy love; and then a sweet and healing shame, like that of her who bathed the Master's feet with her tears, would have bred fresh love, and no wrath."

But again I answered for myself, that my heart had not been the less tender towards her that I had tried to humble her, for it was that she might slip from under the net of her pride. Even when my tongue spoke the hardest things I could find, my heart was yearning over her. If I could but make her feel that she too had been wrong, would not the sense of common wrong between them help her to forgive? And with the first motion of willing pardon, would not a spring of tenderness, grief, and hope, burst from her poor old dried-up heart, and make it young and fresh once more! Thus I reasoned with myself as I followed her back through the darkness.

The wind fell a little as we came near the village, and the rain began to come down in torrents. There must have been a moon somewhere behind the clouds, for the darkness became less dense, and I began to fancy I could again see the dim shape which had rushed from me. I increased my speed, and became certain of it. Suddenly, her strength giving way, or her foot stumbling over something in the road, she fell to the earth with a cry.

I was beside her in a moment. She was insensible. I did what I could for her, and in a few minutes she began to come to herself.

"Where am I? Who is it?" she asked, listlessly.

When she found who I was, she made a great effort to rise, and succeeded.

"You must take my arm," I said, "and I will help you to the vicarage."

"I will go home," she answered.

"Lean on me now, at least; for you must get somewhere."

"What does it matter?" she said, in such a tone of despair, that it went to my very heart.

A wild half-cry, half-sob followed, and then she took my arm, and said nothing more. Nor did I trouble her with any words, except, when we readied the gate, to beg her to come into the vicarage instead of going home. But she would not listen to me, and so I took her home.

She pulled the key of the shop from her pocket. Her hand trembled so that I took it from her, and opened the door. A candle with a long snuff was flickering on the counter; and stretched out on the counter, with his head about a foot from the candle, lay little Gerard, fast asleep.

"Ah, little darling!" I said in my heart, "this is not much like painting the sky yet. But who knows?" And as I uttered the commonplace question in my mind, in my mind it was suddenly changed into the half of a great dim prophecy by the answer which arose to it there, for the answer was "God."

I lifted the little fellow in my arms. He had fallen asleep weeping, and his face was dirty, and streaked with the channels of his tears. Catherine had snuffed the candle, and now stood with it in her hand, waiting for me to go. But, without heeding her, I bore my child to the door that led to their dwelling. I had never been up those stairs before, and therefore knew nothing of the way. But without offering any opposition, his mother followed, and lighted me. What a sad face of suffering and strife it was upon which that dim light fell! She set the candle down upon the table of a small room at the top of the stairs, which might have been comfortable enough but that it was neglected and disordered; and now I saw that she did not even have her child to sleep with her, for his crib stood in a corner of this their sitting-room.

I sat down on a haircloth couch, and proceeded to undress little Gerard, trying as much as I could not to wake him. In this I was almost successful. Catherine stood staring at me without saying a word. She looked dazed, perhaps from the effects of her fall. But she brought me his nightgown notwithstanding. Just as I had finished putting it on, and was rising to lay him in his crib, he opened his eyes, and looked at me; then gave a hurried look round, as if for his mother; then threw his arms about my neck and kissed me. I laid him down and the same moment he was fast asleep. In the morning it would not be even a dream to him.

"Now," I thought, "you are safe for the night, poor fatherless child. Even your mother's hardness will not make you sad now. Perhaps the heavenly Father will send you loving dreams."

I turned to Catherine, and bade her good-night. She just put her hand in mine; but, instead of returning my leave-taking, said:

"Do not fancy you will get the better of me, Mr Walton, by being kind to that boy. I will have my revenge, and I know how. I am only waiting my time. When he is just going to drink, I will dash it from his hand. I will. At the altar I will."

Her eyes were flashing almost with madness, and she made fierce gestures with her arm. I saw that argument was useless.

"You loved him once, Catherine," I said. "Love him again. Love him better. Forgive him. Revenge is far worse than anything you have done yet."

"What do I care? Why should I care?"

And she laughed terribly.

I made haste to leave the room and the house; but I lingered for nearly an hour about the place before I could make up my mind to go home, so much was I afraid lest she should do something altogether insane.

But at length I saw the candle appear in the shop, which was some relief to my anxiety; and reflecting that her one consuming thought of revenge was some security for her conduct otherwise, I went home.

That night my own troubles seemed small to me, and I did not brood over them at all. My mind was filled with the idea of the sad misery which, rather than in which, that poor woman was; and I prayed for her as for a desolate human world whose sun had deserted the heavens, whose fair fields, rivers, and groves were hardening into the frost of death, and all their germs of hope becoming but portions of the lifeless mass. "If I am sorrowful," I said, "God lives none the less. And His will is better than mine, yea, is my hidden and perfected will. In Him is my life. His will be done. What, then, is my trouble compared to hers? I will not sink into it and be selfish."

In the morning my first business was to inquire after her. I found her in the shop, looking very ill, and obstinately reserved. Gerard sat in a corner, looking as far from happy as a child of his years could look. As I left the shop he crept out with me.

"Gerard, come back," cried his mother.

"I will not take him away," I said.

The boy looked up in my face, as if he wanted to whisper to me, and I

293

stooped to listen.

"I dreamed last night," said the boy, "that a big angel with white wings came and took me out of my bed, and carried me high, high up—so high that I could not dream any more."

"We shall be carried up so high one day, Gerard, my boy, that we shall not want to dream any more. For we shall be carried up to God himself. Now go back to your mother."

He obeyed at once, and I went on through the village.

CHAPTER XXIII. THE DEVIL IN THE VICAR.

I wanted just to pass the gate, and look up the road towards Oldcastle Hall. I thought to see nothing but the empty road between the leafless trees, lying there like a dead stream that would not bear me on to the "sunny pleasure-dome with caves of ice" that lay beyond. But just as I reached the gate, Miss Oldcastle came out of the lodge, where I learned afterwards the woman that kept the gate was ill.

When she saw me she stopped, and I entered hurriedly, and addressed her. But I could say nothing better than the merest commonplaces. For her old manner, which I had almost forgotten, a certain coldness shadowed with haughtiness, whose influence I had strongly felt when I began to make her acquaintance, had returned. I cannot make my reader understand how this could be blended with the sweetness in her face and the gentleness of her manners; but there the opposites were, and I could feel them both. There was likewise a certain drawing of herself away from me, which checked the smallest advance on my part; so that—I wonder at it now, but so it was—after a few words of very ordinary conversation, I bade her good morning and went away, feeling like "a man forbid"—as if I had done her some wrong, and she had chidden me for it. What a stone lay in my breast! I could hardly breathe for it. What could have caused her to change her manner towards me? I had made no advance; I could not have offended her. Yet there she glided up the road, and here stood I, outside the gate. That road was now a flowing river that bore from me the treasure of the earth, while my boat was spell-bound, and could not follow. I would run after her, fall at her feet, and intreat to

294

know wherein I had offended her. But there I stood enchanted, and there she floated away between the trees; till at length she turned the slow sweep, and I, breathing deep as she vanished from my sight, turned likewise, and walked back the dreary way to the village. And now I knew that I had never been miserable in my life before. And I knew, too, that I had never loved her as I loved her now.

But, as I had for the last ten years of my life been striving to be a right will, with a thousand failures and forgetfulnesses every one of those years, while yet the desire grew stronger as hope recovered from every failure, I would now try to do my work as if nothing had happened to incapacitate me for it. So I went on to fulfil the plan with which I had left home, including, as it did, a visit to Thomas Weir, whom I had not seen in his own shop since he had ordered me out of it. This, as far as I was concerned, was more accidental than intentional. I had, indeed, abstained from going to him for a while, in order to give him time TO COME ROUND; but then circumstances which I have recorded intervened to prevent me; so that as yet no advance had been made on my part any more than on his towards a reconciliation; which, however, could have been such only on one side, for I had not been in the least offended by the way he had behaved to me, and needed no reconciliation. To tell the truth, I was pleased to find that my words had had force enough with him to rouse his wrath. Anything rather than indifference! That the heart of the honest man would in the end right me, I could not doubt; in the meantime I would see whether a friendly call might not improve the state of affairs. Till he yielded to the voice within him, however, I could not expect that our relation to each other would be quite restored. As long as he resisted his conscience, and knew that I sided with his conscience, it was impossible he should regard me with peaceful eyes, however much he might desire to be friendly with me.

I found him busy, as usual, for he was one of the most diligent men I have ever known. But his face was gloomy, and I thought or fancied that the old scorn had begun once more to usurp the expression of it. Young Tom was not in the shop.

"It is a long time since I saw you, now, Thomas."

"I can hardly wonder at that," he returned, as if he were trying to do me justice; but his eyes dropped, and he resumed his work, and said no more. I thought it better to make no reference to the past even by assuring him that it was not from resentment that I had been a stranger.

"How is Tom?" I asked.

"Well enough," he returned. Then, with a smile of peevishness not unmingled with contempt, he added: "He's getting too uppish for me. I don't think the Latin agrees with him."

I could not help suspecting at once how the matter stood—namely, that the father, unhappy in his conduct to his daughter, and unable to make up his mind to do right with regard to her, had been behaving captiously and unjustly to his son, and so had rendered himself more miserable than ever.

"Perhaps he finds it too much for him without me," I said, evasively; "but I called to-day partly to inform him that I am quite ready now to recommence our readings together; after which I hope you will find the Latin agree with him better."

"I wish you would let him alone, sir—I mean, take no more trouble about him. You see I can't do as you want me; I wasn't made to go another man's way; and so it's very hard—more than I can bear—to be under so much obligation to you."

"But you mistake me altogether, Thomas. It is for the lad's own sake that I want to go on reading with him. And you won't interfere between him and any use I can be of to him. I assure you, to have you go my way instead of your own is the last thing I could wish, though I confess I do wish very much that you would choose the right way for your own way."

He made me no answer, but maintained a sullen silence.

"Thomas," I said at length, "I had thought you were breaking every bond of Satan that withheld you from entering into the kingdom of heaven; but I fear he has strengthened his bands and holds you now as much a captive as ever. So it is not even your own way you are walking in, but his."

"It's no use your trying to frighten me. I don't believe in the devil."

"It is God I want you to believe in. And I am not going to dispute with you now about whether there is a devil or not. In a matter of life and death we have no time for settling every disputed point."

"Life or death! What do you mean?"

"I mean that whether you believe there is a devil or not, you KNOW there is an evil power in your mind dragging you down. I am not speaking in generals; I mean NOW, and you know as to what I mean it. And if you yield to it, that evil power, whatever may be your theory about it, will drag you down to death. It is a matter of life or death, I repeat, not of theory about the devil."

"Well, I always did say, that if you once give a priest an inch he'll take an ell; and I am sorry I forgot it for once."

Having said this, he shut up his mouth in a manner that indicated plainly enough he would not open it again for some time. This, more than his speech, irritated me, and with a mere "good morning," I walked out of the shop.

No sooner was I in the open air than I knew that I too, I as well as poor Thomas Weir, was under a spell; knew that I had gone to him before I had recovered sufficiently from the mingled disappointment and mortification of my interview with Miss Oldcastle; that while I spoke to him I was not speaking with a whole heart; that I had been discharging a duty as if I had been discharging a musket; that, although I had spoken the truth, I had spoken it ungraciously and selfishly.

I could not bear it. I turned instantly and went back into the shop.

"Thomas, my friend," I said, holding out my hand, "I beg your pardon. I was wrong. I spoke to you as I ought not. I was troubled in my own mind, and that made me lose my temper and be rude to you, who are far more troubled than I am. Forgive me!"

He did not take my hand at first, but stared at me as if, not comprehending me, he supposed that I was backing up what I had said last with more of the same sort. But by the time I had finished he saw what I meant; his countenance altered and looked as if the evil spirit were about to depart from him; he held out his hand, gave mine a great grasp, dropped his head, went on with his work, and said never a word.

I went out of the shop once more, but in a greatly altered mood.

On the way home, I tried to find out how it was that I had that morning failed so signally. I had little virtue in keeping my temper, because it was naturally very even; therefore I had the more shame in losing it. I had borne all my uneasiness about Miss Oldcastle without, as far as I knew, transgressing in this fashion till this very morning. Were great sorrows less hurtful to the temper than small disappointments? Yes, surely. But Shakespeare represents Brutus, after hearing of the sudden death of his wife, as losing his temper with Cassius to a degree that bewildered the latter, who said he did not know that Brutus could have been so angry. Is this consistent with the character of the stately-minded Brutus, or with the dignity of sorrow? It is. For the loss of his wife alone would have made him only less irritable; but the whole weight of an army, with its distracting cares and conflicting interests, pressed upon him; and the battle of an empire was to be fought at daybreak, so that he could not be alone with his grief. Between the silence of death in his mind, and the roar of life in his brain, he became irritable.

Looking yet deeper into it, I found that till this morning I had experienced no personal mortification with respect to Miss Oldcastle. It was not the mere disappointment of having no more talk with her, for the sight of her was a blessing I had not in the least expected, that had worked upon me, but the fact that she had repelled or seemed to repel me. And thus I found that self was at the root of the wrong I had done to one over whose mental condition, especially while I was telling him the unwelcome truth, I ought to have been as tender as a mother over her wounded child. I could not say that it was wrong to feel disappointed or even mortified; but something was wrong when one whose especial business it was to serve his people in the name of Him who was full of grace and truth, made them suffer because of his own inward pain.

No sooner had I settled this in my mind than my trouble returned with a sudden pang. Had I actually seen her that morning, and spoken to her, and left her with a pain in my heart? What if that face of hers was doomed ever to bring with it such a pain—to be ever to me no more than a lovely vision radiating grief? If so, I would endure in silence and as patiently as I could, trying to make up for the lack of brightness in my own fate by causing more brightness in the fate of others. I would at least keep on trying to do my work.

That moment I felt a little hand poke itself into mine. I looked down, and there was Gerard Weir looking up in my face. I found myself in the midst of the children coming out of school, for it was Saturday, and a half-holiday. He smiled in my face, and I hope I smiled in his; and so, hand in hand, we went on to the vicarage, where I gave him up to my sister. But I cannot convey to my reader any notion of the quietness that entered my heart with the grasp of that childish hand. I think it was the faith of the boy in me that comforted me, but I could not help thinking of the words of our Lord about receiving a child in His name, and so receiving Him. By the time we reached the vicarage my heart was very quiet. As the little child held by my hand, so I seemed to be holding by God's hand. And a sense of heart-security, as well as soul-safety, awoke in me; and I said to myself,—Surely He will take care of my heart as well as of my mind and my conscience. For one blessed moment I seemed to be at the very centre of things, looking out quietly upon my own troubled emotions as upon something outside of me—apart from me, even as one from the firm rock may look abroad upon the vexed sea. And I thought I then knew something of what the apostle meant when he said, "Your life is hid with Christ in God." I knew that there was a deeper self than that which was thus troubled.

I had not had my usual ramble this morning, and was otherwise ill prepared for the Sunday. So I went early into the church; but finding that the sexton's wife had not yet finished lighting the stove, I sat down by my own fire in the vestry.

Suppose I am sitting there now while I say one word for our congregations in winter. I was very particular in having the church well warmed before Sunday. I think some parsons must neglect seeing after this matter on principle, because warmth may make a weary creature go to sleep here and there about the place: as if any healing doctrine could enter the soul while it is on the rack of the frost. The clergy should see—for it is their business—that their people have no occasion to think of their bodies at all while they are in church. They have enough ado to think of the truth. When our Lord was feeding even their bodies, He made them all sit down on the grass. It is worth noticing that there was much grass in the place—a rare thing I should think in those countries—and therefore, perhaps, it was chosen by Him for their comfort in feeding their souls and bodies both. If I may judge from experiences of my own, one of the reasons why some churches are of all places the least likely for anything good to be found in, is, that they are as wretchedly cold to the body as they are to the soul—too cold every way for anything to grow in them. Edelweiss, "Noble-white"—as they call a plant growing under the snow on some of the Alps—could not survive the winter in such churches. There is small welcome in a cold house. And the clergyman, who is the steward, should look to it. It is for him to give his Master's friends a welcome to his Master's house—for the welcome of a servant is precious, and now-a-days very rare.

And now Mrs Stone must have finished. I go into the old church which looks as if it were quietly waiting for its people. No. She has not done yet. Never mind.—How full of meaning the vaulted roof looks! as if, having gathered a soul of its own out of the generations that have worshipped here for so long, it had feeling enough to grow hungry for a psalm before the end of the week.

Some such half-foolish fancy was now passing through my tranquillized mind or rather heart—for the mind would have rejected it at once—when to my—what shall I call it?—not amazement, for the delight was too strong for amazement—the old organ woke up and began to think aloud. As if it had been brooding over it all the week in the wonderful convolutions of its wooden brain, it began to sigh out the Agnus Dei of Mozart's twelfth mass upon the air of the still church, which lay swept and garnished for the Sunday.—How could it be? I know now; and I guessed then; and my guess was right; and my reader must be content to guess too. I took no step to verify my conjecture, for I felt that I was upon my honour, but sat in one of the pews and listened, till the old organ sobbed itself into silence. Then I heard the steps of the sexton's wife vanish from the church, heard her lock the door, and knew that I was alone in the ancient pile, with the twilight growing thick about me, and felt like Sir Galahad, when, after the "rolling organ-harmony," he heard "wings flutter, voices hover clear." In a moment the mood changed; and I was sorry, not that the dear organ was dead for the night, but actually felt gently-mournful that the wonderful old thing never had and never could have a conscious life of its own. So strangely does the passion—which I had not invented, reader, whoever thou art that thinkest love and a church do not well harmonize—so strangely, I say, full to overflowing of its own vitality, does it radiate life, that it would even of its own superabundance quicken into blessed consciousness the inanimate objects around it, thinking what they would feel had they a consciousness correspondent to their form, were their faculties moved from within themselves instead of from the will and operation of humanity.

I lingered on long in the dark church, as my reader knows I had done often before. Nor did I move from the seat I had first taken till I left the sacred building. And there I made my sermon for the next morning. And herewith I impart it to my reader. But he need not be afraid of another such as I have already given him, for I impart it only in its original germ, its concentrated essence of sermon—these four verses:

Had I the grace to win the grace

Of some old man complete in lore,

My face would worship at his face,

Like childhood seated on the floor.

Had I the grace to win the grace

Of childhood, loving shy, apart,

The child should find a nearer place,

And teach me resting on my heart.

Had I the grace to win the grace

Of maiden living all above,

My soul would trample down the base,

That she might have a man to love.

A grace I have no grace to win

Knocks now at my half-open door:

Ah, Lord of glory, come thou in,

Thy grace divine is all and more.

This was what I made for myself. I told my people that God had created all our worships, reverences, tendernesses, loves. That they had come out of His heart, and He had made them in us because they were in Him first. That otherwise He would not have cared to make them. That all that we could imagine of the wise, the lovely, the beautiful, was in Him, only infinitely more of them than we could not merely imagine, but understand, even if He did all He could to explain them to us, to make us understand them. That in Him was all the wise teaching of the best man ever known in the world and more; all the grace and gentleness and truth of the best child and more; all the tenderness and devotion of the truest type of womankind and more; for there is a love that passeth the love of woman, not the love of Jonathan to David, though David said so: but the love of God to the men and women whom He has made. Therefore, we must be all God's; and all our aspirations, all our worships, all our honours, all our loves, must centre in Him, the Best.

CHAPTER XXIV. AN ANGEL UNAWARES.

Feeling rather more than the usual reaction so well-known to clergymen after the concentrated duties of the Sunday, I resolved on Monday to have the long country walk I had been disappointed of on the Saturday previous. It was such a day as it seems impossible to describe except in negatives. It was not stormy, it was not rainy, it was not sunshiny, it was not snowy, it was not frosty, it was not foggy, it was not clear, it was nothing but cloudy and quiet and cold and generally ungenial, with just a puff of wind now and then to give an assertion to its ungeniality. I should not in the least have cared to tell what sort the day was, had it not been an exact representation of my own mind. It was not the day that made me such as itself. The weather could always easily influence the surface of my mind, my external mood, but it could never go much further. The smallest pleasure would break through the conditions that merely came of such a day. But this morning my whole mind and heart seemed like the day. The summer was thousands of miles off on the other side of the globe. Ethelwyn, up at the old house there across the river, seemed millions of miles away. The summer MIGHT come back; she never would come nearer: it was absurd to expect it. For in such moods stupidity constantly arrogates to itself the qualities and claims of insight. In fact, it passes itself off for common sense, making the most dreary ever appear the most reasonable. In such moods a man might almost be persuaded that it was ridiculous to expect any such poetic absurdity as the summer, with its diamond mornings and its opal evenings, ever to come again; nay, to think that it ever had had any existence except in the fancies of the human heart—one of its castles in the air. The whole of life seemed faint and foggy, with no red in it anywhere; and when I glanced at my present relations in Marshmallows, I could not help finding several circumstances to give some appearance of justice to this appearance of things. I seemed to myself to have done no good. I had driven Catherine Weir to the verge of suicide, while at the same time I could not restrain her from the contemplation of some dire revenge. I had lost the man upon whom I had most reckoned as a seal of my ministry, namely, Thomas Weir. True there was Old Rogers; but Old Rogers was just as good before I found him. I could not dream of having made him any better. And so I went on brooding over all the disappointing portions of my labour, all the time thinking about myself, instead of God and the work that lay for me to do in the days to come.

"Nobody," I said, "but Old Rogers understands me. Nobody would care, as far as my teaching goes, if another man took my place from next Sunday forward. And for Miss Oldcastle, her playing the Agnus Dei on Saturday afternoon, even if she intended that I should hear it, could only indicate at most that she knew how she had behaved to me in the morning, and thought she had gone too far and been unkind, or perhaps was afraid lest she should be accountable for any failure I might make in my Sunday duties, and therefore felt bound to do something to restore my equanimity."

Choosing, though without consciously intending to do so, the dreariest path to be found, I wandered up the side of the slow black river, with the sentinel pollards looking at themselves in its gloomy mirror, just as I was looking at myself in the mirror of my circumstances. They leaned in all directions, irregular as the headstones in an ancient churchyard. In the summer they looked like explosions of green leaves at the best; now they looked like the burnt-out cases of the summer's fireworks. How different, too, was the river from the time when a whole fleet of shining white lilies lay anchored among their own broad green leaves upon its clear waters, filled with sunlight in every pore, as they themselves would fill the pores of a million-caverned sponge! But I could not even recall the past summer as beautiful. I seemed to care for nothing. The first miserable afternoon at Marshmallows looked now as if it had been the whole of my coming relation to the place seen through a reversed telescope. And here I was IN it now.

The walk along the side was tolerably dry, although the river was bankfull. But when I came to the bridge I wanted to cross—a wooden one—I found that the approach to it had been partly undermined and carried away, for here the river had overflowed its banks in one of the late storms; and all about the place was still very wet and swampy. I could therefore get no farther in my gloomy walk, and so turned back upon my steps. Scarcely had I done so, when I saw a man coming hastily towards me from far upon the straight line of the river walk. I could not mistake him at any distance. It was Old Rogers. I felt both ashamed and comforted when I recognized him.

"Well, Old Rogers," I said, as soon as he came within hail, trying to speak cheerfully, "you cannot get much farther this way—without wading a bit, at least."

"I don't want to go no farther now, sir. I came to find you."

"Nothing amiss, I hope?"

"Nothing as I knows on, sir. I only wanted to have a little chat with you.

I told master I wanted to leave for an hour or so. He allus lets me do just as I like."

"But how did you know where to find me?"

"I saw you come this way. You passed me right on the bridge, and didn't see me, sir. So says I to myself, 'Old Rogers, summat's amiss wi' parson to-day. He never went by me like that afore. This won't do. You just go and see.' So I went home and told master, and here I be, sir. And I hope you're noways offended with the liberty of me."

"Did I really pass you on the bridge?" I said, unable to understand it.

"That you did, sir. I knowed parson must be a goodish bit in his own in'ards afore he would do that."

"I needn't tell you I didn't see you, Old Rogers."

"I could tell you that, sir. I hope there's nothing gone main wrong, sir. Miss is well, sir, I hope?"

"Quite well, I thank you. No, my dear fellow, nothing's gone main wrong, as you say. Some of my running tackle got jammed a bit, that's all. I'm a little out of spirits, I believe."

"Well, sir, don't you be afeard I'm going to be troublesome. Don't think I want to get aboard your ship, except you fling me a rope. There's a many things you mun ha' to think about that an ignorant man like me couldn't take up if you was to let 'em drop. And being a gentleman, I do believe, makes the matter worse betuxt us. And there's many a thing that no man can go talkin' about to any but only the Lord himself. Still you can't help us poor folks seeing when there's summat amiss, and we can't help havin' our own thoughts any more than the sailor's jackdaw that couldn't speak. And sometimes we may be nearer the mark than you would suppose, for God has made us all of one blood, you know."

"What ARE you driving at, Old Rogers?" I said with a smile, which was none the less true that I suspected he had read some of the worst trouble of my heart. For why should I mind an honourable man like him knowing

305

what oppressed me, though, as things went, I certainly should not, as he said, choose to tell it to any but one?

"I don't want to say what I was driving at, if it was anything but this—that I want to put to the clumsy hand of a rough old tar, with a heart as soft as the pitch that makes his hand hard—to trim your sails a bit, sir, and help you to lie a point closer to the wind. You're not just close-hauled, sir."

"Say on, Old Rogers. I understand you, and I will listen with all my heart, for you have a good right to speak."

And Old Rogers spoke thus:—

"Oncet upon a time, I made a voyage in a merchant barque. We were becalmed in the South Seas. And weary work it wur, a doin' of nothin' from day to day. But when the water began to come up thick from the bottom of the water-casks, it was wearier a deal. Then a thick fog came on, as white as snow a'most, and we couldn't see more than a few yards ahead or on any side of us. But the fog didn't keep the heat off; it only made it worse, and the water was fast going done. The short allowance grew shorter and shorter, and the men, some of them, were half-mad with thirst, and began to look bad at one another. I kept up my heart by looking ahead inside me. For days and days the fog hung about us as if the air had been made o' flocks o' wool. The captain took to his berth, and several of the crew to their hammocks, for it was just as hot on deck as anywhere else. The mate lay on a sparesail on the quarter-deck, groaning. I had a strong suspicion that the schooner was drifting, and hove the lead again and again, but could find no bottom. Some of the men got hold of the spirits, and THAT didn't quench their thirst. It drove them clean mad. I had to knock one of them down myself with a capstan bar, for he ran at the mate with his knife. At last I began to lose all hope. And still I was sure the schooner was slowly drifting. My head was like to burst, and my tongue was like a lump of holystone in my mouth. Well, one morning, I had just, as I thought, lain down on the deck to breathe my last, hoping I should die before I went quite mad with thirst, when all at once the fog lifted, like the foot of a sail. I sprung to my feet. There was the blue sky overhead; but the terrible burning sun was there. A moment more and a light air blew on my cheek, and, turning my face to it as if it had been the very breath of God, there was an island within half a mile, and I saw the shine of water on the face of a rock on the shore. I cried out, 'Land on the weather-quarter! Water in sight!' In a moment more a boat was lowered, and in a few minutes the boat's crew, of which I was one, were lying, clothes and all, in a little stream that came down from the hills above.—There, Mr Walton! that's what I wanted to say to you."

This is as near the story of my old friend as my limited knowledge of sea affairs allows me to report it.

"I understand you quite, Old Rogers, and I thank you heartily," I said.

"No doubt," resumed he, "King Solomon was quite right, as he always was, I suppose, in what he SAID, for his wisdom mun ha' laid mostly in the tongue—right, I say, when he said, 'Boast not thyself of to-morrow; for thou knowest not what a day may bring forth;' but I can't help thinking there's another side to it. I think it would be as good advice to a man on the other tack, whose boasting lay far to windward, and he close on a lee-shore wi' breakers—it wouldn't be amiss to say to him, 'Don't strike your colours to the morrow; for thou knowest not what a day may bring forth.' There's just as many good days as bad ones; as much fair weather as foul in the days to come. And if a man keeps up heart, he's all the better for that, and none the worse when the evil day does come. But, God forgive me! I'm talking like a heathen. As if there was any chance about what the days would bring forth. No, my lad," said the old sailor, assuming the dignity of his superior years under the inspiration of the truth, "boast nor trust nor hope in the morrow. Boast and trust and hope in God, for thou shalt yet praise Him, who is the health of thy countenance and thy God."

I could but hold out my hand. I had nothing to say. For he had spoken to me as an angel of God.

The old man was silent for some moments: his emotion needed time to still itself again. Nor did he return to the subject. He held out his hand once more, saying—

"Good day, sir. I must go back to my work."

307

"I will go back with you," I returned.

And so we walked back side by side to the village, but not a word did we speak the one to the other, till we shook hands and parted upon the bridge, where we had first met. Old Rogers went to his work, and I lingered upon the bridge. I leaned upon the low parapet, and looked up the stream as far as the mists creeping about the banks, and hovering in thinnest veils over the surface of the water, would permit. Then I turned and looked down the river crawling on to the sweep it made out of sight just where Mr Brownrigg's farm began to come down to its banks. Then I looked to the left, and there stood my old church, as quiet in the dreary day, though not so bright, as in the sunshine: even the graves themselves must look yet more "solemn sad" in a wintry day like this, than they look when the sunlight that infolds them proclaims that God is not the God of the dead but of the living. One of the great battles that we have to fight in this world—for twenty great battles have to be fought all at once and in one—is the battle with appearances. I turned me to the right, and there once more I saw, as on that first afternoon, the weathercock that watched the winds over the stables at Oldcastle Hall. It had caught just one glimpse of the sun through some rent in the vapours, and flung it across to me, ere it vanished again amid the general dinginess of the hour.

CHAPTER XXV. TWO PARISHIONERS.

I HAVE said, near the beginning of my story, that my parish was a large one: how is it that I have mentioned but one of the great families in it, and have indeed confined my recollections entirely to the village and its immediate neighbourhood? Will my reader have patience while I explain this to him a little? First, as he may have observed, my personal attraction is towards the poor rather than the rich. I was made so. I can generally get nearer the poor than the rich. But I say GENERALLY, for I have known a few rich people quite as much to my mind as the best of the poor. Thereupon, of course, their education would give them the advantage with me in the possibilities of communion. But when the heart is right, and there is a good stock of common sense as well,—a gift predominant, as far as I am aware, in no one class over another, education will turn the scale very gently with me.

And then when I reflect that some of these poor people would have made nobler ladies and gentlemen than all but two or three I know, if they had only had the opportunity, there is a reaction towards the poor, something like a feeling of favour because they have not had fair play—a feeling soon modified, though not altered, by the reflection that they are such because God who loves them better than we do, has so ordered their lot, and by the recollection that not only was our Lord himself poor, but He said the poor were blessed. And let me just say in passing that I not only believe it because He said it, but I believe it because I see that it is so. I think sometimes that the world must have been especially created for the poor, and that particular allowances will be made for the rich because they are born into such disadvantages, and with their wickednesses and their miseries, their love of spiritual dirt and meanness, subserve the highest growth and emancipation of the poor, that they may inherit both the earth and the kingdom of heaven.

But I have been once more wandering from my subject.

Thus it was that the people in the village lying close to my door attracted most of my attention at first; of which attention those more immediately associated with the village, as, for instance, the inhabitants of the Hall, came in for a share, although they did not belong to the same class.

Again, the houses of most of the gentlefolk lay considerably apart from the church and from each other. Many of them went elsewhere to church, and I did not feel bound to visit those, for I had enough to occupy me without, and had little chance of getting a hold of them to do them good. Still there were one or two families which I would have visited oftener, I confess, had I been more interested in them, or had I had a horse. Therefore, I ought to have bought a horse sooner than I did. Before this winter was over, however, I did buy one, partly to please Dr Duncan, who urged me to it for the sake of my health, partly because I could then do my duty better, and partly, I confess, from having been very fond of an old mare of my father's, when I was a boy, living, after my mother's death, at a farm of his in B—shire. Happening to come across a gray mare very much like her, I bought her at once.

I think it was the very day after the events recorded in my last chapter that I mounted her to pay a visit to two rich maiden ladies, whose carriage stopped at the Lych-gate most Sundays when the weather was favourable, but whom I had called upon only once since I came to the parish. I should not have thought this visit worth mentioning, except for the conversation I had with them, during which a hint or two were dropped which had an influence in colouring my thoughts for some time after.

I was shown with much ceremony by a butler, as old apparently as his livery of yellow and green, into the presence of the two ladies, one of whom sat in state reading a volume of the Spectator. She was very tall, and as square as the straight long-backed chair upon which she sat. A fat asthmatic poodle lay at her feet upon the hearth-rug. The other, a little lively gray-haired creature, who looked like a most ancient girl whom no power of gathering years would ever make old, was standing upon a high chair, making love to a demoniacal-looking cockatoo in a gilded cage. As I entered the room, the latter all but jumped from her perch with a merry though wavering laugh, and advanced to meet me.

"Jonathan, bring the cake and wine," she cried to the retreating servant.

The former rose with a solemn stiff-backedness, which was more amusing than dignified, and extended her hand as I approached her, without moving from her place.

"We were afraid, Mr Walton," said the little lady, "that you had forgotten we were parishioners of yours."

"That I could hardly do," I answered, "seeing you are such regular attendants at church. But I confess I have given you ground for your rebuke, Miss Crowther. I bought a horse, however, the other day, and this is the first use I have put him to."

"We're charmed to see you. It is very good of you not to forget such uninteresting girls as we are."

"You forget, Jemima," interposed her sister, in a feminine bass, "that time is always on the wing. I should have thought we were both decidedly middle-aged, though you are the elder by I will not say how many years."

310

"All but ten years, Hester. I remember rocking you in your cradle scores of times. But somehow, Mr Walton, I can't help feeling as if she were my elder sister. She is so learned, you see; and I don't read anything but the newspapers."

"And your Bible, Jemima. Do yourself justice."

"That's a matter of course, sister. But this is not the way to entertain Mr Walton."

"The gentlemen used to entertain the ladies when I was young, Jemima. I do not know how it may have been when you were."

"Much the same, I believe, sister. But if you look at Mr Walton, I think you will see that he is pretty much entertained as it is."

"I agree with Miss Hester," I said. "It is the duty of gentlemen to entertain ladies. But it is so much the kinder of ladies when they surpass their duty, and condescend to entertain gentlemen."

"What can surpass duty, Mr Walton? I confess I do not agree with your doctrines upon that point."

"I do not quite understand you, Miss Hester," I returned.

"Why, Mr Walton—I hope you will not think me rude, but it always seems to me—and it has given me much pain, when I consider that your congregation is chiefly composed of the lower classes, who may be greatly injured by such a style of preaching. I must say I think so, Mr Walton. Only perhaps you are one of those who think a lady's opinion on such matters is worth nothing."

"On the contrary, I respect an opinion just as far as the lady or gentleman who holds it seems to me qualified to have formed it first. But you have not yet told me what you think so objectionable in my preaching."

"You always speak as if faith in Christ was something greater than duty. Now I think duty the first thing."

"I quite agree with you, Miss Crowther. For how can I, or any clergyman, urge a man to that which is not his duty? But tell me, is not faith in Christ a duty? Where you have mistaken me is, that you think I speak of faith as higher than duty, when indeed I speak of faith as higher than any OTHER duty. It is the highest duty of man. I do not say the duty he always sees clearest, or even sees at all. But the fact is, that when that which is a duty becomes the highest delight of a man, the joy of his very being, he no more thinks or needs to think about it as a duty. What would you think of the love of a son who, when an appeal was made to his affections, should say, 'Oh yes, I love my mother dearly: it is my duty, of course?'"

"That sounds very plausible, Mr Walton; but still I cannot help feeling that you preach faith and not works. I do not say that you are not to preach faith, of course; but you know faith without works is dead."

"Now, really, Hester," interposed Miss Jemima, "I cannot think how it is, but, for my part, I should have said that Mr Walton was constantly preaching works. He's always telling you to do something or other. I know I always come out of the church with something on my mind; and I've got to work it off somehow before I'm comfortable."

And here Miss Jemima got up on the chair again, and began to flirt with the cockatoo once more, but only in silent signs.

I cannot quite recall how this part of the conversation drew to a close. But I will tell a fact or two about the sisters which may possibly explain how it was that they took up such different notions of my preaching. The elder scarce left the house, but spent almost the whole of her time in reading small dingy books of eighteenth century literature. She believed in no other; thought Shakespeare sentimental where he was not low, and Bacon pompous; Addison thoroughly respectable and gentlemanly. Pope was the great English poet, incomparably before Milton. The "Essay on Man" contained the deepest wisdom; the "Rape of the Lock" the most graceful imagination to be found in the language. The "Vicar of Wakefield" was pretty, but foolish; while in philosophy, Paley was perfect, especially in his notion of happiness, which she had heard objected to, and therefore warmly defended. Somehow or other, respectability—in position, in morals, in religion, in conduct—was everything. The consequence was that her very nature was old-fashioned, and had nothing in it of that lasting youth which is the birthright—so often despised—of every immortal being. But I have already said more about her than her place in my story justifies.

Miss Crowther, on the contrary, whose eccentricities did not lie on the side of respectability, had gone on shocking the stiff proprieties of her younger sister till she could be shocked no more, and gave in as to the hopelessness of fate. She had had a severe disappointment in youth, had not only survived it, but saved her heart alive out of it, losing only, as far as appeared to the eyes of her neighbours at least, any remnant of selfish care about herself; and she now spent the love which had before been concentrated upon one object, upon every living thing that came near her, even to her sister's sole favourite, the wheezing poodle. She was very odd, it must be confessed, with her gray hair, her clear gray eye with wrinkled eyelids, her light step, her laugh at once girlish and cracked; darting in and out of the cottages, scolding this matron with a lurking smile in every tone, hugging that baby, boxing the ears of the other little tyrant, passing this one's rent, and threatening that other with awful vengeances, but it was a very lovely oddity. Their property was not large, and she knew every living thing on the place down to the dogs and pigs. And Miss Jemima, as the people always called her, transferring the MISS CROWTHER of primogeniture to the younger, who kept, like King Henry IV.,—

"*Her presence, like a robe pontifical,*

Ne'er seen but wonder'd at,"

was the actual queen of the neighbourhood; for, though she was the very soul of kindness, she was determined to have her own way, and had it.

Although I did not know all this at the time, such were the two ladies who held these different opinions about my preaching; the one who did nothing but read Messrs Addison, Pope, Paley, and Co., considering that I neglected the doctrine of works as the seal of faith, and the one who was busy helping her neighbours from morning to night, finding little in my preaching, except incentive to benevolence.

The next point where my recollection can take up the conversation, is where Miss Hester made the following further criticism on my pulpit labours.

"You are too anxious to explain everything, Mr Walton."

I pause in my recording, to do my critic the justice of remarking that what she said looks worse on paper than it sounded from her lips; for she was a gentlewoman, and the tone has much to do with the impression made by the intellectual contents of all speech.

"Where can be the use of trying to make uneducated people see the grounds of everything?" she said. "It is enough that this or that is in the Bible."

"Yes; but there is just the point. What is in the Bible? Is it this or that?"

"You are their spiritual instructor: tell them what is in the Bible."

"But you have just been objecting to my mode of representing what is in the Bible."

"It will be so much the worse, if you add argument to convince them of what is incorrect."

"I doubt that. Falsehood will expose itself the sooner that honest argument is used to support it."

"You cannot expect them to judge of what you tell them."

"The Bible urges upon us to search and understand."

"I grant that for those whose business it is, like yourself."

"Do you think, then, that the Church consists of a few privileged to understand, and a great many who cannot understand, and therefore need not be taught?"

"I said you had to teach them."

"But to teach is to make people understand."

"I don't think so. If you come to that, how much can the wisest of us understand? You remember what Pope says,—

> *'Superior beings, when of late they saw*
>
> *A mortal man unfold all Nature's law,*
>
> *Admired such wisdom in an earthly shape,*
>
> *And show'd a Newton as we show an ape?'*"

"I do not know the passage. Pope is not my Bible. I should call such superior beings very inferior beings indeed."

"Do you call the angels inferior beings?"

"Such angels, certainly."

"He means the good angels, of course."

"And I say the good angels could never behave like that, for contempt is one of the lowest spiritual conditions in which any being can place himself. Our Lord says, 'Take heed that ye despise not one of these little ones, for their angels do always behold the face of my Father, who is in heaven.'"

"Now will you even say that you understand that passage?"

"Practically, well enough; just as the poorest man of my congregation may understand it. I am not to despise one of the little ones. Pope represents the angels as despising a Newton even."

"And you despise Pope."

"I hope not. I say he was full of despising, and therefore, if for no other reason, a small man."

"Surely you do not jest at his bodily infirmities?"

"I had forgotten them quite."

"In every other sense he was a great man."

"I cannot allow it. He was intellectually a great man, but morally a small man."

"Such refinements are not easily followed."

"I will undertake to make the poorest woman in my congregation understand that."

"Why don't you try your friend Mrs Oldcastle, then? It might do her a little good," said Miss Hester, now becoming, I thought, a little spiteful at hearing her favourite treated so unceremoniously. I found afterwards that there was some kindness in it, however.

"I should have very little influence with Mrs Oldcastle if I were to make the attempt. But I am not called upon to address my flock individually upon every point of character."

"I thought she was an intimate friend of yours."

"Quite the contrary. We are scarcely friendly."

"I am very glad to hear it," said Miss Jemima, who had been silent during the little controversy that her sister and I had been carrying on. "We have been quite misinformed. The fact is, we thought we might have seen more of you if it had not been for her. And as very few people of her own position in society care to visit her, we thought it a pity she should be your principal friend in the parish."

"Why do they not visit her more?"

"There are strange stories about her, which it is as well to leave alone. They are getting out of date too. But she is not a fit woman to be regarded as the clergyman's friend. There!" said Miss Jemima, as if she had wanted to relieve her bosom of a burden, and had done it.

"I think, however, her religious opinions would correspond with your own, Mr Walton," said Miss Hester.

"Possibly," I answered, with indifference; "I don't care much about opinion."

"Her daughter would be a nice girl, I fancy, if she weren't kept down by her mother. She looks scared, poor thing! And they say she's not quite—the thing, you know," said Miss Jemima.

"What DO you mean, Miss Crowther?"

She gently tapped her forehead with a forefinger.

I laughed. I thought it was not worth my while to enter as the champion of Miss Oldcastle's sanity.

"They are, and have been, a strange family as far back as I can remember; and my mother used to say the same. I am glad she comes to our church now. You mustn't let her set her cap at you, though, Mr Walton. It wouldn't do at all. She's pretty enough, too!"

"Yes," I returned, "she is rather pretty. But I don't think she looks as if she had a cap to set at anybody."

I rose to go, for I did not relish any further pursuit of the conversation in the same direction.

I rode home slowly, brooding on the lovely marvel, that out of such a rough ungracious stem as the Oldcastle family, should have sprung such a delicate, pale, winter-braved flower, as Ethelwyn. And I prayed that I might be honoured to rescue her from the ungenial soil and atmosphere to which the machinations of her mother threatened to confine her for the rest of a suffering life.

CHAPTER XXVI. SATAN CAST OUT.

I was within a mile of the village, returning from my visit to the Misses Crowther, when my horse, which was walking slowly along the soft side of the road, lifted his head, and pricked up his ears at the sound, which he heard first, of approaching hoofs. The riders soon came in sight—Miss Oldcastle, Judy, and Captain Everard. Miss Oldcastle I had never seen on horseback before. Judy was on a little white pony she used to gallop about the fields near the Hall. The Captain was laughing and chatting gaily as they drew near, now to the one, now to the other. Being on my own side of the road I held straight on, not wishing to stop or to reveal the signs of a distress which had almost overwhelmed me. I felt as cold as death, or rather as if my whole being had been deprived of vitality by a sudden exhaustion around me of the ethereal element of life. I believe I did not alter my bearing, but remained with my head bent, for I had been thinking hard just before, till we were on the point of meeting, when I lifted my hat to Miss Oldcastle without drawing bridle, and went on. The Captain returned my salutation, and likewise rode on. I could just see, as they passed me, that Miss Oldcastle's pale face was flushed even to scarlet, but she only bowed and kept alongside of her companion. I thought I had escaped conversation, and had gone about twenty yards farther, when I heard the clatter of Judy's pony behind me, and up she came at full gallop.

"Why didn't you stop to speak to us, Mr Walton?" she said. "I pulled up, but you never looked at me. We shall be cross all the rest of the day, because you cut us so. What have we done?"

"Nothing, Judy, that I know of," I answered, trying to speak cheerfully. "But I do not know your companion, and I was not in the humour for an introduction."

She looked hard at me with her keen gray eyes; and I felt as if the child was seeing through me.

"I don't know what to make of it, Mr Walton. You're very different somehow from what you used to be. There's something wrong somewhere. But I suppose you would all tell me it's none of my business. So I won't ask questions. Only I wish I could do anything for you."

I felt the child's kindness, but could only say—

"Thank you, Judy. I am sure I should ask you if there were anything you could do for me. But you'll be left behind."

"No fear of that. My Dobbin can go much faster than their big horses. But I see you don't want me, so good-bye."

She turned her pony's head as she spoke, jumped the ditch at the side of the road, and flew after them along the grass like a swallow. I likewise roused my horse and went off at a hard trot, with the vain impulse so to shake off the tormenting thoughts that crowded on me like gadflies. But this day was to be one of more trial still.

As I turned a corner, almost into the street of the village, Tom Weir was at my side. He had evidently been watching for me. His face was so pale, that I saw in a moment something had happened.

"What is the matter, Tom?" I asked, in some alarm.

He did not reply for a moment, but kept unconsciously stroking my horse's neck, and staring at me "with wide blue eyes."

"Come, Tom," I repeated, "tell me what is the matter."

I could see his bare throat knot and relax, like the motion of a serpent, before he could utter the words.

"Kate has killed her little boy, sir."

He followed them with a stifled cry—almost a scream, and hid his face in his hands.

"God forbid!" I exclaimed, and struck my heels in my horse's sides, nearly overturning poor Tom in my haste.

"She's mad, sir; she's mad," he cried, as I rode off.

"Come after me," I said, "and take the mare home. I shan't be able to leave your sister."

Had I had a share, by my harsh words, in driving the woman beyond the bounds of human reason and endurance? The thought was dreadful. But I must not let my mind rest on it now, lest I should be unfitted for what might have to be done. Before I reached the door, I saw a little crowd of the villagers, mostly women and children, gathered about it. I got off my horse, and gave him to a woman to hold till Tom should come up. With a little difficulty, I prevailed on the rest to go home at once, and not add to the confusions and terrors of the unhappy affair by the excitement of their presence. As soon as they had yielded to my arguments, I entered the shop, which to my annoyance I found full of the neighbours. These likewise I got rid of as soon as possible, and locking the door behind them, went up to the room above.

To my surprise, I found no one there. On the hearth and in the fender lay two little pools of blood. All in the house was utterly still. It was very dreadful. I went to the only other door. It was not bolted as I had expected to find it. I opened it, peeped in, and entered. On the bed lay the mother, white as death, but with her black eyes wide open, staring at the ceiling: and on her arm lay little Gerard, as white, except where the blood had flowed from the bandage that could not confine it, down his sweet deathlike face. His eyes were fast closed, and he had no sign of life about him. I shut the door behind me, and approached the bed. When Catherine caught sight of me, she showed no surprise or emotion of any kind. Her lips, with automaton-like movement, uttered the words—

"I have done it at last. I am ready. Take me away. I shall be hanged. I don't care. I confess it. Only don't let the people stare at me."

Her lips went on moving, but I could hear no more till suddenly she broke out—

"Oh! my baby! my baby!" and gave a cry of such agony as I hope never to hear again while I live.

At this moment I heard a loud knocking at the shop-door, which was the only entrance to the house, and remembering that I had locked it, I went down to see who was there. I found Thomas Weir, the father, accompanied by Dr Duncan, whom, as it happened, he had had some difficulty in finding. Thomas had sped to his daughter the moment he heard the rumour of what had happened, and his fierceness in clearing the shop had at least prevented the neighbours, even in his absence, from intruding further.

We went up together to Catherine's room. Thomas said nothing to me about what had happened, and I found it difficult even to conjecture from his countenance what thoughts were passing through his mind.

Catherine looked from one to another of us, as if she did not know the one from the other. She made no motion to rise from her bed, nor did she utter a word, although her lips would now and then move as if moulding a sentence. When Dr Duncan, after looking at the child, proceeded to take him from her, she gave him one imploring look, and yielded with a moan; then began to stare hopelessly at the ceiling again. The doctor carried the child into the next room, and the grandfather followed.

"You see what you have driven me to!" cried Catherine, the moment I was left alone with her. "I hope you are satisfied."

The words went to my very soul. But when I looked at her, her eyes were wandering about over the ceiling, and I had and still have difficulty in believing that she spoke the words, and that they were not an illusion of my sense, occasioned by the commotion of my own feelings. I thought it better, however, to leave her, and join the others in the sitting-room. The first thing I saw there was Thomas on his knees, with a basin of water, washing away the blood of his grandson from his daughter's floor. The very sight of the child had hitherto been nauseous to him, and his daughter had been beyond the reach of his forgiveness. Here was the end of it—the blood of the one shed by the hand of the other, and the father of both, who had disdained both, on his knees, wiping it up. Dr Duncan was giving the child brandy; for he had found that he had been sick, and that the loss of blood was the chief cause of his condition. The blood flowed from a wound on the head, extending backwards from the temple, which had evidently been occasioned by a fall upon the fender, where the blood lay both inside and out; and the doctor took the sickness as a sign that the brain had not been seriously injured by the blow. In a few minutes he said—

"I think he'll come round."

"Will it be safe to tell his mother so?" I asked.

"Yes: I think you may."

I hastened to her room.

"Your little darling is not dead, Catherine. He is coming to."

She THREW herself off the bed at my feet, caught them round with her arms, and cried—

"I will forgive him. I will do anything you like. I forgive George Everard. I will go and ask my father to forgive me."

I lifted her in my arms—how light she was!—and laid her again on the bed, where she burst into tears, and lay sobbing and weeping. I went to the other room. Little Gerard opened his eyes and closed them again, as I entered. The doctor had laid him in his own crib. He said his pulse was improving. I beckoned to Thomas. He followed me.

"She wants to ask you to forgive her," I said. "Do not, in God's name, wait till she asks you, but go and tell her that you forgive her."

"I dare not say I forgive her," he answered. "I have more need to ask her to forgive me."

I took him by the hand, and led him into her room. She feebly lifted her arms towards him. Not a word was said on either side. I left them in each other's embrace. The hard rocks had been struck with the rod, and the waters of life had flowed forth from each, and had met between.

I have more than once known this in the course of my experience—the ice and snow of a long estrangement suddenly give way, and the boiling geyser-floods of old affection rush from the hot deeps of the heart. I think myself that the very lastingness and strength of animosity have their origin sometimes in the reality of affection: the love lasts all the while, freshly indignant at every new load heaped upon it; till, at last, a word, a look, a sorrow, a gladness, sets it free; and, forgetting all its claims, it rushes irresistibly towards its ends. Thus was it with Thomas and Catherine Weir.

When I rejoined Dr Duncan, I found little Gerard asleep, and breathing quietly.

"What do you know of this sad business, Mr Walton?" said the doctor.

"I should like to ask the same question of you," I returned. "Young Tom told me that his sister had murdered the child. That is all I know."

"His father told me the same; and that is all I know. Do you believe it?"

"At least we have no evidence about it. It is tolerably certain neither of those two could have been present. They must have received it by report. We must wait till she is able to explain the thing herself."

"Meantime," said Dr Duncan, "all I believe is, that she struck the child, and that he fell upon the fender."

I may as well inform my reader that, as far as Catherine could give an account of the transaction, this conjecture was corroborated. But the smallest reminder of it evidently filled her with such a horror of self-loathing, that I took care to avoid the subject entirely, after the attempt at explanation which she made at my request. She could not remember with any clearness what had happened. All she remembered was that she had been more miserable than ever in her life before; that the child had come to her, as he seldom did, with some childish request or other; that she felt herself seized with intense hatred of him; and the next thing she knew was that his blood was running in a long red finger towards her. Then it seemed as if that blood had been drawn from her own over-charged heart and brain; she knew what she had done, though she did not know how she had done it; and the tide of her ebbed affection flowed like the returning waters of the Solway. But beyond her restored love, she remembered nothing more that happened till she lay weeping with the hope that the child would yet live. Probably more particulars returned afterwards, but I took care to ask no more questions. In the increase of illness that followed, I more than once saw her shudder while she slept, and thought she was dreaming what her waking memory had forgotten; and once she started awake, crying, "I have murdered him again."

To return to that first evening:—When Thomas came from his daughter's room, he looked like a man from whom the bitterness of evil had passed away. To human eyes, at least, it seemed as if self had been utterly slain in him. His face had that child-like expression in its paleness, and the tearfulness without tears haunting his eyes, which reminds one of the feeling of an evening in summer between which and the sultry day preceding it has fallen the gauzy veil of a cooling shower, with a rainbow in the east.

"She is asleep," he said.

"How is it your daughter Mary is not here?" I asked.

"She was taken with a fit the moment she heard the bad news, sir. I left her with nobody but father. I think I must go and look after her now. It's not the first she's had neither, though I never told any one before. You won't mention it, sir. It makes people look shy at you, you know, sir."

"Indeed, I won't mention it.—Then she mustn't sit up, and two nurses will be wanted here. You and I must take it to-night, Thomas. You'll attend to your daughter, if she wants anything, and I know this little darling won't be frightened if he comes to himself, and sees me beside him."

"God bless you, sir," said Thomas, fervently.

And from that hour to this there has never been a coolness between us.

"A very good arrangement," said Dr Duncan; "only I feel as if I ought to have a share in it."

"No, no," I said. "We do not know who may want you. Besides, we are both younger than you."

"I will come over early in the morning then, and see how you are going on."

As soon as Thomas returned with good news of Mary's recovery, I left him, and went home to tell my sister, and arrange for the night. We carried back with us what things we could think of to make the two patients as comfortable as possible; for, as regarded Catherine, now that she would let her fellows help her, I was even anxious that she should feel something of that love about her which she had so long driven from her door. I felt towards her somewhat as towards a new-born child, for whom this life of mingled weft must be made as soft as its material will admit of; or rather, as if she had been my own sister, as indeed she was, returned from wandering in weary and miry ways, to taste once more the tenderness of home. I wanted her to read the love of God in the love that even I could show her. And, besides, I must confess that, although the result had been, in God's great grace, so good, my heart still smote me for the severity with which I had spoken the truth to her; and it was a relief to myself to endeavour to make some amends for having so spoken to her. But I had no intention of going near her that night, for I thought the less she saw of me the better, till she should be a little stronger, and have had time, with the help of her renewed feelings, to get over the painful associations so long accompanying the thought of me. So I took my place beside Gerard, and watched through the night. The little fellow repeatedly cried out in that terror which is so often the consequence of the loss of blood; but when I laid my hand on him, he smiled without waking, and lay quite still again for a while. Once or twice he woke up, and looked so bewildered that I feared delirium; but a little jelly composed him, and he fell fast asleep again. He did not seem even to have headache from the blow.

But when I was left alone with the child, seated in a chair by the fire, my only light, how my thoughts rushed upon the facts bearing on my own history which this day had brought before me! Horror it was to think of Miss Oldcastle even as only riding with the seducer of Catherine Weir. There was torture in the thought of his touching her hand; and to think that before the summer came once more, he might be her husband! I will not dwell on the sufferings of that night more than is needful; for even now, in my old age, I cannot recall without renewing them. But I must indicate one train of thought which kept passing through my mind with constant recurrence:—Was it fair to let her marry such a man in ignorance? Would she marry him if she knew what I knew of him? Could I speak against my rival?—blacken him even with the truth—the only defilement that can really cling? Could I for my own dignity do so? And was she therefore to be sacrificed in ignorance? Might not some one else do it instead of me? But if I set it agoing, was it not precisely the same thing as if I did it myself, only more cowardly? There was but one way of doing it, and that was—with the full and solemn consciousness that it was and must be a barrier between us for ever. If I could give her up fully and altogether, then I might tell her the truth which was to preserve her from marrying such a man as my rival. And I must do so, sooner than that she, my very dream of purity and gentle truth, should wed defilement. But how bitter to cast away my CHANCE! as I said, in the gathering despair of that black night. And although every time I said it—for the same words would come over and over as in a delirious dream—I repeated yet again to myself that wonderful line of Spenser,—

"It chanced—eternal God that chance did guide,"

yet the words never grew into spirit in me; they remained "words, words, words," and meant nothing to my feeling—hardly even to my judgment meant anything at all. Then came another bitter thought, the bitterness of which was wicked: it flashed upon me that my own earnestness with Catherine Weir, in urging her to the duty of forgiveness, would bear a main part in wrapping up in secrecy that evil thing which ought not to be hid. For had she not vowed— with the same facts before her which now threatened to crush my heart into a lump of clay—to denounce the man at the very altar? Had not the revenge which I had ignorantly combated been my best ally? And for one brief, black, wicked moment I repented that I had acted as I had acted. The next I was on my knees by the side of the sleeping child, and had repented back again in shame and sorrow. Then came the consolation that if I suffered hereby, I suffered from doing my duty. And that was well.

Scarcely had I seated myself again by the fire when the door of the room opened softly, and Thomas appeared.

"Kate is very strange, sir," he said, "and wants to see you."

I rose at once.

"Perhaps, then, you had better stay with Gerard."

"I will, sir; for I think she wants to speak to you alone."

I entered her chamber. A candle stood on a chest of drawers, and its light fell on her face, once more flushed in those two spots with the glow of the unseen fire of disease. Her eyes, too, glittered again, but the fierceness was gone, and only the suffering remained. I drew a chair beside her, and took her hand. She yielded it willingly, even returned the pressure of kindness which I offered to the thin trembling fingers.

"You are too good, sir," she said. "I want to tell you all. He promised to marry me, I believed him. But I did very wrong. And I have been a bad mother, for I could not keep from seeing his face in Gerard's. Gerard was the name he told me to call him when I had to write to him, and so I named the little darling Gerard. How is he, sir?"

"Doing nicely," I replied. "I do not think you need be at all uneasy about him now."

"Thank God. I forgive his father now with all my heart. I feel it easier since I saw how wicked I could be myself. And I feel it easier, too, that I have not long to live. I forgive him with all my heart, and I will take no revenge. I will not tell one who he is. I have never told any one yet. But I will tell you. His name is George Everard—Captain Everard. I came to know him when I was apprenticed at Addicehead. I would not tell you, sir, if I did not know that you will not tell any one. I know you so well that I will not ask you not. I saw him yesterday, and it drove me wild. But it is all over now. My heart feels so cool now. Do you think God will forgive me?"

Without one word of my own, I took out my pocket Testament and read these words:—

"For if ye forgive men their trespasses, your heavenly Father will also forgive you."

Then I read to her, from the seventh chapter of St Luke's Gospel, the story of the woman who was a sinner and came to Jesus in Simon's house, that she might see how the Lord himself thought and felt about such. When I had finished, I found that she was gently weeping, and so I left her, and resumed my place beside the boy. I told Thomas that he had better not go near her just yet. So we sat in silence together for a while, during which I felt so weary and benumbed, that I neither cared to resume my former train of thought, nor to enter upon the new one suggested by the confession of Catherine. I believe I must have fallen asleep in my chair, for I suddenly returned to consciousness at a cry from Gerard. I started up, and there was the child fast asleep, but standing on his feet in his crib, pushing with his hands from before him, as if resisting some one, and crying—

"Don't. Don't. Go away, man. Mammy! Mr Walton!"

I took him in my arms, and kissed him, and laid him down again; and he lay as still as if he had never moved. At the same moment, Thomas came again into the room.

"I am sorry to be so troublesome, sir," he said; "but my poor daughter says there is one thing more she wanted to say to you."

I returned at once. As soon as I entered the room, she said eagerly:—

"I forgive him—I forgive him with all my heart; but don't let him take Gerard."

I assured her I would do my best to prevent any such attempt on his part, and making her promise to try to go to sleep, left her once more. Nor was either of the patients disturbed again during the night. Both slept, as it appeared, refreshingly.

In the morning, that is, before eight o'clock, the old doctor made his welcome appearance, and pronounced both quite as well as he had expected to find them. In another hour, he had sent young Tom to take my place, and my sister to take his father's. I was determined that none of the gossips of the village should go near the invalid if I could help it; for, though such might be kind-hearted and estimable women, their place was not by such a couch as that of Catherine Weir. I enjoined my sister to be very gentle in her approaches to her, to be careful even not to seem anxious to serve her, and so to allow her to get gradually accustomed to her presence, not showing herself for the first day more than she could help, and yet taking good care she should have everything she wanted. Martha seemed to understand me perfectly; and I left her in charge with the more confidence that I knew Dr Duncan would call several times in the course of the day. As for Tom, I had equal assurance that he would attend to orders; and as Gerard was very fond of him, I dismissed all anxiety about both, and allowed my mind to return with fresh avidity to the contemplation of its own cares, and fears, and perplexities.

It was of no use trying to go to sleep, so I set out for a walk.

CHAPTER XXVII. THE MAN AND THE CHILD.

It was a fine frosty morning, the invigorating influences of which, acting along with the excitement following immediately upon a sleepless night, overcame in a great measure the depression occasioned by the contemplation of my circumstances. Disinclined notwithstanding for any more pleasant prospect, I sought the rugged common where I had so lately met Catherine

328

Weir in the storm and darkness, and where I had stood without knowing it upon the very verge of the precipice down which my fate was now threatening to hurl me. I reached the same chasm in which I had sought a breathing space on that night, and turning into it, sat down upon a block of sand which the frost had detached from the wall above. And now the tumult began again in my mind, revolving around the vortex of a new centre of difficulty.

For, first of all, I found my mind relieved by the fact that, having urged Catherine to a line of conduct which had resulted in confession,—a confession which, leaving all other considerations of my office out of view, had the greater claim upon my secrecy that it was made in confidence in my uncovenanted honour,—I was not, could not be at liberty to disclose the secret she confided to me, which, disclosed by herself, would have been the revenge from which I had warned her, and at the same time my deliverance. I was relieved I say at first, by this view of the matter, because I might thus keep my own chance of some favourable turn; whereas, if I once told Miss Oldcastle, I must give her up for ever, as I had plainly seen in the watch of the preceding night. But my love did not long remain skulking thus behind the hedge of honour. Suddenly I woke and saw that I was unworthy of the honour of loving her, for that I was glad to be compelled to risk her well-being for the chance of my own happiness; a risk which involved infinitely more wretchedness to her than the loss of my dearest hopes to me; for it is one thing for a man not to marry the woman he loves, and quite another for a woman to marry a man she cannot ever respect. Had I not been withheld partly by my obligation to Catherine, partly by the feeling that I ought to wait and see what God would do, I should have risen that moment and gone straight to Oldcastle Hall, that I might plunge at once into the ocean of my loss, and encounter, with the full sense of honourable degradation, every misconstruction that might justly be devised of my conduct. For that I had given her up first could never be known even to her in this world. I could only save her by encountering and enduring and cherishing her scorn. At least so it seemed to me at the time; and, although I am certain the other higher motives had much to do in holding me back, I am equally certain that this awful vision of the irrevocable fate to follow upon the deed, had great influence, as well, in inclining me to suspend action.

I was still sitting in the hollow, when I heard the sound of horses' hoofs in the distance, and felt a foreboding of what would appear. I was only a few yards from the road upon which the sand-cleft opened, and could see a space of it sufficient to show the persons even of rapid riders. The sounds drew nearer. I could distinguish the step of a pony and the steps of two horses besides. Up they came and swept past—Miss Oldcastle upon Judy's pony, and Mr Stoddart upon her horse; with the captain upon his own. How grateful I felt to Mr Stoddart! And the hope arose in me that he had accompanied them at Miss Oldcastle's request.

I had had no fear of being seen, sitting as I was on the side from which they came. One of the three, however, caught a glimpse of me, and even in the moment ere she vanished I fancied I saw the lily-white grow rosy-red. But it must have been fancy, for she could hardly have been quite pale upon horseback on such a keen morning.

I could not sit any longer. As soon as I ceased to hear the sound of their progress, I rose and walked home—much quieter in heart and mind than when I set out.

As I entered by the nearer gate of the vicarage, I saw Old Rogers enter by the farther. He did not see me, but we met at the door. I greeted him.

"I'm in luck," he said, "to meet yer reverence just coming home. How's poor Miss Weir to-day, sir?"

"She was rather better, when I left her this morning, than she had been through the night. I have not heard since. I left my sister with her. I greatly doubt if she will ever get up again. That's between ourselves, you know. Come in."

"Thank you, sir. I wanted to have a little talk with you.—You don't believe what they say—that she tried to kill the poor little fellow?" he asked, as soon as the study door was closed behind us.

"If she did, she was out of her mind for the moment. But I don't believe it."

And thereupon I told him what both his master and I thought about

330

it. But I did not tell him what she had said confirmatory of our conclusions.

"That's just what I came to myself, sir, turning the thing over in my old head. But there's dreadful things done in the world, sir. There's my daughter been a-telling of me—"

I was instantly breathless attention. What he chose to tell me I felt at liberty to hear, though I would not have listened to Jane herself.—I must here mention that she and Richard were not yet married, old Mr Brownrigg not having yet consented to any day his son wished to fix; and that she was, therefore, still in her place of attendance upon Miss Oldcastle.

"—There's been my daughter a-telling of me," said Rogers, "that the old lady up at the Hall there is tormenting the life out of that daughter of hers— she don't look much like hers, do she, sir?—wanting to make her marry a man of her choosing. I saw him go past o' horseback with her yesterday, and I didn't more than half like the looks on him. He's too like a fair-spoken captain I sailed with once, what was the hardest man I ever sailed with. His own way was everything, even after he saw it wouldn't do. Now, don't you think, sir, somebody or other ought to interfere? It's as bad as murder that, and anybody has a right to do summat to perwent it."

"I don't know what can be done, Rogers. I CAN'T interfere."

The old man was silent. Evidently he thought I might interfere if I pleased. I could see what he was thinking. Possibly his daughter had told him something more than he chose to communicate to me. I could not help suspecting the mode in which he judged I might interfere. But I could see no likelihood before me but that of confusion and precipitation. In a word, I had not a plain path to follow.

"Old Rogers," I said, "I can almost guess what you mean. But I am in more difficulty with regard to what you suggest than I can easily explain to you. I need not tell you, however, that I will turn the whole matter over in my mind."

"The prey ought to be taken from the lion somehow, if it please God," returned the old man solemnly. "The poor young lady keeps up as well as she can before her mother; but Jane do say there's a power o' crying done in her own room."

Partly to hide my emotion, partly with the sudden resolve to do something, if anything could be done, I said:—

"I will call on Mr Stoddart this evening. I may hear something from him to suggest a mode of action."

"I don't think you'll get anything worth while from Mr Stoddart. He takes things a deal too easy like. He'll be this man's man and that man's man both at oncet. I beg your pardon, sir. But HE won't help us."

"That's all I can think of at present, though," I said; whereupon the man-of-war's man, with true breeding, rose at once, and took a kindly leave.

I was in the storm again. She suffering, resisting, and I standing aloof! But what could I do? She had repelled me—she would repel me. Were I to dare to speak, and so be refused, the separation would be final. She had said that the day might come when she would ask help from me: she had made no movement towards the request. I would gladly die to serve her—yea, more gladly far than live, if that service was to separate us. But what to do I could not see. Still, just to do something, even if a useless something, I would go and see Mr Stoddart that evening. I was sure to find him alone, for he never dined with the family, and I might possibly catch a glimpse of Miss Oldcastle.

I found little Gerard so much better, though very weak, and his mother so quiet, notwithstanding great feverishness, that I might safely leave them to the care of Mary, who had quite recovered from her attack, and her brother Tom. So there was something off my mind for the present.

The heavens were glorious with stars,—Arcturus and his host, the Pleiades, Orion, and all those worlds that shine out when ours is dark; but I did not care for them. Let them shine: they could not shine into me. I tried with feeble effort to lift my eyes to Him who is above the stars, and yet holds the sea, yea, the sea of human thought and trouble, in the hollow of His hand. How much sustaining, although no conscious comforting, I got from that region

"Where all men's prayers to Thee raised Return possessed of what

they pray Thee."

I cannot tell. It was not a time favourable to the analysis of feeling—still less of religious feeling. But somehow things did seem a little more endurable before I reached the house.

I was passing across the hall, following the "white wolf" to Mr Stoddart's room, when the drawing-room door opened, and Miss Oldcastle came half out, but seeing me drew back instantly. A moment after, however, I heard the sound of her dress following us. Light as was her step, every footfall seemed to be upon my heart. I did not dare to look round, for dread of seeing her turn away from me. I felt like one under a spell, or in an endless dream; but gladly would I have walked on for ever in hope, with that silken vortex of sound following me. Soon, however, it ceased. She had turned aside in some other direction, and I passed on to Mr Stoddart's room.

He received me kindly, as he always did; but his smile flickered uneasily. He seemed in some trouble, and yet pleased to see me.

"I am glad you have taken to horseback," I said. "It gives me hope that you will be my companion sometimes when I make a round of my parish. I should like you to see some of our people. You would find more in them to interest you than perhaps you would expect."

I thus tried to seem at ease, as I was far from feeling.

"I am not so fond of riding as I used to be," returned Mr Stoddart.

"Did you like the Arab horses in India?"

"Yes, after I got used to their careless ways. That horse you must have seen me on the other day, is very nearly a pure Arab. He belongs to Captain Everard, and carries Miss Oldcastle beautifully. I was quite sorry to take him from her, but it was her own doing. She would have me go with her. I think I have lost much firmness since I was ill."

"If the loss of firmness means the increase of kindness, I do not think you will have to lament it," I answered. "Does Captain Everard make a long stay?"

"He stays from day to day. I wish he would go. I don't know what to do. Mrs Oldcastle and he form one party in the house; Miss Oldcastle and Judy another; and each is trying to gain me over. I don't want to belong to either. If they would only let me alone!"

"What do they want of you, Mr Stoddart?"

"Mrs Oldcastle wants me to use my influence with Ethelwyn, to persuade her to behave differently to Captain Everard. The old lady has set her heart on their marriage, and Ethelwyn, though she dares not break with him, she is so much afraid of her mother, yet keeps him somehow at arm's length. Then Judy is always begging me to stand up for her aunt. But what's the use of my standing up for her if she won't stand up for herself; she never says a word to me about it herself. It's all Judy's doing. How am I to know what she wants?"

"I thought you said just now she asked you to ride with her?"

"So she did, but nothing more. She did not even press it, only the tears came in her eyes when I refused, and I could not bear that; so I went against my will. I don't want to make enemies. I am sure I don't see why she should stand out. He's a very good match in point of property and family too."

"Perhaps she does not like him?" I forced myself to say.

"Oh! I suppose not, or she would not be so troublesome. But she could arrange all that if she were inclined to be agreeable to her friends. After all I have done for her! Well, one must not look to be repaid for anything one does for others. I used to be very fond of her: I am getting quite tired of her miserable looks."

And what had this man done for her, then? He had, for his own amusement, taught her Hindostanee; he had given her some insight into the principles of mechanics, and he had roused in her some taste for the writings of the Mystics. But for all that regarded the dignity of her humanity and her womanhood, if she had had no teaching but what he gave her, her

334

mind would have been merely "an unweeded garden that grows to seed." And now he complained that in return for his pains she would not submit to the degradation of marrying a man she did not love, in order to leave him in the enjoyment of his own lazy and cowardly peace. Really he was a worse man than I had thought him. Clearly he would not help to keep her in the right path, not even interfere to prevent her from being pushed into the wrong one. But perhaps he was only expressing his own discomfort, not giving his real judgment, and I might be censuring him too hardly.

"What will be the result, do you suppose?" I asked.

"I can't tell. Sooner or later she will have to give in to her mother. Everybody does. She might as well yield with a good grace."

"She must do what she thinks right," I said. "And you, Mr Stoddart, ought to help her to do what is right. You surely would not urge her to marry a man she did not love."

"Well, no; not exactly urge her. And yet society does not object to it. It is an acknowledged arrangement, common enough."

"Society is scarcely an interpreter of the divine will. Society will honour vile things enough, so long as the doer has money sufficient to clothe them in a grace not their own. There is a God's-way of doing everything in the world, up to marrying, or down to paying a bill."

"Yes, yes, I know what you would say; and I suppose you are right. I will not urge any opinion of mine. Besides, we shall have a little respite soon, for he must join his regiment in a day or two."

It was some relief to hear this. But I could not with equanimity prosecute a conversation having Miss Oldcastle for the subject of it, and presently took my leave.

As I walked through one of the long passages, but dimly lighted, leading from Mr Stoddart's apartment to the great staircase, I started at a light touch on my arm. It was from Judy's hand.

"Dear Mr Walton——" she said, and stopped.

335

For at the same moment appeared at the farther end of the passage towards which I had been advancing, a figure of which little more than a white face was visible; and the voice of Sarah, through whose softness always ran a harsh thread that made it unmistakable, said,

"Miss Judy, your grandmamma wants you."

Judy took her hand from my arm, and with an almost martial stride the little creature walked up to the speaker, and stood before her defiantly. I could see them quite well in the fuller light at the end of the passage, where there stood a lamp. I followed slowly that I might not interrupt the child's behaviour, which moved me strangely in contrast with the pusillanimity I had so lately witnessed in Mr Stoddart.

"Sarah," she said, "you know you are telling a lie Grannie does NOT want me. You have NOT been in the dining-room since I left it one moment ago. Do you think, you BAD woman, I am going to be afraid of you? I know you better than you think. Go away directly, or I will make you."

She stamped her little foot, and the "white wolf" turned and walked away without a word.

If the mothers among my readers are shocked at the want of decorum in my friend Judy, I would just say, that valuable as propriety of demeanour is, truth of conduct is infinitely more precious. Glad should I be to think that the even tenor of my children's good manners could never be interrupted, except by such righteous indignation as carried Judy beyond the strict bounds of good breeding. Nor could I find it in my heart to rebuke her wherein she had been wrong. In the face of her courage and uprightness, the fault was so insignificant that it would have been giving it an altogether undue importance to allude to it at all, and might weaken her confidence in my sympathy with her rectitude. When I joined her she put her hand in mine, and so walked with me down the stair and out at the front door.

"You will take cold, Judy, going out like that," I said.

"I am in too great a passion to take cold," she answered. "But I have no time to talk about that creeping creature.—Auntie DOESN'T like Captain

336

Everard; and grannie keeps insisting on it that she shall have him whether she likes him or not. Now do tell me what you think."

"I do not quite understand you, my child."

"I know auntie would like to know what you think. But I know she will never ask you herself. So I am asking you whether a lady ought to marry a gentleman she does not like, to please her mother."

"Certainly not, Judy. It is often wicked, and at best a mistake."

"Thank you, Mr Walton. I will tell her. She will be glad to hear that you say so, I know."

"Mind you tell her you asked me, Judy. I should not like her to think I had been interfering, you know."

"Yes, yes; I know quite well. I will take care. Thank you. He's going to-morrow. Good night."

She bounded into the house again, and I walked away down the avenue. I saw and felt the stars now, for hope had come again in my heart, and I thanked the God of hope. "Our minds are small because they are faithless," I said to myself. "If we had faith in God, as our Lord tells us, our hearts would share in His greatness and peace. For we should not then be shut up in ourselves, but would walk abroad in Him." And with a light step and a light heart I went home.

CHAPTER XXVIII. OLD MRS TOMKINS.

Very severe weather came, and much sickness followed, chiefly amongst the poorer people, who can so ill keep out the cold. Yet some of my well-to-do parishioners were laid up likewise—amongst others Mr Boulderstone, who had an attack of pleurisy. I had grown quite attached to Mr Boulderstone by this time, not because he was what is called interesting, for he was not; not because he was clever, for he was not; not because he was well-read, for he was not; not because he was possessed of influence in the parish, though he had that influence; but simply because he was true; he was what he appeared, felt what he professed, did what he said; appearing kind, and feeling and acting kindly. Such a man is rare and precious, were he as stupid as the Welsh giant in "Jack the Giant-Killer." I could never see Mr Boulderstone a mile off, but my heart felt the warmer for the sight.

Even in his great pain he seemed to forget himself as he received me, and to gain comfort from my mere presence. I could not help regarding him as a child of heaven, to be treated with the more reverence that he had the less aid to his goodness from his slow understanding. It seemed to me that the angels might gather with reverence around such a man, to watch the gradual and tardy awakening of the intellect in one in whom the heart and the conscience had been awake from the first. The latter safe, they at least would see well that there was no fear for the former. Intelligence is a consequence of love; nor is there any true intelligence without it.

But I could not help feeling keenly the contrast when I went from his warm, comfortable, well-defended chamber, in which every appliance that could alleviate suffering or aid recovery was at hand, like a castle well appointed with arms and engines against the inroads of winter and his yet colder ally Death,—when, I say, I went from his chamber to the cottage of the Tomkinses, and found it, as it were, lying open and bare to the enemy. What holes and cracks there were about the door, through which the fierce wind rushed at once into the room to attack the aged feet and hands and throats! There were no defences of threefold draperies, and no soft carpet on the brick floor,—only a small rug which my sister had carried them laid down before a weak-eyed little fire, that seemed to despair of making anything of it against the huge cold that beleaguered and invaded the place. True, we had had the little cottage patched up. The two Thomas Weirs had been at work upon it for a whole day and a half in the first of the cold weather this winter; but it was like putting the new cloth on the old garment, for fresh places had broken out, and although Mrs Tomkins had fought the cold well with what rags she could spare, and an old knife, yet such razor-edged winds are hard to keep out, and here she was now, lying in bed, and breathing hard, like the sore-pressed garrison which had retreated to its last defence, the keep of the castle. Poor old Tomkins sat shivering over the little fire.

"Come, come, Tomkins! this won't do," I said, as I caught up a broken shovel that would have let a lump as big as one's fist through a hole in the middle of it. "Why don't you burn your coals in weather like this? Where do you keep them?"

It made my heart ache to see the little heap in a box hardly bigger than the chest of tea my sister brought from London with her. I threw half of it on the fire at once.

"Deary me, Mr Walton! you ARE wasteful, sir. The Lord never sent His good coals to be used that way."

"He did though, Tomkins," I answered. "And He'll send you a little more this evening, after I get home. Keep yourself warm, man. This world's cold in winter, you know."

"Indeed, sir, I know that. And I'm like to know it worse afore long. She's going," he said, pointing over his shoulder with his thumb towards the bed where his wife lay.

I went to her. I had seen her several times within the last few weeks, but had observed nothing to make me consider her seriously ill. I now saw at a glance that Tomkins was right. She had not long to live.

"I am sorry to see you suffering so much, Mrs Tomkins," I said.

"I don't suffer so wery much, sir; though to be sure it be hard to get the breath into my body, sir. And I do feel cold-like, sir."

"I'm going home directly, and I'll send you down another blanket. It's much colder to-day than it was yesterday."

"It's not weather-cold, sir, wi' me. It's grave-cold, sir. Blankets won't do me no good, sir. I can't get it out of my head how perishing cold I shall be when I'm under the mould, sir; though I oughtn't to mind it when it's the will o' God. It's only till the resurrection, sir."

"But it's not the will of God, Mrs Tomkins."

"Ain't it, sir? Sure I thought it was."

"You believe in Jesus Christ, don't you, Mrs Tomkins?"

"That I do, sir, with all my heart and soul."

"Well, He says that whosoever liveth and believeth in Him shall never die."

"But, you know, sir, everybody dies. I MUST die, and be laid in the churchyard, sir. And that's what I don't like."

"But I say that is all a mistake. YOU won't die. Your body will die, and be laid away out of sight; but you will be awake, alive, more alive than you are now, a great deal."

And here let me interrupt the conversation to remark upon the great mistake of teaching children that they have souls. The consequence is, that they think of their souls as of something which is not themselves. For what a man HAS cannot be himself. Hence, when they are told that their souls go to heaven, they think of their SELVES as lying in the grave. They ought to be taught that they have bodies; and that their bodies die; while they themselves live on. Then they will not think, as old Mrs Tomkins did, that THEY will be laid in the grave. It is making altogether too much of the body, and is indicative of an evil tendency to materialism, that we talk as if we POSSESSED souls, instead of BEING souls. We should teach our children to think no more of their bodies when dead than they do of their hair when it is cut off, or of their old clothes when they have done with them.

"Do you really think so, sir?"

"Indeed I do. I don't know anything about where you will be. But you will be with God—in your Father's house, you know. And that is enough, is it not?"

"Yes, surely, sir. But I wish you was to be there by the bedside of me when I was a-dyin'. I can't help bein' summat skeered at it. It don't come nat'ral to me, like. I ha' got used to this old bed here, cold as it has been—many's the night—wi' my good man there by the side of me."

"Send for me, Mrs Tomkins, any moment, day or night, and I'll be with you directly."

"I think, sir, if I had a hold ov you i' the one hand, and my man there, the Lord bless him, i' the other, I could go comfortable."

"I'll come the minute you send for me—just to keep you in mind that a better friend than I am is holding you all the time, though you mayn't feel His hands. If it is some comfort to have hold of a human friend, think that a friend who is more than man, a divine friend, has a hold of you, who knows all your fears and pains, and sees how natural they are, and can just with a word, or a touch, or a look into your soul, keep them from going one hair's-breadth too far. He loves us up to all out need, just because we need it, and He is all love to give."

"But I can't help thinking, sir, that I wouldn't be troublesome. He has such a deal to look after! And I don't see how He can think of everybody, at every minute, like. I don't mean that He will let anything go wrong. But He might forget an old body like me for a minute, like."

"You would need to be as wise as He is before you could see how He does it. But you must believe more than you can understand. It is only common sense to do so. Think how nonsensical it would be to suppose that one who could make everything, and keep the whole going as He does, shouldn't be able to help forgetting. It would be unreasonable to think that He must forget because you couldn't understand how He could remember. I think it is as hard for Him to forget anything as it is for us to remember everything; for forgetting comes of weakness, and from our not being finished yet, and He is all strength and all perfection."

"Then you think, sir, He never forgets anything?"

I knew by the trouble that gathered on the old woman's brow what kind of thought was passing through her mind. But I let her go on, thinking so to help her the better. She paused for one moment only, and then resumed—much interrupted by the shortness of her breathing.

"When I was brought to bed first," she said, "it was o' twins, sir. And oh! sir, it was VERY hard. As I said to my man after I got my head up a bit, 'Tomkins,' says I, 'you don't know what it is to have TWO on 'em cryin' and

341

cryin', and you next to nothin' to give 'em; till their cryin' sticks to your brain, and ye hear 'em when they're fast asleep, one on each side o' you.' Well, sir, I'm ashamed to confess it even to you; and what the Lord can think of me, I don't know."

"I would rather confess to Him than to the best friend I ever had," I said; "I am so sure that He will make every excuse for me that ought to be made. And a friend can't always do that. He can't know all about it. And you can't tell him all, because you don't know all yourself. He does."

"But I would like to tell YOU, sir. Would you believe it, sir, I wished 'em dead? Just to get the wailin' of them out o' my head, I wished 'em dead. In the courtyard o' the squire's house, where my Tomkins worked on the home-farm, there was an old draw-well. It wasn't used, and there was a lid to it, with a hole in it, through which you could put a good big stone. And Tomkins once took me to it, and, without tellin' me what it was, he put a stone in, and told me to hearken. And I hearkened, but I heard nothing,—as I told him so. 'But,' says he, 'hearken, lass.' And in a little while there come a blast o' noise like from somewheres. 'What's that, Tomkins?' I said. 'That's the ston',' says he, 'a strikin' on the water down that there well.' And I turned sick at the thought of it. And it's down there that I wished the darlin's that God had sent me; for there they'd be quiet."

"Mothers are often a little out of their minds at such times, Mrs Tomkins. And so were you."

"I don't know, sir. But I must tell you another thing. The Sunday afore that, the parson had been preachin' about 'Suffer little children,' you know, sir, 'to come unto me.' I suppose that was what put it in my head; but I fell asleep wi' nothin' else in my head but the cries o' the infants and the sound o' the ston' in the draw-well. And I dreamed that I had one o' them under each arm, cryin' dreadful, and was walkin' across the court the way to the draw-well; when all at once a man come up to me and held out his two hands, and said, 'Gie me my childer.' And I was in a terrible fear. And I gave him first one and then the t'other, and he took them, and one laid its head on one shoulder of him, and t'other upon t'other, and they stopped their cryin', and fell fast asleep; and away he walked wi' them into the dark, and I saw him no more. And then I awoke cryin', I didn't know why. And I took my twins to me, and my breasts was full, if ye 'll excuse me, sir. And my heart was as full o' love to them. And they hardly cried worth mentionin' again. But afore they was two year old, they both died o' the brown chytis, sir. And I think that He took them."

"He did take them, Mrs Tomkins; and you'll see them again soon."

"But, if He never forgets anything——"

"I didn't say that. I think He can do what He pleases. And if He pleases to forget anything, then He can forget it. And I think that is what He does with our sins—that is, after He has got them away from us, once we are clean from them altogether. It would be a dreadful thing if He forgot them before that, and left them sticking fast to us and defiling us. How then should we ever be made clean?—What else does the prophet Isaiah mean when he says, 'Thou hast cast my sins behind Thy back?' Is not that where He does not choose to see them any more? They are not pleasant to Him to think of any more than to us. It is as if He said—'I will not think of that any more, for my sister will never do it again,' and so He throws it behind His back."

"They ARE good words, sir. I could not bear Him to think of me and my sins both at once."

I could not help thinking of the words of Macbeth, "To know my deed, 'twere best not know myself."

The old woman lay quiet after this, relieved in mind, though not in body, by the communication she had made with so much difficulty, and I hastened home to send some coals and other things, and then call upon Dr Duncan, lest he should not know that his patient was so much worse as I had found her.

From Dr Duncan's I went to see old Samuel Weir, who likewise was ailing. The bitter weather was telling chiefly upon the aged. I found him in bed, under the old embroidery. No one was in the room with him. He greeted me with a withered smile, sweet and true, although no flash of white teeth broke forth to light up the welcome of the aged head.

"Are you not lonely, Mr Weir?"

"No, sir. I don't know as ever I was less lonely. I've got my stick, you see, sir," he said, pointing to a thorn stick which lay beside him.

"I do not quite understand you," I returned, knowing that the old man's gently humorous sayings always meant something.

"You see, sir, when I want anything, I've only got to knock on the floor, and up comes my son out of the shop. And then again, when I knock at the door of the house up there, my Father opens it and looks out. So I have both my son on earth and my Father in heaven, and what can an old man want more?"

"What, indeed, could any one want more?"

"It's very strange," the old man resumed after a pause, "but as I lie here, after I've had my tea, and it is almost dark, I begin to feel as if I was a child again.—They say old age is a second childhood; but before I grew so old, I used to think that meant only that a man was helpless and silly again, as he used to be when he was a child: I never thought it meant that a man felt like a child again, as light-hearted and untroubled as I do now."

"Well, I suspect that is not what people do mean when they say so. But I am very glad—you don't know how pleased it makes me to hear that you feel so. I will hope to fare in the same way when my time comes."

"Indeed, I hope you will, sir; for I am main and happy. Just before you came in now, I had really forgotten that I was a toothless old man, and thought I was lying here waiting for my mother to come in and say good-night to me before I went to sleep. Wasn't that curious, when I never saw my mother, as I told you before, sir?"

"It was very curious."

"But I have no end of fancies. Only when I begin to think about it, I can always tell when they are fancies, and they never put me out. There's one

I see often—a man down on his knees at that cupboard nigh the floor there, searching and searching for somewhat. And I wish he would just turn round his face once for a moment that I might see him. I have a notion always it's my own father."

"How do you account for that fancy, now, Mr Weir?"

"I've often thought about it, sir, but I never could account for it. I'm none willing to think it's a ghost; for what's the good of it? I've turned out that cupboard over and over, and there's nothing there I don't know."

"You're not afraid of it, are you?"

"No, sir. Why should I be? I never did it no harm. And God can surely take care of me from all sorts."

My readers must not think anything is going to come out of this strange illusion of the old man's brain. I questioned him a little more about it, and came simply to the conclusion, that when he was a child he had found the door open and had wandered into the house, at the time uninhabited, had peeped in at the door of the same room where he now lay, and had actually seen a man in the position he described, half in the cupboard, searching for something. His mind had kept the impression after the conscious memory had lost its hold of the circumstance, and now revived it under certain physical conditions. It was a glimpse out of one of the many stories which haunted the old mansion. But there he lay like a child, as he said, fearless even of such usurpations upon his senses.

I think instances of quiet unSELFconscious faith are more common than is generally supposed. Few have along with it the genial communicative impulse of old Samuel Weir, which gives the opportunity of seeing into their hidden world. He seemed to have been, and to have remained, a child, in the best sense of the word. He had never had much trouble with himself, for he was of a kindly, gentle, trusting nature; and his will had never been called upon to exercise any strong effort to enable him to walk in the straight path. Nor had his intellect, on the other hand, while capable enough, ever been so active as to suggest difficulties to his faith, leaving him, even theoretically, far nearer the truth than those who start objections for their own sakes, liking to feel themselves in a position of supposed antagonism to the generally acknowledged sources of illumination. For faith is in itself a light that lightens even the intellect, and hence the shield of the complete soldier of God, the shield of faith, is represented by Spenser as "framed all of diamond, perfect, pure, and clean," (the power of the diamond to absorb and again radiate light being no poetic fiction, but a well-known scientific fact,) whose light falling upon any enchantment or false appearance, destroys it utterly: for

> "all that was not such as seemed in sight.
>
> Before that shield did fade, and suddaine fall."

Old Rogers had passed through a very much larger experience. Many more difficulties had come to him, and he had met them in his own fashion and overcome them. For while there is such a thing as truth, the mind that can honestly beget a difficulty must at the same time be capable of receiving that light of the truth which annihilates the difficulty, or at least of receiving enough to enable it to foresee vaguely some solution, for a full perception of which the intellect may not be as yet competent. By every such victory Old Rogers had enlarged his being, ever becoming more childlike and faithful; so that, while the childlikeness of Weir was the childlikeness of a child, that of Old Rogers was the childlikeness of a man, in which submission to God is not only a gladness, but a conscious will and choice. But as the safety of neither depended on his own feelings, but on the love of God who was working in him, we may well leave all such differences of nature and education to the care of Him who first made the men different, and then brought different conditions out of them. The one thing is, whether we are letting God have His own way with us, following where He leads, learning the lessons He gives us.

I wished that Mr Stoddart had been with me during these two visits. Perhaps he might have seen that the education of life was a marvellous thing, and, even in the poorest intellectual results, far more full of poetry and wonder than the outcome of that constant watering with the watering-pot of self-education which, dissociated from the duties of life and the influences of his fellows, had made of him what he was. But I doubt if he would have seen it.

A week had elapsed from the night I had sat up with Gerard Weir, and his mother had not risen from her bed, nor did it seem likely she would ever rise again. On a Friday I went to see her, just as the darkness was beginning to gather. The fire of life was burning itself out fast. It glowed on her cheeks, it burned in her hands, it blazed in her eyes. But the fever had left her mind. That was cool, oh, so cool, now! Those fierce tropical storms of passion had passed away, and nothing of life was lost. Revenge had passed away, but revenge is of death, and deadly. Forgiveness had taken its place, and forgiveness is the giving, and so the receiving of life. Gerard, his dear little head starred with sticking-plaster, sat on her bed, looking as quietly happy as child could look, over a wooden horse with cylindrical body and jointless legs, covered with an eruption of red and black spots.—Is it the ignorance or the imagination of children that makes them so easily pleased with the merest hint at representation? I suspect the one helps the other towards that most desirable result, satisfaction.—But he dropped it when he saw me, in a way so abandoning that—comparing small things with great—it called to my mind those lines of Milton:—

> "*From his slack hand the garland wreathed for Eve,*
>
> *Down dropt, and all the faded roses shed.*"

The quiet child FLUNG himself upon my neck, and the mother's face gleamed with pleasure.

"Dear boy!" I said, "I am very glad to see you so much better."

For this was the first time he had shown such a revival of energy. He had been quite sweet when he saw me, but, until this evening, listless.

"Yes," he said, "I am quite well now." And he put his hand up to his head.

"Does it ache?"

"Not much now. The doctor says I had a bad fall."

"So you had, my child. But you will soon be well again."

347

The mother's face was turned aside, yet I could see one tear forcing its way from under her closed eyelid.

"Oh, I don't mind it," he answered. "Mammy is so kind to me! She lets me sit on her bed as long as I like."

"That IS nice. But just run to auntie in the next room. I think your mammy would like to talk to me for a little while."

The child hurried off the bed, and ran with overflowing obedience.

"I can even think of HIM now," said the mother, "without going into a passion. I hope God will forgive him. I do. I think He will forgive me."

"Did you ever hear," I asked, "of Jesus refusing anybody that wanted kindness from Him? He wouldn't always do exactly what they asked Him, because that would sometimes be of no use, and sometimes would even be wrong; but He never pushed them away from Him, never repulsed their approach to Him. For the sake of His disciples, He made the Syrophenician woman suffer a little while, but only to give her such praise afterwards and such a granting of her prayer as is just wonderful."

She said nothing for a little while; then murmured,

"Shall I have to be ashamed to all eternity? I do not want not to be ashamed; but shall I never be able to be like other people—in heaven I mean?"

"If He is satisfied with you, you need not think anything more about yourself. If He lets you once kiss His feet, you won't care to think about other people's opinion of you even in heaven. But things will go very differently there from here. For everybody there will be more or less ashamed of himself, and will think worse of himself than he does of any one else. If trouble about your past life were to show itself on your face there, they would all run to comfort you, trying to make the best of it, and telling you that you must think about yourself as He thinks about you; for what He thinks is the rule, because it is the infallible right way. But perhaps rather, they would tell you to leave that to Him who has taken away our sins, and not trouble yourself any more about it. But to tell the truth, I don't think such thoughts will come to you at all when once you have seen the face of Jesus Christ. You will be so filled with His glory and goodness and grace, that you will just live in Him and not in yourself at all."

"Will He let us tell Him anything we please?"

"He lets you do that now: surely He will not be less our God, our friend there."

"Oh, I don't mind how soon He takes me now! Only there's that poor child that I've behaved so badly to! I wish I could take him with me. I have no time to make it up to him here."

"You must wait till he comes. He won't think hardly of you. There's no fear of that."

"What will become of him, though? I can't bear the idea of burdening my father with him."

"Your father will be glad to have him, I know. He will feel it a privilege to do something for your sake. But the boy will do him good. If he does not want him, I will take him myself."

"Oh! thank you, thank you, sir."

A burst of tears followed.

"He has often done me good," I said.

"Who, sir? My father?"

"No. Your son."

"I don't quite understand what you mean, sir."

"I mean just what I say. The words and behaviour of your lovely boy have both roused and comforted my heart again and again."

She burst again into tears.

"That is good to hear. To think of your saying that! The poor little innocent! Then it isn't all punishment?"

"If it were ALL punishment, we should perish utterly. He is your punishment; but look in what a lovely loving form your punishment has come, and say whether God has been good to you or not."

"If I had only received my punishment humbly, things would have been very different now. But I do take it—at least I want to take it—just as He would have me take it. I will bear anything He likes. I suppose I must die?"

"I think He means you to die now. You are ready for it now, I think. You have wanted to die for a long time; but you were not ready for it before."

"And now I want to live for my boy. But His will be done."

"Amen. There is no such prayer in the universe as that. It means everything best and most beautiful. Thy will, O God, evermore be done."

She lay silent. A tap came to the chamber-door. It was Mary, who nursed her sister and attended to the shop.

"If you please, sir, here's a little girl come to say that Mrs Tomkins is dying, and wants to see you."

"Then I must say good-night to you, Catherine. I will see you to-morrow morning. Think about old Mrs Tomkins; she's a good old soul; and when you find your heart drawn to her in the trouble of death, then lift it up to God for her, that He will please to comfort and support her, and make her happier than health—stronger than strength, taking off the old worn garment of her body, and putting upon her the garment of salvation, which will be a grand new body, like that the Saviour had when He rose again."

"I will try. I will think about her."

For I thought this would be a help to prepare her for her own death. In thinking lovingly about others, we think healthily about ourselves. And the things she thought of for the comfort of Mrs Tomkins, would return to comfort herself in the prospect of her own end, when perhaps she might not be able to think them out for herself.

CHAPTER XXIX. CALM AND STORM.

But of the two, Catherine had herself to go first. Again and again was I sent for to say farewell to Mrs Tomkins, and again and again I returned home leaying her asleep, and for the time better. But on a Saturday evening, as I sat by my vestry-fire, pondering on many things, and trying to make myself feel that they were as God saw them and not as they appeared to me, young Tom came to me with the news that his sister seemed much worse, and his father would be much obliged if I would go and see her. I sent Tom on before, because I wished to follow alone.

It was a brilliant starry night; no moon, no clouds, no wind, nothing but stars. They seemed to lean down towards the earth, as I have seen them since in more southern regions. It was, indeed, a glorious night. That is, I knew it was; I did not feel that it was. For the death which I went to be near, came, with a strange sense of separation, between me and the nature around me. I felt as if nature knew nothing, felt nothing, meant nothing, did not belong to humanity at all; for here was death, and there shone the stars. I was wrong, as I knew afterwards.

I had had very little knowledge of the external shows of death. Strange as it may appear, I had never yet seen a fellow-creature pass beyond the call of his fellow-mortals. I had not even seen my father die. And the thought was oppressive to me. "To think," I said to myself, as I walked over the bridge to the village-street—"to think that the one moment the person is here, and the next—who shall say WHERE? for we know nothing of the region beyond the grave! Not even our risen Lord thought fit to bring back from Hades any news for the human family standing straining their eyes after their brothers and sisters that have vanished in the dark. Surely it is well, all well, although we know nothing, save that our Lord has been there, knows all about it, and does not choose to tell us. Welcome ignorance then! the ignorance in which he chooses to leave us. I would rather not know, if He gave me my choice, but preferred that I should not know." And so the oppression passed from me, and I was free.

But little as I knew of the signs of the approach of death, I was certain, the moment I saw Catherine, that the veil that hid the "silent land" had begun to lift slowly between her and it. And for a moment I almost envied her that she was so soon to see and know that after which our blindness and ignorance were wondering and hungering. She could hardly speak. She looked more patient than calm. There was no light in the room but that of the fire, which flickered flashing and fading, now lighting up the troubled eye, and now letting a shadow of the coming repose fall gently over it. Thomas sat by the fire with the child on his knee, both looking fixedly into the glow. Gerard's natural mood was so quiet and earnest, that the solemnity about him did not oppress him. He looked as if he were present at some religious observance of which he felt more than he understood, and his childish peace was in no wise inharmonious with the awful silence of the coming change. He was no more disquieted at the presence of death than the stars were.

And this was the end of the lovely girl—to leave the fair world still young, because a selfish man had seen that she was fair! No time can change the relation of cause and effect. The poison that operates ever so slowly is yet poison, and yet slays. And that man was now murdering her, with weapon long-reaching from out of the past. But no, thank God! this was not the end of her. Though there is woe for that man by whom the offence cometh, yet there is provision for the offence. There is One who bringeth light out of darkness, joy out of sorrow, humility out of wrong. Back to the Father's house we go with the sorrows and sins which, instead of inheriting the earth, we gathered and heaped upon our weary shoulders, and a different Elder Brother from that angry one who would not receive the poor swine-humbled prodigal, takes the burden from our shoulders, and leads us into the presence of the Good.

She put out her hand feebly, let it lie in mine, looked as if she wanted me to sit down by her bedside, and when I did so, closed her eyes. She said nothing. Her father was too much troubled to meet me without showing the signs of his distress, and his was a nature that ever sought concealment for its emotion; therefore he sat still. But Gerard crept down from his knee, came to me, clambered up on mine, and laid his little hand upon his mother's, which I was holding. She opened her eyes, looked at the child, shut them again, and tears came out from between the closed lids.

"Has Gerard ever been baptized?" I asked her.

Her lips indicated a NO.

"Then I will be his godfather. And that will be a pledge to you that I will never lose sight of him."

She pressed my hand, and the tears came faster.

Believing with all my heart that the dying should remember their dying Lord, and that the "Do this in remembrance of me" can never be better obeyed than when the partaker is about to pass, supported by the God of his faith, through the same darkness which lay before our Lord when He uttered the words and appointed the symbol, we kneeled, Thomas and I, and young Tom, who had by this time joined us with his sister Mary, around the bed, and partook with the dying woman of the signs of that death, wherein our Lord gave Himself entirely to us, to live by His death, and to the Father of us all in holiest sacrifice as the high-priest of us His people, leading us to the altar of a like self-abnegation. Upon what that bread and that wine mean, the sacrifice of our Lord, the whole world of humanity hangs. It is the redemption of men.

After she had received the holy sacrament, she lay still as before. I heard her murmur once, "Lord, I do not deserve it. But I do love Thee." And about two hours after, she quietly breathed her last. We all kneeled, and I thanked the Father of us aloud that He had taken her to Himself. Gerard had been fast asleep on his aunt's lap, and she had put him to bed a little before. Surely he slept a deeper sleep than his mother's; for had she not awaked even as she fell asleep?

When I came out once more, I knew better what the stars meant. They looked to me now as if they knew all about death, and therefore could not be sad to the eyes of men; as if that unsympathetic look they wore came from this, that they were made like the happy truth, and not like our fears.

But soon the solemn feeling of repose, the sense that the world and all its cares would thus pass into nothing, vanished in its turn. For a moment I had been, as it were, walking on the shore of the Eternal, where the tide of time had left me in its retreat. Far away across the level sands I heard it moaning, but I stood on the firm ground of truth, and heeded it not. In a few moments more it was raving around me; it had carried me away from my rest, and I was filled with the noise of its cares.

For when I returned home, my sister told me that Old Rogers had called, and seemed concerned not to find me at home. He would have gone to find me, my sister said, had I been anywhere but by a deathbed. He would not leave any message, however, saying he would call in the morning.

I thought it better to go to his house. The stars were still shining as brightly as before, but a strong foreboding of trouble filled my mind, and once more the stars were far away, and lifted me no nearer to "Him who made the seven stars and Orion." When I examined myself, I could give no reason for my sudden fearfulness, save this: that as I went to Catherine's house, I had passed Jane Rogers on her way to her father's, and having just greeted her, had gone on; but, as it now came back upon me, she had looked at me strangely— that is, with some significance in her face which conveyed nothing to me; and now her father had been to seek me: it must have something to do with Miss Oldcastle.

But when I came to the cottage, it was dark and still, and I could not bring myself to rouse the weary man from his bed. Indeed it was past eleven, as I found to my surprise on looking at my watch. So I turned and lingered by the old mill, and fell a pondering on the profusion of strength that rushed past the wheel away to the great sea, doing nothing. "Nature," I thought, "does not demand that power should always be force. Power itself must repose. He that believeth shall—not make haste, says the Bible. But it needs strength to be still. Is my faith not strong enough to be still?" I looked up to the heavens once more, and the quietness of the stars seemed to reproach me. "We are safe up here," they seemed to say: "we shine, fearless and confident, for the God who gave the primrose its rough leaves to hide it from the blast of uneven spring, hangs us in the awful hollows of space. We cannot fall out of His safety. Lift up your eyes on high, and behold! Who hath created

354

these things—that bringeth out their host by number! He calleth them all by names. By the greatness of His might, for that He is strong in power, not one faileth. Why sayest thou, O Jacob! and speakest, O Israel! my way is hid from the Lord, and my judgment is passed over from my God?"

The night was very still; there was, I thought, no one awake within miles of me. The stars seemed to shine into me the divine reproach of those glorious words. "O my God!" I cried, and fell on my knees by the mill-door.

What I tried to say more I will not say here. I MAY say that I cried to God. What I said to Him ought not, cannot be repeated to another.

When I opened my eyes I saw the door of the mill was open too, and there in the door, his white head glimmering, stood Old Rogers, with a look on his face as if he had just come down from the mount. I started to my feet, with that strange feeling of something like shame that seizes one at the very thought of other eyes than those of the Father. The old man came forward, and bowed his head with an unconscious expression of humble dignity, but would have passed me without speech, leaving the mill-door open behind him. I could not bear to part with him thus.

"Won't you speak to me, Rogers?" I said.

He turned at once with evident pleasure.

"I beg your pardon, sir. I was ashamed of having intruded on you, and I thought you would rather be left alone. I thought—I thought—" hesitated the old man, "that you might like to go into the mill, for the night's cold out o' doors."

"Thank you, Rogers. I won't now. I thought you had been in bed. How do you come to be out so late?"

"You see, sir, when I'm in any trouble, it's no use to go to bed. I can't sleep. I only keep the old 'oman wakin'. And the key o' the mill allus hangin' at the back o' my door, and knowin' it to be a good place to—to—shut the door in, I came out as soon as she was asleep; but I little thought to see you, sir."

"I came to find you, not thinking how the time went. Catherine Weir is gone home."

"I am right glad to hear it, poor woman. And perhaps something will come out now that will help us."

"I do not quite understand you," I said, with hesitation.

But Rogers made no reply.

"I am sorry to hear you are in trouble to-night. Can I help you?" I resumed.

"If you can help yourself, sir, you can help me. But I have no right to say so. Only, if a pair of old eyes be not blind, a man may pray to God about anything he sees. I was prayin' hard about you in there, sir, while you was on your knees o' the other side o' the door."

I could partly guess what the old man meant, and I could not ask him for further explanation.

"What did you want to see me about?" I inquired.

He hesitated for a moment.

"I daresay it was very foolish of me, sir. But I just wanted to tell you that—our Jane was down here from the Hall this arternoon——"

"I passed her on the bridge. Is she quite well?"

"Yes, yes, sir. You know that's not the point."

The old man's tone seemed to reprove me for vain words, and I held my peace.

"The captain's there again."

An icy spear seemed to pass through my heart. I could make no reply. The same moment a cold wind blew on me from the open door of the mill.

Although Lear was of course right when he said,

"*The tempest in my mind*

Doth from my senses take all feeling else

Save what beats there,"

    yet it is also true, that sometimes, in the midst of its greatest pain, the mind takes marvellous notice of the smallest things that happen around it. This involves a law of which illustrations could be plentifully adduced from Shakespeare himself, namely, that the intellectual part of the mind can go on working with strange independence of the emotional.

    From the door of the mill, as from a sepulchral tavern, blew a cold wind like the very breath of death upon me, just when that pang shot, in absolute pain, through my heart. For a wind had arisen from behind the mill, and we were in its shelter save where a window behind and the door beside me allowed free passage to the first of the coming storm.

    I believed I turned away from the old man without a word. He made no attempt to detain me. Whether he went back into his closet, the old mill, sacred in the eyes of the Father who honours His children, even as the church wherein many prayers went up to Him, or turned homewards to his cottage and his sleeping wife, I cannot tell. The first I remember after that cold wind is, that I was fighting with that wind, gathered even to a storm, upon the common where I had dealt so severely with her who had this very night gone into that region into which, as into a waveless sea, all the rivers of life rush and are silent. Is it the sea of death? No. The sea of life—a life too keen, too refined, for our senses to know it, and therefore we call it death—because we cannot lay hold upon it.

    I will not dwell upon my thoughts as I wandered about over that waste. The wind had risen to a storm charged with fierce showers of stinging hail, which gave a look of gray wrath to the invisible wind as it swept slanting by, and then danced and scudded along the levels. The next point in that night of pain is when I found myself standing at the iron gate of Oldcastle Hall. I had left the common, passed my own house and the church, crossed the river, walked through the village, and was restored to self-consciousness—that is, I knew that I was there—only when first I stood in the shelter of one of those great pillars and the monster on its top. Finding the gate open, for they were not precise about having it fastened, I pushed it and entered. The wind was roaring in the trees as I think I have never heard it roar since; for the hail clashed upon the bare branches and twigs, and mingled an unearthly hiss with the roar. In the midst of it the house stood like a tomb, dark, silent, without one dim light to show that sleep and not death ruled within. I could have fancied that there were no windows in it, that it stood, like an eyeless skull, in that gaunt forest of skeleton trees, empty and desolate, beaten by the ungenial hail, the dead rain of the country of death. I passed round to the other side, stepping gently lest some ear might be awake—as if any ear, even that of Judy's white wolf, could have heard the loudest step in such a storm. I heard the hailstones crush between my feet and the soft grass of the lawn, but I dared not stop to look up at the back of the house. I went on to the staircase in the rock, and by its rude steps, dangerous in the flapping of such storm-wings as swept about it that night, descended to the little grove below, around the deep-walled pool. Here the wind did not reach me. It roared overhead, but, save an occasional sigh, as if of sympathy with their suffering brethren abroad in the woild, the hermits of this cell stood upright and still around the sleeping water. But my heart was a well in which a storm boiled and raged; and all that "pother o'er my head" was peace itself compared to what I felt. I sat down on the seat at the foot of a tree, where I had first seen Miss Oldcastle reading. And then I looked up to the house. Yes, there was a light there! It must be in her window. She then could not rest any more than I. Sleep was driven from her eyes because she must wed the man she would not; while sleep was driven from mine because I could not marry the woman I would. Was that it? No. My heart acquitted me, in part at least, of thinking only of my own sorrow in the presence of her greater distress. Gladly would I have given her up for ever, without a hope, to redeem her from such a bondage. "But it would be to marry another some day," suggested the tormentor within. And then the storm, which had a little abated, broke out afresh in my soul. But before I rose from her seat I was ready even for that—at least I thought so—if only I might deliver her from the all but destruction that seemed to be impending over her. The same moment in which my mind seemed to have arrived at the possibility of such a resolution, I rose almost involuntarily, and glancing once more at the dull light in her window—for I did not doubt that it was her window, though it was much too dark to discern, the shape of the house—almost felt my way to the stair, and climbed again into the storm.

But I was quieter now, and able to go home. It must have been nearly morning, though at this season of the year the morning is undefined, when I reached my own house. My sister had gone to bed, for I could always let myself in; nor, indeed, did any one in Marshmailows think the locking of the door at night an imperative duty.

When I fell asleep, I was again in the old quarry, staring into the deep well. I thought Mrs Oldcastle was murdering her daughter in the house above, while I was spell-bound to the spot, where, if I stood long enough, I should see her body float into the well from the subterranean passage, the opening of which was just below where I stood. I was thus confusing and reconstructing the two dreadful stories of the place—that told me by old Weir, about the circumstances of his birth; and that told me by Dr Duncan, about Mrs Oldcastle's treatment of her elder daughter. But as a white hand and arm appeared in the water below me, sorrow and pity more than horror broke the bonds of sleep, and I awoke to less trouble than that of my dreams, only because that which I feared had not yet come.

CHAPTER XXX. A SERMON TO MYSELF.

It was the Sabbath morn. But such a Sabbath! The day seemed all wan with weeping, and gray with care. The wind dashed itself against the casement, laden with soft heavy sleet. The ground, the bushes, the very outhouses seemed sodden with the rain. The trees, which looked stricken as if they could die of grief, were yet tormented with fear, for the bare branches went streaming out in the torrent of the wind, as cowering before the invisible foe. The first thing I knew when I awoke was the raving of that wind. I could lie in bed not a moment longer. I could not rest. But how was I to do the work of my office? When a man's duty looks like an enemy, dragging him into the dark mountains, he has no less to go with it than when, like a friend with loving face, it offers to lead him along green pastures by the river-side. I had little power over my feelings; I could not prevent my mind from mirroring itself in the nature around me; but I could address myself to the work I had to do. "My God!" was all the prayer I could pray ere I descended to join my sister at the breakfast-table. But He knew what lay behind the one word.

Martha could not help seeing that something was the matter. I saw by her looks that she could read so much in mine. But her eyes alone questioned me, and that only by glancing at me anxiously from, time to time. I was grateful to her for saying nothing. It is a fine thing in friendship to know when to be silent.

The prayers were before me, in the hands of all my friends, and in the hearts of some of them; and if I could not enter into them as I would, I could yet read them humbly before God as His servant to help the people to worship as one flock. But how was I to preach? I had been in difficulty before now, but never in so much. How was I to teach others, whose mind was one confusion? The subject on which I was pondering when young Weir came to tell me his sister was dying, had retreated as if into the far past; it seemed as if years had come between that time and this, though but one black night had rolled by. To attempt to speak upon that would have been vain, for I had nothing to say on the matter now. And if I could have recalled my former thoughts, I should have felt a hypocrite as I delivered them, so utterly dissociated would they have been from anything that I was thinking or feeling now. Here would have been my visible form and audible voice, uttering that as present to me now, as felt by me now, which I did think and feel yesterday, but which, although I believed it, was not present to my feeling or heart, and must wait the revolution of months, or it might be of years, before I should feel it again, before I should be able to exhort my people about it with the fervour of a present faith. But, indeed, I could not even recall what I had thought and felt. Should I then tell them that I could not speak to them that morning?—There would be nothing wrong in that. But I felt ashamed of yielding to personal trouble when the truths of God were all about me, although I could not feel them. Might not some hungry soul go away without being satisfied, because I was faint and down-hearted? I confess I had a desire likewise to avoid giving rise to speculation and talk about myself, a desire which, although not wrong, could neither have strengthened me to speak the truth, nor have justified me in making the attempt.—What was to be done?

All at once the remembrance crossed my mind of a sermon I had preached before upon the words of St Paul: "Thou therefore which teachest another, teachest thou not thyself?" a subject suggested by the fact that on the preceding Sunday I had especially felt, in preaching to my people, that I was exhorting myself whose necessity was greater than theirs—at least I felt it to be greater than I could know theirs to be. And now the converse of the thought came to me, and I said to myself, "Might I not try the other way now, and preach to myself? In teaching myself, might I not teach others? Would it not hold? I am very troubled and faithless now. If I knew that God was going to lay the full weight of this grief upon me, yet if I loved Him with all my heart, should I not at least be more quiet? There would not be a storm within me then, as if the Father had descended from the throne of the heavens, and 'chaos were come again.' Let me expostulate with myself in my heart, and the words of my expostulation will not be the less true with my people."

All this passed through my mind as I sat in my study after breakfast, with the great old cedar roaring before my window. It was within an hour of church-time. I took my Bible, read and thought, got even some comfort already, and found myself in my vestry not quite unwilling to read the prayers and speak to my people.

There were very few present. The day was one of the worst—violently stormy, which harmonized somewhat with my feelings; and, to my further relief, the Hall pew was empty. Instead of finding myself a mere minister to the prayers of others, I found, as I read, that my heart went out in crying to God for the divine presence of His Spirit. And if I thought more of myself in my prayers than was well, yet as soon as I was converted, would I not strengthen my brethren? And the sermon I preached to myself and through myself to my people, was that which the stars had preached to me, and thereby driven me to my knees by the mill-door. I took for my text, "The glory of the Lord shall be revealed;" and then I proceeded to show them how the glory of the Lord was to be revealed. I preached to myself that throughout this fortieth chapter of the prophecies of Isaiah, the power of God is put side by side with the weakness of men, not that He, the perfect, may glory over His feeble children; not that He may say to them—"Look how mighty I am, and go down upon your knees and worship"—for power alone was never yet

361

worthy of prayer; but that he may say thus: "Look, my children, you will never be strong but with MY strength. I have no other to give you. And that you can get only by trusting in me. I cannot give it you any other way. There is no other way. But can you not trust in me? Look how strong I am. You wither like the grass. Do not fear. Let the grass wither. Lay hold of my word, that which I say to you out of my truth, and that will be life in you that the blowing of the wind that withers cannot reach. I am coming with my strong hand and my judging arm to do my work. And what is the work of my strong hand and ruling arm? To feed my flock like a shepherd, to gather the lambs with my arm, and carry them in my bosom, and gently lead those that are with young. I have measured the waters in the hollow of my hand, and held the mountains in my scales, to give each his due weight, and all the nations, so strong and fearful in your eyes, are as nothing beside my strength and what I can do. Do not think of me as of an image that your hands can make, a thing you can choose to serve, and for which you can do things to win its favour. I am before and above the earth, and over your life, and your oppressors I will wither with my breath. I come to you with help I need no worship from you. But I say love me, for love is life, and I love you. Look at the stars I have made. I know every one of them. Not one goes wrong, because I keep him right. Why sayest thou, O Jacob, and speakest, O Israel—my way is HID from the Lord, and my judgment is passed over from my God! I give POWER to the FAINT, and to them that have no might, plenty of strength."

"Thus," I went on to say, "God brings His strength to destroy our weakness by making us strong. This is a God indeed! Shall we not trust Him?"

I gave my people this paraphrase of the chapter, to help them to see the meanings which their familiarity with the words, and their non-familiarity with the modes of Eastern thought, and the forms of Eastern expression, would unite to prevent them from catching more than broken glimmerings of. And then I tried to show them that it was in the commonest troubles of life, as well as in the spiritual fears and perplexities that came upon them, that they were to trust in God; for God made the outside as well as the inside, and they altogether belonged to Him; and that when outside things, such as pain or loss of work, or difficulty in getting money, were referred to

God and His will, they too straightway became spiritual affairs, for nothing in the world could any longer appear common or unclean to the man who saw God in everything. But I told them they must not be too anxious to be delivered from that which troubled them: but they ought to be anxious to have the presence of God with them to support them, and make them able in patience to possess their souls; and so the trouble would work its end—the purification of their minds, that the light and gladness of God and all His earth, which the pure in heart and the meek alone could inherit, might shine in upon them. And then I repeated to them this portion of a prayer out of one of Sir Philip Sidney's books:—

"O Lord, I yield unto Thy will, and joyfully embrace what sorrow Thou wilt have me suffer. Only thus much let me crave of Thee, (let my craving, O Lord, be accepted of Thee, since even that proceeds from Thee,) let me crave, even by the noblest title, which in my greatest affliction I may give myself, that I am Thy creature, and by Thy goodness (which is Thyself) that Thou wilt suffer some beam of Thy majesty so to shine into my mind, that it may still depend confidently on Thee."

All the time I was speaking, the rain, mingled with sleet, was dashing against the windows, and the wind was howling over the graves all about. But the dead were not troubled by the storm; and over my head, from beam to beam of the roof, now resting on one, now flitting to another, a sparrow kept flying, which had taken refuge in the church till the storm should cease and the sun shine out in the great temple. "This," I said aloud, "is what the church is for: as the sparrow finds there a house from the storm, so the human heart escapes thither to hear the still small voice of God when its faith is too weak to find Him in the storm, and in the sorrow, and in the pain." And while I spoke, a dim watery gleam fell on the chancel-floor, and the comfort of the sun awoke in my heart. Nor let any one call me superstitious for taking that pale sun-ray of hope as sent to me; for I received it as comfort for the race, and for me as one of the family, even as the bow that was set in the cloud, a promise to the eyes of light for them that sit in darkness. As I write, my eye falls upon the Bible on the table by my side, and I read the words, "For the Lord God is a sun and shield, the Lord will give grace and glory." And I lift my eyes from my paper and look abroad from my window, and the sun is shining in its strength. The leaves are dancing in the light wind that gives them each its share of the sun, and my trouble has passed away for ever, like the storm of that night and the unrest of that strange Sabbath.

Such comforts would come to us oftener from Nature, if we really believed that our God was the God of Nature; that when He made, or rather when He makes, He means; that not His hands only, but His heart too, is in the making of those things; that, therefore, the influences of Nature upon human minds and hearts are because He intended them. And if we believe that our God is everywhere, why should we not think Him present even in the coincidences that sometimes seem so strange? For, if He be in the things that coincide, He must be in the coincidence of those things.

Miss Oldcastle told me once that she could not take her eyes off a butterfly which was flitting about in the church all the time I was speaking of the resurrection of the dead. I told the people that in Greek there was one word for the soul and for a butterfly—Psyche; that I thought as the light on the rain made the natural symbol of mercy—the rainbow, so the butterfly was the type in nature, and made to the end, amongst other ends, of being such a type—of the resurrection of the human body; that its name certainly expressed the hope of the Greeks in immortality, while to us it speaks likewise of a glorified body, whereby we shall know and love each other with our eyes as well as our hearts.—My sister saw the butterfly too, but only remembered that she had seen it when it was mentioned in her hearing: on her the sight made no impression; she saw no coincidence.

I descended from the pulpit comforted by the sermon I had preached to myself. But I was glad to feel justified in telling my people that, in consequence of the continued storm, for there had been no more of sunshine than just that watery gleam, there would be no service in the afternoon, and that I would instead visit some of my sick poor, whom the weather might have discomposed in their worn dwellings.

The people were very slow in dispersing. There was so much putting on of clogs, gathering up of skirts over the head, and expanding of umbrellas, soon to be taken down again as worse than useless in the violence of the wind, that the porches were crowded, and the few left in the church detained till the others made way. I lingered with these. They were all poor people.

"I am sorry you will have such a wet walk home," I said to Mrs Baird, the wife of old Reginald Baird, the shoemaker, a little wizened creature, with more wrinkles than hairs, who the older and more withered she grew, seemed like the kernels of some nuts only to grow the sweeter.

"It's very good of you to let us off this afternoon, sir. Not as I minds the wet: it finds out the holes in people's shoes, and gets my husband into more work."

This was in fact the response of the shoemaker's wife to my sermon. If we look for responses after our fashion instead of after people's own fashion, we ought to be disappointed. Any recognition of truth, whatever form it may take, whether that of poetic delight, intellectual corroboration, practical commonplace; or even vulgar aphorism, must be welcomed by the husbandmen of the God of growth. A response which jars against the peculiar pitch of our mental instrument, must not therefore be turned away from with dislike. Our mood of the moment is not that by which the universe is tuned into its harmonies. We must drop our instrument and listen to the other, and if we find that the player upon it is breathing after a higher expression, is, after his fashion, striving to embody something he sees of the same truth the utterance of which called forth this his answer, let us thank God and take courage. God at least is pleased: and if our refinement and education take away from our pleasure, it is because of something low, false, and selfish, not divine in a word, that is mingled with that refinement and that education. If the shoemaker's wife's response to the prophet's grand poem about the care of God over His creatures, took the form of acknowledgment for the rain that found out the holes in the people's shoes, it was the more genuine and true, for in itself it afforded proof that it was not a mere reflex of the words of the prophet, but sprung from the experience and recognition of the shoemaker's wife. Nor was there anything necessarily selfish in it, for if there are holes in people's shoes, the sooner they are found out the better.

While I was talking to Mrs Baird, Mr Stoddart, whose love for the old organ had been stronger than his dislike to the storm, had come down into the church, and now approached me.

"I never saw you in the church before, Mr Stoddart," I said, "though I have heard you often enough. You use your own private door always."

"I thought to go that way now, but there came such a fierce burst of wind and rain in my face, that my courage failed me, and I turned back—like the sparrow—for refuge in the church."

"A thought strikes me," I said. "Come home with me, and have some lunch, and then we will go together to see some of my poor people. I have often wished to ask you."

His face fell.

"It is such a day!" he answered, remonstratingly, but not positively refusing. It was not his way ever to refuse anything positively.

"So it was when you set out this morning," I returned; "but you would not deprive us of the aid of your music for the sake of a charge of wind, and a rattle of rain-drops."

"But I shan't be of any use. You are going, and that is enough."

"I beg your pardon. Your very presence will be of use. Nothing yet given him or done for him by his fellow, ever did any man so much good as the recognition of the brotherhood by the common signs of friendship and sympathy. The best good of given money depends on the degree to which it is the sign of that friendship and sympathy. Our Lord did not make little of visiting: 'I was sick, and ye visited me.' 'Inasmuch as ye did it not to one of the least of these, ye did it not to me.' Of course, if the visitor goes professionally and not humanly,—as a mere religious policeman, that is—whether he only distributes tracts with condescending words, or gives money liberally because he thinks he ought, the more he does not go the better, for he only does harm to them and himself too."

"But I cannot pretend to feel any of the interest you consider essential: why then should I go?"

"To please me, your friend. That is a good human reason. You need not say a word—you must not pretend anything. Go as my companion, not as their visitor. Will you come?"

"I suppose I must."

"You must, then. Thank you. You will help me. I have seldom a companion."

So when the storm-fit had abated for the moment, we hurried to the vicarage, had a good though hasty lunch, (to which I was pleased to see Mr Stoddart do justice; for it is with man as with beast, if you want work out of him, he must eat well—and it is the one justification of eating well, that a man works well upon it,) and set out for the village. The rain was worse than ever. There was no sleet, and the wind was not cold, but the windows of heaven were opened, and if the fountains of the great deep were not broken up, it looked like it, at least, when we reached the bridge and saw how the river had spread out over all the low lands on its borders. We could not talk much as we went along.

"Don't you find some pleasure in fighting the wind?" I said.

"I have no doubt I should," answered Mr Stoddart, "if I thought I were going to do any good; but as it is, to tell the truth, I would rather be by my own fire with my folio Dante on the reading desk."

"Well, I would rather help the poorest woman in creation, than contemplate the sufferings of the greatest and wickedest," I said.

"There are two things you forget," returned Mr Stoddart. "First, that the poem of Dante is not nearly occupied with the sufferings of the wicked; and next, that what I have complained of in this expedition—which as far as I am concerned, I would call a wild goose chase, were it not that it is your doing and not mine—is that I am not going to help anybody."

"You would have the best of the argument entirely," I replied, "if your expectation was sure to turn out correct."

As I spoke, we had come within a few yards of the Tomkins's cottage, which lay low down from the village towards the river, and I saw that the water was at the threshold. I turned to Mr Stoddart, who, to do him justice, had not yet grumbled in the least.

"Perhaps you had better go home, after all," I said; "for you must wade into Tomkins's if you go at all. Poor old man! what can he be doing, with his wife dying, and the river in his house!"

"You have constituted yourself my superior officer, Mr Walton. I never turned my back on my leader yet. Though I confess I wish I could see the enemy a little clearer."

"There is the enemy," I said, pointing to the water, and walking into it.

Mr Stoddart followed me without a moment's hesitation.

When I opened the door, the first thing I saw was a small stream of water running straight from the door to the fire on the hearth, which it had already drowned. The old man was sitting by his wife's bedside. Life seemed rapidly going from the old woman. She lay breathing very hard.

"Oh, sir," said the old man, as he rose, almost crying, "you're come at last!"

"Did you send for me?" I asked.

"No, sir. I had nobody to send. Leastways, I asked the Lord if He wouldn't fetch you. I been prayin' hard for you for the last hour. I couldn't leave her to come for you. And I do believe the wind 'ud ha' blown me off my two old legs."

"Well, I am come, you see. I would have come sooner, but I had no idea you would be flooded."

"It's not that I mind, sir, though it IS cold sin' the fire went. But she IS goin' now, sir. She ha'n't spoken a word this two hours and more, and her breathin's worse and worse. She don't know me now, sir."

A moan of protestation came from the dying woman.

"She does know you, and loves you too, Tomkins," I said. "And you'll both know each other better by and by."

The old woman made a feeble motion with her hand. I took it in mine. It was cold and deathlike. The rain was falling in large slow drops from the roof upon the bedclothes. But she would be beyond the reach of all the region storms before long, and it did not matter much.

"Look if you can find a basin or plate, Mr Stoddart, and put it to catch the drop here," I said.

For I wanted to give him the first chance of being useful.

"There's one in the press there," said the old man, rising feebly.

"Keep your seat," said Mr Stoddart. "I'll get it."

And he got a basin from the cupboard, and put it on the bed to catch the drop.

The old woman held my hand in hers; but by its motion I knew that she wanted something; and guessing what it was from what she had said before, I made her husband sit on the bed on the other side of her and take hold of her other hand, while I took his place on the chair by the bedside. This seemed to content her. So I went and whispered to Mr Stoddart, who had stood looking on disconsolately:—

"You heard me say I would visit some of my sick people this afternoon. Some will be expecting me with certainty. You must go instead of me, and tell them that I cannot come, because old Mrs Tomkins is dying; but I will see them soon."

He seemed rather relieved at the commission. I gave him the necessary directions to find the cottages, and he left me.

I may mention here that this was the beginning of a relation between Mr Stoddart and the poor of the parish—a very slight one indeed, at first, for it consisted only in his knowing two or three of them, so as to ask after their health when he met them, and give them an occasional half-crown. But it led to better things before many years had passed. It seems scarcely more than yesterday—though it is twenty years ago—that I came upon him in the avenue, standing in dismay over the fragments of a jug of soup which he had dropped, to the detriment of his trousers as well as the loss of his soup. "What am I to do?" he said. "Poor Jones expects his soup to-day."—"Why, go back and get some more."—"But what will cook say?" The poor man was more afraid of the cook than he would have been of a squadron of cavalry. "Never mind the cook. Tell her you must have some more as soon as it can be got ready." He stood uncertain for a moment. Then his face brightened. "I will tell her I want my luncheon. I always have soup. And I'll get out through the greenhouse, and carry it to Jones."—"Very well," I said; "that will do capitally." And I went on, without caring to disturb my satisfaction by determining whether the devotion of his own soup arose more from love to Jones, or fear of the cook. He was a great help to me in the latter part of his life, especially after I lost good Dr Duncan, and my beloved friend Old Rogers. He was just one of those men who make excellent front-rank men, but are quite unfit for officers. He could do what he was told without flinching, but he always required to be told.

I resumed my seat by the bedside, where the old woman was again moaning. As soon as I took her hand she ceased, and so I sat till it began to grow dark.

"Are you there, sir?" she would murmur.

"Yes, I am here. I have a hold of your hand."

"I can't feel you, sir."

"But you can hear me. And you can hear God's voice in your heart. I am here, though you can't feel me. And God is here, though you can't see Him."

She would be silent for a while, and then murmur again—

"Are you there, Tomkins?"

"Yes, my woman, I'm here," answered the old man to one of these questions; "but I wish I was there instead, wheresomever it be as you're goin', old girl."

And all that I could hear of her answer was, "Bym by; bym by."

Why should I linger over the death-bed of an illiterate woman, old and plain, dying away by inches? Is it only that she died with a hold of my hand, and that therefore I am interested in the story? I trust not. I was interested in HER. Why? Would my readers be more interested if I told them of the death of a young lovely creature, who said touching things, and died amidst a circle of friends, who felt that the very light of life was being taken away from them? It was enough for me that here was a woman with a heart like my own; who needed the same salvation I needed; to whom the love of God was the one blessed thing; who was passing through the same dark passage into the light that the Lord had passed through before her, that I had to pass through after her. She had no theories—at least, she gave utterance to none; she had few thoughts of her own—and gave still fewer of them expression; you might guess at a true notion in her mind, but an abstract idea she could scarcely lay hold of; her speech was very common; her manner rather brusque than gentle; but she could love; she could forget herself; she could be sorry for what she did or thought wrong; she could hope; she could wish to be better; she could admire good people; she could trust in God her Saviour. And now the loving God-made human heart in her was going into a new school that it might begin a fresh beautiful growth. She was old, I have said, and plain; but now her old age and plainness were about to vanish, and all that had made her youth attractive to young Tomkins was about to return to her, only rendered tenfold more beautiful by the growth of fifty years of learning according to her ability. God has such patience in working us into vessels of honour! in teaching us to be children! And shall we find the human heart in which the germs of all that is noblest and loveliest and likest to God have begun to grow and manifest themselves uninteresting, because its circumstances have been narrow, bare, and poverty-stricken, though neither sordid nor unclean; because the woman is old and wrinkled and brown, as if these were more than the transient accidents of humanity; because she has neither learned grammar nor philosophy; because her habits have neither been delicate nor self-indulgent? To help the mind of such a woman to unfold to the recognition of the endless delights of truth; to watch the dawn of the rising intelligence upon the too still face, and the transfiguration of the whole form, as the gentle rusticity vanishes in yet gentler grace, is a labour and a delight worth the time and mind of an archangel. Our best living poet says— but no; I will not quote. It is a distinct wrong that befalls the best books to have many of their best words quoted till in their own place and connexion they cease to have force and influence. The meaning of the passage is that the communication of truth is one of the greatest delights the human heart can experience. Surely this is true. Does not the teaching of men form a great part of the divine gladness?

Therefore even the dull approaches of death are full of deep significance and warm interest to one who loves his fellows, who desires not to be distinguished by any better fate than theirs; and shrinks from the pride of supposing that his own death, or that of the noblest of the good, is more precious in the sight of God than that of "one of the least of these little ones."

At length, after a long silence, the peculiar sounds of obstructed breathing indicated the end at hand. The jaw fell, and the eyes were fixed. The old man closed the mouth and the eyes of his old companion, weeping like a child, and I prayed aloud, giving thanks to God for taking her to Himself. It went to my heart to leave the old man alone with the dead; but it was better to let him be alone for a while, ere the women should come to do the last offices for the abandoned form.

I went to Old Rogers, told him the state in which I had left poor Tomkins, and asked him what was to be done.

"I'll go and bring him home, sir, directly. He can't be left there."

"But how can you bring him in such a night?"

"Let me see, sir. I must think. Would your mare go in a cart, do you think?"

"Quite quietly. She brought a load of gravel from the common a few days ago. But where's your cart? I haven't got one."

"There's one at Weir's to be repaired, sir. It wouldn't be stealing to borrow it."

372

How he managed with Tomkins I do not know. I thought it better to leave all the rest to him. He only said afterwards, that he could hardly get the old man away from the body. But when I went in next day, I found Tomkins sitting, disconsolate, but as comfortable as he could be, in the easy chair by the side of the fire. Mrs Rogers was bustling about cheerily. The storm had died in the night. The sun was shining. It was the first of the spring weather. The whole country was gleaming with water. But soon it would sink away, and the grass be the thicker for its rising.

CHAPTER XXXI. A COUNCIL OF FRIENDS.

My reader will easily believe that I returned home that Sunday evening somewhat jaded, nor will he be surprised if I say that next morning I felt disinclined to leave my bed. I was able, however, to rise and go, as I have said, to Old Rogers's cottage.

But when I came home, I could no longer conceal from myself that I was in danger of a return of my last attack. I had been sitting for hours in wet clothes, with my boots full of water, and now I had to suffer for it. But as I was not to blame in the matter, and had no choice offered me whether I should be wet or dry while I sat by the dying woman, I felt no depression at the prospect of the coming illness. Indeed, I was too much depressed from other causes, from mental strife and hopelessness, to care much whether I was well or ill. I could have welcomed death in the mood in which I sometimes felt myself during the next few days, when I was unable to leave my bed, and knew that Captain Everard was at the Hall, and knew nothing besides. For no voice reached me from that quarter any more than if Oldcastle Hall had been a region beyond the grave. Miss Oldcastle seemed to have vanished from my ken as much as Catherine Weir and Mrs Tomkins—yes, more—for there was only death between these and me; whereas, there was something far worse—I could not always tell what—that rose ever between Miss Oldcastle and myself, and paralysed any effort I might fancy myself on the point of making for her rescue.

One pleasant thing happened. On the Thursday, I think it was, I felt better. My sister came into my room and said that Miss Crowther had called, and wanted to see me.

"Which Miss Crowther is it?" I asked.

"The little lady that looks like a bird, and chirps when she talks."

Of course I was no longer in any doubt as to which of them it was.

"You told her I had a bad cold, did you not?"

"Oh, yes. But she says if it is only a cold, it will do you no harm to see her."

"But you told her I was in bed, didn't you?"

"Of course. But it makes no difference. She says she's used to seeing sick folk in bed; and if you don't mind seeing her, she doesn't mind seeing you."

"Well, I suppose I must see her," I said.

So my sister made me a little tidier, and introduced Miss Crowther.

"O dear Mr Walton, I am SO sorry! But you're not very ill, are you?"

"I hope not, Miss Jemima. Indeed, I begin to think this morning that I am going to get off easier than I expected."

"I am glad of that. Now listen to me. I won't keep you, and it is a matter of some importance. I hear that one of your people is dead, a young woman of the name of Weir, who has left a little boy behind her. Now, I have been wanting for a long time to adopt a child——"

"But," I interrupted her, "What would Miss Hester say?"

"My sister is not so very dreadful as perhaps you think her, Mr Walton; and besides, when I do want my own way very particularly, which is not often, for there are not so many things that it's worth while insisting upon— but when I DO want my own way, I always have it. I then stand upon my right of—what do you call it?—primo—primogeniture—that's it! Well, I think I know something of this child's father. I am sorry to say I don't know much good of him, and that's the worse for the boy. Still——"

"The boy is an uncommonly sweet and lovable child, whoever was his

374

father," I interposed.

"I am very glad to hear it. I am the more determined to adopt him. What friends has he?"

"He has a grandfather, and an uncle and aunt, and will have a godfather— that's me—in a few days, I hope."

"I am very glad to hear it. There will be no opposition on the part of the relatives, I presume?"

"I am not so sure of that. I fear I shall object for one, Miss Jemima."

"You? I didn't expect that of you, Mr Walton, I must say."

And there was a tremor in the old lady's voice more of disappointment and hurt than of anger.

"I will think it over, though, and talk about it to his grandfather, and we shall find out what's best, I do hope. You must not think I should not like you to have him."

"Thank you, Mr Walton. Then I won't stay longer now. But I warn you I will call again very soon, if you don't come to see me. Good morning."

And the dear old lady shook hands with me and left me rather hurriedly, turning at the door, however, to add—

"Mind, I've set my heart upon having the boy, Mr Walton. I've seen him often."

What could have made Miss Crowther take such a fancy to the boy? I could not help associating it with what I had heard of her youthful disappointment, but never having had my conjectures confirmed, I will say no more about them. Of course I talked the matter over with Thomas Weir; but, as I had suspected, I found that he was now as unwilling to part with the boy as he had formerly disliked the sight of him. Nor did I press the matter at all, having a belief that the circumstances of one's natal position are not to be rudely handled or thoughtlessly altered, besides that I thought Thomas and his daughter ought to have all the comfort and good that were to be got from the presence of the boy whose advent had occasioned them so much trouble and sorrow, yea, and sin too. But I did not give a positive and final refusal to Miss Crowther. I only said "for the present;" for I did not feel at liberty to go further. I thought that such changes might take place as would render the trial of such a new relationship desirable; as, indeed, it turned out in the end, though I cannot tell the story now, but must keep it for a possible future.

I have, I think, entirely as yet, followed, in these memoirs, the plan of relating either those things only at which I was present, or, if other things, only in the same mode in which I heard them. I will now depart from this plan—for once. Years passed before some of the following facts were reported to me, but it is only here that they could be interesting to my readers.

At the very time Miss Crowther was with me, as nearly as I can guess, Old Rogers turned into Thomas Weir's workshop. The usual, on the present occasion somewhat melancholy, greetings having passed between them, Old Rogers said—

"Don't you think, Mr Weir, there's summat the matter wi' parson?"

"Overworked," returned Weir. "He's lost two, ye see, and had to see them both safe over, as I may say, within the same day. He's got a bad cold, I'm sorry to hear, besides. Have ye heard of him to-day?"

"Yes, yes; he's badly, and in bed. But that's not what I mean. There's summat on his mind," said Old Rogers.

"Well, I don't think it's for you or me to meddle with parson's mind," returned Weir.

"I'm not so sure o' that," persisted Rogers. "But if I had thought, Mr Weir, as how you would be ready to take me up short for mentionin' of the thing, I wouldn't ha' opened my mouth to you about parson—leastways, in that way, I mean."

"But what way DO you mean, Old Rogers?"

"Why, about his in'ards, you know."

"I'm no nearer your meanin' yet."

376

"Well, Mr Weir, you and me's two old fellows, now—leastways I'm a deal older than you. But that doesn't signify to what I want to say."

And here Old Rogers stuck fast—according to Weir's story.

"It don't seem easy to say no how, Old Rogers," said Weir.

"Well, it ain't. So I must just let it go by the run, and hope the parson, who'll never know, would forgive me if he did."

"Well, then, what is it?"

"It's my opinion that that parson o' ours—you see, we knows about it, Mr Weir, though we're not gentlefolks—leastways, I'm none."

"Now, what DO you mean, Old Rogers?"

"Well, I means this—as how parson's in love. There, that's paid out."

"Suppose he was, I don't see yet what business that is of yours or mine either."

"Well, I do. I'd go to Davie Jones for that man."

A heathenish expression, perhaps; but Weir assured me, with much amusement in his tone, that those were the very words Old Rogers used. Leaving the expression aside, will the reader think for a moment on the old man's reasoning? My condition WAS his business; for he was ready to die for me! Ah! love does indeed make us all each other's keeper, just as we were intended to be.

"But what CAN we do?" returned Weir.

Perhaps he was the less inclined to listen to the old man, that he was busy with a coffin for his daughter, who was lying dead down the street. And so my poor affairs were talked of over the coffin-planks. Well, well, it was no bad omen.

"I tell you what, Mr Weir, this here's a serious business. And it seems to me it's not shipshape o' you to go on with that plane o' yours, when we're talkin' about parson."

"Well, Old Rogers, I meant no offence. Here goes. NOW, what have you to say? Though if it's offence to parson you're speakin' of, I know, if I were parson, who I'd think was takin' the greatest liberty, me wi' my plane, or you wi' your fancies."

"Belay there, and hearken."

So Old Rogers went into as many particulars as he thought fit, to prove that his suspicion as to the state of my mind was correct; which particulars I do not care to lay in a collected form before my reader, he being in no need of such a summing up to give his verdict, seeing the parson has already pleaded guilty. When he had finished,

"Supposing all you say, Old Rogers," remarked Thomas, "I don't yet see what WE'VE got to do with it. Parson ought to know best what he's about."

"But my daughter tells me," said Rogers, "that Miss Oldcastle has no mind to marry Captain Everard. And she thinks if parson would only speak out he might have a chance."

Weir made no reply, and was silent so long, with his head bent, that Rogers grew impatient.

"Well, man, ha' you nothing to say now—not for your best friend—on earth, I mean—and that's parson? It may seem a small matter to you, but it's no small matter to parson."

"Small to me!" said Weir, and taking up his tool, a constant recourse with him when agitated, he began to plane furiously.

Old Rogers now saw that there was more in it than he had thought, and held his peace and waited. After a minute or two of fierce activity, Thomas lifted up a face more white than the deal board he was planing, and said,

"You should have come to the point a little sooner, Old Rogers."

He then laid down his plane, and went out of the workshop, leaving Rogers standing there in bewilderment. But he was not gone many minutes. He returned with a letter in his hand.

"There," he said, giving it to Rogers.

"I can't read hand o' write," returned Rogers. "I ha' enough ado with straight-foret print But I'll take it to parson."

"On no account," returned Thomas, emphatically "That's not what I gave it you for. Neither you nor parson has any right to read that letter; and I don't want either of you to read it. Can Jane read writing?"

"I don't know as she can, for, you see, what makes lasses take to writin' is when their young man's over the seas, leastways not in the mill over the brook."

"I'll be back in a minute," said Thomas, and taking the letter from Rogers's hand, he left the shop again.

He returned once more with the letter sealed up in an envelope, addressed to Miss Oldcastle.

"Now, you tell your Jane to give that to Miss Oldcastle from me—mind, from ME; and she must give it into her own hands, and let no one else see it. And I must have it again. Mind you tell her all that, Old Rogers."

"I will. It's for Miss Oldcastle, and no one else to know on't. And you're to have it again all safe when done with."

"Yes. Can you trust Jane not to go talking about it?"

"I think I can. I ought to, anyhow. But she can't know anythink in the letter now, Mr Weir."

"I know that; but Marshmallows is a talkin' place. And poor Kate ain't right out o' hearin' yet.—You'll come and see her buried to-morrow, won't ye, Old Rogers?"

"I will, Thomas. You've had a troubled life, but thank God the sun came out a bit before she died."

"That's true, Rogers. It's all right, I do think, though I grumbled long and sore. But Jane mustn't speak of that letter."

"No. That she shan't."

"I'll tell you some day what's in it. But I can't bear to talk about it yet."

And so they parted.

I was too unwell still either to be able to bury my dead out of my sight or to comfort my living the next Sunday. I got help from Addicehead, however, and the dead bodies were laid aside in the ancient wardrobe of the tomb. They were both buried by my vestry-door, Catherine where I had found young Tom lying, namely, in the grave of her mother, and old Mrs Tomkins on the other side of the path.

On Sunday, Rogers gave his daughter the letter, and she carried it to the Hall. It was not till she had to wait on her mistress before leaving her for the night that she found an opportunity of giving it into her own hands.

Then when her bell rang, Jane went up to her room, and found her so pale and haggard that she was frightened. She had thrown herself back on the couch, with her hands lying by her sides, as if she cared for nothing in this world or out of it. But when Jane entered, she started and sat up, and tried to look like herself. Her face, however, was so pitiful, that honest-hearted Jane could not help crying, upon which the responsive sisterhood overcame the proud lady, and she cried too. Jane had all but forgotten the letter, of the import of which she had no idea, for her father had taken care to rouse no suspicions in her mind. But when she saw her cry, the longing to give her something, which comes to us all when we witness trouble—for giving seems to mean everything-brought to her mind the letter she had undertaken to deliver to her. Now she had no notion, as I have said, that the letter had anything to do with her present perplexity, but she hoped it might divert her thoughts for a moment, which is all that love at a distance can look for sometimes.

"Here is a letter," said Jane, "that Mr Weir the carpenter gave to my father to give to me to bring to you, miss."

"What is it about, Jane?" she asked listlessly.

Then a sudden flash broke from her eyes, and she held out her hand eagerly to take it. She opened it and read it with changing colour, but when she had finished it, her cheeks were crimson, and her eyes glowing like fire.

"The wretch," she said, and threw the letter from her into the middle of the floor.

Jane, who remembered the injunctions of her father as to the safety and return of the letter, stooped to pick it up: but had hardly raised herself when the door opened, and in came Mrs Oldcastle. The moment she saw her mother, Ethelwyn rose, and advancing to meet her, said,

"Mother, I will NOT marry that man. You may do what you please with me, but I WILL NOT."

"Heigho!" exclaimed Mrs Oldcastle with spread nostrils, and turning suddenly upon Jane, snatched the letter out of her hand.

She opened and read it, her face getting more still and stony as she read. Miss Oldcastle stood and looked at her mother with cheeks now pale but with still flashing eyes. The moment her mother had finished the letter, she walked swiftly to the fire, tearing the letter as she went, and thrust it between the bars, pushing it in fiercely with the poker, and muttering—

"A vile forgery of those low Chartist wretches! As if he would ever have looked at one of THEIR women! A low conspiracy to get money from a gentleman in his honourable position!"

And for the first time since she went to the Hall, Jane said, there was colour in that dead white face.

She turned once more, fiercer than ever, upon Jane, and in a tone of rage under powerful repression, began:—

"You leave the house—THIS INSTANT."

The last two words, notwithstanding her self-command, rose to a scream. And she came from the fire towards Jane, who stood trembling near the door, with such an expression on her countenance that absolute fear drove her from the room before she knew what she was about. The locking of the door behind her let her know that she had abandoned her young mistress to the madness of her mother's evil temper and disposition. But it was too late. She lingered by the door and listened, but beyond an occasional hoarse tone of suppressed energy, she heard nothing. At length the lock—as suddenly turned, and she was surprised by Mrs Oldcastle, if not in a listening attitude, at least where she had no right to be after the dismissal she had received.

Opposite Miss Oldcastle's bedroom was another, seldom used, the door of which was now standing open. Instead of speaking to Jane, Mrs Oldcastle gave her a violent push, which drove her into this room. Thereupon she shut the door and locked it. Jane spent the whole of the night in that room, in no small degree of trepidation as to what might happen next. But she heard no noise all the rest of the night, part of which, however, was spent in sound sleep, for Jane's conscience was in no ways disturbed as to any part she had played in the current events.

It was not till the morning that she examined the door, to see if she could not manage to get out and escape from the house, for she shared with the rest of the family an indescribable fear of Mrs Oldcastle and her confidante, the White Wolf. But she found it was of no use: the lock was at least as strong as the door. Being a sensible girl and self-possessed, as her parents' child ought to be, she made no noise, but waited patiently for what might come. At length, hearing a step in the passage, she tapped gently at the door and called, "Who's there?" The cook's voice answered.

"Let me out," said Jane. "The door's locked." The cook tried, but found there was no key. Jane told her how she came there, and the cook promised to get her out as soon as she could. Meantime all she could do for her was to hand her a loaf of bread on a stick from the next window. It had been long dark before some one unlocked the door, and left her at liberty to go where she pleased, of which she did not fail to make immediate use.

Unable to find her young mistress, she packed her box, and, leaving it behind her, escaped to her father. As soon as she had told him the story, he came straight to me.

CHAPTER XXXII. THE NEXT THING.

As I sat in my study, in the twilight of that same day, the door was hurriedly opened, and Judy entered. She looked about the room with a quick glance to see that we were alone, then caught my hand in both of hers, and burst out crying.

"Why, Judy!" I said, "what IS the matter?" But the sobs would not allow her to answer. I was too frightened to put any more questions, and so stood silent—my chest feeling like an empty tomb that waited for death to fill it. At length with a strong effort she checked the succession of her sobs, and spoke.

"They are killing auntie. She looks like a ghost already," said the child, again bursting into tears.

"Tell me, Judy, what CAN I do for her?"

"You must find out, Mr Walton. If you loved her as much as I do, you would find out what to do."

"But she will not let me do anything for her."

"Yes, she will. She says you promised to help her some day."

"Did she send you, then?"

"No. She did not send me."

"Then how—what—what can I do!"

"Oh, you exact people! You must have everything square and in print before you move. If it had been me now, wouldn't I have been off like a shot! Do get your hat, Mr Walton."

"Come, then, Judy. I will go at once.—Shall I see her?"

And every vein throbbed at the thought of rescuing her from her persecutors, though I had not yet the smallest idea how it was to be effected.

"We will talk about that as we go," said Judy, authoritatively.

In a moment more we were in the open air. It was a still night, with an odour of damp earth, and a hint of green buds in it. A pale half-moon hung in the sky, now and then hidden by the clouds that swept across it, for there was wind in the heavens, though upon earth all was still. I offered Judy my arm, but she took my hand, and we walked on without a word till we had got through the village and out upon the road.

"Now, Judy," I said at last, "tell me what they are doing to your aunt?"

"I don't know what they are doing. But I am sure she will die."

"Is she ill?"

"She is as white as a sheet, and will not leave her room. Grannie must have frightened her dreadfully. Everybody is frightened at her but me, and I begin to be frightened too. And what will become of auntie then?"

"But what can her mother do to her?"

"I don't know. I think it is her determination to have her own way that makes auntie afraid she will get it somehow; and she says now she will rather die than marry Captain Everard. Then there is no one allowed to wait on her but Sarah, and I know the very sight of her is enough to turn auntie sick almost. What has become of Jane I don't know. I haven't seen her all day, and the servants are whispering together more than usual. Auntie can't eat what Sarah brings her, I am sure; else I should almost fancy she was starving herself to death to keep clear of that Captain Everard."

"Is he still at the Hall?"

"Yes. But I don't think it is altogether his fault. Grannie won't let him go. I don't believe he knows how determined auntie is not to marry him. Only, to be sure, though grannie never lets her have more than five shillings in her pocket at a time, she will be worth something when she is married."

"Nothing can make her worth more than she is, Judy," I said, perhaps with some discontent in my tone.

"That's as you and I think, Mr Walton; not as grannie and the captain think at all. I daresay he would not care much more than grannie whether she

384

was willing or not, so long as she married him."

"But, Judy, we must have some plan laid before we reach the Hall; else my coming will be of no use."

"Of course. I know how much I can do, and you must arrange the rest with her. I will take you to the little room up-stairs—we call it the octagon. That you know is just under auntie's room. They will be at dinner—the captain and grannie. I will leave you there, and tell auntie that you want to see her."

"But, Judy,——-"

"Don't you want to see her, Mr Walton?"

"Yes, I do; more than you can think."

"Then I will tell her so."

"But will she come to me?"

"I don't know. We have to find that out."

"Very well. I leave myself in your hands."

I was now perfectly collected. All my dubitation and distress were gone, for I had something to do, although what I could not yet tell. That she did not love Captain Everard was plain, and that she had as yet resisted her mother was also plain, though it was not equally certain that she would, if left at her mercy, go on to resist her. This was what I hoped to strengthen her to do. I saw nothing more within my reach as yet. But from what I knew of Miss Oldcastle, I saw plainly enough that no greater good could be done for her than this enabling to resistance. Self-assertion was so foreign to her nature, that it needed a sense of duty to rouse her even to self-defence. As I have said before, she was clad in the mail of endurance, but was utterly without weapons. And there was a danger of her conduct and then of her mind giving way at last, from the gradual inroads of weakness upon the thews which she left unexercised. In respect of this, I prayed heartily that I might help her.

Judy and I scarcely spoke to each other from the moment we entered the gate till I found myself at a side door which I had never observed till now. It was fastened, and Judy told me to wait till she went in and opened it. The moon was now quite obscured, and I was under no apprehension of discovery. While I stood there I could not help thinking of Dr Duncan's story, and reflecting that the daughter was now returning the kindness shown to the mother.

I had not to wait long before the door opened behind me noiselessly, and I stepped into the dark house. Judy took me by the hand, and led me along a passage, and then up a stair into the little drawing-room. There was no light. She led me to a seat at the farther end, and opening a door close beside me, left me in the dark.

There I sat so long that I fell into a fit of musing, broken ever by startled expectation. Castle after castle I built up; castle after castle fell to pieces in my hands. Still she did not come. At length I got so restless and excited that only the darkness kept me from starting up and pacing the room. Still she did not come, and partly from weakness, partly from hope deferred, I found myself beginning to tremble all over. Nor could I control myself. As the trembling increased, I grew alarmed lest I should become unable to carry out all that might be necessary.

Suddenly from out of the dark a hand settled on my arm. I looked up and could just see the whiteness of a face. Before I could speak, a voice said brokenly, in a half-whisper:—

"WILL you save me, Mr Walton? But you're trembling; you are ill; you ought not to have come to me. I will get you something."

And she moved to go, but I held her. All my trembling was gone in a moment. Her words, so careful of me even in her deep misery, went to my heart and gave me strength. The suppressed feelings of many months rushed to my lips. What I said I do not know, but I know that I told her I loved her. And I know that she did not draw her hand from mine when I said so.

But ere I ceased came a revulsion of feeling.

"Forgive me," I said, "I am selfishness itself to speak to you thus now, to

386

take advantage of your misery to make you listen to mine. But, at least, it will make you sure that if all I am, all I have will save you—"

"But I am saved already," she interposed, "if you love me—for I love you."

And for some moments there were no words to speak. I stood holding her hand, conscious only of God and her. At last I said:

"There is no time now but for action. Nor do I see anything but to go with me at once. Will you come home to my sister? Or I will take you wherever you please."

"I will go with you anywhere you think best. Only take me away."

"Put on your bonnet, then, and a warm cloak, and we will settle all about it as we go."

She had scarcely left the room when Mrs Oldcastle came to the door.

"No lights here!" she said. "Sarah, bring candles, and tell Captain Everard, when he will join us, to come to the octagon room. Where can that little Judy be? The child gets more and more troublesome, I do think. I must take her in hand."

I had been in great perplexity how to let her know that I was there; for to announce yourself to a lady by a voice out of the darkness of her boudoir, or to wait for candles to discover you where she thought she was quite alone— neither is a pleasant way of presenting yourself to her consciousness. But I was helped out of the beginning into the middle of my difficulties, once more by that blessed little Judy. I did not know she was in the room till I heard her voice. Nor do I yet know how much she had heard of the conversation between her aunt and myself; for although I sometimes see her look roguish even now that she is a middle-aged woman with many children, when anything is said which might be supposed to have a possible reference to that night, I have never cared to ask her.

"Here I am, grannie," said her voice. "But I won't be taken in hand by you or any one else. I tell you that. So mind. And Mr Walton is here, too, and

387

Aunt Ethelwyn is going out with him for a long walk."

"What do you mean, you silly child?"

"I mean what I say," and "Miss Judy speaks the truth," fell together from her lips and mine.

"Mr Walton," began Mrs Oldcastle, indignantly, "it is scarcely like a gentleman to come where you are not wanted——"

Here Judy interrupted her.

"I beg your pardon, grannie, Mr Walton WAS wanted—very much wanted. I went and fetched him."

But Mrs Oldcastle went on unheeding.

"——and to be sitting in my room in the dark too!"

"That couldn't be helped, grannie. Here comes Sarah with candles."

"Sarah," said Mrs Oldcastle, "ask Captain Everard to be kind enough to step this way."

"Yes, ma'am," answered Sarah, with an untranslatable look at me as she set down the candles.

We could now see each other. Knowing words to be but idle breath, I would not complicate matters by speech, but stood silent, regarding Mrs Oldcastle. She on her part did not flinch, but returned my look with one both haughty and contemptuous. In a few moments, Captain Everard entered, bowed slightly, and looked to Mrs Oldcastle as if for an explanation. Whereupon she spoke, but to me.

"Mr Walton," she said, "will you explain to Captain Everard to what we owe the UNEXPECTED pleasure of a visit from you?"

"Captain Everard has no claim to any explanation from me. To you, Mrs Oldcastle, I would have answered, had you asked me, that I was waiting for Miss Oldcastle."

"Pray inform Miss Oldcastle, Judy, that Mr Walton insists upon seeing her at once."

"That is quite unnecessary. Miss Oldcastle will be here presently," I said.

Mrs Oldcastle turned slightly livid with wrath. She was always white, as I have said: the change I can describe only by the word I have used, indicating a bluish darkening of the whiteness. She walked towards the door beside me. I stepped between her and it.

"Pardon me, Mrs Oldcastle. That is the way to Miss Oldcastle's room. I am here to protect her."

Without saying a word she turned and looked at Captain Everard. He advanced with a long stride of determination. But ere he reached me, the door behind me opened, and Miss Oldcastle appeared in her bonnet and shawl, catrying a small bag in her hand. Seeing how things were, the moment she entered, she put her hand on my arm, and stood fronting the enemy with me. Judy was on my right, her eyes flashing, and her cheek as red as a peony, evidently prepared to do battle a toute outrance for her friends.

"Miss Oldcastle, go to your room instantly, I COMMAND you," said her mother; and she approached as if to remove her hand from my arm. I put my other arm between her and her daughter.

"No, Mrs Oldcastle," I said. "You have lost all a mother's rights by ceasing to behave like a mother, Miss Oldcastle will never more do anything in obedience to your commands, whatever she may do in compliance with your wishes."

"Allow me to remark," said Captain Everard, with attempted nonchalance, "that that is strange doctrine for your cloth."

"So much the worse for my cloth, then," I answered, "and the better for yours if it leads you to act more honourably."

Still keeping himself entrenched in the affectation of a supercilious indifference, he smiled haughtily, and gave a look of dramatic appeal to Mrs Oldcastle.

"At least," said that lady, "do not disgrace yourself, Ethelwyn, by leaving the house in this unaccountable manner at night and on foot. If you WILL leave the protection of your mother's roof, wait at least till tomorrow."

"I would rather spend the night in the open air than pass another under your roof, mother. You have been a strange mother to me—and Dorothy too!"

"At least do not put your character in question by going in this unmaidenly fashion. People will talk to your prejudice—and Mr Walton's too."

Ethelwyn smiled.—She was now as collected as I was, seeming to have cast off all her weakness. My heart was uplifted more than I can say.—She knew her mother too well to be caught by the change in her tone.

I had not hitherto interrupted her once when she took the answer upon herself, for she was not one to be checked when she chose to speak. But now she answered nothing, only looked at me, and I understood her, of course.

"They will hardly have time to do so, I trust, before it will be out of their power. It rests with Miss Oldcastle herself to say when that shall be."

As if she had never suspected that such was the result of her scheming, Mrs Oldcastle's demeanour changed utterly. The form of her visage was altered. She made a spring at her daughter, and seized her by the arm.

"Then I forbid it," she screamed; "and I WILL be obeyed. I stand on my rights. Go to your room, you minx."

"There is no law human or divine to prevent her from marrying whom she will. How old are you, Ethelwyn?"

I thought it better to seem even cooler than I was.

"Twenty-seven," answered Miss Oldcastle.

"Is it possible you can be so foolish, Mrs Oldcastle, as to think you have the slightest hold on your daughter's freedom? Let her arm go."

But she kept her grasp.

"You hurt me, mother," said Miss Oldcastle.

"Hurt you? you smooth-faced hypocrite! I will hurt you then!"

But I took Mrs Oldcastle's arm in my hand, and she let go her hold.

"How dare you touch a woman?" she said.

"Because she has so far ceased to be a woman as to torture her own daughter."

Here Captain Everard stepped forward, saying,—

"The riot-act ought to be read, I think. It is time for the military to interfere."

"Well put, Captain Everard," I said. "Our side will disperse if you will only leave room for us to go."

"Possibly I may have something to say in the matter."

"Say on."

"This lady has jilted me."

"Have you, Ethelwyn?"

"I have not."

"Then, Captain Everard, you lie."

"You dare to tell me so?"

And he strode a pace nearer.

"It needs no daring. I know you too well; and so does another who trusted you and found you false as hell."

"You presume on your cloth, but—" he said, lifting his hand.

"You may strike me, presuming on my cloth," I answered; "and I will not return your blow. Insult me as you will, and I will bear it. Call me coward, and I will say nothing. But lay one hand on me to prevent me from doing my duty, and I knock you down—or find you more of a man than I take you for."

It was either conscience or something not so good that made a coward of him. He turned on his heel.

"I really am not sufficiently interested in the affair to oppose you. You may take the girl for me. Both your cloth and the presence of ladies protect your insolence. I do not like brawling where one cannot fight. You shall hear from me before long, Mr Walton."

"No, Captain Everard, I shall not hear from you. You know you dare not write to me. I know that of you which, even on the code of the duellist, would justify any gentleman in refusing to meet you. Stand out of my way!"

I advanced with Miss Oldcastle on my arm. He drew back; and we left the room.

As we reached the door, Judy bounded after us, threw her arms round her aunt's neck, then round mine, kissing us both, and returned to her place on the sofa. Mrs Oldcastle gave a scream, and sunk fainting on a chair. It was a last effort to detain her daughter and gain time. Miss Oldcastle would have returned, but I would not permit her.

"No," I said; "she will be better without you. Judy, ring the bell for Sarah."

"How dare you give orders in my house?" exclaimed Mrs Oldcastle, sitting bolt upright in the chair, and shaking her fist at us. Then assuming the heroic, she added, "From this moment she is no daughter of mine. Nor can you touch one farthing of her money, sir. You have married a beggar after all, and that you'll both know before long."

"Thy money perish with thee!" I said, and repented the moment I had said it. It sounded like an imprecation, and I know I had no correspondent feeling; for, after all, she was the mother of my Ethelwyn. But the allusion to money made me so indignant, that the words burst from me ere I could consider their import.

The cool wind greeted us like the breath of God, as we left the house and closed the door behind us. The moon was shining from the edge of a vaporous mountain, which gradually drew away from her, leaving her alone in the midst of a lake of blue. But we had not gone many paces from the house when Miss Oldcastle began to tremble violently, and could scarcely get along with all the help I could give her. Nor, for the space of six weeks did one word pass between us about the painful occurrences of that evening. For all that time she was quite unable to bear it.

When we managed at last to reach the vicarage, I gave her in charge to my sister, with instructions to help her to bed at once, while I went for Dr Duncan.

CHAPTER XXXIII. OLD ROGERS'S THANKSGIVING.

I found the old man seated at his dinner, which he left immediately when he heard that Miss Oldcastle needed his help. In a few words I told him, as we went, the story of what had befallen at the Hall, to which he listened with the interest of a boy reading a romance, asking twenty questions about the particulars which I hurried over. Then he shook me warmly by the hand, saying—

"You have fairly won her, Walton, and I am as glad of it as I could be of anything I can think of. She is well worth all you must have suffered. This will at length remove the curse from that wretched family. You have saved her from perhaps even a worse fate than her sister's."

"I fear she will be ill, though," I said, "after all that she has gone through."

But I did not even suspect how ill she would be.

As soon as I heard Dr Duncan's opinion of her, which was not very definite, a great fear seized upon me that I was destined to lose her after all. This fear, however, terrible as it was, did not torture me like the fear that had preceded it. I could oftener feel able to say, "Thy will be done" than I could before.

Dr Duncan was hardly out of the house when Old Rogers arrived, and was shown into the study. He looked excited. I allowed him to tell out his story, which was his daughter's of course, without interruption. He ended by

393

saying:—

"Now, sir, you really must do summat. This won't do in a Christian country. We ain't aboard ship here with a nor'-easter a-walkin' the quarter-deck."

"There's no occasion, my dear old fellow, to do anything."

He was taken aback.

"Well, I don't understand you, Mr Walton. You're the last man I'd have expected to hear argufy for faith without works. It's right to trust in God; but if you don't stand to your halliards, your craft 'll miss stays, and your faith 'll be blown out of the bolt-ropes in the turn of a marlinspike."

I suspect there was some confusion in the figure, but the old man's meaning was plain enough. Nor would I keep him in a moment more of suspense.

"Miss Oldcastle is in the house, Old Rogers," I said.

"What house, sir?" returned the old man, his gray eyes opening wider as he spoke.

"This house, to be sure."

I shall never forget the look the old man cast upwards, or the reality given to it by the ordinarily odd sailor-fashion of pulling his forelock, as he returned inward thanks to the Father of all for His kindness to his friend. And never in my now wide circle of readers shall I find one, the most educated and responsive, who will listen to my story with a more gracious interest than that old man showed as I recounted to him the adventures of the evening. There were few to whom I could have told them: to Old Rogers I felt that it was right and natural and dignified to tell the story even of my love's victory.

How then am I able to tell it to the world as now? I can easily explain the seeming inconsistency. It is not merely that I am speaking, as I have said before, from behind a screen, or as clothed in the coat of darkness of an anonymous writer; but I find that, as I come nearer and nearer to the invisible world, all my brothers and sisters grow dearer and dearer to me; I feel towards them more and more as the children of my Father in heaven; and although some of them are good children and some naughty children, some very lovable and some hard to love, yet I never feel that they are below me, or unfit to listen to the story even of my love, if they only care to listen; and if they do not care, there is no harm done, except they read it. Even should they, and then scoff at what seemed and seems to me the precious story, I have these defences: first, that it was not for them that I cast forth my precious pearls, for precious to me is the significance of every fact in my history—not that it is mine, for I have only been as clay in the hands of the potter, but that it is God's, who made my history as it seemed and was good to Him; and second, that even should they trample them under their feet, they cannot well get at me to rend me. And more, the nearer I come to the region beyond, the more I feel that in that land a man needs not shrink from uttering his deepest thoughts, inasmuch as he that understands them not will not therefore revile him.—"But you are not there yet. You are in the land in which the brother speaketh evil of that which he understandeth not."—True, friend; too true. But I only do as Dr Donne did in writing that poem in his sickness, when he thought he was near to the world of which we speak: I rehearse now, that I may find it easier then.

> *"Since I am coming to that holy room,*
>
> *Where, with the choir of saints for evermore,*
>
> *I shall be made thy music, as I come,*
>
> *I tune the instrument here at the door;*
>
> *And what I must do then, think here before."*

When Rogers had thanked God, he rose, took my hand, and said:—

"Mr Walton, you WILL preach now. I thank God for the good we shall all get from the trouble you have gone through."

"I ought to be the better for it," I answered.

"You WILL be the better for it," he returned. "I believe I've allus been the better for any trouble as ever I had to go through with. I couldn't quite say the same for every bit of good luck I had; leastways, I considei trouble the best luck a man can have. And I wish you a good night, sir. Thank God! again."

"But, Rogers, you don't mean it would be good for us to have bad luck always, do you? You shouldn't be pleased at what's come to me now, in that case."

"No, sir, sartinly not."

"How can you say, then, that bad luck is the best luck?"

"I mean the bad luck that comes to us—not the bad luck that doesn't come. But you're right, sir. Good luck or bad luck's both best when HE sends 'em, as He allus does. In fac', sir, there is no bad luck but what comes out o' the man hisself. The rest's all good."

But whether it was the consequence of a reaction from the mental strain I had suffered, or the depressing effect of Miss Oldcastle's illness coming so close upon the joy of winning her; or that I was more careless and less anxious to do my duty than I ought to have been—I greatly fear that Old Rogers must have been painfully disappointed in the sermons which I did preach for several of the following Sundays. He never even hinted at such a fact, but I felt it much myself. A man has often to be humbled through failure, especially after success. I do not clearly know how my failures worked upon me; but I think a man may sometimes get spiritual good without being conscious of the point of its arrival, or being able to trace the process by which it was wrought in him. I believe that my failures did work some humility in me, and a certain carelessness of outward success even in spiritual matters, so far as the success affected me, provided only the will of God was done in the dishonour of my weakness. And I think, but I am not sure, that soon after I approached this condition of mind, I began to preach better. But still I found for some time that however much the subject of my sermon interested me in my study or in the church or vestry on the Saturday evening; nay, even although my heart was full of fervour during the prayers and lessons; no sooner had I begun to speak than the glow died out of the sky of my thoughts; a dull clearness of the intellectual faculties took its place; and I was painfully aware that what I could speak without being moved myself was not the most likely utterance to move the feelings of those who only listened. Still a man may occasionally be used by the Spirit of God as the inglorious "trumpet of a prophecy" instead of being inspired with the life of the Word, and hence speaking out of a full heart in testimony of that which he hath known and seen.

I hardly remember when or how I came upon the plan, but now, as often as I find myself in such a condition, I turn away from any attempt to produce a sermon; and, taking up one of the sayings of our Lord which He himself has said "are spirit and are life," I labour simply to make the people see in it what I see in it; and when I find that thus my own heart is warmed, I am justified in the hope that the hearts of some at least of my hearers are thereby warmed likewise.

But no doubt the fact that the life of Miss Oldcastle seemed to tremble in the balance, had something to do with those results of which I may have already said too much. My design had been to go at once to London and make preparation for as early a wedding as she would consent to; but the very day after I brought her home, life and not marriage was the question. Dr Duncan looked very grave, and although he gave me all the encouragement he could, all his encouragement did not amount to much. There was such a lack of vitality about her! The treatment to which she had been for so long a time subjected had depressed her till life was nearly quenched from lack of hope. Nor did the sudden change seem able to restore the healthy action of what the old physicians called the animal spirits. Possibly the strong reaction paralysed their channels, and thus prevented her gladness from reaching her physical nature so as to operate on its health. Her whole complaint appeared in excessive weakness. Finding that she fainted after every little excitement, I left her for four weeks entirely to my sister and Dr Duncan, during which time she never saw me; and it was long before I could venture to stay in her room more than a minute or two. But as the summer approached she began to show signs of reviving life, and by the end of May was able to be wheeled into the garden in a chair.

During her aunt's illness, Judy came often to the vicarage. But Miss Oldcastle was unable to see her any more than myself without the painful consequence which I have mentioned. So the dear child always came to me in the study, and through her endless vivacity infected me with some of her hope. For she had no fears whatever about her aunt's recovery.

I had had some painful apprehensions as to the treatment Judy herself might meet with from her grandmother, and had been doubtful whether I ought not to hive carried her off as well as her aunt; but the first time she came, which was the next day, she set my mind at rest on that subject.

"But does your grannie know where you are come?" I had asked her.

"So well, Mr Walton," sne replied, "that there was no occasion to tell her. Why shouldn't I rebel as well as Aunt Wynnie, I wonder?" she added, looking archness itself.

"How does she bear it?"

"Bear what, Mr Walton?"

"The loss of your aunt."

"You don't think grannie cares about that, do you! She's vexed enough at the loss of Captain Everard,—Do you know, I think he had too much wine yesterday, or he wouldn't have made quite such a fool of himself."

"I fear he hadn't had quite enough to give him courage, Judy. I daresay he was brave enough once, but a bad conscience soon destroys a man's courage."

"Why do you call it a bad conscience, Mr Walton? I should have thought that a bad conscience was one that would let a girl go on anyhow and say nothing about it to make her uncomfortable."

"You are quite right, Judy; that is the worst kind of conscience, certainly. But tell me, how does Mrs Oldcastle bear it?"

"You asked me that already."

Somehow Judy's words always seem more pert upon paper than they did upon her lips. Her naivete, the twinkling light in her eyes, and the smile flitting about her mouth, always modified greatly the expression of her words.

"—Grannie never says a word about you or auntie either."

"But you said she was vexed: how do you know that?"

"Because ever since the captain went away this morning, she won't speak a word to Sarah even."

"Are you not afraid of her locking you up some day or other?"

"Not a bit of it. Grannie won't touch me. And you shouldn't tempt me to run away from her like auntie. I won't. Grannie is a naughty old lady, and I don't believe anybody loves her but me—not Sarah, I'm certain. Therefore I can't leave her, and I won't leave her, Mr Walton, whatever you may say about her."

"Indeed, I don't want you to leave her, Judy."

And Judy did not leave her as long as she lived. And the old lady's love to that child was at least one redeeming point in her fierce character. No one can tell how mucn good it may have done her before she died—though but a few years passed before her soul was required of her. Before that time came, however, a quarrel took place between her and Sarah, which quarrel I incline to regard as a hopeful sign. And to this day Judy has never heard how her old grannie treated her mother. When she learns it now from these pages I think she will be glad that she did not know it before her death.

The old lady would see neither doctor nor parson; nor would she hear of sending for her daughter. The only sign of softening that she gave was that once she folded her granddaughter in her arms and wept long and bitterly. Perhaps the thought of her dying child came back upon her, along with the reflection that the only friend she had was the child of that marriage which she had persecuted to dissolution.

CHAPTER XXXIV. TOM'S STORY.

My reader will perceive that this part of my story is drawing to a close. It embraces but a brief period of my life, and I have plenty more behind not altogether unworthy of record. But the portions of any man's life most generally interesting are those in which, while the outward history is most stirring, it derives its chief significance from accompanying conflict within. It is not the rapid change of events, or the unusual concourse of circumstances that alone can interest the thoughtful mind; while, on the other hand, internal change and tumult can be ill set forth to the reader, save they be accompanied and in part, at least, occasioned by outward events capable of embodying and elucidating the things that are of themselves unseen. For man's life ought to be a whole; and not to mention the spiritual necessities of our nature—to leave the fact alone that a man is a mere thing of shreds and patches until his heart is united, as the Psalmist says, to fear the name of God—to leave these considerations aside, I say, no man's life is fit for representation as a work of art save in proportion as there has been a significant relation between his outer and inner life, a visible outcome of some sort of harmony between them. Therefore I chose the portion in which I had suffered most, and in which the outward occurrences of my own life had been most interesting, for the fullest representation; while I reserve for a more occasional and fragmentary record many things in the way of experience, thought, observation, and facts in the history both of myself and individuals of my flock, which admit of, and indeed require, a more individual treatment than would be altogether suitable to a continuous story. But before I close this part of my communications with those whom I count my friends, for till they assure me of the contrary I mean to flatter myself with considering my readers generally as such, I must gather up the ends of my thread, and dispose them in such a manner that they shall neither hang too loose, nor yet refuse length enough for what my friend Rogers would call splicing.

It was yet summer when Miss Oldcastle and I were married. It was to me a day awful in its gladness. She was now quite well, and no shadow hung upon her half-moon forehead. We went for a fortnight into Wales, and then returned to the vicarage and the duties of the parish, in which my wife was quite ready to assist me.

Perhaps it would help the wives of some clergymen out of some difficulties, and be their protection against some reproaches, if they would at once take the position with regard to the parishioners which Mrs Walton took, namely, that of their servant, but not in her own right—in her husband's.

She saw, and told them so, that the best thing she could do for them was to help me, that she held no office whatever in the parish, and they must apply to me when anything went amiss. Had she not constantly refused to be a "judge or a divider," she would have been constantly troubled with quarrels too paltry to be referred to me, and which were the sooner forgotten that the litigants were not drawn on further and further into the desert of dispute by the mirage of a justice that could quench no thirst. Only when any such affair was brought before me, did she use her good offices to bring about a right feeling between the contending parties, generally next-door neighbours, and mostly women, who, being at home all day, found their rights clash in a manner that seldom happened with those that worked in the fields. Whatever her counsel could do, however, had full scope through me, who earnestly sought it. And whatever she gave the poor, she gave as a private person, out of her own pocket. She never administered the communion offering—that is, after finding out, as she soon did, that it was a source of endless dispute between some of the recipients, who regarded it as their common property, and were never satisfied with what they received. This is the case in many country parishes, I fear. As soon as I came to know it, I simply told the recipients that, although the communion offering belonged to them, yet the distribution of it rested entirely with me; and that I would distribute it neither according to their fancied merits nor the degree of friendship I felt for them, but according to the best judgment I could form as to their necessities; and if any of them thought these were underrated, they were quite at liberty to make a fresh representation of them to me; but that I, who knew more about their neighbours than it was likely they did, and was not prejudiced by the personal regards which they could hardly fail to be influenced by, was more likely than they were to arrive at an equitable distribution of the money—upon my principles if not on theirs. And at the same time I tried to show them that a very great part of the disputes in the world came from our having a very keen feeling of our own troubles, and a very dull feeling of our neighbour's; for if the case was reversed, and our neighbour's condition became ours, ten to one our judgment would be reversed likewise. And I think some of them got some sense out of what I said. But I ever found the great difficulty in my dealing with my people to be the preservation of the authority which was needful for service; for when the elder serve the younger—and in many cases it is not age that determines seniority—they must not forget that without which the service they offer will fail to be received as such by those to whom it is offered. At the same time they must ever take heed that their claim to authority be founded on the truth, and not on ecclesiastical or social position. Their standing in the church accredits their offer of service: the service itself can only be accredited by the Truth and the Lord of Truth, who is the servant of all.

But it cost both me and my wife some time and some suffering before we learned how to deport ourselves in these respects.

In the same manner she avoided the too near, because unprofitable, approaches of a portion of the richer part of the community. For from her probable position in time to come, rather than her position in time past, many of the fashionable people in the county began to call upon her—in no small degree to her annoyance, simply from the fact that she and they had so little in common. So, while she performed all towards them that etiquette demanded, she excused herself from the closer intimacy which some of them courted, on the ground of the many duties which naturally fell to the parson's wife in a country parish like ours; and I am sure that long before we had gained the footing we now have, we had begun to reap the benefits of this mode of regarding our duty in the parish as one, springing from the same source, and tending to the same end. The parson's wife who takes to herself authority in virtue of her position, and the parson's wife who disclaims all connexion with the professional work of her husband, are equally out of place in being parsons' wives. The one who refuses to serve denies her greatest privilege; the one who will be a mistress receives the greater condemnation. When the wife is one with her husband, and the husband is worthy, the position will soon reveal itself.

But there cannot be many clergymen's wives amongst my readers; and I may have occupied more space than reasonable with this "large discourse." I apologize, and, there is room to fear, go on to do the same again.

As I write I am seated in that little octagonal room overlooking the quarry, with its green lining of trees, and its deep central well. It is my study now. My wife is not yet too old to prefer the little room in which she thought and suffered so much, to every other, although the stair that leads to it is high and steep. Nor do I object to her preference because there is no ready way to reach it save through this: I see her the oftener. And although I do not like any one to look over my shoulder while I write—it disconcerts me somehow—yet the moment the sheet is finished and flung on the heap, it is her property, as the print, reader, is yours. I hear her step overhead now. She is opening her window. Now I hear her door close; and now her foot is on the stair.

"Come in, love. I have just finished another sheet. There it is. What shall I end the book with? What shall I tell the friends with whom I have been conversing so often and so long for the last thing ere for a little while I bid them good-bye?"

And Ethelwyn bends her smooth forehead—for she has a smooth forehead still, although the hair that crowns it is almost white—over the last few sheets; and while she reads, I will tell those who will read, one of the good things that come of being married. It is, that there is one face upon which the changes come without your seeing them; or rather, there is one face which you can still see the same through all the shadows which years have gathered and heaped upon it. No, stay; I have got a better way of putting it still: there is one face whose final beauty you can see the mere clearly as the bloom of youth departs, and the loveliness of wisdom and the beauty of holiness take its place; for in it you behold all that you loved before, veiled, it is true, but glowing with gathered brilliance under the veil ("Stop one moment, my dear") from which it will one day shine out like the moon from under a cloud, when a stream of the upper air floats it from off her face.

"Now, Ethelwyn, I am ready. What shall I write about next?"

"I don't think you have told them anywhere about Tom."

"No more I have. I meant to do so. But I am ashamed of it."

"The more reason to tell it."

"You are quite right. I will go on with it at once. But you must not stand

403

there behind me. When I was a child, I could always confess best when I hid my face with my hands."

"Besides," said Ethelwyn, without seeming to hear what I said, "I do not want to have people saying that the vicar has made himself out so good that nobody can believe in him."

"That would be a great fault in my book, Ethelwyn. What does it come from in me? Let me see. I do not think I want to appear better than I am; but it sounds hypocritical to make merely general confessions, and it is indecorous to make particular ones. Besides, I doubt if it is good to write much about bad things even in the way of confession——"

"Well, well, never mind justifying it," said Ethelwyn. "I don't want any justification. But here is a chance for you. The story will, I think, do good, and not harm. You had better tell it, I do think. So if you are inclined, I will go away at once, and let you go on without interruption. You will have it finished before dinner, and Tom is coming, and you can tell him what you have done."

So, reader, now my wife has left me, I will begin. It shall not be a long story.

As soon as my wife and I had settled down at home, and I had begun to arrange my work again, it came to my mind that for a long time I had been doing very little for Tom Weir. I could not blame myself much for this, and I was pretty sure neither he nor his father blamed me at all; but I now saw that it was time we should recommence something definite in the way of study. When he came to my house the next morning, and I proceeded to acquaint myself with what he had been doing, I found to my great pleasure that he had made very considerable progress both in Latin and Mathematics, and I resolved that I would now push him a little. I found this only brought out his mettle; and his progress, as it seemed to me, was extraordinary. Nor was this all. There were such growing signs of goodness in addition to the uprightness which had first led to our acquaintance, that although I carefully abstained from making the suggestion to him, I was more than pleased when I discovered, from some remark he made, that he would gladly give himself to the service of the Church. At the same time I felt compelled to be the more cautious in anything I said, from the fact that the prospect of the social elevation which would be involved in the change might be a temptation to him, as no doubt it has been to many a man of humble birth. However, as I continued to observe him closely, my conviction was deepened that he was rarely fitted for ministering to his fellows; and soon it came to speech between his father and me, when I found that Thomas, so far from being unfavourably inclined to the proposal, was prepared to spend the few savings of his careful life upon his education. To this, however, I could not listen, because there was his daughter Mary, who was very delicate, and his grandchild too, for whom he ought to make what little provision he could. I therefore took the matter in my own hands, and by means of a judicious combination of experience and what money I could spare, I managed, at less expense than most parents suppose to be unavoidable, to maintain my young friend at Oxford till such time as he gained a fellowship. I felt justified in doing so in part from the fact that some day or other Mrs Walton would inherit the Oldcastle property, as well as come into possession of certain moneys of her own, now in the trust of her mother and two gentlemen in London, which would be nearly sufficient to free the estate from incumbrance, although she could not touch it as long as her mother lived and chose to refuse her the use of it, at least without a law-suit, with which neither of us was inclined to have anything to do. But I did not lose a penny by the affair. For of the very first money Tom received after he had got his fellowship, he brought the half to me, and continued to do so until he had repaid me every shilling I had spent upon him. As soon as he was in deacon's orders, he came to assist me for a while as curate, and I found him a great help and comfort. He occupied the large room over his father's shop which had been his grandfather's: he had been dead for some years.

I was now engaged on a work which I had been contemplating for a long time, upon the development of the love of Nature as shown in the earlier literature of the Jews and Greeks, through that of the Romans, Italians, and other nations, with the Anglo-Saxon for a fresh starting-point, into its latest forms in Gray, Thomson, Cowper, Crabbe, Wordsworth, Keats, and Tennyson; and Tom supplied me with much of the time which I bestowed upon this object, and I was really grateful to him. But, in looking back, and trying to account to myself for the snare into which I fell, I see plainly enough that I thought too much of what I had done for Tom, and too little of the honour God had done me in allowing me to help Tom. I took the high-dais-throne over him, not consciously, I believe, but still with a contemptible condescension, not of manner but of heart, so delicately refined by the innate sophistry of my selfishness, that the better nature in me called it only fatherly friendship, and did not recognize it as that abominable thing so favoured of all those that especially worship themselves. But I abuse my fault instead of confessing it.

One evening, a gentle tap came to my door, and Tom entered. He looked pale and anxious, and there was an uncertainty about his motions which I could not understand.

"What is the matter, Tom?" I asked.

"I wanted to say something to you, sir," answered Tom.

"Say on," I returned, cheerily.

"It is not so easy to say, sir," rejoined Tom, with a faint smile. "Miss Walton, sir—"

"Well, what of her? There's nothing happened to her? She was here a few minutes ago—though, now I think of it—"

Here a suspicion of the truth flashed on me, and struck me dumb. I am now covered with shame to think how, when the thing approached myself on that side, it swept away for the moment all my fine theories about the equality of men in Christ their Head. How could Tom Weir, whose father was a joiner, who had been a lad in a London shop himself, dare to propose marrying my sister? Instead of thinking of what he really was, my regard rested upon this and that stage through which he had passed to reach his present condition. In fact, I regarded him rather as of my making than of God's.

Perhaps it might do something to modify the scorn of all classes for those beneath them, to consider that, by regarding others thus, they justify those above them in looking down upon them in their turn. In London shops, I am credibly informed, the young women who serve in the show-rooms, or behind the counters, are called LADIES, and talk of the girls who make up the articles for sale as PERSONS. To the learned professions, however, the distinction between the shopwomen and milliners is, from their superior height, unrecognizable; while doctors and lawyers are again, I doubt not, massed by countesses and other blue-blooded realities, with the literary lions who roar at soirees and kettle-drums, or even with chiropodists and violin-players! But I am growing scornful at scorn, and forget that I too have been scornful. Brothers, sisters, all good men and true women, let the Master seat us where He will. Until he says, "Come up higher," let us sit at the foot of the board, or stand behind, honoured in waiting upon His guests. All that kind of thing is worth nothing in the kingdom; and nothing will be remembered of us but the Master's judgment.

I have known a good churchwoman who would be sweet as a sister to the abject poor, but offensively condescending to a shopkeeper or a dissenter, exactly as if he was a Pariah, and she a Brahmin. I have known good people who were noble and generous towards their so-called inferiors and full of the rights of the race—until it touched their own family, and just no longer. Yea I, who had talked like this for years, at once, when Tom Weir wanted to marry my sister, lost my faith in the broad lines of human distinction judged according to appearances in which I did not even believe, and judged not righteous judgment.

"For," reasoned the world in me, "is it not too bad to drag your wife in for such an alliance? Has she not lowered herself enough already? Has she not married far below her accredited position in society? Will she not feel injured by your family if she see it capable of forming such a connexion?"

What answer I returned to Tom I hardly know. I remember that the poor fellow's face fell, and that he murmured something which I did not heed. And then I found myself walking in the garden under the great cedar, having stepped out of the window almost unconsciously, and left Tom standing there alone. It was very good of him ever to forgive me.

Wandering about in the garden, my wife saw me from her window, and met me as I turned a corner in the shrubbery.

And now I am going to have my revenge upon her in a way she does not expect, for making me tell the story: I will tell her share in it.

"What is the matter with you, Henry?" she asked.

"Oh, not much," I answered. "Only that Weir has been making me rather uncomfortable."

"What has he been doing?" she inquired, in some alarm. "It is not possible he has done anything wrong."

My wife trusted him as much as I did.

"No—o—o," I answered. "Not anything exactly wrong."

"It must be very nearly wrong, Henry, to make you look so miserable."

I began to feel ashamed and more uncomfortable.

"He has been falling in love with Martha," I said; "and when I put one thing to another, I fear he may have made her fall in love with him too." My wife laughed merrily.

"Whal a wicked curate!"

"Well, but you know it is not exactly agreeable."

"Why?"

"You know why well enough."

"At least, I am not going to take it for granted. Is he not a good man?"

"Yes."

"Is he not a well-educated man?"

"As well as myself—for his years."

"Is he not clever?"

"One of the cleverest fellows I ever met"

"Is he not a gentleman?"

"I have not a fault to find with his manners."

"Nor with his habits?" my wife went on.

"No."

"Nor with his ways of thinking?"

"No.—But, Ethelwyn, you know what I mean quite well. His family, you know."

"Well, is his father not a respectable man?"

"Oh, yes, certainly. Thoroughly respectable."

"He wouldn't borrow money of his tailor instead of paying for his clothes, would he?"

"Certainly not"

"And if he were to die to-day he would carry no debts to heaven with him?"

"I believe not."

"Does he bear false witness against his neighbour?"

"No. He scorns a lie as much as any man I ever knew."

"Which of the commandments is it in particular that he breaks, then?"

"None that I know of; excepting that no one can keep them yet that is only human. He tries to keep every one of them I do believe."

"Well, I think Tom very fortunate in having such a father. I wish my mother had been as good."

"That is all true, and yet—"

"And yet, suppose a young man you liked had had a fashionable father who had ruined half a score of trades-people by his extravagance—would you object to him because of his family?"

"Perhaps not."

"Then, with you, position outweighs honesty—in fathers, at least."

To this I was not ready with an answer, and my wife went on.

"It might be reasonable if you did though, from fear lest he should turn out like his father.—But do you know why I would not accept your offer of taking my name when I should succeed to the property?"

"You said you liked mine better," I answered.

"So I did. But I did not tell you that I was ashamed that my good husband should take a name which for centuries had been borne by hard-hearted, worldly minded people, who, to speak the truth of my ancestors to my husband, were neither gentle nor honest, nor high-minded."

"Still, Ethelwyn, you know there is something in it, though it is not so easy to say what. And you avoid that. I suppose Martha has been talking you over to her side."

"Harry," my wife said, with a shade of solemnity, "I am almost ashamed of you for the first time. And I will punish you by telling you the truth. Do you think I had nothing of that sort to get over when I began to find that I was thinking a little more about you than was quite convenient under the circumstances? Your manners, dear Harry, though irreproachable, just had not the tone that I had been accustomed to. There was a diffidence about you also that did not at first advance you in my regard."

"Yes, yes," I answered, a little piqued, "I dare say. I have no doubt you thought me a boor."

"Dear Harry!"

"I beg your pardon, wifie. I know you didn't. But it is quite bad enough to have brought you down to my level, without sinking you still lower."

"Now there you are wrong, Harry. And that is what I want to show you.

410

I found that my love to you would not be satisfied with making an exception in your favour. I must see what force there really was in the notions I had been bred in."

"Ah!" I said. "I see. You looked for a principle in what you had thought was an exception."

"Yes," returned my wife; "and I soon found one. And the next step was to throw away all false judgment in regard to such things. And so I can see more clearly than you into the right of the matter.—Would you hesitate a moment between Tom Weir and the dissolute son of an earl, Harry?"

"You know I would not."

"Well, just carry out the considerations that suggests, and you will find that where there is everything personally noble, pure, simple, and good, the lowliness of a man's birth is but an added honour to him; for it shows that his nobility is altogether from within him, and therefore is his own. It cannot then have been put on him by education or imitation, as many men's manners are, who wear their good breeding like their fine clothes, or as the Pharisee his prayers, to be seen of men."

"But his sister?"

"Harry, Harry! You were preaching last Sunday about the way God thinks of things. And you said that was the only true way of thinking about them. Would the Mary that poured the ointment on Jesus's head have refused to marry a good man because he was the brother of that Mary who poured it on His feet? Have you thought what God would think of Tom for a husband to Martha?"

I did not answer, for conscience had begun to speak. When I lifted my eyes from the ground, thinking Ethelwyn stood beside me, she was gone. I felt as if she were dead, to punish me for my pride. But still I could not get over it, though I was ashamed to follow and find her. I went and got my hat instead, and strolled out.

What was it that drew me towards Thomas Weir's shop? I think it must have been incipient repentance—a feeling that I had wronged the man. But just as I turned the corner, and the smell of the wood reached me, the picture so often associated in my mind with such a scene of human labour, rose before me. I saw the Lord of Life bending over His bench, fashioning some lowly utensil for some housewife of Nazareth. And He would receive payment for it too; for He at least could see no disgrace in the order of things that His Father had appointed. It is the vulgar mind that looks down on the earning and worships the inheriting of money. How infinitely more poetic is the belief that our Lord did His work like any other honest man, than that straining after His glorification in the early centuries of the Church by the invention of fables even to the disgrace of his father! They say that Joseph was a bad carpenter, and our Lord had to work miracles to set the things right which he had made wrong! To such a class of mind as invented these fables do those belong who think they honour our Lord when they judge anything human too common or too unclean for Him to have done.

And the thought sprung up at once in my mind—"If I ever see our Lord face to face, how shall I feel if He says to me; 'Didst thou do well to murmur that thy sister espoused a certain man for that in his youth he had earned his bread as I earned mine? Where was then thy right to say unto me, Lord, Lord?'"

I hurried into the workshop.

"Has Tom told you about it?" I said.

"Yes, sir. And I told him to mind what he was about; for he was not a gentleman, and you was, sir."

"I hope I am. And Tom is as much a gentleman as I have any claim to be."

Thomas Weir held out his hand.

"Now, sir, I do believe you mean in my shop what you say in your pulpit; and there is ONE Christian in the world at least.—But what will your good lady say? She's higher-born than you—no offence, sir."

"Ah, Thomas, you shame me. I am not so good as you think me. It was my wife that brought me to reason about it."

"God bless her."

"Amen. I'm going to find Tom."

At the same moment Tom entered the shop, with a very melancholy face. He started when he saw me, and looked confused.

"Tom, my boy," I said, "I behaved very badly to you. I am sorry for it. Come back with me, and have a walk with my sister. I don't think she'll be sorry to see you."

His face brightened up at once, and we left the shop together. Evidently with a great effort Tom was the first to speak.

"I know, sir, how many difficulties my presumption must put you in."

"Not another word about it, Tom. You are blameless. I wish I were. If we only act as God would have us, other considerations may look after themselves—or, rather, He will look after them. The world will never be right till the mind of God is the measure of things, and the will of God the law of things. In the kingdom of Heaven nothing else is acknowledged. And till that kingdom come, the mind and will of God must, with those that look for that kingdom, over-ride every other way of thinking, feeling, and judging. I see it more plainly than ever I did. Take my sister, in God's name, Tom, and be good to her."

Tom went to find Martha, and I to find Ethelwyn.

"It is all right," I said, "even to the shame I feel at having needed your reproof."

"Don't think of that. God gives us all time to come to our right minds, you know," answered my wife.

"But how did you get on so far a-head of me, wifie?"

Ethelwyn laughed.

"Why," she said, "I only told you back again what you have been telling me for the last seven or eight years."

So to me the message had come first, but my wife had answered first with the deed.

And now I have had my revenge on her.

Next to her and my children, Tom has been my greatest comfort for many years. He is still my curate, and I do not think we shall part till death part us for a time. My sister is worth twice what she was before, though they have no children. We have many, and they have taught me much.

Thomas Weir is now too old to work any longer. He occupies his father's chair in the large room of the old house. The workshop I have had turned into a school-room, of the external condition of which his daughter takes good care, while a great part of her brother Tom's time is devoted to the children; for he and I agree that, where it can be done, the pastoral care ought to be at least equally divided between the sheep and the lambs. For the sooner the children are brought under right influences—I do not mean a great deal of religious speech, but the right influences of truth and honesty, and an evident regard to what God wants of us—not only are they the more easily wrought upon, but the sooner do they recognize those influences as right and good. And while Tom quite agrees with me that there must not be much talk about religion, he thinks that there must be just the more acting upon religion; and that if it be everywhere at hand in all things taught and done, it will be ready to show itself to every one who looks for it. And besides that action is more powerful than speech in the inculcation of religion, Tom says there is no such corrective of sectarianism of every kind as the repression of speech and the encouragement of action.

Besides being a great help to me and everybody else almost in Marshmallows, Tom has distinguished himself in the literary world j and when I read his books I am yet prouder of my brother-in-law. I am only afraid that Martha is not good enough for him. But she certainly improves, as I have said already.

Jane Rogers was married to young Brownrigg about a year after we

414

were married. The old man is all but confined to the chimney-corner now, and Richard manages the farm, though not quite to his father's satisfaction, of course. But they are doing well notwithstanding. The old mill has been superseded by one of new and rare device, built by Richard; but the old cottage where his wife's parents lived has slowly mouldered back to the dust.

For the old people have been dead for many years.

Often in the summer days as I go to or come from the vestry, I sit down for a moment on the turf that covers my old friend, and think that every day is mouldering away this body of mine till it shall fall a heap of dust into its appointed place. But what is that to me? It is to me the drawing nigh of the fresh morning of life, when I shall be young and strong again, glad in the presence of the wise and beloved dead, and unspeakably glad in the presence of my God, which I have now but hope to possess far more hereafter.

I will not take a solemn leave of my friends iust yet. For I hope to hold a little more communion with them ere I go hence. I know that my mental faculty is growing weaker, but some power yet remains; and I say to myself, "Perhaps this is the final trial of your faith—to trust in God to take care of your intellect for you, and to believe, in weakness, the truths He revealed to you in strength. Remember that Truth depends not upon your seeing it, and believe as you saw when your sight was at its best. For then you saw that the Truth was beyond all you could see." Thus I try to prepare for dark days that may come, but which cannot come without God in them.

And meantime I hope to be able to communicate some more of the good things experience and thought have taught me, and it may be some more of the events that have befallen my friends and myself in our pilgrimage. So, kind readers, God be with you. That is the older and better form of GOOD-BYE.

About Author

Elizabeth Yates wrote of Sir Gibbie, "It moved me the way books did when, as a child, the great gates of literature began to open and first encounters with noble thoughts and utterances were unspeakably thrilling."

Even Mark Twain, who initially disliked MacDonald, became friends with him, and there is some evidence that Twain was influenced by him. The Christian author Oswald Chambers wrote in his "Christian Disciplines" that "it is a striking indication of the trend and shallowness of the modern reading public that George MacDonald's books have been so neglected".

Early life

George MacDonald was born on 10 December 1824 at Huntly, Aberdeenshire, Scotland. His father, a farmer, was one of the MacDonalds of Glen Coe and a direct descendant of one of the families that suffered in the massacre of 1692.

MacDonald grew up in an unusually literate environment: one of his maternal uncles was a notable Celtic scholar, editor of the Gaelic Highland Dictionary and collector of fairy tales and Celtic poetry. His paternal grandfather had supported the publication of an Ossian edition, the controversial Celtic text believed by some to have contributed to the starting of European Romanticism. MacDonald's step-uncle was a Shakespeare scholar, and his paternal cousin another Celtic academic. Both his parents were readers, his father harbouring predilections for Newton, Burns, Cowper, Chalmers, Coleridge, and Darwin, to quote a few, while his mother had received a classical education which included multiple languages.

An account cited how the young George suffered lapses in health in his early years and was subject to problems with his lungs such as asthma, bronchitis and even a bout of tuberculosis. This last illness was considered a family disease and two of MacDonald's brothers, his mother, and later three of his own children actually died from the ailment. Even in his adult life, he was constantly travelling in search of purer air for his lungs.

MacDonald grew up in the Congregational Church, with an atmosphere of Calvinism. However, his family was atypical, with his paternal grandfather a Catholic-born, fiddle-playing, Presbyterian elder; his paternal grandmother an Independent church rebel; his mother was a sister to the Gallic-speaking radical who became moderator of the disrupting Free Church, while his step-mother, to whom he was also very close, was the daughter of a Scottish Episcopalian priest.

MacDonald graduated from the University of Aberdeen in 1845 with a master's degree in chemistry and physics. He spent the next several years struggling with matters of faith and deciding what to do with his life. His son, biographer Greville MacDonald stated that his father could have pursued a career in the medical field but he speculated that lack of money put an end to this prospect. It was only in 1848 when MacDonald began theological training at Highbury College for the Congregational ministry.

Early career

MacDonald was appointed minister of Trinity Congregational Church, Arundel, in 1850, after briefly serving as a locum minister in Ireland. However, his sermons—which preached God's universal love and that everyone was capable of redemption —met with little favour and his salary was cut in half. In May 1853, MacDonald tendered his resignation from his pastoral duties at Arundel. Later he was engaged in ministerial work in Manchester, leaving that because of poor health. An account cited the role of Lady Byron in convincing MacDonald to travel to Algiers in 1856 with the hope that the sojourn would help turn his health around. When he got back, he settled in London and taught for some time at the University of London. MacDonald was also for a time editor of Good Words for the Young.

Writing Career

MacDonald's first novel David Elginbrod was published in 1863.

George MacDonald is often regarded as the founding father of modern fantasy writing. George MacDonald's best-known works are Phantastes, The Princess and the Goblin, At the Back of the North Wind, and Lilith (1895), all fantasy novels, and fairy tales such as "The Light Princess", "The Golden Key", and "The Wise Woman". "I write, not for children," he wrote, "but for

418

the child-like, whether they be of five, or fifty, or seventy-five." MacDonald also published some volumes of sermons, the pulpit not having proved an unreservedly successful venue.

After his literary success, MacDonald went on to do a lecture tour in the United States in 1872–1873, after being invited to do so by a lecture company, the Boston Lyceum Bureau. On the tour, MacDonald lectured about other poets such as Robert Burns, Shakespeare, and Tom Hood. He performed this lecture to great acclaim, speaking in Boston to crowds in the neighborhood of three thousand people.

MacDonald served as a mentor to Lewis Carroll (the pen-name of Charles Lutwidge Dodgson); it was MacDonald's advice, and the enthusiastic reception of Alice by MacDonald's many sons and daughters, that convinced Carroll to submit Alice for publication. Carroll, one of the finest Victorian photographers, also created photographic portraits of several of the MacDonald children. MacDonald was also friends with John Ruskin, and served as a go-between in Ruskin's long courtship with Rose La Touche. While in America he was befriended by Longfellow and Walt Whitman.

MacDonald's use of fantasy as a literary medium for exploring the human condition greatly influenced a generation of notable authors, including C. S. Lewis, who featured him as a character in his The Great Divorce. In his introduction to his MacDonald anthology, Lewis speaks highly of MacDonald's views:

This collection, as I have said, was designed not to revive MacDonald's literary reputation but to spread his religious teaching. Hence most of my extracts are taken from the three volumes of Unspoken Sermons. My own debt to this book is almost as great as one man can owe to another: and nearly all serious inquirers to whom I have introduced it acknowledge that it has given them great help—sometimes indispensable help toward the very acceptance of the Christian faith. ...

I know hardly any other writer who seems to be closer, or more continually close, to the Spirit of Christ Himself. Hence his Christ-like union of tenderness and severity. Nowhere else outside the New Testament have I found terror and comfort so intertwined. ...

In making this collection I was discharging a debt of justice. I have never concealed the fact that I regarded him as my master; indeed I fancy I have never written a book in which I did not quote from him. But it has not seemed to me that those who have received my books kindly take even now sufficient notice of the affiliation. Honesty drives me to emphasize it.

Others he influenced include J. R. R. Tolkien and Madeleine L'Engle. MacDonald's non-fantasy novels, such as Alec Forbes, had their influence as well; they were among the first realistic Scottish novels, and as such MacDonald has been credited with founding the "kailyard school" of Scottish writing.

Chesterton cited The Princess and the Goblin as a book that had "made a difference to my whole existence", in showing "how near both the best and the worst things are to us from the first... and making all the ordinary staircases and doors and windows into magical things."

Later life

In 1877 he was given a civil list pension. From 1879 he and his family moved to Bordighera, in a place much loved by British expatriates, the Riviera dei Fiori in Liguria, Italy, almost on the French border. In that locality there also was an Anglican church, All Saints, which he attended. Deeply enamoured of the Riviera, he spent 20 years there, writing almost half of his whole literary production, especially the fantasy work. MacDonald founded a literary studio in that Ligurian town, naming it Casa Coraggio (Bravery House). It soon became one of the most renowned cultural centres of that period, well attended by British and Italian travellers, and by locals, with presentations of classic plays and readings of Dante and Shakespeare often being held.

In 1900 he moved into St George's Wood, Haslemere, a house designed for him by his son, Robert, its building overseen by his eldest son, Greville.

George MacDonald died on 18 September 1905 in Ashtead, Surrey, England. He was cremated in Woking, Surrey, England and his ashes were buried in Bordighera, in the English cemetery, along with his wife Louisa and daughters Lilia and Grace.

Personal life

MacDonald married Louisa Powell in Hackney in 1851, with whom he raised a family of eleven children: Lilia Scott (1852), Mary Josephine (1853-1878), Caroline Grace (1854), Greville Matheson (1856-1944), Irene (1857), Winifred Louise (1858), Ronald (1860–1933), Robert Falconer (1862–1913), Maurice (1864), Bernard Powell (1865–1928), and George Mackay (1867–1909?).

His son Greville became a noted medical specialist, a pioneer of the Peasant Arts movement, wrote numerous fairy tales for children, and ensured that new editions of his father's works were published. Another son, Ronald, became a novelist. His daughter Mary was engaged to the artist Edward Robert Hughes until her death in 1878. Ronald's son, Philip MacDonald (George MacDonald's grandson), became a Hollywood screenwriter.

Tuberculosis caused the death of several family members, including Lilia, Mary Josephine, Grace, Maurice as well as one granddaughter and a daughter-in-law. MacDonald was said to have been particularly affected by the death of Lilia, her eldest.

Theology

According to biographer William Raeper, MacDonald's theology "celebrated the rediscovery of God as Father, and sought to encourage an intuitive response to God and Christ through quickening his readers' spirits in their reading of the Bible and their perception of nature."

MacDonald's oft-mentioned universalism is not the idea that everyone will automatically be saved, but is closer to Gregory of Nyssa in the view that all will ultimately repent and be restored to God.

MacDonald appears to have never felt comfortable with some aspects of Calvinist doctrine, feeling that its principles were inherently "unfair"; when the doctrine of predestination was first explained to him, he burst into tears (although assured that he was one of the elect). Later novels, such as Robert Falconer and Lilith, show a distaste for the idea that God's electing love is limited to some and denied to others.

Chesterton noted that only a man who had "escaped" Calvinism could say that God is easy to please and hard to satisfy.

MacDonald rejected the doctrine of penal substitutionary atonement as developed by John Calvin, which argues that Christ has taken the place of sinners and is punished by the wrath of God in their place, believing that in turn it raised serious questions about the character and nature of God. Instead, he taught that Christ had come to save people from their sins, and not from a Divine penalty for their sins: the problem was not the need to appease a wrathful God, but the disease of cosmic evil itself. MacDonald frequently described the atonement in terms similar to the Christus Victor theory. MacDonald posed the rhetorical question, "Did he not foil and slay evil by letting all the waves and billows of its horrid sea break upon him, go over him, and die without rebound—spend their rage, fall defeated, and cease? Verily, he made atonement!"

MacDonald was convinced that God does not punish except to amend, and that the sole end of His greatest anger is the amelioration of the guilty. As the doctor uses fire and steel in certain deep-seated diseases, so God may use hell-fire if necessary to heal the hardened sinner. MacDonald declared, "I believe that no hell will be lacking which would help the just mercy of God to redeem his children." MacDonald posed the rhetorical question, "When we say that God is Love, do we teach men that their fear of Him is groundless?" He replied, "No. As much as they were will come upon them, possibly far more. ... The wrath will consume what they call themselves; so that the selves God made shall appear."

However, true repentance, in the sense of freely chosen moral growth, is essential to this process, and, in MacDonald's optimistic view, inevitable for all beings (see universal reconciliation).

MacDonald states his theological views most distinctly in the sermon "Justice", found in the third volume of Unspoken Sermons. (Source: Wikipedia)

Printed in July 2019
by Rotomail Italia S.p.A., Vignate (MI) - Italy